MW01204751

Shadow of the Father

by Kyell Gold

This is a work of fiction. All characters and events portrayed within are fictitious.

SHADOW OF THE FATHER

Published by Sofawolf Press
St. Paul, Minnesota
http://www.sofawolf.com

ISBN 978-0-9819883-4-4
Printed in the United States of America
First trade paperback edition
Second printing, December 2012

Cover and interior art by Sara Palmer

For my father,

who taught me

"don't be normal."

Contents

Foreword

If this is your first introduction to the world of Argaea, welcome. It's my third full novel and umpteenth story in the Renaissance-era furry universe I created with the story "The Prisoner's Release" back in Heat #1, years and years ago. The world then was the size of a prison cell, its population a fox named Volle and two jailers.

In Heat #2, "The Prisoner's Release" concluded, bringing us out of the prison cell and into the city of Divalia, the capital of the country of Tephos. From that story, the novels "Volle" and "Pendant of Fortune," set before and after it respectively, came about. Both centered around Volle, a lord in the royal court at Tephos, and expanded on the Panbestian Church and its six major deities, imaginatively named Ursis, Canis, Felis, Rodenta, Mustela, and Herbivora, as well as the royal succession in Tephos, which passes not from father to son, but circulates between the six Houses of the church.

Lordship, however, does pass from father to son. In "Pendant of Fortune," we meet Volle's first son, Volyan, and are witness to the conception of what will hopefully be his second. For years, I've known that Yilon was conceived that day, and would have his own trials and tribulations growing up, though he would not be in line to succeed to his father's title. I had the first two paragraphs of his story written for a long time, and late in 2008, I had enough of the rest of the story planned that I could start writing.

"Shadow of the Father" explores new parts of Argaea and introduces new characters, alongside some old friends, if you're a return visitor. It is a somewhat younger book than "Volle"; Yilon is several years younger than his father was at the start of his adventure, and has a bit more growing to do. It was a wonderful experience for me, finding out more about my world, and I hope you will enjoy it just as much. I think it is more than a worthy successor to "Volle" and "Pendant of Fortune."

"Shadow" is the first novel in years that I wrote completely as a novel, following the episodic "Waterways" and "Out of Position." I documented the writing of it at kyellgold.livejournal.com (it was called "Sins of the Father" at the time), sharing it with the community there. I continue to learn about writing with every book, a journey larger than Argaea that I hope I never come to the end of. As always, I deeply appreciate your company on this journey. It's much more fun than making it alone.

--Kyell, January 2010

Chapter 1: The Steward of Dewanne

By the time the second month of summer had come and gone, the novelty of the locusts had faded, but Yilon still relished the bitter taste and crunch of them. They flew stupidly into the darkness of his black-furred paw, as though anxious for their short lives to be over. Volyan ate them cooked and honey-coated, but Yilon preferred plucking them from the air, like fruit from invisible trees. He wasn't the only one, either; most of the population of the palace could be seen crunching locusts when walking outside, even the mice, rats, and deer.

Yilon chewed on one he'd retrieved from his russet head fur as he walked beneath the shady vines out into the gardens. Despite the stifling heat, he still wore a full tunic, albeit a loose cotton one that breathed well. Volyan, he knew, would be wearing nothing but shorts as a grudging concession to propriety, one of many points on which they differed. Even if he'd had the older fox's developed physique and stature, Yilon still would have worn a tunic. Often he wondered if they really shared the parentage they both claimed.

For example, Yilon would never have missed a history lesson of his own volition, certainly not to lounge by the fountain in the garden and entertain a pair of airheaded girls. But that was the first place he looked today when sent to find his older brother. A number of lords had sought shelter from the heat in the shady arbors around the fountain, while the younger generation splashed around in it. Volyan was with neither.

If he wasn't in the garden, and he wasn't in their chambers, then he was likely down in the armory practicing his swordplay. Yilon slipped into a side door of the palace and took a shortcut down the two flights of the Rabbit stair to the lower levels.

"Held up in History again?" said a voice behind him as he stepped off the last stair.

"Oh, right." Yilon held out his paw. His friend Sinch, a short, smiling mouse, slapped it and then held his own out for a return slap. "Sorry, I didn't tell you. Father canceled my weapons practice today."

Sinch looked around. "There isn't anything but the armory down here."

"I'm looking for my brother. I'm supposed to bring him back."

"Oh." Sinch pointed up the stair. "I just saw him leaving."

"He wasn't in the garden." Yilon turned and hurried up the stairs, Sinch following.

"Not the garden. Out of the palace."

Yilon stopped on the landing. "Teeth and Tail," he swore. He pulled himself around the bust of a rabbit to run up the second flight, not bothering to quiet the clicking of his claws on stone. "I'm not going into that tavern to find him."

Sinch stood three inches shorter than Yilon on level ground. On the stairs, running up behind him, the mouse had to reach up a foot just to grab Yilon's elbow. "He might not have gone there."

"Of course he did," Yilon said, shaking free. He grasped the rabbit statue on the main floor and whirled around it, dodging between servants and lords on his way further up.

Sinch ran up in his wake. "Did he know your father wanted to see you both?"

"Probably." Yilon had already been thinking that if Volyan had found out about the meeting somehow, that he would've gone out of his way to avoid it. "I'm just going to see if I can see him on the street, and then I'll go back to Father."

The flight of stairs ended at the third floor corridor. Yilon spun to his left, hurrying past doorways until he got to a small archway on his right. He ducked into the shadowy space, not waiting for his eyes to adjust before finding the bottom of the ladder and swarming up. At the top, he whispered down, "All clear?"

"Clear," Sinch's voice floated up to him. He pushed the trap door open, flooding the space with light. Of course other people in the palace knew about the way to the roof, but Yilon liked pretending it was their secret. He clambered out into the shimmering heat, stepping aside immediately to let Sinch hop out. By the time Sinch had lowered the door closed, Yilon had already made it across the roof, peering out over the waist-high wall.

Below him and to the right lay the front gardens, filled with strolling lords and bustling servants. Around them rose the true palace walls, and beyond them, the bustling streets of Divalia.. "How long ago?" Yilon asked as Sinch came up to his side.

The mouse rested his elbows on the wall. "Not long. Fifteen minutes, perhaps. He was leaving the armory, and he had on his vest, the yellow one, so I knew he was going outside." They stared at the street ahead of them. If Volyan had gone that way, they should be seeing him soon.

Light sparkled to Yilon's left, sunlight reflecting off the river. His attention drifted from searching for a fox in a yellow vest out on the street to watching a small barge float by. He wondered where it was on its way to, heading southward on the Lurine. Maybe Villutian, or Tistunish, or even...

He heard a soft whoosh and then the thunk of wood on stone. His ears flicked to catch the sound just as Sinch tackled him from the side, knocking him to the ground. "What the—" He struggled against the mouse, finally shoving him to the side. "Are you crazy?"

"Get down!" Sinch's eyes were wide. He pointed to the small object, a few feet from them, that had made the sound.

Yilon had seen plenty of things like this, had been handling some just yesterday, in fact. But the arrows he shot were fletched with pigeon feathers, not black crow's. He reached out and took the small shaft in his paws, turning it over. "It's not from the palace," he said.

Sinch shook his head. He hissed, "It came from out there! Someone shot at you!"

The arrow itself was perfectly ordinary. Yilon frowned. "Don't be ridiculous. Who would shoot at me? It got away from someone, that's all."

"It almost hit you!"

He closed his paw around the arrow, brandishing it as if it were a pointer and he a tutor. "Do you know how good someone would have to be to get that close to me intentionally from outside the palace? Besides, it's not a longbow arrow, and a regular bow wouldn't be able to shoot that far."

"So, what?" Sinch's voice was still high, frightened. "Someone snuck into the palace to shoot at you?"

Yilon tossed the arrow to one side. "Don't be stupid," he said. "You can't sneak into the palace. Well, *you* can. But you know what I mean."

Sinch continued to look fearfully at the wall. He crept up to it and peered over it. "There's rooftops across the way," he said. "You could shoot a regular bow from there."

The rooftops seemed too far away, but Yilon only had a glimpse before Sinch pulled him down again. "Let me!" he said.

"You're being silly." Yilon shook free of the mouse and brushed his clothes and tail off. Rather than look back over the wall, he strode quickly to the trap door. "I'm going back to Father," he said. "If you're sure Volyan was going out, I'll just tell him that."

Sinch hurried after him, with glances back at the street and rooftops. "I'm pretty sure," he said. "He never wears the vest."

"And when Father's done with whatever he wants to tell me, I'll bring a bow up here and we can shoot arrows at the rooftops. Okay?" He clambered through the trap door and down the ladder.

"Um," Sinch said, "I'm not sure..." He swung through and shut the trap door above him, plunging them into darkness.

"We won't hit them. That'll prove that it's just an accident."

"But..."

Yilon reached the bottom of the ladder and stepped back. When Sinch reached the floor, Yilon put a paw on his shoulder and squeezed. "Don't worry so much," he said. "When we come back, we can maybe spend a little more time up there."

He felt Sinch relax under his paw, turning to nuzzle it briefly. "It was really disturbing," he said.

"It's the roof of the palace. It's safe." He patted the mouse's rear. "Now come on, I need to get back to my chambers or Father'll throw a fit."

They emerged into the third floor hallway, passing Lord and Lady Quirn, a bear couple who took up most of the space. Yilon squeezed by and hurried around to the Wolf Stair, sprinting down it with Sinch close behind.

"I'll wait for you by the armory," Sinch said as they reached the main floor. Yilon waved acknowledgment, dashing around the corner to his chambers.

"Sorry!" he said, throwing open the inner door. "I went to look for Volyan, but he took off, probably out at that..." He skidded to a halt.

At the desk sat his father, Lord Vinton, chair turned around to face the interior of the room. Leaning against the wall beside the desk, the breeze from the window ruffling his white cheek fur, his father's lover Streak, a wolf in a green jerkin and vest, watched Yilon with amusement. On the other side of the desk, a short, thin fox ruffled through a sheaf of papers, apparently oblivious to Yilon. He wasn't anyone Yilon had seen around the palace before, but he was dressed in traveling clothes: a leather jerkin with a faded crest on the front, loose leggings, and a small cap. And next to the desk, at one of the chairs around the small table there, his brother Volyan sat smirking, his arms folded across a yellow vest that was open enough to show off most of his chest.

"Have a seat," his father said, gesturing to the empty chair opposite Volyan.

Yilon glared at his brother. He took one step to the side and slouched against the wall, next to the doorway.

His father sighed and stood. He looked like he'd just come from a council meeting, dressed in a green velvet doublet that matched Streak's green vest. His reddish-brown tail, more brown than Yilon's, swayed slowly behind him. "I'd hoped to put this day off," he said. "At least for another year or two. But we got the word today." He gestured to the thin fox, who looked up. "This is Maxon, the steward of Dewanne."

Yilon stared at the papers, dread prickling his fur. He kept his ears up, but couldn't stop his tail from curling around his leg. Maxon cleared his throat. "It is with deep regret that I announce the passing of Sheffin, thirty-first Lord of Dewanne. We...mourn him and salute the Lady Dewanne, who will be serving as Lady Regent until his designated heir can take his place." Yilon's fingers felt numb. The steward cleared his throat again. "As you know, Lord Dewanne died without official issue. He did designate an official heir, whose selection has been confirmed by the Lady Regent. In accordance with the laws of the realm, the designated heir must present himself at the court in Dewanne for his Confirmation; he can then return to Divalia to be sworn in by the King."

It was him, of course it was him. His father had told him it would be him, but still he couldn't suppress the tension of hope that maybe Lord Dewanne had changed his mind at the last minute. Maybe he'd figured Volyan was a better choice, since he was older. And then Volyan could go to Dewanne, and he could go back to Vinton, live there as long as he wanted. Maybe...

"The designated heir is Yilon, second son of Volle, seventeenth Lord of Vinton, and Ilyana Rodion."

All eyes in the room turned to Yilon. He looked at the floor, at his claws, anywhere but back at his family or Maxon. He didn't hear most of what the steward said next through the rushing in his ears, something about taking the high road and the court in Dewanne.

"We'll have dinner tomorrow and see you off the day after," Yilon's father said. "I expect you'll want to say good-bye to some people. And we'll arrange with Master Ovile for some books to take along with you."

"The day after tomorrow?" Yilon's head snapped up.

Maxon coughed into his paw. "It is imperative that you present yourself for Confirmation at the earliest possible convenience."

"What's the matter?" Volyan said. "Don't want to take a nice trip?"

Volle turned to him. "You'll be leaving at the same time," he said.

Volyan half-rose from his chair. "Why? I'm already the heir."

His father waved a paw at Maxon's papers. "We were waiting for Dewanne's official pronouncement. For various reasons, it was..."

Maxon coughed. "Lord Dewanne wisely took the time to evaluate every option, the better to decide which would be best for the land."

"He didn't want to commit to anything," Streak snorted. "No matter how..."

Volle laid a paw on his arm. "He's gone now," he said quietly. "Nobody's harmed."

They held each other's eyes. Yilon looked away, at Maxon's papers, and said loudly, "Fine. I'll go start getting ready."

"Yilon," Volle said, but Yilon was already stalking out into the foyer, where his father caught him by the shoulder and spun him around.

In the past year, Yilon had shot up by eight inches. That still left him half a foot shy of his father and a full foot shorter than Volyan. When he faced his father now, he found himself stretching his legs to try to make up that half foot. His father's ears were forward, in contrast to Yilon's, which were pinned back. They stared at each other without speaking, until Volle said what Yilon knew he was going to say. "Ever since you came of age, I've been waiting for you to act like it."

"I thought when I came of age I wouldn't be ordered around any more."

He watched the familiar wrinkles appear in his father's muzzle. Volle lifted a paw and rubbed his whiskers. "I'm not the one ordering you..."

"Oh? That's what it sounded like."

"Don't interrupt me," Volle snapped. "Whether or not you want this obligation, you have to go to Dewanne. He designated you."

"With your permission."

"Yes."

Streak poked his head out of the parlor. "Is everything okay?"

Yilon heaved an exaggerated sigh. Volle turned, his voice softer. "Fine. I'll be back in a second." The white wolf nodded and disappeared.

"Why wasn't Mother here for this?" Yilon demanded.

"There wasn't time to send for her," Volle said.

"She would've wanted to come." Yilon's ears came up. "I'll go see her on the way to Dewanne."

"You won't," Volle said. "It's weeks out of the way."

"It's only three days."

"Each way. And you won't spend just one day there, if you go back."

"I thought you weren't going to order me around any more."

His father looked directly back at him, amber eyes firm. "I guess you thought wrong."

Yilon lowered his head, staring at his feet. "It's not fair," he muttered. "I just want to go home for a bit. It won't hurt anyone."

"Your Confirmation's to be in three weeks. Besides the discourtesy of leaving an entire land waiting for a ruler, you'll risk being stuck in Dewanne all winter. The pass through the mountains closes early."

Yilon curled his tail tightly under him. "It wouldn't take that long."

"You can stop by and see your mother on the way back," Volle said. "In fact, since Volyan will be down there, perhaps Streak and I will visit as well. Send a message when you're ready to leave Dewanne."

"Volyan gets to go," he growled.

"He's going to be their lord."

"He doesn't even like it there."

Volle leaned forward. "Nonetheless. He has accepted his duty."

Yilon picked with the claws on his toes at a worn patch in the carpet. "Can I go now?"

It seemed ages before his father broke the silence. "Go ahead," he said. "We're having dinner here tomorrow night, in the chambers. I want to talk to you before you go."

"Isn't that what we're doing now?"

"There are a couple things I need to tell you." At that, Yilon looked up at his father's muzzle. Volle gave him a small smile. "Not now. So I'll see you tomorrow?"

"Do I have a choice?"

Volle reached out, squeezing Yilon's shoulder briefly. "You always have a choice. It may not look that way to you right now, and most of your choices may not seem very attractive, but you always have a choice." He lifted his paw. "Go on, say your good-byes. If there's anything you need for your journey, let Maxon or Jinna know. You have a certain amount of credit."

Yilon nodded. "Thanks," he said quickly, and went to go find Sinch.

He found him feinting and lunging with a dull, worn dagger at the base of the stairs opposite the practice space near the armory. "I'll be right out," Yilon said, waving as he ducked into the armory.

He knew the shelves well enough that it only took him a moment to find a dagger, a short bow and a quiver of arrows. He held them up for the armorer at the entrance to see. "Have 'em back tonight," the old bear said. Yilon nodded, slinging the quiver over his shoulder.

Meeting Sinch outside, he handed him the dagger. "Here," he said. "Want to head back up to the roof, or out to the practice range?"

"Thanks." Sinch slipped the older dagger into his belt and hefted the one Yilon had given him, which was visibly sharper. The handle, though worn, still maintained its polished sheen, and a small emerald in the pommel reflected the light. "This is a nice one."

Yilon tested the tension in the bowstring. "I figured, why not?" he said. "It's my last night of weapons practice here."

Sinch lowered the dagger. "Really? You're going home?"

"No. I'm going to Dewanne." Yilon stomped up the stairs, the bow dangling from his paw.

Footsteps scurried after him. "Dewanne? So he, uh..."

"Yes. And I have to go be confirmed or whatever is going to happen."

"That's exciting!" Sinch bounded up to walk alongside him. "You're gonna be a Lord."

"I guess." Yilon paused. "I'll have my own chambers here."

"And money!" Sinch said. "More than Volyan."

Yilon grinned. "I could buy you that dagger."

The mouse's ears flicked halfway back. "Aw, don't waste your money on that," he said. "My dagger's fine. I only use it to pick locks anyway."

"You're good with it. You should have a nice one you can throw, and fight with."

Sinch's grin showed off his prominent front teeth. He jogged up two more stairs, thin tail whipping behind him, and said, "Let's go to the practice range. Bet I can score more hits than you."

Yilon rubbed black paws together. "You've got a bet," he said.

At this time of the afternoon, it took them half an hour to get space on the large practice range by the outer wall. Yilon aimed for the far target, at a hundred feet, while Sinch chose the twenty-foot target. They always played best out of five, because a standard practice quiver held five arrows. Sinch had to run and retrieve his dagger after every toss, so Yilon had to wait while the mouse was on the range before firing his next shot.

Distracted by thoughts of Dewanne and his upcoming trip, Yilon missed his first two shots while Sinch made one. Focus, he barked to himself, and made the next two, while Sinch again made one and missed one.

Two ten-year-old fawns, daughters of one of the cervine lords, stood behind them and watched Sinch. Every noble cub was trained in archery, but not many people of any age in the palace threw daggers. The fawns chattered together, and behind them, a small party was coming in through the outer gates. Yilon tried to ignore them. "You go," he told the mouse, who was waiting for him to shoot.

"Okay." Sinch cocked his arm, tongue sticking out of the side of his mouth as he hefted the dagger and let it go. It sped through the air, landing in the heart of the target.

He turned to Yilon with almost an apologetic smile. "It's a really nice dagger," he said. "Flies really well."

"I just have to make this one," Yilon said. He drew the bowstring back, sighting along the imaginary arc which ended at the target.

A cough sounded behind them just as he let go. The arrow sailed through the air, brushing the edge of the target before hitting the ground. The fawns snickered and sauntered away.

"That didn't count," Sinch was saying as Yilon turned around. "You were distracted."

"No," Yilon said. "I let go where I aimed it. You win." He looked up into Maxon's narrow muzzle. "What is it?"

Maxon inclined his head. "So sorry to have interrupted your lordship's practice." He cleared his throat. "In order to prepare the carriage for our return to Dewanne, I need to know how many possessions you will be bringing."

"I'll get the arrows," Sinch said. He jogged toward the long target while Yilon scratched his head.

At this distance, Yilon could now see the matted white fur at Maxon's collarbone. It looked as though it hadn't been washed in days, and smelled strongly of the steward's own musk and the dirt of the road. He could also make out the crest on the leather jerkin, now, a scripted 'D' atop the star of Canis, with a leafy branch on either side, the whole atop three diamonds. "Clothes...weapons..." He counted on his fingers. "Two trunks?"

Maxon followed Sinch with his eyes, nodding. "Very good. And is that your lordship's personal servant?"

Yilon laughed. "Sinch? No, no, he's just a friend."

"Excellent." Maxon straightened and smiled. His bushy tail uncurled; only then did Yilon realize it had been tucked against the taller fox's leg. "I had been going to suggest to his lordship that the court of Dewanne will be delighted to assign a personal servant to him."

"I'll have a servant?" Yilon grinned.

Maxon nodded shortly. "Of course. Now, if his lordship will excuse me, I have preparations of my own to make."

"Sure," Yilon said, but Maxon was already turning on his heel. He'd barely rounded the corner of the hedge at the entrance to the practice range when Sinch was back. He dropped the arrows in Yilon's quiver, panting slightly.

"What'd you tell him to do?" Sinch asked. His dark eyes gleamed with reflections of the setting sun.

"Nothing. Another round?"

"Sure." Sinch flipped the dagger neatly in the air and caught it by the pommel. "But you already owe me."

"Don't think I've forgotten." Yilon reached for an arrow, nocked it, and let fly.

Chapter 2: Chiona's Request

Because he was supposed to have dinner with his family the next night, Yilon left the palace with Sinch after their practice session to have a quick meal in the local pub. Over stews (roast fowl for Yilon, vegetables for Sinch) and fresh-baked bread at the Cup and Crown, they talked about Dewanne. "All I know about it is it's in the mountains, to the southwest," Sinch said, scooping up vegetables with a slice of bread. "You told me they border Delford."

Yilon chewed a piece of fowl. "During the war, there was some fighting. But it's been peaceful since then. They send us berries and wine, and the mountains around the city have mines. Mostly silver and copper. It's been ruled by foxes for as long as anyone can remember."

"You'll be a good fit." Sinch grinned.

Yilon flicked an ear. "It's about a two-week trip."

At that, Sinch looked down and pushed his bread around his bowl. "You'll be gone for a month and a half."

"Maybe more," Yilon said. "I'm going to stop and see Mother on the way home."

"Oh." Sinch nibbled on his bread.

"Father and Streak are going to come down." Yilon broke off a piece of his own bread to scoop up bits of fowl and vegetable. "Do you think you could come down with them?"

"Maybe."

Yilon looked up at the mouse's drooping whiskers and lowered muzzle. "I'm sure they wouldn't mind."

Sinch turned from side to side, scanning the room. It was moderately crowded, but the only people near them were a pair of ragged-looking raccoons, absorbed in some discussion of their own. The noise level kept their conversation private: the general background chatter, the clank of plates and tankards, and the noise in the street outside, coming in through the open windows. His ears swiveled from side to side and then cupped forward toward Yilon. "I don't think so."

"Why not?" Yilon pushed his bowl forward and licked his fingers before rubbing his muzzle fur clean with them. "All right, I'll see you when I get back here this winter, then."

Sinch smiled, but Yilon could tell it was forced. He pushed his bowl back as well, dropping the remainder of his bread into a napkin and folding it over.

Yilon emptied a silver coin into his paw. He turned it over, looking at it, and then left it on the table. "Ready to collect your winnings?"

"Sure," Sinch said again, with a little more enthusiasm. He waited until Yilon had stood to push back his own chair.

Divalia's streets bustled with activity at dusk. Day workers hurried home while the few nocturnals made their way down to the river docks and the King's Guard stations. Yilon slipped through the crowd with a fox's grace, Sinch following with practiced hops and darts. Even as they dodged around people, they were able to keep up a conversation.

"Mother's going to want to make you cakes," Sinch called around a portly beaver. He'd recovered some of his energy upon leaving the Cup and Crown.

Yilon licked his lips, already feeling hungry again. "I wonder how long they'll keep." He ducked behind a wolf and slipped between a pair of stags. Hopping over a pile of refuse at the side of the street, he turned down a less heavily traveled alley. Sinch followed.

"You can get food along the way, can't you?"

"Sure," Yilon said. "There's pubs and stuff. Maxon will know where to stop."

Sinch sniffed. "He doesn't look like he knows good food."

"I'll order him to find some."

They emerged into another crowded street. Yilon weaved across it to another alley, where he scaled a decrepit gate and dropped to the ground in a filthy garden. Sinch landed beside him a moment later. They crossed together, cut through the corner of the next yard, and opened the gate onto a garden as neatly kept as the others were overgrown. Herbs grew in rows along the edges, tiered with the largest bushes at the top, the green broken up with splashes of purple and red flowers. In the corners nearest the house, two small fruit trees rose. The tree on the left bore only leaves, but the stains and pits below it gave off a thick, sweet fragrance that reminded Yilon of the evenings he'd spent a few months before with Sinch sitting below it, popping cherries into their muzzles and tossing them at each other.

The other tree sagged under the weight of bright green apples, not yet ripe. Yilon's mouth watered at the memory of the sweet, crunchy fruit. He felt a wave of sadness that he would be missing the apple harvest this year. "Save me one, will you?" he said, pointing at the tree.

"Sure." Sinch walked in the back door ahead of Yilon, his tail dragging on the ground again.

Yilon followed him into a small, neat kitchen. Racks of dried herbs and fruits hanging from the ceiling filled the space with a delicious medley of scent that he'd never smelled elsewhere, even in the palace kitchens. The room was warm, as it always was; Yilon had never seen the stove cold.

Chiona, Sinch's mother, wasn't bent over the stove as they walked in. She was talking to a young badger, about twelve from the look of him, who was just her height. "Here," she was saying, "and tell your father he can make up the difference next week when he's feeling better."

She placed a cloth-wrapped package into the badger's paws, topping it with a small cake. "Thank you, miss!" the badger said.

"Off with you, now." She patted his shoulder as he left, then turned. "Good evening, boys. How was your day?"

"I won this time." Sinch stepped forward for a hug, and then dropped the leftover bread into her paw. "We ate at the Cup and Crown."

She lifted the bread to her nose, then took a nibble of it. "Good, reliable Jesse," she said, setting it on the counter beside the stove. "Nothing new with him." Yilon stepped forward, hugging the small mouse to his chest. She looked up at him as they drew apart. "But you, there's something new with you."

Yilon smiled down at her. "They're sending me away, finally."

She tilted her head, a small sparkle in her eyes behind her wire spectacles. "How nice of the old Lord to wait until you'd come of age. Consideration is not common among Lords."

"Tell me about it." He ducked his head, scratching behind one ear.

"Oh, you'll be different." She turned back to the stove, reaching into one of her cabinets. "You wouldn't be here if you didn't have compassion."

Yilon felt Sinch's paw at the base of his tail. He wagged it slowly. "I'm leaving tomorrow."

She pulled out two small sacks, smelling of flour and sugar. "I'll make you some cakes to take with you. Never know what you're going to find on the road. Let's see, you like cinnamon, right? And I can spare a little bit of this..." Her paws lifted a small pouch delicately from the spice rack.

Yilon leaned forward to sniff, but only caught a whiff of an exotic scent when she shooed him out. "Go on with you both. You'll smell when they're ready."

Sinch grabbed his paw and pulled. "Thanks!" Yilon waved, trotting after his friend. They mounted the narrow wooden staircase, boards creaking under their hind paws. Yilon kept one finger on the wall, tracing the pitted holes in the wood. Halfway up the first flight, he paused next to a small portrait of the family, Sinch's mother standing behind her three children.

His friend stopped patiently, tail flicking along the stair. Yilon smiled up. "Wonder if they'd let me make a copy to take to the court at Dewanne."

"You could take that one," Sinch said. "It is yours."

"No, it's yours. Maybe by the time I get back." Yilon patted Sinch's rump, starting the mouse on his way back up.

They passed the room his sisters shared, but even Yilon's ear caught no sound from inside. They were most likely still out at their jobs. Sinch's room, at the very top of the narrow house, was the smallest, but it was his alone, and it was this as much as his mother's affection and cooking that made Yilon's tail wag whenever he visited. He had to share a room with Volyan, in the servant's quarters of his father's chambers, which was awkward whenever Volyan brought back one of his conquests for the night. It was one of those nights that had prompted him to visit Sinch, at the mouse's urging.

The small room was almost as familiar to him as his own: the narrow bed of straw-stuffed cloth, the tiny table piled with tunics, the stool tucked neatly under it. With the door closed, there was barely room for the two of them to stand together on the floor. Which was okay, because they rarely stood together for longer than it took to rub the sides of their muzzles against each other.

Sinch sat down on the bed and leaned back against the wall as Yilon closed the door. His tail flicked along the cloth. "You know, since it's your last night and all, if you don't want to..."

Yilon slid the lock across the door frame. When he turned, he knelt immediately in front of the mouse, his muzzle wide in a grin. "Why would I not want to?"

"Oh, I was just saying." Sinch closed his eyes as Yilon's paws tugged at the laces of his pants, slipping them apart easily.

"I lost fair and square," Yilon said. "So I go first." His paws pulled gently on the waist of the trousers, sliding them down Sinch's narrow, grey-furred thighs. He leaned forward, one paw holding the fringe of the mouse's tunic up while the other slipped along the white space between those thighs to cup the soft white sac. Sinch was already pretty hard, pink shaft showing above his white sheath, so Yilon got right to it, brushing his tongue up the sheath and then up the warm skin above it to the tip.

Sinch's narrow frame shuddered. He reached around to hold Yilon's arm, spreading his legs as much as the half-removed trousers would allow. Yilon closed his eyes, inhaling his friend's light scent. He settled himself on the floor more comfortably, resting both elbows on the mouse's thighs.

With slow, even strokes, he licked up the warm hardness in front of him, brushing Sinch's tight white stomach with his other paw as he did.

When he felt Sinch squeeze his arm, he slid his lips around the mouse's erection, taking the narrow shaft completely in, rubbing his tongue against it the way Sinch liked. Yilon enjoyed the rhythms of pleasing his friend, the breathing getting harsher, the feel of the skin sliding through his lips, even the curl of Sinch's whiplike tail when it wound around his wrist, as it did now. He wasn't as fond of the taste of the climax (compared to his own, at least), but it certainly wasn't bad. Besides, the connection he felt would have been worth it even if it tasted like locusts.

This close to Sinch, he could really feel the mouse's warmth through his short fur. Yilon's thicker fur was cooler to the touch, but even at the skin, Sinch was always warm. On the nights when they'd begun sharing the small bed, Yilon usually ended up waking early from the heat. The mouse was, if anything, warmer during their intimate sessions. Now, sliding his muzzle up and down over an erection that felt as if it had been out in the sun for hours, Yilon tightened his paw and fancied he felt the shaft in his muzzle grow warmer still.

He slowed just a bit, just enough to prolong Sinch's trembling and soft squeaks, but it was already too late for him to stop. The squeaks grew louder, interspersed with ragged inhalations, until the mouse's hips bucked up against Yilon's muzzle, warmth splashing onto his tongue in time with Sinch's moans of pleasure.

Yilon held him, sucking gently as Sinch arched. He lowered his muzzle with his friend's hips when it was over, washing with his tongue until Sinch squirmed and moaned. Yilon lifted his muzzle and smiled up. "Good?"

Sinch didn't answer right away, panting. "Yes," he said. "I'll miss ya."

The words drove home to Yilon that this might be the last time he knelt here, in this small room at the top of the house. He looked away from the mouse's eyes and around to the warped wood walls, the neatly piled clothes, the window looking out onto the buildings across the street. It reminded him of his own room, the one he'd moved into when he turned ten. That room had a view of the gardens, and the city of Vinton beyond.

"Your turn." Sinch interrupted his reverie, sliding off the bed and patting the cloth. Yilon smiled and stood, gazing absently out the window at the street below before sitting down in the same position the mouse had just vacated. He didn't look down as Sinch reached up to his waist, even when he felt the mouse's nimble fingers at his pants laces.

Sinch's paw closed around his sheath, squeezing the softness. "You okay?"

At that, Yilon did look down along his slender muzzle at Sinch's anxious expression. "I'm fine," he said. "Just thinking."

"Don't think so much." Sinch smiled, trailing a finger up and down Yilon's sheath.

The fox drove the nebulous thoughts out of his head and focused on the light brushing, the tickling sensation in his fur. His sheath tingled, getting harder. "There you are," he said.

"Mmm. There *you* are." The fingers on his sheath met more resistance in their squeezing. Yilon spread his legs and leaned back, letting Sinch caress him to full hardness. As soon as he felt the opening of his sheath spread and cool air on his tip, he felt the mouse's fingers brushing his skin, and then it was much easier to relax and let himself feel the tingles building in his groin, the pressure in the swelling knot at the base of his shaft.

Sinch liked to use his paws first, before applying his tongue. He slid a paw up Yilon's sheath, ruffling the fur and then smoothing it down again. When he reached the top, he brushed a furry finger up the protruding shaft, then teased with a claw on the way down. The sharp touch made the fox shiver every time he felt it, made the fur on his arms lift in arousal and his fingertips twitch. His tail thumped against the bed.

"I like when your tail wags," Sinch said softly. He slid one paw under Yilon's sac, rubbing lightly there. His other paw stroked smoothly up and down Yilon's now-full erection, pausing to squeeze the tip between his fingers and thumb, then lowering to rest against the swollen knot. Yilon laid a hind paw against Sinch's thigh, his toes curling at the mounting arousal. Any moment now, Sinch would ask if he were close. His whiskers twitched. *Not yet...not yet...*

Warm breath on his sheath. He heard Sinch inhale as the mouse's paw moved faster, building heat in his shaft, building pressure in his knot. Yilon's hips trembled. "Are you close?" Sinch asked.

"Yes," Yilon breathed. "Yes."

"Mmm." Warmth enveloped him. Sinch could never stop his front teeth from brushing skin, but Yilon liked that, and though he'd never said so, he suspected Sinch knew. He gasped at the press of the mouse's tongue along his tip. Even though it sometimes took him a while to bring himself to climax, depending on his state of mind, he never lasted long once he was in Sinch's muzzle. Tonight was no exception. With a panting moan, he arched his back away from the wall, his whole body tense in that moment before his passion crested. And then he sucked in his breath and moaned, convulsing and spurting out into the warm muzzle around him, over and over.

When he sagged back against the wall, Sinch lifted his head, rubbing a paw along his smile. "Nice," he said. He brushed a finger along Yilon's sheath. "You want a cloth?"

Yilon shook his head, still panting. "I'll be okay. Thanks."

His friend climbed up onto the bed and sat beside him, his pants at mid-thigh as well. He leaned against the fox and curled his thin tail over Yilon's bushy one. "When you're a Lord," he said a moment later, "will you have to stay in the palace all the time?"

Yilon turned his muzzle slowly. "Probably," he said. "But I'll have my own chambers. If there are any."

"There's empty ones on the first floor, by the Weasel Stair."

"I'd rather be on the third floor." He looked the mouse in the eye. "Wait, was that where you were hiding that one time?"

Sinch smiled. "No. I found those when I was wandering one day."

"I never noticed them."

The mouse traced paths through the red fur on Yilon's exposed thigh. "Going to stay here tonight?"

"Sure." Yilon said it without pausing to think.

"Your father won't be upset?"

Yilon shrugged. "You think your mother's done with the cakes?"

"She won't have started them baking yet," Sinch said, but he scooted away from Yilon and pulled his pants up.

He was right, as it turned out. Chiona was just mixing ingredients into a large bowl. Her nose twitched as they entered the kitchen. "Sinchon," she said, "would you taste this and see if there's anything you'd add to it? Yilon, come help me gather a couple things in the garden, be a dear?"

"Of course." Sinch took the bowl.

"Wash your paws first," his mother said. Sinch dipped his ears and gave Yilon an abashed grin, putting the bowl down again. Yilon lifted his own paws to his nose, trying to be nonchalant about it, and smelled mostly his own saliva and a bit of Sinch's musk. It wasn't too bad. Still, he wiped them self-consciously on his tunic as he followed Chiona outside.

"What are you collecting?" he asked her, but she motioned him to the far side of the garden, near the gate. The drone of locusts overwhelmed the sounds of the far-off busy street. Yilon's ears tracked them, in case one came close enough to grab.

"I just need some of these flowers," she said. She bent to pick small purple flowers from a large bush. "Hold out your paws."

He held them out, cupped together. One by one, she dropped the blossoms into them. "You're leaving tomorrow?"

"Day after." A small noise outside the gate, a scrape of claw on pavement, turned his ear. Someone passing by, he thought idly. Someone else who knows our shortcut.

She nodded. Three more blossoms fell into his paws. "I want you to take Sinchon with you."

He almost dropped the flowers. His ears swung around to face her full on. "What?"

"He has nobody else. He won't ask you for fear of troubling you. But he has no other friends, really."

The blossoms in his paw filled his nose with fragrance, sweet and delicate. "I know that, but I thought..."

Chiona moved to another section of the bush. When he didn't finish, she said, "You've always seemed older than him, more sure of your place in the world. Before you met him, he was quiet and shy, never told me where he was going. When he's with you, I don't worry."

Another noise behind the gate. Yilon had never stood here for this long, so he hadn't realized it was such a popular shortcut. "But he helps you in the kitchen. He can't leave his...his family."

"It's woman's work, what he does. And he has so little family as it is. Just me, and his sisters, when they're home." Her fingers worked dexterously to extract blossoms from the inside of the bush.

"He sees his father."

She turned from the bush to peer up at him. Her wise, dark eyes reminded him so much of Sinch's that even had he not known her, he would have known they were related. "In passing, in corridors and gardens. Not to come home to. Not to tell him when he's doing well, or keep him from doing ill."

"But there's you," he said.

"There is me," she agreed. "But I've taught him all I can. Bellia can help me in the kitchen. If Sinchon stays around here, he'll end up a cook or a kitchen boy."

"A cook is an honorable profession," Yilon began, but stopped when Chiona laughed.

"Rodenta bless you, my boy, I'm not ashamed of what I do. It's fine work, for a woman. But Sinchon can be more." She rested her paws on his, over top of the blossoms. "He's got much of his father in him, just as you have of yours."

"You know my father?"

She winked. "When I worked in the kitchens, he and that Lord Ikling were in there every morning to snatch a piece of bread or a small cake, seemed like. He always paid me compliments and asked after me. Not many Lords do that."

Yilon stared down at her silver-furred paws, covering the purple blossoms, with his black fingers beneath. "That's what people say."

She put a finger to his lips. It smelled of the warmth of her kitchen, the fragrance of the blossoms. "You're a good cub, honest and true. Sinchon needs more friends like you. Will you take him with you?"

Yilon pictured taking Sinch with him, thought about how good it would be to have a friend along, and then he heard another scraping, a little different this time. His ears flicked toward the gate. What if it wasn't just a busy road? When Chiona lowered her paw, he caught another scent, one stronger than it would've been if the person on the other side of the gate were just passing by. Rat, he could tell, but not much more.

He tipped the blossoms into Chiona's paws and put his finger to his lips. Quickly, he yanked the gate open, just in time to see a light brown rat tail disappearing over the fence into the adjacent garden. In a second, he was across the alley, leaping for the top of the fence. He hung there, looking into the garden on the other side. Nothing stirred among the few ragged flowers, the pile of garbage by the house, or the overgrown weeds. The wooden door into the house was shut tight.

He debated whether to jump into the garden. Locusts buzzed overhead, but no other sound reached him. The smell of garbage overwhelmed any traces the rat might have left. Besides that, he was starting to remember the arrow on the roof top, and realizing how exposed he was hanging on top of a fence in a back alley of Divalia. He dropped to the ground.

"Sorry," he said, returning to Chiona's yard and closing the door. She gave him a curious look from the same spot near the flowery bush. "Your garden's really nice."

"Sinchon and the girls help me with it." She tilted her head. "Are you in any sort of trouble?"

He shook his head. "I don't know. I think someone was listening outside the gate."

She frowned. "Listening at my gate?"

Yilon flicked his ears. "I don't know. Maybe it's just a coincidence."

Sinchon called through the open door, "I think it's done, Ma."

They both turned toward the kitchen. Chiona looked up at Yilon. "Please," she said. "He won't ask you himself."

He nodded. "If I can."

"Thank you." She made her way along the little stone path back to the kitchen. Yilon followed, his mind awhirl with thoughts of Sinch coming with him, the arrow on the roof, and the rat in the alley. He was too distracted to talk much to Sinch, or his sisters when they arrived home a short time later. Finally, Chiona shooed them off to bed, fending off their motions toward the delicious-smelling pastries.

"The cakes will be done in the morning," she said. "And you both have a busy day tomorrow." Her brown eyes twinkled as she hustled them up the stairs.

"What did she mean, we have a busy day tomorrow?" Sinch closed the door behind them.

Yilon leaned against the wall beside the window, tail swishing behind him. "I was thinking," he said. "How would you like to come with me to Dewanne?"

Sinch gaped, his head tilting. "I...with you? But..." He glanced at his door, looking downward.

"Your mom..." Yilon stopped. "Um, I asked her already. That's what we were talking about in the garden," he said, inspired.

"She said yes?" Yilon nodded. Sinch paced toward the small table, where he set down a paw on his pile of clothes. "And...you want me to come?"

"Of course." Yilon smiled. "It'll be more fun that way."

"Really?"

Yilon sat on the bed. "Didn't I just say that?"

"Sorry." Sinch's face spread into a grin. "I'd love to." He took two steps to the bed and knelt astride one of Yilon's legs. His nose bounced an inch from the fox's.

Yilon grasped his friend's arms and pulled him down to the bed. "All right," he said. "Then let's get some sleep. We both have to pack tomorrow."

The bed was small, but they were used to fitting together on it. Yilon squeezed back against the wall, and Sinch squeezed back against him. It was crowded and warm, but this late in the summer, the night brought a cooling breeze in through the open window. Yilon was more comfortable in Sinch's bed than he'd ever been in his own bed at the palace.

Chapter 3: The Crown of Dewanne

In the morning, Chiona gave Yilon a napkin folded around a warm pile of cakes. The aroma of fresh baking and honey rose to his nostrils; the strong cinnamon and underlying vanilla made his nose twitch. "Now, mind you don't eat them all the first day," she said, turning back to the stove. "They'll keep for a week."

"Mmmf," Yilon said, holding the napkin out to Sinch.

Chiona snatched the parcel back. "Honestly, you two. I have cakes made for you to eat this morning! Hmph. I'll just put them in here and you can have them tomorrow."

"We could have those now, too," Yilon said, taking the wrapped cakes and swallowing the one in his mouth.

The mouse laughed. "Growing boys. Here, take them and go on about your day. Sinchon, I'll see you for dinner. Yilon, will you be back to say good-bye?"

"I don't know." He leaned in close and rubbed his muzzle along hers. "If I don't, good-bye, and thank you."

She put her arms around him. "You take care, and remember what I said."

Yilon looked more carefully outside when he left than he normally did. "What's the matter?" Sinch asked, behind him, but Yilon didn't want to worry him any more. He'd already over-reacted to the arrow on the roof. And the streets in the morning were clearer than they had been at night. He could see almost all the way to the river. All the rats he could see were intent on their own errands.

Sinch was very chattery on the way back, talking about the trip and the country they'd see. Yilon kept the conversation going with a word here and there, but in the back of his mind he was puzzling over why a rat might want to spy on him. Who could he turn to to ask about that kind of thing? Sinch would overreact, his father would either overreact or tell him he was being silly, and his tutors all lived in their own abstract worlds.

They showed their papers at the gate and walked into the palace garden. Halfway to the door, Yilon grabbed Sinch's arm and pulled him down a side path. "Father," he said, jerking his head in the direction they were turning away from. His father ran with Lord Ikling every morning, and Yilon didn't have any desire to meet up with him before dinner.

"So what are you going to take along?" Sinch asked, holding open the side door.

Yilon slipped through. The palace was just beginning to wake up, lords strolling down the hallways to breakfast or out to morning errands as the servants hurried to get their work done. "Clothes," he said, "all those formal outfits I have, and I'm going to the armory now to get a bow. Then I've got the armband my mother gave me, all my books...of course, my comportment and diplomacy classes don't even have books..."

They walked down to the armory, where Yilon found it surprisingly easy to talk the old bear into letting him have not only a short bow for the trip to Dewanne, but also the knife he'd loaned Sinch the day before. He kept it hidden in his belt so that Sinch wouldn't see it when he came out, but he needn't have worried. Sinch was standing at the base of the stair, looking up, and didn't seem to have noticed him at all.

Yilon edged around until he could see what Sinch was looking at: a mouse lord strolling down the stair, giving instructions to his servant. Sinch shrank back behind the large post, peering around it as the lord passed by.

Yilon came to stand behind his friend, watching the lord walk away. He thought the lord hadn't seen them at all, but just before he stepped into a side passage, he turned his head, his dark eyes looking directly at the two of them.

Sinch froze where he was, even his tail going limp and falling to the marble. Yilon couldn't think of anything to say to his friend. The moment stretched out, the two of them and the lord moving with the slowness of cold honey. Finally, the lord moved his head back, and continued walking down the side passage, out of sight.

They stood watching the empty passage. Sinch's shoulders sagged. Yilon put a paw on the nearer one to him. "Wanna help me pack?" he said. The mouse nodded, following him around to his chambers without a word.

By the time they reached the room, he'd perked up. Volyan wasn't there, no doubt having spent the night with one of his friends, but four empty trunks had appeared overnight, two on Yilon's side of the room and two on Volyan's. Sinch helped Yilon fold his clothes and pack them into the first trunk, which took them about until Volyan returned, his tunic balled up under his arm. The fluffy white fur on his chest was tousled, his stomach fur matted, but his ears were perked, and below his sleepy eyes, his muzzle curved in a satisfied smile.

"Good morning, brother," he said, tossing the tunic into one of the trunks. "Packed already?"

"Almost." Yilon glanced at his empty trunk.

Volyan looked around the small room. "Can't believe I have to go too. I was hoping to have my room to myself again."

"You'll have it when you get back," Sinch said. "Yilon's gonna be a lord and he'll have his own chambers."

"Maybe." Volyan opened his wardrobe. When he turned around, arms full of rumpled tunics, Yilon saw his grin. "If there aren't any other lords who need rooms."

"Oh, be quiet," Yilon said.

"Don't worry. I'm sure there's a closet somewhere." Volyan tossed the tunics into his trunk.

"Come on, Sinch." Yilon waved to his friend.

The mouse tagged along dutifully behind him as he visited all his tutors, collecting books and well-wishes. It took most of the afternoon, but this time of year, the sun was still halfway on its journey down the sky when Sinch had to leave for dinner. "Back here at sunup?" he said.

Yilon nodded, tail wagging. "Excited?"

He didn't really need to ask. Sinch nodded, eyes bright. "And," he said, lowering his voice, "I haven't forgotten about that arrow. I'm going to get a couple weapons to bring along, just in case..."

"No, listen," Yilon said. "We'll have guards, I'm sure."

Sinch nodded. "But how do you know you can trust them?"

"Maxon wouldn't bring someone untrustworthy," Yilon started to argue, but the mouse was so earnest, and what harm would it do? "All right," he said. "I feel safer already."

"Don't get hurt tonight." Sinch looked behind him, into the palace main hall.

"I just hope I can get through dinner without Father making a scene." Yilon clapped his friend on the shoulder. "See you in the morning."

Despite his flippant words, Sinch's comment bothered him, bringing up again the nagging worry that he might really be in some danger. He watched the mouse walk through the long shadows created by the sun across the garden. The familiar setting had never felt so sinister. He imagined an arrow flying out of nowhere towards his heart, a rat stepping out of the shadows with a knife...

He hadn't realized he was holding his breath until Sinch was out of sight, when he let it out in a slow exhale, relaxing. He'd no sooner turned back to the main hall than a paw landed on his shoulder.

He jumped. A raspy voice said, "Ah, Yilon, just who I've been looking for."

The familiar voice reassured him. Jinna, the porcupine who currently served as palace Steward, always looked harried; her paws rarely stopped fidgeting, and the small decorative beads that weighted down her long quills always seemed to have been scrambled from some basic pattern into randomness. "I've had a busy day," he said.

She clacked her front teeth at him, a habit he was happy Sinch hadn't developed. "*You've* had a busy day? Let me tell you, between trying to arrange the king's dinner for the visiting Ferrenian nobles next week and issuing new papers and preparing for the annual winter retreat and on top of all that I'm told I have to prepare your papers to be sworn in before tomorrow morning..."

"I have to be sworn in tonight?" Yilon yelped.

"No, no, I had to prepare the *papers* tonight, because you're leaving in the morning." She clacked her teeth again. "Come on, come on, I need to give them to you."

He followed her up to her office and took the papers, a bundle sealed with the king's seal. "Now, you'll need to have them re-sealed, of course. Maxon will take care of that. And I will see you again when you come back. Now. Maxon has your maps, and your father has the crown."

Yilon stopped nodding automatically. "The what?"

"Crown, the crown of Dewanne, you need it to be confirmed, didn't Maxon tell you that?"

"No." Yilon touched the top of his head, between his ears. "I need a crown?"

"Maxon will explain all that. He has all the papers you'll need between here and Dewanne, and he knows the way. Is there anything else you need from me?"

Yilon's ears folded down. "I don't know. I hope not."

She patted him on the shoulder, bustling him out the door. "I hope not, too, because you won't want to turn around and come back for it. Have a good trip and I'll see you back here in a few months."

She'd already turned to go back inside when he had an idea. "Wait!" He ran back into the office after her.

Her beads rattled as she sat down at her desk. The smile on her short muzzle was tired but warm. "What is it, dear?"

"Well..." He hesitated. It had seemed perfect a second ago, that he would ask sensible, efficient Jinna about the arrow and the rat, but now that he had to make the words come out, he felt as if he were trying to tell her about a dream he'd had, something ridiculous and childish. When he'd first arrived at the palace two years ago, he'd asked several stupid questions about life there, to the delight of his brother, and now he prided himself on knowing everything about his world.

Jinna picked up a piece of paper from the desk. "I'm fairly busy," she said softly.

"Could someone shoot an arrow onto the roof?" he blurted out.

She looked up from the paper and laughed, shortly. "You would know that better than I would, wouldn't you?"

"I mean," he said, "I was on the roof and an arrow landed there. Sinch thinks someone was shooting at me, but that's silly. It was just a regular arrow, not a longbow one."

Jinna's smile faded. "Did the arrow just land there? Or did it come in," she moved her broad paw horizontally across her desk, "at you?"

"More at me," he said. "I think. I didn't really see it. Sinch knocked me down. So he must have been able to see it coming."

Beads rattled as Jinna shook her shoulders. "It's troublesome," she said. "Back in the time of King Halloran, a merchant scaled the wall outside and hit a lord with a stone from a sling. Broke his arm. And in the fourth year of King Calinon's reign, someone killed a lord with an arrow shot from the top of the Knight's Rest."

"Is that a tavern?"

She nodded. "It was. King Calinon ordered it torn down. But both those nobles were in the garden at the time. I don't know of anyone being shot at on the roof." She peered at him. "That might be because nobody ever goes up there. Why were you on the roof?"

"It's nice up there." Yilon rubbed one hind paw along the floor. "Quiet. Nobody told me I couldn't go up there."

Jinna chuckled. "You can. Most people don't. Hm. It's certainly odd that, the timing coming the day after we received the news of Lord Dewanne's passing."

"You mean..." Yilon furrowed his brow, his ears flattening. "But how could anyone know? Why would someone attack me?"

"That's the question. It could be your bloodline, if there's some distant relative with a claim to the title. Nobody's had time to build up a grudge against you, have they?"

Yilon shook his head. "Is anyone else from Dewanne even here?"

Jinna clacked her teeth. "I suspect it is merely a coincidence and an accident, but I will do some research. If I find anything that seems important, I will send a messenger to find you in Dewanne."

Out in the hall, Yilon clutched the bundle of paper, his head spinning. He walked down to his father's chambers, hurrying as he got closer and smelled the food, the aroma so fresh it must have been brought down just a few minutes before. His stomach was growling by the time he opened the door.

His father, Streak, Volyan, and Maxon were already seated around a table that had been brought into the parlor. His father's servant, a quiet grey fox named Vinnix, pulled out the last empty chair as Yilon walked in.

Yilon swept his tail back and sat down, setting the papers on the table, where they were immediately removed to the desk by Vinnix. "Finally," Volyan grumbled. "I'm starving."

"I had to go see Jinna," Yilon explained.

His father waved a paw. "We haven't been waiting for long."

Vinnix lifted the lid from the serving dish and filled each of their plates from it, with roasted fowl in a honey glaze, an assortment of roasted vegetables, candied sweet potatoes, and a freshly-baked wheat bun. Yilon had to wait until their guest was served, then his father and Streak, and finally Volyan before he got his plate.

"It feels like you only just arrived here," Volle said to Yilon. "And now you're leaving already."

"All grown up," Streak said. Maxon coughed into his paw.

Yilon shrugged, taking a bite of his roll. It wasn't as good as Chiona's.

Volle looked over at Volyan. "You're both leaving," he said. "Off to be official heirs."

His voice sounded funny. When Yilon looked up, he saw his father's ears splayed, his muzzle resting on both paws. He wasn't touching his food. Yilon looked at Volyan, who met his gaze with a serious expression and then looked back at Volle. "We'll be back soon," he said. "And we'll be staying in the same places."

Their father nodded, smiling. "I know." He lifted his fork and took a bite of the fowl. "It's just all happening so quickly."

"Tell me about it." Yilon had managed to avoid thinking about the fact that he was leaving home for most of the day, busying himself with errands and packing. Now, looking around the parlor he'd thought he'd be glad to leave, he found himself nervous at the prospect of the journey. Don't be silly, he told himself. Sinch will be with you, and besides, you've left home to go live in a new place before.

Yes, he reminded himself, and look how well that went. He speared a vegetable and chewed on it, looking down at his plate.

His father said his name and Volyan's, and when they lifted their heads, went on, "I want you both to know how very proud I am of you. You are both quick learners and quick on your paws." The first, Yilon knew, was

"I meant no offense."

more true of him, while the second was more fitting for his brother. "I wish we'd had more time to spend together."

"We'll have plenty of time, Father," Volyan said.

Yilon pushed around the food on his plate, his stomach suddenly churning with worry. He wished Sinch were eating with them, so he could turn to his friend and see someone else who was taking the trip with them. That reminded him that he needed to tell Maxon, so he turned to the thin fox. "Maxon," he said, "I do have someone coming with me after all."

The three adults stared at him. Maxon cleared his throat. "Er, your father informed me that you do not have a personal servant."

"I don't. The one who's coming with me is my friend, Sinch. Sinchon. He's the mouse who was practicing with me yesterday when you saw us."

Streak put a paw on Volle's shoulder, but Yilon paid them little attention. He couldn't quite figure out why Maxon's muzzle curved down as if his last bite of fowl had been spoiled. "I see," Maxon said. "I must advise you that I would consider that decision unwise."

"Unwise?" Yilon echoed. "Why? He's my friend."

"I am not in a position to criticize your lordship's choice of friends here in Divalia, but I must point out that a ruling Lord of Dewanne is expected to associate with a certain class of people." Maxon coughed, and took a bite of fowl, apparently considering that the last word on the matter.

"He's got noble blood," Yilon said with some heat. "He's not just common. He's as good as you or me. Maybe better than you."

Maxon put his fork down and turned his full attention on Yilon. "I *beg* your pardon?"

"What my son meant to say," Volle put in, "is that his friend is certainly in his class. For all that matters."

"I said what I meant," Yilon muttered, but his ears came up.

Maxon coughed. "I meant no offense," he said. "I did not intend to cast doubt upon the bloodline of Master Sinchon. I merely meant that..." He looked around the table. "The nobility of Dewanne are all of good vulpine lineage. No offense, sir."

Streak nodded in return. "None taken."

"Think how it would look to have the future Lord of Dewanne arrive in town in the company of..."

Yilon took a certain amount of pleasure from seeing the rest of the table staring at Maxon with the same mix of bewilderment and irritation he felt. "Of what?" Volle said. "His best friend?"

Maxon's ears folded back. He appeared to be searching for something to say. Volle went on. "Listen to me, Steward. My son is your future lord.

He has told you that his friend will be accompanying him. Your advice has been heard. I expect to hear no more on the matter."

"Of course, sir," Maxon said, his voice low. He lifted a paw and rubbed his whiskers. "My apologies."

Volle pointed across the table. "Apologize to him."

Maxon turned to Yilon. "My deepest apologies, my lord. Please understand that I had only your well-being in mind."

Yilon glanced at his father, who nodded. "I accept your apology," he said. "But don't let it happen again."

"Of course not, my lord."

The grin came unbidden to his muzzle, though he tried to restrain it. He snuck a sideways glance at Volyan, who was similarly grinning, and who gave him an encouraging head-bob and flick of the ears. Next to him, his father's russet muzzle still held a warm smile, giving Yilon an unexpected sympathetic warmth in his chest. Then his gaze slid over to the white wolf at his father's side, and his grin became a scowl. He stabbed at his vegetables and filled his muzzle, chewing hard.

For the rest of the meal, his father didn't attempt any more speeches about his children. Maxon cleared his throat several times, but didn't speak. Though Yilon preferred small talk to emotionally-charged tearful good-byes, he still couldn't believe they were calmly discussing the weather and the quality of the food when he and Volyan were going to be leaving the next day. For his last dinner in Vinton, his mother had prepared his favorite meal, barbecued mountain sheep with the local sour sunberries, and she'd brought him his first taste of wine. They'd eaten on the large patio of the small mountainside palace under the stars, and she'd talked about all the challenges he was going to face in Divalia. He hadn't cried until the next day, alone in the carriage.

After dinner, Streak and Volyan went to walk in the gardens and talk together, as they often did. Yilon tried to retire to his room, but his father asked him to wait, with a gesture to Maxon. The thin fox nodded, coughed, and reached for a satchel slung over the back of his chair. It was a plain leather traveling bag of the sort Yilon had used to bring his personal effects from Vinton, patched and worn, but Maxon opened the laces as carefully as if they were the finest silk.

He reached inside and drew out a polished wooden box as large as Yilon's head. The top of the box was inlaid with a gleaming pattern, intricate copper with gold highlights, of a fox's head in the frontal view of a star of Canis, the points of the ears touching the back corners, the nose positioned just above the clasp that Maxon undid with gentle precision. He lifted the hinged lid slowly. Yilon noticed that he was not coughing nor clearing his throat, and in fact had done neither since Volle had gestured to him to begin.

"This," Maxon said, raising the lid to its fullest extent, "is the crown of Dewanne."

On a bed of black silk, a gleaming wrought gold headpiece shone in the dim parlor. Yilon leaned forward for a better look. The base of the crown formed a "U" of solid gold, the top prongs of which curved down and around to fit around the base of a fox's ears. Atop this base sat a smaller copper circlet that supported three golden peaks at the front, the middle one higher than the ends. Thin copper wire inside each of the peaks traced different patterns.

"The peaks represent the mountains that are our home," Maxon said, indicating them with a finger without touching them. "This is the crest of the House of Dewanne." Yilon had already recognized the pattern in the center peak from Maxon's jerkin, the circular emblem with the star of Canis. "On this peak, symbolizing our past, is the ancient star of Fox-Canis. And on this side," his finger moved from the left peak to the right, "symbolizing our future, is the current crest of the King of Divalia. It is re-worked every time the Circle moves along."

"Tail and Teeth," Yilon breathed. He reached out for it, but Maxon intercepted his paw.

"Ahem. Begging his lordship's pardon, but the heir should not touch the crown until the Confirmation ceremony. It is tradition." He turned his muzzle away from Yilon and the crown to cough.

Yilon drew his paw back. "Sorry," he said.

"It is only worn on ceremonial occasions," Maxon said, closing the box.

Yilon's father met his eye. "Why did you need to bring it on this errand, Maxon? Wouldn't it have been safer remaining in Dewanne?" Yilon had the feeling that his father knew the answer and was only asking the question for his benefit.

Maxon replaced the crown in its bag as carefully as he'd removed it. "The crown has great importance to the people. It is unlikely that a confirmed heir would be accepted should he attempt to undergo the ceremony without wearing it."

Yilon frowned. "You mean if I don't have the crown, I can't become lord of Dewanne?"

"Nothing is impossible," Maxon said. "However, as I said, it would be much more difficult. Needlessly so, may I add, because the crown is in my care and will remain so until the confirmation ceremony, after which it will be locked in the palace treasury in its normal place."

"Wouldn't it have been safer just to leave it there?" Yilon eyed the plain leather bag. It seemed so vulnerable.

"The treasury is normally quite secure," Maxon said. "However, in this case, when the next lord has not yet been confirmed, the location of the crown is of paramount importance."

"You mean that someone else could take over the lordship," Yilon said. Maxon inclined his head. "Has that ever happened?"

"Twice in our remembered history, the crown was stolen and a confirmation ceremony performed for a lord who was not the official heir. In one case, the lordship was taken by the heir's brother with the help of the local Cantor. In the second case, the old Lord had died suddenly and without issue, so there was no official heir. There was a certain amount of unpleasantness over the succession for a number of years."

Unpleasantness. Yilon's fur prickled. He'd read about wars of succession in his history lessons: protracted, bloody affairs with high passions driving both sides to ridiculous lengths. He would certainly never raise an army to wrest the title of Lord Vinton from his brother.

"It is a blessing," Maxon proceeded after a clearing of his throat, "that Lord Dewanne named his heir before passing. Though of course," he said, lowering his voice and leaning in with a glance at the doorway through which Vinnix had disappeared, "there was little doubt who would be chosen."

"I was wondering about that," Yilon said. "Why—"

Volle coughed suddenly. "Excuse me," he said. He pushed back his chair and stood. Maxon immediately followed suit. "I was just thinking I should go check on your carriage for tomorrow," Volle said, tail swaying.

"Oh, my lord, I should do that." Maxon volunteered immediately.

Yilon's father nodded. "Very well. Thank you, Maxon."

"I'll return in a moment." The thin fox bowed to both of them. He started to pick up the crown, then reconsidered and left it sitting on the floor.

Yilon, who'd remained in his chair, watched his father sit back down. "You never meant to go," he said. "You just wanted to get rid of him."

His father looked pleased. "Always remember that people will behave according to their station," he said. "If I'd simply asked him to leave, he would have wondered what I wanted to say to you without him present."

"So what do you want to say to me?" Yilon leaned back in his chair, slumping.

His father looked at the door the same way Maxon had when checking that Vinnix had gone. "You've never asked why you were named the heir to Dewanne."

Yilon shrugged. "He didn't have any cubs. You have a spare one."

"You're not a "spare," and don't let me hear you say that again," Volle snapped. "Understand?"

"Yes, sir." Yilon sagged further down in his chair.

His father stared at him until Yilon squirmed, looking around the parlor, at the shadows outside the window, at the plain leather satchel, anywhere but his father's green eyes, dark in the parlor. "All right," Volle said finally. "I'm going to tell you why you're the heir to Dewanne. I expect you to keep this in the closest confidence."

Yilon perked his ears despite the sullen resentment he was trying to foster. "Yes, sir."

"The reason is that Lord Dewanne and Lady Dewanne thought that you were Lord Dewanne's son."

At that, Yilon bolted upright in his chair. "You mean, that Mother just took me in, raised me—"

His father held out a paw. "Let me finish. They thought—Lady Dewanne still thinks—that Lord Dewanne sired you by your mother. That is not the case. You are my son. But Dewanne needed an heir, and publicly he has said that he would prefer the land remain held by a fox of noble birth. Since he and his wife had no cubs of their own, and he and I were good friends, that left you." He checked the door again, but no sound or scent came from beyond it. "There was no reason to tell you before now. I'd intended to tell you later tonight, but I hadn't realized that Lord Dewanne had told Maxon about your supposed heritage." His ears flicked, matching the annoyance that briefly clouded his muzzle.

"Wait," Yilon said, his head whirling. "So he thought...but that means that he must have...he and Mother? While she was married to you?" His father nodded. "She wouldn't, though. Not with another fox." He gulped, ears flattening in guilt as the words spilled out. His mother's affairs had always been discreet, and with a careless sentence, he'd just told his father about them. He curled his tail under his chair, wishing he could snatch the words back.

His father nodded as if he'd always known, though his ears drooped. "Your mother and I have long had an understanding. I have no illusions that she keeps herself faithful to me."

"She hasn't made a commitment to anyone else." Yilon folded his arms.

"That would be her right," Volle said. "But regardless, it was her honor that led her to confess to me what Dewanne had planned. She arranged to trick him so that he would believe he'd sired a cub with her, a cub he intended me to believe was mine, but who would bear his blood."

"Why?" Yilon said. "Why wouldn't she just say no?"

Volle smiled. "She wanted the best for her cubs. She wants to be the mother to Lords, and she saw a chance to do well for another of her sons."

That sounded like his mother, more than the vixen who would cheat on her husband and then double-cross the cheater. Slowly, he relaxed. "So I'm not his son?"

His father's smile grew wider. He shook his head. "Your nose should tell you that."

He hadn't put much thought into it, but looking back on his arrival at the palace and the ease with which he'd fallen into a familial relationship with his father and brother, he knew that scent was part of that. He took one deep breath through his nose and felt the familiarity of his father's scent that went beyond simple species recognition. Of course, he thought, he'd never met Lord Dewanne. So it was possible he'd have felt the same with him, wasn't it?

"So I wanted you to be prepared for that," his father was saying. "Because Lady Dewanne for certain, and perhaps some other influential people at the court, will tell you you're his son. Play along. Nobody need know the truth but for us and your mother."

"Does Volyan know?" He couldn't say why he asked, but it was one of the first things that came to mind.

"If it's important to you, we can tell him," his father said. "I doubt he'll ever hear otherwise, though."

Yilon shrugged. "I was just wondering." He tilted his head. "Why didn't Lord Dewanne have cubs of his own?"

His father folded his ears down. "That would be his family's business. I would suggest you not bring it up with Lady Dewanne. There's no remedying it now, no matter what the reason."

Yilon determined that he would ask her at the first opportunity. He pushed back his chair. "Fine. Thanks for telling me."

"There's one more thing." His father looked away from him, ears folding back.

Yilon felt a tremor in his chest. He sat down. "What?"

"Well..." His father lowered his muzzle. "As a Lord, you know, you will have certain duties. Now, I've never had the chance to talk to you about... about how a fox and a vixen..."

"You don't have to," Yilon said quickly. "I, uh, Volyan explained it all."

His father didn't look much comforted by that. "Good, good. I suppose he probably already knew when I had that talk with him, too. He's certainly wasted little time broadening his experience. But I've noticed that you don't seem to have the same...enthusiasm that he does."

The conversation was taking a steep turn that made Yilon feel like he were looking off the edge of the roof. He scuffed his paws along the floor and wished he could run away, wished for Volyan or Maxon to come back into the room and put an end to this.

"I've been through some of the same things you have. I wanted to tell you that even if you do prefer males, there's no reason you can't be a proper, beloved lord. I hope you've seen the life that I have with Streak as an example..."

Yilon snorted. His father paused, then went on. "If you want to stay close to Sinch—"

"Leave him out of it," Yilon said.

Volle paused. "I'm just saying, you and he could have a good life together."

"He's just a friend of mine." Yilon felt himself growling. "We're not going to have a *life* together, or anything like that."

"Okay," his father said slowly. "You don't seem interested in anyone else. There was Haley..."

"She was as bad as the empty-headed idiots Volyan likes."

Now his father frowned, his tone becoming more stern. "There's no need to be rude to your brother's companions."

"He says the same thing about them, or haven't you listened?" Yilon sat up in his chair. "Or don't you care because he's so perfect?"

"Yilon," his father said warningly. His brow lowered, his muzzle almost snarling.

"No, really! He never does anything wrong! He gets to be lord of Vinton. He's in love with girls just like a lord is supposed to be. Maybe I like them too. Maybe I just don't like any of the ones in this place."

"That doesn't excuse rudeness."

Yilon barely heard him. "Just because there's only one person who I really like spending time with, one worthwhile person in this whole stupid city, you *assume* I'm like you."

His father's eyes darkened further. "You don't have to be like me."

"I don't want to be like you!" Yilon stood in his chair. "I don't want to be lord of Dewanne and I don't want to live in this stupid palace in this stupid city! The only good thing about this whole stupid ordeal is that it gets me out of here."

"Sit down," Volle said quietly.

Yilon's tail curled down. He remained standing. "I'm a lord now."

"Not yet," Volle said. "And I'm still your father."

"So you think," Yilon said.

"I know. I trust your mother."

"You don't even know her!" He was almost shouting.

His father glared at him. "I know her well enough."

"Sure." Yilon scowled at the table.

"You think you're the only one who's ever gone through something like this?"

"I'm the only one who seems to care."

His father took a breath. "I've tried for two years to be a good father, to get through to you. I thought we'd reached an understanding these last few months."

Anger and guilt swirled within him. He felt the decision to retort come and go without being conscious of having made it. "Maybe I just stopped caring enough to fight."

"That would make me sad," his father said. He lifted his head. Although Yilon was still staring down at the dark wood of the table, he knew his father was looking right at him. "One thing I never thought of you is that you didn't care."

"You don't even know me! You have no idea what I care about." He returned his father's look, daring him to disagree.

A wry smile twisted his father's muzzle. "You're not as mysterious as you think. I know you care about Vinton, and miss it. I know you care about your mother. I know you care about Sinch."

"I told you, leave him out of it."

"I just don't want you to cast him aside because you think he doesn't fit into the life of a lord."

"Lords have friends, don't they?" Yilon said.

"Of course they do, but—"

He heard a cough outside and smelled the Dewanne steward. He leaned down. "Don't assume everyone's like you. I don't want to be anything like you. I'll have a wife because I have to, and I'll be true to her."

His father's eyes clouded. Yilon steeled himself against the stab of guilt, straightening as Maxon entered the room. The steward started to talk, then looked from one to the other of them and broke off. "Should I come back?"

Yilon folded his arms and waited for his father to speak. "No," Volle said. "You have to leave early. You should get your sleep."

It was curious. He had gotten in the last word, but as he lay down on his bed for the last time, he didn't have the feeling of having won. He turned over and stared at the ceiling in the dark room. The padding in the bed smelled musty, but not as bad as Sinch's, and over that smell lay his own musk and Volyan's. And in those two vulpine scents, he caught the relationship not just between the two of them, but also with their father.

He missed the warmth of Sinch at his side. But he couldn't miss it, or he'd just drive himself crazy. He was to be a lord with a wife, whether he wanted one or not. If he'd learned nothing else from history, he'd learned the importance of succession.

He closed his eyes and tried to push away all the thoughts crowding his head. Volyan was breathing evenly, already asleep, but it took Yilon the better part of an hour to relax. He wasn't even aware of having fallen asleep in the windowless room, but a moment later, Volyan was shaking him awake and the blackness outside the doorway was tinged with grey.

The sun hadn't quite risen. They walked out to the stables all together, where Maxon was already waiting for them. The palace grooms had prepared two carriages, each with two mounts stamping the ground impatiently. Their breath steamed in barely visible puffs in the slight chill of the morning air. A plump raccoon supervised the fitting of the harnesses on Yilon's carriage, while a wiry fox with a crossbow slung across his back sat atop and watched, his paws curled around a bowl from which he lapped occasionally. Yilon thought the fox was staring at him, but as soon as their eyes met, the other looked away.

Vinnix and three footservants brought down Yilon's two trunks and Volyan's one. Maxon had only one case with him as well as the plain leather bag. Yilon followed that one as the servants loaded the bags onto the coaches.

A paw landed on his shoulder. He turned to his father, whose other paw rested similarly on Volyan's shoulder.

"This day is far too quickly come," he said. "I would've liked to have kept you young for a little longer."

Yilon rolled his eyes, while Volyan just laughed and hugged their father back. "I'll see you in a couple weeks," he said.

"I know, but you're going off to take your responsibilities." Volle paused to take a breath. Yilon looked away from the shine in his eyes. "To grow up and be lords."

"Not me." Volyan looked at Yilon. "Not for a while."

"Maybe sooner than you think." Their father cut off Volyan's protest with a wave. "I don't intend to step down or die any time soon. I just want you both to know that you're not alone. You'll always be part of this family."

At that, Volyan reached his other arm to include Streak in the group. Yilon huffed, slipping away from his father's paw to walk over to Maxon. As he reached the other fox's side, he saw Sinch hurrying through the garden, with Jinna at his side. He waved for his father's benefit, pretending he'd seen them coming and that was why he'd broken away.

His father came over to him anyway, as Volyan and Streak embraced and murmured to each other. Maxon stepped back discreetly at a look from Volle, who took Yilon to one side. "I know how you feel," he said, "and I just want you to remember that there will come a time when you will want this family. Don't say anything right now. All I ask is that you remember that when you do, it will be here."

"Fine," Yilon said.

"And there's one more thing I wanted to tell you before you go," Volle said.

"Am I late?" Sinch ran up, breathless, his bag slung over his shoulder. He looked around eagerly at the foxes.

"You run fast enough," Jinna grumbled, coming up behind him. Her beads rattled, a colorful mess in the grey morning light.

"Just in time," Maxon said, and coughed.

Yilon glanced at the steward, frowning at his tone, but didn't say anything. Jinna was beckoning him to one side. He hoped his father wouldn't follow them, but he did, and she didn't stop him.

"I wanted to catch you before you left," she said. "I pulled out some of our files on Dewanne last night. There's a history of some factions there, dating from the old pre-Unification time, renewed again when we conquered Delford. It's primarily foxes and mice, though there may be some factions within the foxes as well. I didn't have time to go through all the notes."

"Why did you ask about factions?" Volle's muzzle tilted, studying his son.

"Shouldn't I find out about the land I'm going to be lord of?" Yilon asked. He saw immediately from Jinna's look that she wouldn't keep the secret from his father, but he didn't care.

"And nobody else has arrived at the palace from Dewanne in the past week. I sent Burberry to ask around the merchants, but that will take a few days. It's okay, he doesn't have much else to do at the moment except get in Cofi's way. If I find anything, I'll send it on."

"Thank you," Yilon said.

She nodded, making her beads rattle. "I thought you should know about the factions." She looked past him at the carriages, quite deliberately, but when he turned he saw only Maxon and Sinch, ignoring each other. By the time he turned back, she was already waving to him. "Now I have to get back and see if I can finish Lord Fuster's guest's papers before she wakes up."

He and his father watched her scurry down the garden path in a *ssshk-ssshk* of bouncing beads. "Good," Volle said, "I admire your diligence in researching Dewanne. It makes me feel that I don't have to tell you this last thing."

Yilon waited. His father said, "Listen."

He cocked his ears, but his father said nothing more. "I'm listening."

Volle smiled. "No. Just that: listen. To the people who greet you, those who offer you favors, and those who offer scorn. Master Xoren tells me you are already practiced at that, but I thought—"

"You thought you'd remind me."

"Yes." Volle's smile faded. "And now, I think Maxon and Sinch are ready for you."

Yilon paused, the moment of separation calling up echoes of two years ago. "Thanks," he said, awkwardly. "I'll write when I get to Dewanne."

His father smiled. "Travel safe."

"We can take care of ourselves," Sinch said, walking up to them. "Come on, Yilon, I think he wants to go."

Volyan and Streak came back over for good-byes as well. Yilon hugged his brother and then waved to his family as he stepped up into the carriage, Sinch close behind him. Maxon had already seated himself on the rear bench, the leather satchel at his side, so Yilon and Sinch took the facing seats, their backs to the mounts. The plump raccoon climbed up next to the crossbow-wielding fox, and within moments, they were driving through the gates and into the city of Divalia.

By Yilon's count, Maxon either coughed or cleared his throat nineteen times in the short drive to the walls of Divalia, even though he said not a word, his nose buried in his small book. Yilon stared out the window and tried to figure out in his head how many times it would happen on the whole trip.

Sinch finally spoke, looking out of his window at the receding buildings of Divalia. "I've never been outside the city," he said. "Thank you for allowing me to come along."

Maxon coughed, staring firmly down at his book. Yilon spoke up when it was clear the steward wasn't about to. "Of course I wanted you along," he said. "In fact, I brought something for you."

Sinch's eyes widened as Yilon brought the dagger out from under his belt. "For me?"

Yilon nodded. "What, like I'm going to carry a dagger around? What would I do with it?"

"Defend yourself?" Maxon suggested.

Yilon grinned. "I feel safer with Sinch having the dagger."

"Really." Maxon looked scornful.

"You should show him what you can do," Yilon told Sinch.

"Maybe later." The mouse turned the dagger over in his paws. "We'll be driving for two weeks, right?"

Again, Maxon remained quiet. Yilon gave him a chance, and then said, "Depending on how fast the horses go. At this pace, that's about right."

"It'll go fast," Sinch said.

One of the things Yilon liked about the mouse was his general optimism, which is why it had been so strange that he was worried about the arrow. That led him to thinking about what Jinna had said, about the factions and the other people who'd traveled from Dewanne. There couldn't be many, not at this time of year. Merchants wouldn't be going home yet, and they were the majority of travelers on the roads.

Now that he had a chance to relax in the safety of the carriage, he couldn't seriously entertain the idea that someone was trying to hurt him. It was possible, of course, but who would travel all the way from Dewanne when he was going there himself? Why not just stay and wait for him? In Divalia, Yilon was surrounded by family and friends and the palace guards. Every mile put between him and the palace made him more isolated, less secure.

He shifted on his seat. Sinch, next to him, gazed raptly at the countryside, the cultivated fields with copses of trees defining their edges. Yilon had never asked whether his friend had left the city before. He himself thought the fields looked much the same as the fields between Vinton and Divalia, no real difference noticeable driving west rather than south from the capital. It was all bright green, dark green, with no real order to it, a field of brown here and there breaking the pattern where the early harvest had been taken in. He pretended, for an hour or two, that they were in fact driving south. That cheered him almost as much as Sinch's presence beside him.

By the time the sun had nearly set, they'd seen three small villages and one large town, where they'd stopped for necessity and lunch. Maxon remained taciturn, clearing his throat though he never followed the sound with words. He was the one who chose the inn where they were to stay the night, saying only that he'd stayed there on the way in to the city and that it was clean. Yilon thought the name was curious: The Silent Muskrat. The inn stood by itself on the bank of a river, an hour or more from the last small town they'd seen. No picture indicated what a muskrat was or once had been, and the innkeeper, a large stag, and his young rabbit helper both scurried around too busily for Yilon to ask. But the name didn't matter; the food was good, though entirely made up of vegetables, and the beds were well-made and clean.

The sleeping arrangements were somewhat difficult. Maxon insisted that he and Yilon stay together, with Sinch in the second room. Yilon protested, but Sinch said that he didn't mind. "Fine," Yilon said. "Let's take a walk before bed, then." Maxon showed no inclination to join them, which was good as Yilon had no intention of inviting him.

"I really don't mind staying in a different room," Sinch said. "As long as..."

Yilon pushed the door open and ushered his friend outside. The light of the inn died down behind them as the door swung closed. "As long as what?"

"As long as you're careful," the mouse whispered.

The concern in his tone stopped Yilon short just outside the door. "Did you hear what Jinna told me?" he asked in a quick, low whisper.

"Yes," Sinch confessed.

Yilon flicked his ears. "And?"

"Did you think it might be Maxon? Who shot the arrow?"

The darkness outside the inn was nearly absolute. Clouds hid the moon and stars, so the only light came from the room in the inn where Maxon lay reading. Yilon's eyes adjusted slowly, picking shapes out of the gloom. The river burbled quietly to their left, and the chilly air had a freshness he hadn't smelled since Vinton: trees and grass, unpolluted by other people. "I thought about it."

"He came from Dewanne. And he's been acting weird. He insisted on sleeping with you."

Yilon nodded. "But the guard's in the room with us."

"What if he's in on it too?"

Now he could see Sinch twist his paws. He patted his friend on the shoulder. "If that were the case, they'd have killed us both and dumped us off on the road somewhere, blamed it on bandits. You've heard all the bandit warnings, right?"

Sinch dropped his paws to his sides. "Maybe you're right," he said. "But be careful, okay? There's something strange about him."

Yilon nodded. "I agree. We'll just have to stick together."

"In separate rooms."

He shrugged. "For the night."

Sinch walked at his side without saying anything more, until they'd passed the inn. "We should go back," he said.

Yilon nodded and turned with his friend, back along the path. On their way back into the inn, they passed the stag and rabbit, walking out into the night. Sinch waved to them, but they were deep in a quiet conversation and barely noticed him.

At the door to Yilon's room, Sinch leaned in and whispered, "Take care of yourself."

Yilon grinned. "Sleep well," he said, and opened the door quietly. He slipped inside, nodded to the guard, and crawled into the empty bed.

Chapter 4: The City in the Mountains

Sinch didn't join them for breakfast the next morning. When Yilon rose to check on him, Maxon rose at the same time. "Please, your lordship, allow me."

Yilon stayed where he was, one paw on the table. Maxon looked sincere, his ears up, his expression perfectly composed. "It's no trouble," Yilon said. He glanced at their guard, who stood next to the table. He was wearing his leather jerkin and a focused, attentive expression, scanning the room even though he didn't have his crossbow with him.

The steward indicated the bread and honey on the desk. "Your lordship is in the middle of eating."

"He's usually down by now." Yilon half-lowered himself back to his chair.

"You came to sleep at a rather late hour," Maxon reminded him. "Perhaps his lordship's friend was tired."

"Perhaps." It didn't sound very likely, but Yilon was tired. And Sinch hadn't had anyone to wake him up.

Maxon waved to the guard. The fox nodded crisply. He turned on his heel and marched up the stairs. Yilon sat down slowly in his chair and nibbled on his bread.

The guard returned, alone. "The young master requested another several moments of rest," he said, before resuming his previous attentive position.

Yilon frowned. "Really?"

"He seemed very tired," the guard said.

Maxon had already finished eating. "I shall prepare the carriage," he said. "We have a long day of traveling." He rose, bowed stiffly, and left the inn.

The bread was thick and chewy, the honey flavored with mint, but Yilon barely tasted it. He kept looking at the stairs waiting for Sinch to come down, his fur prickling with every second that passed. He finished his bread, finished the weak cup of tea, and the young rabbit cleared the dishes away, and still Sinch hadn't shown up. Yilon looked at the guard, but the taller fox looked everywhere but at him. Finally, he got up. "I'm going to go check on Sinch," he said.

The guard waved a paw toward the door, where Maxon had just come back in. "I will go fetch the young master," he said. "Your lordship should board the carriage."

"This is ridiculous," Yilon said. "I'm not getting on without Sinch. Why don't you want me to go upstairs?"

"Your lordship is welcome to," Maxon said smoothly, glancing around at the other patrons, who were taking notice of them. "But the carriage is ready. Take his lordship out to the carriage," he said to the guard, "and I will fetch his lordship's companion."

"I'm happy to go up," Yilon said.

Maxon started for the stairs. "There is really no need, your lordship," he said.

"He's my friend." Yilon paced the steward, trying to get to the stairs ahead of him, but Maxon was faster.

"My lord," he said, holding out a paw to stop Yilon, "you must understand that this was for your benefit."

Yilon stopped cold. "What was for my benefit?"

"His lordship may have underestimated the friendship of his companion. Or his love of the great city of Divalia."

"What are you talking about?" The hackles on the back of Yilon's neck prickled. He pushed up the stairs, past the steward, who hurried to keep up with him.

"Or there might have been some other reason," Maxon said. "Who can know the mind of...any of us?"

Yilon barely heard him. He nearly ran down the hall, stopping dead in front of the open door of the room Sinch had been in.

It was completely empty. Yilon sagged against the door frame, staring in and lifting his nose to smell the air. Sinch's scent was strong, recent. He hadn't been gone long. But how could he be gone at all? Hadn't they walked through the previous night and said they would have to stick together? At least, Yilon had said that. Had Sinch agreed? He must have, he always would.

Maxon put a paw on his shoulder. "The life of a lord is often difficult," he said, steering Yilon away from the open doorway. "Many people will present a false face in order to win his lordship's favor. Discerning them is a skill that can take a lifetime to acquire. I had hoped to spare his lordship the hurt of being abandoned."

Of course he had. Maxon, who had been so friendly and caring since Yilon had met him. The young fox stopped in the hallway and folded his arms. The steward took two more steps and then turned. "How did you know he'd gone?" Yilon asked.

Maxon looked around him at the doorway. He paused and cleared his throat, and Yilon realized suddenly that that was the first time he'd done that since coming back in from the carriage. "The, ah, room was empty, your lordship."

Yilon looked steadily at the other fox. "So did you tell him that I told him to leave?"

The steward stiffened. "My lord, I assure you I had no contact with—"

Yilon had been watching his eyes, and had noticed his quick glance at the closed door across the hall from Sinch's open door, the one where the two of them had spent the night. He didn't wait for the steward to finish; with a quick motion, he reached for the latch and pushed the door open.

The room was empty of their bags, but a small, plain, familiar satchel sat against the foot of the bed Yilon had slept in. Sprawled out on the bed, just lifting his head at the opening of the door, Sinch blinked at his friend.

"Is the carriage fixed already?" he mumbled.

Maxon coughed, in the ensuing silence. "Your lordship—"

Yilon brushed past him and strode down the stairs. "Barkeep!" he called, walking over to the large stag. "How much would it cost to hire a carriage for Divalia?"

"Three Royals," the stag said, "but there isn't one for—"

"Your lordship." Maxon came up behind him. "I had already left enough to hire a carriage for the mouse."

"It doesn't matter," Yilon said to the stag. "We'll wait as long as it takes. I can draw on the Treasury if need be. We'll be staying until the carriage arrives."

Maxon cleared his throat. "It is imperative that we reach Dewanne as soon as possible. The passes—"

"We will only need one room," Yilon said. "The steward and the guard will be continuing on to Dewanne."

The stag looked back and forth between him and Maxon. "Er..."

"Please excuse us," Maxon said. "We need to discuss this."

"There's nothing to discuss." Yilon faced the older fox, finally. "You and the guard can go back to Dewanne. You can find someone else to run your benighted city. Sinch and I are going back to Divalia."

Maxon put a paw on Yilon's arm. Yilon jerked his arm free, but allowed himself to be led to a vacant table. Maxon started to sit down, but Yilon folded his arms and remained standing. Maxon straightened. "You cannot leave the lordship."

The guard came in, looking around. When he spotted them, he took up a position behind Maxon. Yilon ignored him. "I don't want to travel with you any more. I don't feel safe."

Maxon's eyes flicked back to the guard. "The lordship is a responsibility as well as a privilege," he said. "You have been chosen to lead the province. You cannot simply abandon it on a whim."

"This is not a whim!" Yilon shouted. He got a moment of satisfaction from seeing the steward and guard's ears pin back. Heads around the tavern turned. The serving rabbit had stopped dead with a tray of bread and water to stare at them.

"Control yourself," Maxon said tightly.

"I am in perfect control," Yilon said. "I am not the one who lied in order to attempt to leave behind one of my companions."

"That is not—"

The guard touched Maxon's arm. "We should be on our way, sir."

Maxon snapped without turning, "I will tell you when we are ready to leave."

The other returned his stare for a moment, then looked down. "Yes, sir," he said. He turned to leave, but Yilon heard him say, quite clearly, "doesn't deserve it anyway."

The remark nettled Yilon even further, so he glared at Maxon as the thin fox said, "I will not leave here without you. I apologize if my actions appeared malicious, but I can assure you—"

"Fine," Yilon said. "You won't leave here without me. I won't leave here without Sinch."

Maxon took a breath. "If that is how his lordship feels—"

"It is."

They stared at each other. For the first time, Yilon felt that his authority was being tested. He held the steward's eyes, trying to force his resolve onto the other. Sinch appeared at the top of the stairs, a flicker of grey in his peripheral vision, but he didn't react. Maxon stared back, brown eyes unblinking.

Sinch crossed the floor to them, but didn't get closer than the next table. He looked curiously up at Yilon, but Yilon didn't shift his gaze. "Is... everything okay?" Sinch said timidly.

"It's fine," Yilon said.

Maxon coughed. The movement broke his concentration. He looked down, back at Sinch. His ears folded back, but he brought them up quickly. "Everything is fine," he said. "We are just preparing to leave. If your lordship...and his companion...are ready."

Yilon allowed himself a small smile.

He ignored Maxon for the entire carriage ride that day. When they stopped at an inn, he took the room with Sinch without even asking. The steward, for his part, had withdrawn into himself and his book during the day, even muting his cough. It wasn't until the following day over lunch, when Sinch had gone to use the necessary, that Maxon cleared his throat and followed it with words.

"If his lordship will permit—"

"I will not," Yilon said.

"—I would like to explain my actions."

Yilon tore another bite out of the meat pastry they'd bought. It was stale and somewhat fatty, so he chewed as loudly as he could. "If it were up to me, I would have left *you* back at the Quiet Muskrat."

"I understand his lordship's feelings, but—"

"You are supposed to be following my orders. You're supposed to be loyal to me." Yilon pointed a finger at him.

"I *am* loyal. To the Lord Dewanne and the court of Dewanne," Maxon snapped.

"Which is me!"

"Not yet."

They glared at each other. Maxon dipped his muzzle first. "My lord," he said, "we have several more days of travel remaining, and although it would be within your right to dismiss me once you are confirmed as Lord, I believe your lordship would be remiss in doing so without hearing my motivations for my actions."

Yilon ripped into the meat pastry. He chewed and swallowed a full bite before saying, "All right. Speak."

"Thank you, my lord." Maxon cleared his throat. "It has become clear that his lordship, while of quick wit and great education, does not possess a full understanding of the land whose lordship he is about to inherit. There are certain factors which would make it easier for his lordship to assume the transition to power, and others which would make it more difficult. My actions, I promise you, were only intended to ease that transition and provide his lordship with the smoothest possible path to..."

He turned his head, his words trailing off. Following his gaze, Yilon saw Sinch strolling back. "What," he said, "you can't say it in front of him?"

"Please, allow me to conclude at a later time, your lordship."

Sinch looked from one to the other of them, rubbing his paws together as he sat down. "You were talking?"

"Briefly," Yilon said, finishing his meat pastry. He leaned back in his chair. "After all, we'll all have to travel together for another two weeks. Isn't that right, Maxon?"

"Indeed, your lordship," the steward said, muffling a cough into his paw.

Sinch ate the rest of his lunch without comment, but when Maxon left to use the necessary, the mouse whispered, "Are you sure we can trust him?"

"No," Yilon said. "But at least we know we can't."

On the evening of the eighth day, they stayed in a town called Havial, and in the morning they turned south. The ride became considerably bumpier, so that Yilon and Sinch were constantly shifting to avoid getting bruises on their rears from the bouncing. Maxon remained still, reading through his book, apparently immune to the attempts of the carriage to throw him around. Yilon wasn't sure that Maxon even noticed the conditions, until near midday, when he rapped on the ceiling to signal the driver to stop. He looked across at Yilon and said, "From Havial, the road is less traveled, and therefore less even. It will be this bad the rest of the way. And no churches for services, even at Frontier."

"Whose land is this?" Yilon asked.

"Barclaw, your lordship," Maxon said, and lowered his head to his book.

They hadn't talked since the previous day's lunch, but Yilon wasn't terribly anxious to hear Maxon's explanation. People had all kinds of ways of justifying their actions. Anyway, they weren't alone very often; when Sinch left them, the driver or guard always seemed to be around. At night, Yilon stayed in Sinch's room, the two of them talking about the day's events with a freedom Maxon's presence made impossible.

"Do you think you'll have a servant when you get there?" Sinch asked.

Yilon lay on his back, staring at the ceiling. The room they'd taken was the smallest in the inn, over Maxon's protests, because it was the only one left with two beds. Clearly it was intended for servants. Yilon didn't care, but it had spurred Sinch to ask his question. "I suppose," Yilon said.

"I guess you can order them to do things like make your favorite food." Sinch sighed.

"You're pickier than I am," Yilon said.

"That's 'cause you eat meat." The mouse made a gagging noise. "It makes your breath stink."

Yilon grinned. "Makes me stronger." That's what his mother'd told him.

Sinch remained quiet, his mind obviously moving on. Yilon would have known that even if he hadn't changed the subject. "What do you think it's like?"

"Kind of chewy, but juicy," Yilon said, deliberately misinterpreting.

"Not that." Sinch threw a wadded-up cloth across the room at him. "Being a lord."

"Not that much different from not." Yilon laced his paws behind his head. "My father mostly spends his days talking to people."

"But when he talks to people, things happen." Sinch rolled over on his bed. "And people look up to him and respect him."

"Not everyone."

"You know what I mean." Sinch sighed again. "When he walks around the palace, everyone knows he's important. Imagine when he walks around in his home land. How you'll walk around Dewanne. There won't be anyone more important than you within miles. It'll be your city."

"I don't know about that." Yilon scraped his claws against each other. The rafters of the ceiling were very close to his head. Even in the dim light of the evening, he could see spiderwebs.

"Aren't you looking forward to it?"

He swung his tail over the edge of the bed and swished it back and forth. "Not especially."

Sinch rolled out of bed and padded to his side, sitting on the floor next to him. "Rather be going home?"

"I was important there, too." Yilon rubbed his eyes. "This was exciting at first, but this business with Maxon is...it's tiring. I don't want to have to think about that."

"You're good at it, though." Sinch's small, brown nose and whiskers bobbed a foot or so from Yilon's. "Look how you made him respect you."

"I don't think I'm so good at it. I almost left you behind."

"But you didn't."

"Next time..."

Sinch put a paw on his shoulder. "There won't be a next time. 'cause we're watching out now."

"Back in Divalia, even, we didn't have to watch out. Volyan won't have to watch out."

The mouse's fingers felt good in his fur, squeezing. "It's not so bad. There's two of us. And like I said, you're good at it."

If only Maxon had gone on without them both, Yilon thought some nights, they could have made their way stealthily to Vinton and left all this behind. But no matter what the obligations of his duty would require in the future, Yilon knew he felt a lot better about things with Sinch by his side. So he remained vigilant whenever Maxon suggested a plan, looking for the twist that would let the steward get rid of the mouse. Whether through his vigilance, or because Maxon felt it was not prudent to try again, they did not run into any more problems until they arrived in Frontier, late on the second Gaiaday of their journey.

The sun was two hours from setting when the carriage rattled into the small collection of wooden buildings, but Maxon closed his book, coughed, and said, "We stop here."

"There's still plenty of light," Yilon said.

"The journey from Frontier to Dewanne takes over half a day, my lord."

"We don't have half a day of daylight left," Sinch said, looking out the window.

Maxon rapped on the ceiling of the carriage. They stopped a few moments later, in front of a public house whose sign bore a picture of a waterfall and the name Lower Falls Inn. When the door opened, the first thing Yilon noted was that the characteristic scent of the town owed most of its character to fox. They had stayed in towns that were predominantly cougar, and predominantly skunk, but neither had been as singularly strong as the smell of fox was here.

The second thing he saw was the mountains. At first, when he turned and saw the jagged range just below the sun, he thought for one wild moment that they'd taken a wrong turn and ended up in Vinton. But the mountains in Vinton were low and worn, with rounded caps and trees almost to the top. The mountains that rose over the rooftops of Frontier scraped the sky, their edges sharp and bare, their tips gleaming white tinged with orange. To his right, one peak rose high above the others, the triangular peak listing to one side as if grasped by a giant and carelessly bent.

"Up there, your lordship." Maxon had come up behind Yilon and Sinch and unfolded an angular arm to point to the gap between the two nearest peaks. The black fur on his finger shone in the low sun. "Dewanne lies through that pass in a mountain valley."

"It's beautiful," Sinch said.

"Yes, it is." Maxon's voice, though soft, carried in the silent afternoon air, and he did not clear his throat at all.

Yilon saw nobody in Frontier who was not a fox save for Sinch and their driver, the raccoon. The innkeeper was a silver fox, his winter coat just growing in. His two helpers were young vixens. Every other patron of the inn, from the regulars who worked the port on the nearby river to the merchants just setting out from Dewanne, were foxes. Sinch talked cheerfully enough over dinner, but Yilon saw the flicking of his ears and eyes, and knew that as comfortably as his senses rested among his species, Sinch's were all a-jangle.

They ate in the inn, Sinch taking only the potatoes from the meal they were served, dumping his spitted goat meat onto Yilon's plate. Anxious to reach Dewanne, they retired early and woke before the sun, setting out on the hilly road in near-darkness.

Sunrise caught them before they'd ascended far into the mountains. Light gradually illuminated the path, enough so that Yilon could see the plants and flowers, only a few of them familiar. He knew the ones around Vinton well from countless hikes and walks, so seeing the same terrain with different decoration felt confusing, as if he'd walked into his father's chambers and found Sinch's mother there.

To Sinch, it was all new, and after the monotonous days of grassland, forest, and field, he couldn't restrain his enthusiasm. "Look how red that is!" he'd say, calling Yilon to his side of the carriage. Or, "do you know what kind of bird that is?" Yilon leaned across the mouse's wiry body, looking at the things he was pointing at, not because he thought he might identify them, but because he wanted to have seen them too.

Maxon could have identified them, no doubt, but he remained silent. He did look up from his book to the foliage outside, and once, Yilon actually caught him smiling.

There was no question about his smile when, after hours of a steep ascent that forced all three of them to sit on the back bench, the carriage began descending again. As it rounded a curve, Maxon lifted a finger to point out the window. "There," he said, "is Dewanne."

The bouncing of the carriage made the view difficult to process. Yilon rapped on the ceiling, hopping out of his door as soon as the carriage slowed. Maxon and Sinch followed. The driver looked back. "Something wrong, sirs?"

Yilon shook his head. "Just wanted to get a better view." He couldn't have articulated the impulse that urged him to get a look at Dewanne before entering it, only that he knew it was there.

The air had been noticeably colder in the carriage; out here, in the wind, it was frigid. He wrapped his arms around himself and stared down into the valley below them. On all sides, the ground rose up around the town of Dewanne, which spread in a crescent around the southern shore of a large lake. The nearest buildings had been built along the highest water mark, which was now perhaps a hundred feet from the actual shore of the lake. They were looking down from the northeast, perhaps two hours ride from the town.

"Wow," Sinch breathed. He pointed beyond the lake. "Is Delford over there?"

"Other side of the mountain." Yilon tried to match the layout of the town to what he knew of Vinton and Divalia, to figure out which building was which. The multi-room mansion on the small hill at the far end of the town from the lake must be the palace, with the wide square in front of it ready for the daily market. He couldn't see any buildings with Gaia's six-in-one symbol atop them, but there was a round building atop a lower hill, near the plaza, that looked church-like. Between the plaza and the lake, densely packed buildings and winding streets formed what he thought was similar to Divalia's Old Town, while the houses that spread to either side along the lake shore were larger, probably newer.

On the west side of the town, directly opposite the lake from their position, a large cluster of small buildings sat on the western edge of the town, darker and more closely packed than the rest of the city. Beyond them, Yilon saw several large artificial scrapes in the ground, at the feet of the mountains. He nudged Maxon, pointing down. "What's that cluster on the west side?"

"That, your lordship, is the Warren," the steward said, and coughed. "Your lordship would do well to keep clear of it."

"Why?" Yilon wanted to know.

Maxon turned back toward the carriage with a small cough. "We will try to arrange a tour of the city for his lordship once we have arrived." He stepped up and pulled himself inside again.

Sinch rubbed his paws together. "Chilly up here." He panted. "But I'm glad we stopped."

Yilon nodded, feeling short of breath himself. "Let's get back inside."

The three of them had to crowd together again on the way down, this time on the front bench. Yilon felt his stomach lurch anyway, with more than just the uneven road. The closer they drew to Dewanne, the closer he came to having to think about being a lord, and the farther he drifted from Vinton. The stopover on the way back was a mistake, he decided, staring out the window without seeing the low scrub bouncing by. All it would do would be to rub in his nose that it was Volyan's now, no longer his. He wondered whether his mother would want to come visit in Dewanne. And that made him think of Lady Dewanne.

He'd never met her, but his mother had talked about her several times, as the only other noble vixen she'd met. She described her as good-natured, but aloof, a vixen very much at home in her role as a lady. But she'd also spoken of her with pity, though at the time Yilon hadn't understood why, and his mother hadn't elaborated. Now, in light of what his father had told him, he wondered. What would it be like to be married to someone who would rather scheme to have a cub with some other vixen than to have one with his own wife? And how would she feel when that cub, now grown, arrived to claim the title to the land she'd held all her life?

Maxon, next to him, sat straight up, paws on his knees. Was that what Maxon had meant when he'd said his loyalty was to the court of Dewanne? Had he been instructed by Lady Dewanne to isolate Yilon from his friends? There was no good reason Yilon could come up with for that, but that didn't mean it hadn't happened.

The steward's tail twitched. Probably, Yilon thought, that was as close as he came to wagging.

The humid, fresh air of the lake shore crept in through the doors of the carriage as they descended. If the air had been thin at the top of the mountain, it felt much thicker here. It reminded him of Divalia more than Vinton, despite the mountains all around. The only water in Vinton was a small river, barely worthy of the name, that snaked through the town and down to the plains below. The Lurine in Divalia, wide and powerful, had fascinated him when he'd first arrived in the city.

They entered the outskirts of the city, where smaller fields broke up the scrubby vegetation. Farmhouses appeared here and there, more square and squat than the farms they'd seen on the plains. Beyond the farms, trails led up the sides of the mountains, ending in small dark holes. Yilon saw small figures working in the fields, and foxes in carts, pulling off the road to let them pass.

After that, he saw more buildings and fewer fields, until there were no fields at all. Yilon was more reminded of Vinton than Divalia, watching the houses and storefronts pass by his window; they were smaller than in the capital. Still, there was something strange about them, something he couldn't quite place.

It wasn't just that they were plastered white over grey stone, because many of the buildings in Vinton were too. It might have been the green limestone trim, but that was simply a little different. The names he could see reminded him of home, things like Joni's Grocer and Lakeside Smithy, and the Silver Minnow, a pub whose sign made him thirsty.

"What do they drink here?" he asked.

"Wine," Maxon replied. "Vineyards on the slopes." His thin fingers gestured beyond the buildings, to rows of green vines in the distance.

"I like wine," Sinch piped up from the other side of the carriage.

Maxon did not say anything as the carriage slowed. Yilon saw two red foxes in grey uniforms with green trim at the shoulders and cuffs approach the carriage. They talked briefly with the driver, and then the door to the carriage opened and one of them stepped up to look inside.

The crest of Dewanne, embroidered in green, adorned his left breast. He looked back and forth between Yilon and Maxon, but when he saw Sinch, his paw dropped to the pommel of the short weapon at his side. "Sir," he said to Maxon, without taking his eyes from Sinch, "is everything all right?"

Maxon looked at Yilon as if to say, *see?*, but nodded his head. "Yes, Turon. This is Yilon, who is to be the heir of Dewanne."

Turon spared Yilon a brief glance, enough for Yilon to see the fear and suspicion in the widened eyes. He lowered his voice to almost a whisper pitch. "If you are being threatened," he murmured, "flick your ears back."

Maxon kept them deliberately forward, as Sinch strained forward to hear. "Everything is fine, Turon," he said. "Thank you."

"Yes, sir." The guard glanced at Yilon and said, "Welcome to Dewanne," then dismounted and closed the carriage door.

Yilon met Sinch's eyes. The mouse's ears were back as he settled into the seat, his tail curled around in his lap. I can protect you, Yilon wanted to assure him, but he remembered the guard's expression and couldn't bring himself to say the words.

Several blocks of silence later, the carriage slowed again. Two more guards outside stopped the driver, and while they were, Yilon saw another one amidst a thin crowd of foxes down the street he was facing. This time, the guard did not come in, and the carriage went on its way. "We are almost to the castle," Maxon said.

"What's that?" Yilon watched a large three-story building with an elaborate arched entryway roll by.

"The Silver Building." Maxon coughed.

"What about that one?" Sinch called from the other side of the carriage. Yilon twisted around to see what Sinch was pointing to, but caught only the corner of the building before they passed it.

Maxon settled back on the bench. "I will be sure to arrange a tour of Dewanne for his lordship. I believe Corwin will be available."

"Who's Corwin?" Sinch asked.

Maxon yawned and cleared his throat as if about to answer, but said nothing. Yilon was about to echo the question when the carriage bounced into the wide square they'd seen from the pass. The mansion rose ahead of them, more like a castle than a house, with tall turreted walls and a wide, squat tower on either end. Only the structure between the towers looked like a house, plastered with the same white coating as the other buildings, with glass windows and sloped roofs.

The carriage pulled up in front. Two foxes in the now-familiar livery trotted out from the front gate to help Yilon down, and Maxon behind him. "Welcome home, sir," one of them said to the steward.

"Thank you, Caffin." Maxon grasped the first servant's paw as he stepped down. "Hello, Min."

The second servant bowed. "A pleasure to have you back, sir."

Yilon reached back to help Sinch down, but Maxon pushed Yilon forward. "May I introduce Yilon."

Both servants came to attention immediately, ears perking up, tails arched. They bowed together, straightening quickly. One of them—Caffin—seemed to be struggling not to smile. Yilon, at a loss for how to respond, said, "You can relax?" Why hadn't his diplomacy classes taught him simple things like this?

"Tails down," Maxon said, and both servants relaxed into wagging tails and broad smiles. The driver had dismounted and begun pulling the luggage down from the carriage. Caffin and Min hurried to help him. "Into the Broad Room, I think," Maxon directed them as they carried the trunks down. "And mine into my chambers." He picked up the leather satchel and held it in his arms.

"The Broad Room," Yilon murmured to Sinch, falling behind the others. "Sounds...big."

Maxon turned to face the two of them. He coughed into his paw. "I regret to inform his lordship that mice are not allowed in the castle."

Chapter 5: Sordid Histories

Yilon and Sinch stopped. "What?" Yilon said. Sinch shrank back, lowering his bag to the ground.

The steward looked down his muzzle at them. "It is by decree of the Lord Dewanne."

"I'm the lord," Yilon said.

Sinch put a paw on his arm. "It's okay," he said.

Maxon cleared his throat. "Not yet."

"Well, I'll change it when I am." Yilon glared up defiantly.

The steward nodded. "In the meantime, may I instruct the driver to convey your friend to a more appropriate residence?"

Yilon met Sinch's eyes. The mouse gave him a quick smile. He squeezed Yilon's arm. "I'll find you later."

Yilon smiled broadly. "I'll be there." He waved toward the castle.

"Listen," the driver said. "I've got to turn around if I'm going to get back to Frontier. Don't want to stay here overnight."

"It is a short detour." Maxon stepped closer to the raccoon, pointing to the far side of the plaza. Yilon heard the raccoon ask something about guards, and Maxon say something in a reassuring tone in response.

"It better not be too far," Yilon muttered to Sinch.

"Jinna said there are other mice here," Sinch said, looking at the large square. It occurred to Yilon that they had not seen a single mouse on the whole trip in. "Maybe they're taking me where the mice are."

"Come find me tonight." Yilon whispered. He squeezed his friend's paw. "Be safe."

The raccoon clambered back up onto the carriage. "You too," Sinch whispered. He raised his paw to Yilon and climbed back in. As the carriage pulled away, heading west, it occurred to Yilon that he hadn't seen the guard dismount. He looked around, but the thin fox must already have gone into the castle with the footservants. His eyes lingered on the carriage as it crossed the square, rounded a dingy pub, and disappeared from sight. Then he hurried after the servants and Maxon, who had paused at the gates to wait for him.

"Are mice never allowed in the castle?" He had come up level with the steward as they entered the central building, the large house in the center of the castle grounds. There were no gardens inside the walls here, just a wide central plaza of grey slate. Around the base of the left-hand tower, a pair of foxes strolled toward them, but otherwise the courtyard was deserted.

"In the past, there have been special occasions upon which the courtyard was open to all residents of Dewanne, but never the castle proper." Maxon nodded his head to Min, who was holding the door for both of them.

"That's ridiculous." Yilon let his gaze wander along the paintings in the hallway, portraits of noble foxes in various valiant poses. The large centerpieces on either side depicted epic battle scenes in which the noble foxes were slaughtering hordes of red-eyed, vicious-looking mice.

"Surely his lordship has heard of cities with traditions."

"Of course." Yilon remembered a northern city entirely inhabited by bears. "But most of the ones I've learned about have embraced the Church's teachings."

Maxon stared straight ahead. "We are proud of our traditions here in Dewanne."

"I'm sure most of them are fine. Just this one about mice is so prehistoric."

The servants in front of him laid their ears back. Maxon put a paw on Yilon's shoulder, stopping him until Caffin and Min were further ahead. "You may be the heir," the steward hissed softly, "but you are a stranger here. You would do well to watch very carefully where your paws land until you grow surer of your footing."

"I'm..." The words 'the lord' withered under the intense glare of the steward. He remembered his father's advice to listen, and lowered his ears. "I'll be careful."

They emerged from the hallway into a large open room, lit by skylights. In the center of the ceiling, an elaborate relief of green vines wound around the pattern of grey stones. On each wall, elaborate murals depicted battles and courtly events, each mural rimmed with silver, which caught the light and reflected a glow through the room.

Caffin and Min took the trunks to a staircase to their left, but when Yilon turned to follow, Maxon steered him forward. "I'll have them show you to your room later," he said. "We're to see Lady Dewanne."

"Does she know we're here?" Yilon followed the steward across the polished slate floor.

The steward's ears flicked. He cleared his throat. "She will have been awaiting our arrival."

And indeed, when they'd climbed the grand staircase and walked along the balcony overlooking the foyer, Yilon looked through an open door at the end of the balcony and saw a tall vixen in a white dress, one paw resting on a large wooden desk beside some papers and a twisting, delicate ornament of clear glass, with a ribbon of green running through it. Behind her, a large window facing the courtyard showed the lake and the mountains beyond. She was not looking out of the window, but directly at them.

Maxon did not hurry his steps, but Yilon saw the twitching of his tail and the lift at the corner of his muzzle. "My lady," he said, entering the room ahead of Yilon. He paused to bow, blocking the doorway, his tail arching up much as the servants' had done.

"Tails down, Maxon," the vixen said. Her voice, high and fluting, carried across the long study. "Welcome back."

The steward rose and stepped into the study. Yilon followed, unsure of whether he was expected to bow or not. To be safe, he bowed shallowly.

"I appreciate the courtesy," Lady Dewanne said. "But there is no need to bow to me, Yilon."

He straightened, meeting her eyes. Her muzzle bore a warm smile, and one paw was extended to him. Maxon stood to one side as Yilon walked the length of the study, across the rough carpet woven in regular colored patterns. Along the walls, dark wooden bookshelves and cabinets that matched the desk held books, scrolls, and small stone figurines. A series of grey stone busts of foxes stared down at him from atop the cabinets, but he did not take the time to examine them more closely, keeping his eyes on the smiling vixen.

He stopped beside the desk and took her paw. She leaned forward; he lifted his muzzle to meet hers, and sniffed.

She smelled of the mountains and the lake, but also of something else, something familiar. He pulled back, taking another breath. The familiar smell was not another species, but a combination of species. It was the smell of the palace of Divalia. Stepping back, he tilted his head to get a better look at her, startled that the scent of the palace could linger on someone that long. Did he still smell of Vinton, he wondered, even two years later?

Now that he was closer, he could see the grey creeping up her muzzle, lining the edge of her ears, and touching the corners of her eyes. "So delighted to see you here finally," she said. Her tail swished slowly under her dress. The white fabric shimmered in the sunlight, sparkling with beaded swirls that ran from her right shoulder to her left hip. "I hope you had a pleasant trip."

"It was very nice." Yilon looked beyond her to the lake, reflecting the clouds overhead. From here, with little city visible beyond it, it looked pristine and beautiful. The only part of Dewanne he could see was the dark sprawl Maxon had called the Warren.

"It was indeed, your ladyship." The steward padded up behind him. "I noticed the guard around the city has been doubled again."

She inclined her head. "There have been twelve more robberies in the past month, six the week after you left. Velkan ordered the guard conscription, but it has not been popular. Without Sheffin, Velkan is doing the best he can to collect revenues and maintain order, but the governor holds only so much authority."

"Perhaps if you, my lady—"

She shook her head. "I visited the Grain Depository myself three weeks ago. Taxes are not being paid, the treasury is running short, and the guards suspect this. Velkan has kept desertion to a minimum, but the next round of pay will be the last we can make without dangerously depleting our funds. But the Confirmation will inspire the farmers to make their payments, and the guards to persuade the ones who are not inspired." Almost as an afterthought, she added, "Oh, and Dinah's run off again."

"Oh, dear." For some reason, Maxon sounded more distressed at this news than at the rest.

"Her parents claim she's been kidnapped, but that is ludicrous. Dinah has always been wilful."

"Given the timing, though..." Maxon coughed, lowering his muzzle.

"I'm certain she has simply taken a mount and ridden off somewhere."

Yilon flicked his ears back from one of them to the other. "If your ladyship is certain," Maxon said.

"I am." She half-turned, looking out of the window down at the town. "All this nonsense about ransom notes is just that: nonsense."

"Ransom notes?" Yilon spoke up.

Lady Dewanne returned her attention to him. "Maxon, please have lunch drawn up in the front parlor. Yilon and I will take it in twenty minutes."

"Yes, my lady." Maxon turned on his toes and marched smartly out of the room.

"Come here," Lady Dewanne said to Yilon after Maxon had left. She pulled him to the window, one paw on his shoulder. "This will be your city. I do hope you will have time to get to know it before you return to Divalia."

"Maxon said he would arrange a tour for me tomorrow," Yilon said. "With Corvin?"

"Corwin," Lady Dewanne corrected. "The former governor. He'll be an excellent guide."

Yilon looked at her rather than out at the town. She was not looking at the buildings; rather, her muzzle was raised to give her a view of the mountain beyond the lake. He saw her nostrils flare, as if smelling the lake air through the glass. "Are you from here, too?"

She nodded. "My family still lives there, in our ancestral home." She pointed to the right; pressing close to the window, Yilon saw a cluster of large houses on the lake shore.

"But you're still living here?"

Her paw fell from his shoulder. He saw her smile. "The people need to have a Lord or a Regent in residence."

"So once I take on the lordship, you'll move back in with them?"

She laughed. "Do you want me to?"

"I was thinking it would be nicer if you stayed. Everyone here seems so..." he lowered his voice. "Provincial."

Her ears flicked back. "We are in the provinces."

"Yes, but still."

Her gaze traveled out beyond the lake. "I plan to leave Dewanne before too long. But I will stay long enough to see you established here, never fear."

Yilon stepped away from her, toward the window. Knowing she was leaving made him feel even more alone. Without Sinch, knowing nobody but Maxon, with nothing to look forward to but the return to Divalia for the winter, he laid his ears back and stared out at the landscape upon which nothing seemed to be moving.

When he looked closer, though, he saw boats out on the lake, small skiffs that moved so slowly they'd appeared immobile at first. And when he dropped his eyes to the large open plaza in front of the palace, now empty of any carriages or carts, he saw figures moving along the edges, out of the sun. They wore leather jerkins, and some wore thick traveling cloaks like the one Yilon had left packed in his trunk, the weather still too warm for it until the mountain travel on the last day. But each one had a sharp red muzzle and a bushy red tail.

That made him feel better, if only slightly. He still felt the wrongness of not belonging, removed from being able to smell the people he was supposed to govern. How would he go about doing that if there were no connection between them?

"The first thing I should do is explain your situation." At Lady Dewanne's words, Yilon turned from the window to face her. She'd moved to stand beside the closest stone bust. "I presume your father has told you that Sheffin—that was the late Lord Dewanne—named you as his heir."

When she spoke her husband's name, she said it slowly, and her eyes slid briefly to one side before coming back to rest on his. She waited for him to nod, and when he did, she went on. "He has most likely told you that you were so named because there are few noble fox families, and none others with a male child of suitable age."

Here it comes, Yilon thought, and indeed, when he nodded, she hesitated before going on, composing herself to deliver what she thought would be earth-shattering news. He took the time to prepare himself to react appropriately. "You should know the truth," she said, "so that you can be best prepared to govern this city and this province. The truth is..."

He waited. She turned her head, facing the stone bust, and then lowered her muzzle. "It is so easy to make these plans when the fruition is years away. One does not anticipate the moment when one will have to lay bare the principles that seemed so reasonable then." She might have been talking to the bust or to Yilon, or to the world outside the window. "In the daylight, in the eyes of the innocent..."

She took a breath and looked Yilon directly in the eye. Hers were light blue, strong and clear. "Lord Vinton is not your father," she said.

Yilon found that his first pretend reaction, if he were truly hearing the news and believing it, would be considerably happier than she was likely expecting. He let his jaw drop while he was thinking of what to say next. She let him have all the time he needed. "You mean..." he managed finally, noncommittal yet as confused as she might expect.

She nodded, lifting a finger to point at the stone bust. "There is your father."

He fixed his gaze on the stone fox, whose expression was not as severe nor as aloof as the other busts. Its eyes opened wide, ears slightly asplay, as though trying earnestly to look back at the viewer. The muzzle, shorter and wider than his father's, did not have his father's characteristic smile, but perhaps the sculptor had insisted on as stern an expression as he could muster. There was no way of knowing, but he thought that the fox who'd sat for that piece would not be such a bad father to have.

"Sheffin, your mother, and myself are the only ones who knew." He shifted his gaze to her. She avoided his eyes. "Maxon now knows, because it was necessary for him to know. And now you know, because it is your right."

He let another period of silence crawl by, because he honestly had no idea what to say to her. When it became clear that she would not speak again until he did, he rubbed his muzzle. "It gives me a better connection to this place. I wish I could have met him."

"There is your father."

"He wanted to meet you." She lifted her head, encouraged. "I believe your mother kept you in Vinton as long as she did so that you would not develop a close attachment to Lord Vinton."

"That worked."

He'd let a little more sharpness into his tone than he'd intended. Her ears flicked. "She is your true mother, of course. But I hope you will think of me as your mother as well, in some way."

He froze for a second, then forced his muzzle into a diplomatic smile. "Of course," he said, bowing to conceal the ice in his eyes. By the time he'd straightened, he'd managed to banish it. "May I ask a question?"

She inclined her head, her own smile fading just a bit. Had she noticed his reaction? "Why did you and Lord Dewanne not have any cubs of your own?"

Now her expression became completely serious, and her eyes clouded over. "I was—I am not favored by Canis. Barren. Sheffin chose to keep me at his side rather than find a wife who could give him an heir."

"He must have loved you very much."

Both of them turned to the stone bust. "He did," she said, tenderly. "I am still discovering just how much."

Her affection meant little to Yilon. She was going to leave Dewanne, and anyway, she was nothing to him, even if her husband had been his real father. Her unintentional reminder that his mother, his real mother, was an entire country away had solidified his resolve to take Sinch and follow her out of this valley at the earliest possible opportunity. When Maxon joined them for lunch, Yilon was still trying to figure out how to manage it. As it turned out, it was Maxon who provided him with the idea.

The steward told them that he had sent for Corwin, and for Velkan, who turned out to be the current governor. "Velkan tends to the day-to-day business affairs of Dewanne," Lady Dewanne told him. "As you heard me describe to Maxon. No doubt you had a governor in Vinton as well."

Yilon nodded. "A raccoon named Anton. He'd been governor since forever. Do you have any honey for the bread?"

"I regret that we do not, my lord." Maxon reached out for a piece of the heavy, yellowish bread and sopped up the meat sauce with it.

"I brought some honey from Divalia," Lady Dewanne said, "but it has been exhausted. Sheffin particularly liked it. I would like you to meet with Velkan. Tomorrow you can take the tour with Corwin in the morning and meet further with Velkan in the afternoon."

"What kind of bread is this, anyway?" Yilon liked the taste, a sweet, rich flavor that reminded him more of thick vegetable cakes than bread.

"It is made with potato root." Maxon indicated some actual potatoes in the stew. "They grow abundantly here."

"It's good. And this," Yilon poked at the shredded meat, "this is goat, right? We ate that in Vinton, too."

"Mountain sheep." Lady Dewanne leaned forward. "I planned to have the Confirmation in four days' time. If you would prefer it sooner..."

"No, no." Yilon took another chunk of bread and chewed pensively. "What about cakes?"

"I beg your pardon?" Lady Dewanne's ears folded back.

"Cakes," Yilon said. "Do you make cakes from potatoes? You don't have honey. What do you do for dessert?" he said, when it was clear that neither of them understood what he was getting at.

"Your lordship," Maxon said, "we farm a sweet tuber from which we fashion cakes and candies. There are vineberries and grapes which make for quite pleasant flavoring."

"We'll have dessert in a bit," Lady Dewanne said. "May I have Maxon send invitations to the Confirmation?" Without waiting for him to answer, she said, "Maxon, please come see me after the meal, so we can arrange that."

Yilon nodded. "One thing, though. I would like the mice invited to it."

Lady Dewanne sighed. Maxon cleared his throat, laying his ears back. "My lord, I would strongly advise that you wait—"

"Am I not going to be their lord as well?"

"Of course, your lordship."

"Then they should be present to see me Confirmed."

Lady Dewanne pushed her half-finished plate away from her. "We cannot invite mice, not here. I understand your concern. Growing up in Divalia, this must be strange to you. But there is a very good chance that if you invite mice to your Confirmation ceremony, there will not be a Confirmation ceremony."

"I will go prepare the invitations. My lady, when you are finished, please send for me." Maxon rose in the ensuing silence. Only then did Yilon notice the leather satchel slung over his shoulder.

"You're carrying the crown around with you?" Wheels turned in his head. He began to see a possible way home. If he could...with Sinch's help... yes, it might work.

"As I mentioned to his lordship, this is a particularly sensitive time. Until the Confirmation takes place, it is best for the crown to remain on the person of a trustworthy, er, person."

Yilon leaned back and made a show of appraising the steward. "But how do I know I can trust you?"

The steward's ears folded back, his eyes wide. "Me?"

Lady Dewanne leaned forward to say, "Maxon is very dependable."

Maxon must have been flustered, because he nearly cut off Lady Dewanne's words. "Your lordship—your lordship to be—I have served the court of Dewanne for years!"

"Yes," Yilon drawled, "but there was that incident back at the Muskrat."

"Incident?" Lady Dewanne's ears perked up. "What incident?" The softness in her voice was nearly totally gone.

"That," Maxon said coldly, "was for his lordship's benefit, as I have explained and as I hope is apparent now."

"He tried to abandon my best friend in the middle of nowhere," Yilon said to Lady Dewanne.

"There was ample transportation back to Divalia." Maxon's ears lay flat against his head. "Your—his lordship's friend was in no danger."

"Except of being abandoned."

Lady Dewanne frowned. "Maxon?"

The steward took a deep breath. "My lady, his best friend is a mouse."

She put a paw to her muzzle, turning back to Yilon. "I presume you now understand why that might have become a problem. Where is he now?"

"I don't know." Yilon glared at Maxon. "He's being taken to a "more appropriate residence"."

"Oh," she said. "He was the other figure...I thought that was your servant."

"My lady, I was only thinking of the smooth transition of the title." Maxon placed both paws on the table, the satchel swinging from his shoulder. "I did what I did in the best interests of the court of Dewanne."

She favored him with a smile. "I understand." To Yilon, she said, "Is your mind at rest now?"

"No."

Maxon had given up appealing to him. "My lady—"

She held up a paw, her eyes still fixed on Yilon. "What are you proposing?"

Her gaze searched inside him for his secret purpose. He flinched, just for a second, then cursed himself for doing so. "I want to carry the crown."

"My lady!"

"A moment, Maxon." She studied Yilon. "Do you really feel that is wise?"

He spread his paws. "If you don't trust me to keep the crown safe, how are you going to trust me to rule this land?"

She sat back in her chair, frowning. Maxon, too, looked taken aback. Yilon watched them meet each other's eyes, communicating silently, and when they turned back to him, he could read their decision even before Maxon unslung the satchel and placed it carefully on the table.

"I suppose I need not warn your lordship not to treat it as overly valuable," he said, "lest others note the attention paid and infer its value of their own accord." Without waiting for a response, he turned on his toes and stalked out of the hall.

"You're going to have to work with Maxon for a long time," Lady Dewanne said. "You should think about how to get him on your side."

"I'll do that," Yilon said, more focused on the delight at his plan actually working. At least the first part, and that was the hardest, in his opinion.

"He and Velkan will be your representatives when you are in Divalia representing their interests. So you will have to be on good terms with them, or things will be difficult for you."

"I know." He said it more peevishly than he'd intended, his mind already racing ahead to that night and the next morning. "I'll have a talk with Maxon later. And I'll see Velkan this afternoon, won't I?"

She leaned back, rubbing her whiskers thoughtfully. "Yes, you will."

"All right." He put his ears up and smiled. "So, what's for dessert?"

After a sweet cake topped with a sugary paste whose strange aftertaste Yilon didn't particularly like, they repaired to the study again. Velkan was the first to arrive, a short, dry fox who deferred to Yilon during the short conversation, which consisted mostly of a recitation of current tax policies, a series of questions about relationships with neighboring provinces, and a list of issues currently under consideration for presentation to the king in Divalia.

He liked Corwin better, because there was no agenda behind their conversation. The plump old fox introduced himself by saying, "So you're the new lord, eh?"

Yilon brushed muzzles with him and said, "I am." The old fox smelled of mead and paper, and another male fox. Initially, that made Yilon wary of his friendly nature; he had experience with older males in Divalia who thought they knew right away that he preferred males.

But Corwin sat back, paws linked behind his head, tail swishing freely, showing no interest in Yilon at all, at least of that sort. "It's a lovely little province, if perhaps a little stifling. We hope you'll have the fortitude to come back and visit every so often, just so we know we're not neglected. I've experienced the night life of Divalia and I know how hard it is to tear oneself away."

His eyes twinkled. Yilon grinned. "I'm not much one for night life," he said, relaxing in his own chair. "I have only a couple friends and we don't go out much."

"Oh? What do you do for fun?"

Yilon's tail swung back and forth. "We drink in pubs and practice our weapons."

Corwin's paw went to his muzzle, his eyes wide, though he was smiling. "Oh, my poor dear," he said. "You are so young, and missing out on so much."

Yilon laughed. "I suppose Dewanne is the place for you to show me what I could be doing."

"Darling," Corwin said, "I could show you such things here, your tail would curl and your fur would turn a lovely shade of purple."

"As it happens, you're going to be giving me a tour tomorrow morning."

The sunlight glinted off of Corwin's spectacles as he adjusted them. "I've already got it all planned out."

"That's the first thing I've looked forward to since I arrived here," Yilon said.

"Oh, come now." The older fox leaned forward, his baggy silk shirt rustling as he moved. "Being a lord isn't all that bad. I know the Confirmation is tedious, but you've not even been to one yet. How can you have any idea how bad it is?"

"I have a good imagination," Yilon said.

"You wouldn't know it from your outfit." Corwin clucked, leaning forward to rub a corner of Yilon's leather jerkin between his fingers. "That's all right. First stop tomorrow will be a tailor I know, a divine little fellow on Market Street. He'll know just what to fit you with."

"Is that where you got that shirt? I love the shade."

The light blue fabric shimmered in the light from the window. Corwin brushed it with a paw. "This shirt actually came from Divalia. A gift from the late Lord Dewanne upon my retirement. He was quite considerate, always. Every time he returned from Divalia, a gift for me, something for the castle staff."

"I'm sorry I never got to meet him."

"Oh, he wasn't a terribly good conversationalist." Corwin glanced up at the bust. "My apologies, m'lord. But he cared deeply about those around him."

And how, Yilon wondered, did that include a scheme to deceive one family, betray a fellow lord, and raise a cub under false pretenses to be thrust into a lordship he wasn't ready for? At least he could have had the consideration to stay his death for a few more years. But all he said was, "With you around, I don't imagine he needed much more in the way of conversational skills."

And Corwin laughed and said, "My dear boy, we are going to get along splendidly." And indeed they did, talking until Min came to take Yilon to his chambers.

The Broad Room, on the northeast corner of the castle, looked out onto the east side of the city from one set of windows, the lake and the plaza from the other. His clothes had been hung in the wardrobe, except for one set of nightclothes that had been laid out on the bed. The other furniture in the room, a large desk made of the same dark wood as the desk in Lady Dewanne's study, was completely bare except for two fountain pens. He placed the leather satchel containing the crown onto the bed, and stood there with one paw on the desk, looking out of the window.

"Is everything to your liking, sir?" Min said. When Yilon nodded, he went on, "I will come inform you when dinner is served. If there is anything else you require, please ring the bell."

Yilon touched the cord, which hung from the ceiling near the head of the bed. "Are you to be my personal servant?"

"If your lordship desires it."

"I was told a servant would be assigned to me," Yilon said.

Min bowed. "Your lordship has the power to request any assignment, if he wishes."

Now Yilon wondered if Min would be offended if he didn't request it. He decided there was nothing he could do about it. "I will wait and see who's been assigned to me. But if that servant isn't suitable, I'm certain you would be splendid."

"Thank you, sir." The footservant's ears flicked forward. He bowed and turned to leave, his tail held up at a jaunty angle.

Yilon turned his attention to the room. The first thing he did was select his bright red shirt and hang it in the window, facing the plaza. That done, he sat down at the desk facing the window. A quick search of the desk drawers turned up no ink, nor any paper to accompany the pens. He took his own ink and paper from the case that sat atop his stack of books, and began a letter to his mother.

He'd gotten as far as telling her about the incident with Sinch at the Silent Muskrat when Min returned to summon him to dinner. Like lunch, he found the meal lacking, not only compared to the cooking in Divalia, but also compared to the cooking in Vinton. Maxon had declined to eat with them, but Velkan and Corwin, who had been visiting with Lady Dewanne, remained for dinner. Corwin kept the conversation lively, which was fortunate, because Yilon was starting to feel the effects of the afternoon's meetings on top of the morning's travel, and Velkan was far from an engaging dinner companion.

Min accompanied him back to his room. "I will ensure that your personal servant is assigned by the morning, sir," he said.

"Thank you." Yilon sat on the bed and yawned. "Does the window open? This room is rather stuffy."

"Indeed, sir." Min crossed the room and cracked open the window facing the city, then stood with ears at attention. "Will there be anything else?"

Yilon shook his head. "I wish not to be disturbed until the morning."

"Certainly." Min bowed and closed the door behind him. Yilon didn't see a lock on it, so after opening the window in front of which he'd hung the red shirt, he stripped off his clothes, put on his nightdress, and lay back on the bed.

It seemed he'd no sooner closed his eyes than he was awakened by a soft scratching. He sat up in bed and looked around in the grey night. "Sinch?" he whispered.

The mouse clambered in through the window, pushing his shirt aside and landing on the bed. His eyes shone. "Hi," he whispered back.

Yilon's tail thumped the bed under the sheet. He reached out and clasped Sinch's arm. "Was it hard to get in?"

"Much easier than the palace in Divalia." The mouse crawled up the bed to lie next to Yilon. "There's only guards at the entrance, and the walls are old and easy to climb."

"You shouldn't stay," Yilon said, though he put his arm around the mouse's shoulders. "I just want to tell you my plan."

"Okay," Sinch said. He rested his muzzle against Yilon's cheekruff. "I can always come back. It's easy, like I said."

"You won't have to for many more nights." Yilon yawned. "Here's what I had in mind."

Sinch let him talk, interrupting only to say, "That sounds dangerous," and, "In broad daylight?" When Yilon was done, he said, "I know someone who might help. But he's dangerous, too."

"It's only temporary," Yilon said. "On our way out of town we can tell them. By then he won't be able to get you."

"Yeah, but 'til then..." Sinch drifted off, thinking.

"Can you manage it in time?"

Sinch's dark eyes looked back at him. "I'll manage it."

Yilon smiled and relaxed, resting fingers along Sinch's arm. "Where are you staying?"

"They dropped me off at the edge of the Warren," Sinch said. "It's the place where all the mice live. I walked around and found a boarding-house that had room. I found it on the first try. It's not very clean, or big, but it is cheap. With the money my mother gave me, I could live there for half a year. You wouldn't have liked the dinner. It was all boiled potatoes. But all the mice there are very friendly. They don't like the foxes very much, though. When the carriage dropped me off, a couple kits threw stones at it..."

Yilon closed his eyes, both listening and not listening to Sinch. He drifted off again into a half-dream in which Sinch was explaining to him how the lordship of Dewanne worked, a convoluted explanation that involved him boiling potatoes and drizzling them with honey. That made no sense, Yilon thought, because they didn't have honey here, but then Sinch noticed he wasn't paying attention and started rapping on the counter of the small kitchen.

He started and sat up in the small bed. The rapping was coming from the door of the bedroom. Sinch lay on the bed next to him, and the room was full of light.

"Just a minute!" he yelled. Sinch stirred. Yilon grabbed his shoulder and shook. "Get up!" he hissed. "You gotta go!"

"Sir," Min's voice called. "There is porridge being served downstairs, and Corwin is expected to arrive shortly."

Sinch blinked and then sat up quickly. "All right," Yilon said loudly. "Can you send up my personal servant to help me dress?"

Scrambling out of bed, Sinch stopped to stare at him, covering his mouth to stifle a giggle. Yilon aimed a kick at him as Min opened the door. "Your lordship, I have been selected to be your personal servant," he said. "I will be happy to assist you."

At the sound of the door opening, Sinch had slid under the bed. Yilon could hear him breathing there, so the only thing that he could think to do was make as much noise as possible while Min was in the room. "Oh!" he said, stretching, "I had a wonderful night's sleep. I'm looking forward to breakfast. What should one wear to breakfast? Will I need to change before I leave on my tour?"

He kept up as much of the chatter as he could, trying his best to engage Min and keep him from looking around the room, or sniffing too much. Sinch had the good sense to keep still, waiting for them to clear out the room before making his escape.

Yilon was sure that Min was regretting his assignment as personal servant by the time the two of them left. After all the fuss he'd made over the clothes, he couldn't even have said what the other fox had picked out by the time he slung the crown's leather bag over his shoulder and followed Min out of the room.

They'd closed his bedroom door behind them. With his first chance to relax, he took in the concept that this other fox was bound to him by duty, that his only job was to help Yilon. They walked along the corridor to the stairs.

"Listen," he said to Min, who was short enough that he didn't have to look up to look him in the eye, "I've never had a personal servant before. So I don't really know what's expected of me, or of you. I hope I didn't appear too strange back there. I'm just nervous about how to present myself here."

"Indeed, sir."

"Would it be okay if you didn't call me 'sir'?"

Min paused, his ears flicking. "If his lordship wishes it."

Yilon almost laughed. "No 'his lordship' either. Just 'Yilon.' Can you do that?"

"If...if you wish." The words obviously took an effort for the guard to say.

"Why were you selected to be my servant?"

Min turned the corner and started down the stairs. His ears flicked back for a moment. "There are no dedicated personal servants in the castle since the late Lord Dewanne's servant retired."

"So you drew the short stick?"

Min flicked his ears again. "I volunteered."

Yilon examined the other fox more closely. He'd assumed that he was older, but he realized now that Min was probably no more than two or three years his senior. He still had the slender build of youth, and when he spoke, he hesitated often, gathering confidence. "I'm flattered," Yilon said. "I'm sure we'll get along well."

They'd reached the bottom of the stairs. Min stopped and half-turned. "There are some who feel a foreigner has no business in our castle. I think it is a good omen. Since Lord Dewanne fell ill, the city has been...uneasy. I wanted to be able to do something about it. I want to help." He looked away, as if embarrassed by the outburst, but then went on. "I do have one question. In your room, your things...there was a scent of...of a mouse?"

Yilon froze. "Ah..."

"I know his lordship—my apologies, I know that you were traveling with a mouse. But was the mouse so intimate that his scent would remain so strongly?"

Remembering the feel of Sinch's body against, him, Yilon's ears flushed. "How do you feel about mice?" he said.

Min tilted his muzzle. "The idea of friendship with a mouse is not repugnant." His tail twitched.

"I'm happy to hear that." Yilon relaxed. Maybe not everyone in this backwards town was quite so uptight. "I think we're going to get along very well indeed."

Only Lady Dewanne was seated in the small dining hall, paws folded above her empty plate. A servant held out a chair for Yilon to sit, while another placed dishes of porridge before them both. It wasn't all that bad, especially when seasoned with some of the sugar paste from the night before and a pawful of berries. While Yilon ate, Lady Dewanne asked if he were happy with his assigned servant. Yilon thought this rather rude when Min was standing right there, but fortunately he didn't have to lie.

Corwin joined them in the middle of breakfast, at first refusing even to sit. Yilon, just finishing his bowl, saw the look Corwin was giving it, so he insisted the older fox join them, to give Sinch as much time as possible to get out of the castle. Yilon already knew the fox well enough to know that the slightest excuse was enough for him to launch into a story. Sure enough, he'd no sooner mentioned how fresh the berries tasted than Corwin began to tell him about a fox he knew who owned a small berry farm. "His berries were so good that he once traded a single basket of them for an evening of services from a young vixen. He could've had mine for half that," the older fox told Yilon with a wink. And when that story faltered, Yilon asked about the glassware, and was treated to a lengthy recounting of how Corwin had met the handsome young glassblower and had inspired him to create the lovely delicate glass ornament he'd seen in Lady Dewanne's study. "I gave it to Sheffin to give to her," he said with a wink at Lady Dewanne. "On their anniversary."

"I knew where it came from, of course." She smiled. "For Canis's sake, if you don't leave soon, Yilon won't be back in time for his Confirmation. And it wasn't our anniversary. It was for my birthday."

"Of course," Corwin said, smiling and going on with the story as if she hadn't spoken.

They did finish before the sun was too high in the sky, just a paw's breadth above the peak of the eastern mountain. Min returned to Yilon's chambers to finish organizing his books and to air out the room, while Lady Dewanne walked with them as far as the castle gate, where an open cart and bored driver were waiting. "Enjoy what remains of your morning," she said, leaning close to Yilon again.

"I don't think he'll allow me to do otherwise." Yilon grinned at Corwin, one hind paw on the riding board.

"How quickly he sees through me," Corwin said ruefully. "All the mystery gone and unraveled."

"You aren't exactly known for being guarded," Lady Dewanne said, stepping back to lean against the gate.

Corwin put a paw to his chest. "I have hidden depths, my lady. Not to match yours, of course, but then, who could match you in anything?"

She laughed. "Flatterer. It's good you retired when you did, else I'd find it much harder to take my leave."

"Then would I could be governor again for just one day, long enough to change your mind, but not so long as to interrupt my life of indolence." He hoisted himself up into the cart, which creaked as he settled himself next to Yilon. He raised a paw to the driver, then waved to Lady Dewanne. She waved back, watching as the mounts snorted and the cart rumbled across the plaza.

"She likes you," Yilon observed.

Corwin leaned back and stretched in the sunlight. "The feeling is mutual, dear boy. Many's the time I sat all afternoon with her husband on some affair of state and then stayed up all night with the both of them throwing greenstones."

"Greenstones?"

"A diversion. Some night when you're in need of entertainment...of a slightly tamer variety...oh, speaking of which, look up here to the right." He pointed to a three-story building with stone balconies on the third floor. "It was on that balcony to the right there that a vixen whose name has been lost to history locked out Kilkenic Durenin, who was in line to become the next lord. Sadly, the vixen who locked him out there was not his wife, but rather a tempestuous young thing who took objection to some salacious act Kilkenic had asked her to perform—no doubt something the much more proper Gillia Durenin would have refused to do as well."

"Surely he could climb down," Yilon said.

"If only she had locked his clothes out there with him." Corwin shook his head and clucked. "Of course, the alternative version of that legend is that it was not a vixen at all." Yilon raised an eyebrow. Corwin answered the gesture with a wink.

"If you think that's shocking...turn left here," he called to the driver. The cart swung around the corner onto a narrower street. Foxes scurried out of their way. "See the small shrine there?"

Yilon followed his finger to a round stone building. "The one with the Canis star on the door curtain?"

"That's the one. The Lord of Dewanne at the time—this was sixty years ago—was discovered in there with not one, but two young males. One in each end, as it were."

Yilon stared at the shrine, and the thing that was strange about the buildings in the town clicked into place for him, but he had other questions crowding his head. "What happened?"

"He was removed, in favor of Sheffin's father."

Yilon blinked. "It's that easy?"

"Far from it. The council of nobles had to convene and determine that he was unfit, which they had already thought, more or less, because he'd been married for five years and had yet to produce an heir. And it came out that he'd never so much as seen his wife in the marital bed, which scandalized most of the nobles who saw her there in their dreams more or less every night. Except for Hada Buleva, but even he had the good sense to shut his eyes and produce an heir before going off to his muscular plaything. I shouldn't say that, they were actually very sweet together from all accounts, and Juni Buleva told me that she was raised to think of Poli as a second father, and he came with them to Rekindling."

"Rekindling?" Yilon was having trouble keeping all his questions in his head at once.

"Local festival, quite a happy time. Takes place at midsummer when there isn't much planting to be done. All the clans and families spend a day at relaxing and playing. The pools up the slope are a popular place to go; many of the trade clans go out on the lake or up the pass, and the occasional adventuresome group goes to the top of the mountain."

"Trade clans?"

"The tradesmen for a particular trade, their journeymen, and their apprentices."

Yilon shook his head, tracking the conversation back another level. "So this...muscular plaything..."

"Poli."

"He was accepted by the family?"

Corwin nodded. "As I said, Hada had the sense to take care of his familial duties."

Yilon felt a question, whether one was there or not. "I know how important that is," he said, and then, to change the direction of the conversation, "Is there no wood in this town? All the doorways are curtained, except in the palace."

"Castle," Corwin corrected. "We don't have a palace here. As for wood..." He gestured to the mountainsides. "Do you see any? We have enough scrub to make tools and implements, but real wood has to be brought up from the plains. We like our curtains. Doors feel very confining."

"They feel private," Yilon said. He was reflecting on how much wood there was in the castle, and what that meant.

"Oh, look." They'd passed the shrine, approaching the lake shore. The cart made a right turn around a pub called "Wind's End." Corwin pointed across Yilon at it. "That's where Lord Whassel spent a steamy night with a local young fox, when he was in town on a diplomatic visit some forty years ago. That's how to do it right. Save your perversions for your vacations away. Then nobody in your home hears about it, and nobody where you did it cares."

"Except for you, apparently." Yilon grinned.

"Of course I cared." Corwin put his paw to his chest again, in what Yilon was coming to see as his favorite dramatic gesture. "That's why he took me back there."

Startled, Yilon couldn't help but laugh. "Really?" Corwin assumed an innocent expression. "Amazing. Are all the lords secretly gay?"

"Oh, goodness, no. Sheffin—the late Lord Dewanne—he was straight as an arrow. Straighter, actually. But their gossip is so much less creative. Sheffin never strayed from the path, as far as I know. He thought the world of his wife, would do anything for her."

Yilon rubbed his muzzle. "She's leaving once I'm confirmed."

"Canis bless her, she deserves it. She tended to him these last two years when he was ailing. I wouldn't have expected it myself, but people never fail to surprise you. Look, over there is the Grain and Wine Exchange. All the numbers for the harvest are tallied there."

"Where do they keep the grain and wine?" Yilon craned his neck as they passed the small two-story building, looking at the detailed stone reliefs of wheat and grapes.

"The farmers keep them. We send out inspectors to verify the numbers. Only sheepskin is stored here."

Yilon grinned. "Any famous historical figures caught in compromising positions there?"

"Only financial ones, sadly." Corwin pointed to the adjacent building, a small, non-descript home. "But that there is a lovely place for a discreet dinner and a lakeside view. There's a fireplace and a nice thick bed. Should you ever need it, let me know, I'll get the key from the owner. He's a friend of mine. Driver! Stop up ahead here."

They'd reached an intersection with a small, busy street. The windows on the street held brightly colored bolts of cloth, each doorway emblazoned with a name. Corwin instructed the driver to wait, then followed Yilon down to the flagstones. "Hello, Findley," he said, waving to an older fox passing them while Yilon was pulling the leather satchel from the cart. As they turned onto the street, a pair of young vixens called out his name, and he lifted his paw to wave cheerily back.

Where the lakeside road had been nearly empty of people, the small shopping street was so crowded that it was easy to see why Corwin had asked the driver to stop outside it. Corwin had no difficulty making his way through the shoppers, who parted for him and regroup after he'd passed. Yilon stayed at his side, benefiting from his wake.

The tailors were bunched at the head of the street, but he could smell baking and roasted meat further down, and in one window just past the doorway where Corwin stopped them, he saw the glitter of gems and baubles. "Is this the main shopping street?" he asked as they walked under the sign that read, "H. Damasky."

"It is," Corwin said, "and these are the best locations in it. Hallo, Henri."

A thin fox with more grey than russet on his muzzle looked up from the cloth he was measuring and nodded, beaming. "Corwin!"

The short, plump vixen in front of the counter turned as well, a smile on her broad muzzle. The tailor's eyes moved to Yilon, and his tone grew more distant. "This must be the young new Lord, I wager."

"You'd win. Good morning, Madame Colet. How are the boys?"

The vixen smiled. "Lovely, thank you. How are your grapes?"

"This will be a year like no other." Corwin put his fingers to his muzzle and kissed them. "The dry summer has made them small and potent. Much like yourself."

She laughed. "Be sure to favor us with a bottle, when it's ready."

Corwin bowed. "You'll be at the front of the line. Madame, Henri, may I present Yilon." Yilon bowed. "He's to be our new lord in a few days, and a finer young fox I've not had the pleasure of knowing."

The tailor's smile warmed. "A pleasure to meet you, sir."

Madame Colet curtsied. "And how well *do* you know him, hm, Corwin?"

Corwin laughed. "We've only just met. But I might help him try on some clothes." He winked at her.

"I just have to finish with Henri, and then he's all yours." She turned back to the tailor. "So: the blue, in addition to those."

"I'll have it measured in just a moment," Henri said. "These fingers don't work as fast as they used to."

Corwin waggled his own. "Neither do these, old friend," he said. To Yilon, he motioned toward the back of the store with his head. They walked over toward the window.

Yilon inhaled the scent of fabric, a mingled smell of flax plants and of animal wool. Behind the counter, piles of cloth rolls formed a colorful mountain range, and on either side of the walls of the store, shirts and trousers hung with small sheepskin labels. He read the closest one: it said, "Divalia style, Barris 24. In these or other colors." The small, neat lettering left no doubt in his mind that Henri had printed each label himself.

"From the twenty-fourth year of King Barris's reign," Corwin said. "Not the best time for fashion, honestly. It caught on here because of the sleeves, you see how they flare out like that? The people here like that look." He snorted. "What you want is something more like that one, near the front, with the slender shoulders. See it, the one in blue and white? But we'll need to get it in green, of course."

Yilon let his finger brush a section of the cloth in the window, keeping his eye on the crowd outside. He saw no mice among the passers-by, and wondered if that would hamper his plan. But no, Sinch was smart and reliable. He would have to depend on him. "There must be a lot of people who would want to be Lord," he said, as though he'd been musing over the weight of his title.

"Many would want to, but few are qualified, and even fewer acceptable." Corwin glanced at the leather bag whose strap Yilon kept wrapped around his paw. "There are five noble families in Dewanne, six if you count Vitchen Durenin, who changed his name to Kolled and moved out another street over from the castle, but until he's married with issue, nobody really does. But you shouldn't worry about that. Listen." He moved closer to Yilon and lowered his voice. "I am, if I may say so, an excellent judge of character. I have been very impressed by you, and I think you are just what this city needs."

"How can you know that?" Yilon was half-amused, half-startled.

Corwin smiled and touched a finger to his own nose. "Well. You prefer males, for one. That elevates you right away. But second, you stand very much apart from this land. Sheffin was an admirable Lord once he moved to Divalia. When he lived here, he was constantly besieged by requests from his family for favors. Living afar, he was able to know everybody and treat everyone fairly. Third, you have experience of the world beyond, and it is past time that Dewanne broke out of its provincial cradle. We sit in a strategic position between Delford and Tephos, a position that could bring a great deal of power and influence to the city and the Lord who knows how to cultivate it." He nodded toward Yilon. "I think you could."

Yilon glanced toward the front of the shop, where Madame Colet was finishing her transaction. Neither she nor Henri appeared to have heard them. He tried to imitate Corwin's low whisper. "I'll have to get married, right?"

"Oh, yes. In fact, I know there is a bride picked out for you."

Madame Colet bustled past them with a cheery, "You must come to dinner next week, Corwin, and bring the young Lord with you." While Corwin was nodding, she stepped up closer to him and whispered in his ear, clearly not intending Yilon to hear. He caught two phrases thanks to the reflected sound from the glass of the front window: "for my daughter," and something that sounded like "wormwood."

"Of course," Corwin said, as softly, but the angle of his muzzle made his words more audible. "I have a preparation ready."

"What would we do without you?" she said cheerily, and then she was out the door without waiting to hear the end of Corwin's quick response.

"Lovely, lovely," Henri murmured when Corwin brought Yilon up to the counter.

"None of that Barris trash," Corwin said. "Give us last year's."

The old tailor smiled, bringing his measuring tape around to Yilon, scribbling numbers on sheepskin. "Always the eye, you have. Yes, the Barris period, well, the king being a bear and all, the clothes are looser, flaring, designed to hide by billowing outward. With our King Pontion on the throne, the slimmer look is coming back into fashion, and hopefully will remain so through the Musteline King." He gave a dry chuckle. "By which time I will be long past caring about fashion."

"You think they don't need to look their best in the next world?" Corwin leaned on the counter, watching the measuring.

"There's no vanity in His Pack," Henri said. "Canis will dictate the fashion, and I can simply enjoy it. Oh, you'll look splendid in these." His paws circled Yilon's hips and then measured his legs, with a gentle touch that sparked the thought that he and Corwin had been more than just friends at one time. To distract himself from the light touches in his sensitive areas, Yilon looked fixedly out the window, watching the crowd move past the small shop.

He hoped for a glimpse of Sinch outside, but every person that passed, young and old, short and tall, fat and thin, was a fox. Even in Vinton, he'd never seen so many. Some had light orange fur that was almost beige, while others sported a deep sunset red, and still others carried streaks of brown and gold, like fall leaves. He saw one silver fox, still in his black summer coat, and one whose head fur was dark enough that he might be a cross fox. Two guards in their grey-and-green uniforms strode by them, both acknowledging Corwin with a smile. But there were no mice, not a single one.

While Henri finished the measurements, Corwin laid four shirts on the counter along with two trousers. "Two each of the shirts," he said, "and three each of the pants. You like?"

The shirts all looked the same to Yilon, but he didn't want to get into a discussion about the differences between them. They did look nicer than anything he'd owned apart from his one set of formal dress clothes, unworn since his arrival in Divalia two years before, so he nodded. "They look wonderful."

Corwin patted his shoulder. "I told you you have good taste. Now, one set in green primary, grey secondary, of course. What other colors do you like?"

They stepped aside to show Yilon the dizzying pile of colors behind the counter. "Um," he said. "Yellow?"

Henri and Corwin exchanged a look. "We'll pick you out something nice," Corwin said.

Yilon, still tense over Sinch and wanting to give him additional time, asked what was wrong with yellow, and was treated to a discussion of the history of the color yellow, including a thorough examination of the different shades available. They settled on a nice color that Henri called "golden ocher," with a darker brown as the secondary that Corwin said was perfect to set off Yilon's lighter red fur. They shook paws and sniffed muzzles as they left, Henri promising the clothes would be ready within the week, with one outfit done for the Confirmation.

"Goodness!" Corwin said as they left. He looked up at the sun. "We don't have much time for me to show you the rest of the town. I suppose we should hurry along. I do need to show you where the other noble families live, and the mining exchange, at least. Oh! That shop, just down there..."

He pointed to a small window with jewels glittering in it. "That's where... no, never mind, no time to tell the story."

For as pudgy as he was, he moved with speed when he needed to. Yilon found it much more difficult to follow him through the street on the way back to the cart. At the intersection where the cart was waiting, beneath a street sign marking it the corner of Market Street and Lake Side Road, Yilon glimpsed a trio of mice in ragged, dirty cloaks. He didn't recognize any of them, but their presence where there had been only foxes half an hour before made him sure that Sinch was involved.

Indeed, once they had pulled themselves into the cart, the mice followed them. The foxes on the street gave them a wider berth than they'd given Corwin, with additional dirty looks. The governor spotted the mice and looked down the street for guards. Yilon, following him, saw no uniforms. When Corwin had sat, his ears folded down. "Driver," he said, even though Yilon wasn't all the way in the cart yet, "go on."

But the driver didn't move. The mice were at Corwin's side of the cart now, leaning over it. They smelled wretched. "Help us, old friend," one of them said. "Just a copper for the three of us. Please, please."

"Help us, young prince," another said across Corwin to Yilon. "My brothers and I have not eaten in days."

Corwin's ears flattened further. "Driver!" he called. "Why aren't we moving?"

The driver turned around and gestured to the mounts, "Can't, sir," he said.

Yilon craned his neck and saw that a fourth mouse had planted himself in front of the mounts. Corwin threw himself back in the seat, ignoring the mice as best he could. "Where are the guard? Call them."

"Already done, sir," the driver said. "I hailed the one down the street. He's on his way."

"They're not doing anything," Yilon said. He leaned back in his seat too. The beggar mice were remaining politely out of the cart, mostly. It was clear that this was a time-worn tactic to get money, but his heart pounded anyway. It couldn't be a coincidence, not here outside Market Street where he'd told Sinch to be. The urge to look behind him was nearly overwhelming, but he reminded himself that he had to act natural.

"I do apologize for this further delay," Corwin said. It was the first time Yilon had seen him without even a hint of a smile, his eyes fixed dead ahead of him.

"We had beggars in Divalia," Yilon said. "They were all over."

"What do we pay those guards for?" Corwin muttered.

Yilon was about to press further when he felt a touch on his ear, no more than a breath. He started, and turned despite himself. No mouse was in sight, but a tall cloaked figure was striding quickly away from his cart, a bushy red tail dragging on the ground behind it.

The beggar mice stepped back in unison, and the cart lurched forward. "Finally," Corwin grumbled, as Yilon was thrown back into the bench, his paw landing on the empty spot where his leather satchel had been.

Chapter 6: The Warren

Sinch lay still under the bed, listening to Yilon and the servant-fox discuss clothes. Yilon, bless him, was talking loudly, no doubt to distract the servant from any sounds Sinch might make. But Sinch was very good at being quiet. The only thing he couldn't do anything about was his scent, especially around foxes, and especially without any of the powders that were in the small bag of tools under the loose floorboard in the room he'd rented half a mile away.

Still, either Yilon's noise or his authority kept the servant from looking under the bed to see the huddled mouse there. Once the bedroom door clicked shut and Sinch could see the empty floor, he scurried out to the open window, flipped through, and made his way quickly down. In the morning light, someone might see him, but he had no alternative, really.

Rodenta was with him. No sound met him at the bottom of the wall. He followed the line of the building to the place where the lawn between the house and outer wall was narrowest, and then followed the wall to the unattended door in the back. Nobody was watching on either side, so he slipped through the narrow entrance and out into the city. It would've been no big trick to climb the wall, but it was easier still to find an unguarded door. He liked impressing Yilon with accomplishments that were easier than they appeared.

In the still of morning, the city lay quiet. He'd noticed last night that the crowds persisted in the streets into the evening and well into the night, which was reasonable when you considered the city was made up entirely of foxes and mice. In fact, he hadn't slept at all between the time the driver had left him at the edge of the Warren and the time he'd crept into Yilon's room.

The Warren was the most fascinating place he'd ever been. From the time he'd stepped past the squad of fox guards, across the boundary the driver wouldn't cross, and breathed in the scent of what must be a thousand mice, he'd been entranced. The mice, at first suspicious of him, thawed quickly when he explained that he was new in town and had been arrested. They sent him to Miss Chakray's boarding-house, and one, warning him to keep away from "a troublemaker and thief by the name of Balinni, or any of his gang," had given him without meaning to the name of someone who might be able to help him. He'd boasted, "I'm not afraid of any thief in this town," hoping word would get back to this Balinni mouse. Otherwise, he'd have to find him, and he had an idea that would be difficult in the Warren for someone who didn't know it.

The boarding-house, two stories tall, consisted of a moderately-sized common room on the ground floor where the four tenants and the landlady spent most of their time, three rooms in the basement which were the cheaper ones on account of the mold (according to one of the residents), and three rooms on the second story, one of which was Miss Chakray's residence. Sinch gathered that that room was also available to boarders, with a slightly enhanced array of services offered. He declined that option politely, took the empty second-story room, and secured his belongings as best he could in the featureless space that was barely enough for him to turn around in. The straw pallet by the window took up one entire wall, and the only other furniture was a chair with a broken leg—not that there was room for much else. Spiderwebs filled the corners, and the straw pallet smelled of everyone who'd stayed there before, though not strongly. It took him only a few moments to find a floorboard he could pry up to hide his money below. His clothes he left in his satchel, but he took the dagger from the Divalia armory. He had a feeling it might come in handy when he went to find Balinni.

As it happened, Balinni came to see him before he'd been in the common room of the boarding house for more than half an hour. He'd barely finished the thin root soup Miss Chakray had served when the two mice he'd been talking to got up in mid-sentence and left the table. Sinch looked up, into the hard eyes of a seasoned thief. "He wants to see you," he said.

With no more than a nod, trying not to show his nerves, Sinch followed the mouse outside, around one corner and then another, through cramped alleys. Despite being alert, he didn't hear the approach of the mouse who seized him from behind and spun him around. Sinch had his knife drawn before he registered the torn ear and scarred muzzle of a mouse who was so thin he might have been described as emaciated if his shoulders and arms hadn't been so muscular.

"New in town," Balinni'd said, and it wasn't a question. "Let's see."

He pointed Sinch to a painted target in the wooden side of a crate fifteen feet down the alley, and handed him five rusty knives. When he'd thrown the last one, hitting the target four times, Balinni jumped him and grappled him to the ground, but Sinch got out of the hold. He didn't manage to pin the other mouse, but Balinni chuckled and said, "Good," so no more was expected of him.

The scarred mouse leaned against the brick wall of the alley. "Where you from?" he asked, while his henchmouse fetched the knives. Sinch talked about Divalia, but Balinni cut him off in mid-sentence.

"You've not improved your lot," he started. "Life in the Warren is hard. Best you realize that now. If it's not for you, get yourself back to Frontier and catch the next coach east. But there are opportunities here for a mouse who can avail himself of them. The redtails hate us, but won't get rid of us, and we can live off them if we keep our eyes open and keep a step ahead of them."

"Do they all hate you—us?"

"Every last one." Balinni's eyes glinted. "They blame us for all the ills that befall them, from the ones we caused to the ones we suffer from along with them. So we might as well cause as many as possible."

It was Balinni that Sinch thought of as he crept from the palace back to the Warren in the dawn light. Yilon had told him his plan, but not how Sinch was supposed to pull off his part of it. The mouse's head ran through one idea after another, but he was missing the information necessary to decide which one would work best. He had been able to sneak past the guards once, but could he do it again? Could a whole crew do it, if necessary? How much time, realistically, would he have?

The Warren already felt comfortable to him. The narrow alleys and hidey-holes, the buildings that were just pass-throughs to another street, the streets choked with cleverly placed piles of garbage, pools of filthy water, or ramshackle barricades, all of it was like an immense puzzle that he had to solve every time he wanted to travel somewhere. Being comfortable didn't mean he could find his way, though. Just getting to the small house where Balinni had told him he could be found took him a good half hour, though it was only a hundred yards from Miss Chakray's house.

The small one-story house, flat-roofed and damp, appeared to be Balinni's alone. Despite the damp, it smelled clean, though again it smelled of dozens, if not hundreds, of mice. Two of them lounged in the front room on cots stuffed with straw. Though they looked asleep, huddled under patched cloaks, one of them spoke up as soon as Sinch walked in.

She got up when he'd told her his business and walked into the back room, "to see if Mister Balinni is awake." A moment later, she poked her head back out. "You Sinch?" When he nodded, she jerked her head toward the back. "C'mon in."

Balinni was awake, and listened to Sinch's plans over a breakfast of delicious-smelling bread that he did not offer to share, laid out on a low stone desk that was otherwise cluttered with parchment and ink bottles.

"That's good an' interesting," he said. "Got some good thoughts there. I like the distraction one. Speaks to our strengths. But I'd add one little twist to it."

He raised a paw for the female mouse, who'd stayed in the room. "Run over to Marisco's and get Kishin," he said, wiggling his paw behind and over his head. She was gone in a moment.

"Now," he said to Sinch, "this is pretty big. What's this thing you're to take? And how do you know so much about where it will be?"

"I don't know exactly what it is," Sinch said. "When the guards arrested me yesterday, I heard them talking about the new lord in town, and how he felt he didn't have to have guards to go around with. And one of them said, "Carrying that around with him with no guards, it's just begging for trouble.""

Balinni rolled the breadcrumbs below his slender fingers. "They just said that, right in earshot of you."

"Those guards didn't know I was there," Sinch said. "They threw me into the cart and those other foxes were talking outside."

"Hm." Balinni rolled the breadcrumb ball back and forth, collecting the rest of the crumbs. "It is true that there's a new lord, arrived just yesterday. We don't know much about him. But he might be taken around the city tomorrow. Might be our last chance for a big score. Been a nice couple years for us, old Lord sick and no heir around. And the last couple weeks! Never been busier. So if your information proves true, so much the better. You don't strike me a mouse in the habit of lying." He picked up the breadcrumb ball and popped it into his mouth.

"I'm not," Sinch said, hoping his voice and tail didn't betray his nervousness. "I just want to share in whatever it is."

"You'll get a share, all right." Balinni licked his fingers. "Might take a little while to get it to you. We couldn't sell a royal treasure here in the city."

Sinch nodded, his mind leaping ahead to the problem of what to give Balinni once the theft was accomplished. Hopefully he could stall him and then leave with Yilon, and it wouldn't be a problem. His whiskers tingled at the danger in that plan, but he couldn't think of anything else to do. He'd have to ask Yilon for something from the treasury, something valuable.

He was rather startled when the female mouse returned barely a few moments later. She must be better at navigating the streets than he was. She did not have any person in her company; rather, held away from her body, she carried a large parcel wrapped in sackcloth, about as large as her chest, that reeked of fox.

"Thank you," Balinni said, clearing a space in the center of his desk. "On here."

She set it down and slouched back into a corner of the room. Balinni smiled at Sinch and pulled the sackcloth away to reveal red fur. He lifted three items out and laid them carefully side by side: a wooden pole with a leather harness on one end, about the length of Sinch's arm; a long red-furred tail with a white tip on one end and another leather harness on the other. Sinch barely had time to register that the tail appeared to be a real fox tail, because when Balinni lifted out the last item, all other thoughts flew from his head, and he jerked back from the table.

Facing him was the empty, staring head of a dead fox.

"Beautiful, no?" Balinni caressed the ears fondly. "Marisco does lovely work. Cleaned up all the smell of death, brushed with musk from a couple different foxes so nobody can clearly identify the scent. You wear a cloak over it—never the same one, unless you're on the same job—and wear this on your head. Strap the tail around your midsection, and you can pass for one of them at a glance."

Sinch couldn't take his eyes off the head. It was the most grisly thing he'd ever seen. The eyes had been replaced by glass baubles, and all the fur was neatly brushed and clean, but the nose was dry and wrinkled. He wanted more than anything for Balinni to put the head back in the sackcloth; he wanted never to have to see it again, let alone touch it. But Balinni had attached the wooden pole to the base of the hideous thing and was holding it out to him.

"Try it on," the scarred mouse said, with almost fatherly pride.

There was nothing Sinch could do but close his eyes and take it in his paws. The cheek ruffs felt dry and dead. He couldn't help thinking about Yilon's cheek ruffs, so warm, and how they'd felt a couple hours ago. He forced a smile to his muzzle and lifted it over his head. Balinni fastened the harness around Sinch's neck.

The weight balanced over him so that when he nodded his head forward, it felt about to fall off. He kept his head carefully upright after that, while Balinni chuckled. "It takes a bit of getting used to, but it works well. We've used it a few times now." His eyes, rather than meeting Sinch's, rested above, as though he were talking to the dead fox head. "We call him Kishin."

Sinch swallowed. "Was that...was that his name?"

Balinni laughed. "Rodenta's teats, no. No idea who he was. He came in and died on our doorstep a decade ago. Kishin was one of the nobles who particularly hated us." He traced a finger over his most prominent scar, a gash running from his eye halfway down the right side of his muzzle. "I got this from his soldiers, five years ago. They came in and tried to burn down the Warren one night."

Sinch tried to imagine being woken up in the night, smoke in his nostrils, fire licking at his home. "What...what happened after that?"

"We fought them, lost more than a few good mice, but saved our homes." His eyes glittered. "The redtails may have forgotten him, but we have not."

"Is he...what is he doing now?" Sinch felt the weight of the head pressing down on his neck and shoulders.

Balinni's expression remained impassive. "The darkness he wished on others took him."

There didn't seem to be anything Sinch could say to that.

Balinni called four other mice to help them: the female who'd brought "Kishin," whose name was Valix; the hulking mouse named Bog who'd accompanied him the previous day; and a pair named Cal and Mal, who echoed each other's words to the point that Sinch lost track of which was which. Valix was put in charge, so she brought the five of them to the edge of the Warren near the lake, where steps led down into a foul-smelling trench. "Keep your paws out of the water," she told Sinch, unnecessarily, because he was stepping as carefully as possible. "The rest of us may smell like filth, but you should not. And don't drag the sack."

He hadn't been, but now he hefted it higher. They made their way through narrow twists and turns, until they came to a place where Sinch could just see the ears of three uniformed foxes on the ground above the trench, one bend further along. Valix held up her paw for silence and motioned them into a small hole in the right side of the trench, which fortunately was dry.

The hole smelled of mice, but faintly, and there was another smell tickling Sinch's nose that he couldn't quite identify. If Yilon were here, he'd have been able to figure it out. Light glimmered ahead of them and to the left, but as they walked along, a waft of cooler air brushed Sinch's whiskers, and he looked to his right. He saw nothing but blackness there, and while waiting for his eyes adjust, Valix grabbed his paw and yanked him forward.

He jerked his paw away from her. She glared at him, her eyes glinting with faint light, and motioned for him to put on his disguise.

The passage was relatively dry. Sinch put the sack down, unpacking while Bog, Cal, and Mal kept going toward the faint light of the entrance.

All a matter of quickness and practice.

He got the harness on, fastened the tail around his midsection, making sure it wasn't dragging in the water, and then pulled out the cloak Balinni'd given him. Valix watched him with folded arms, tapping her tail against the wall.

"They can't hear us down here," Sinch whispered.

At the sound of his words, her eyes widened and she lurched forward, slapping a paw over his muzzle. "It's not the guards I'm worried about," she said in words as quiet as a breath, so that even though her lips were an inch from his ear, he had to strain to hear them.

When he nodded, she stepped back, allowing him to lift the hood of the cloak over the dead fox's ears. He adjusted it, but before he could, Valix grabbed his paw and dragged him forward.

They emerged into weak sunlight, in the sewage trench. Looking back, Sinch saw they must be a good ways past where the guards had been standing. Valix, relaxed now, looking him over and gave an approving nod. "Come on," she said, and led him around another bend, to a narrower, straight trench. She hurried him past a hole on the right side to where Cal, or Mal, waited partway down it. "It's there," he said, and then scurried up brick handholds to the surface.

"At least you're not a complete liar," Valix said, but quietly. "They'll signal when it's time."

"How?" Sinch asked, but she just nodded at the surface without further clarification.

The fox's head felt heavier and heavier. With the cloak around him, in the enclosed space of the sewer, he kept sensing someone sneaking up on him. The feeling grew stronger despite the complete silence in the trench. He would hear any movement from yards away. But the smell of the sewers overwhelmed his nose, and that made him nervous. In Divalia, he'd learned about scent-masking, using stinkclouds to obscure one's scent. He'd never descended to the sewers there, though he'd heard they were immense labyrinths crawling under the city, through which you could get anywhere. He'd also heard that the people who used them in Divalia were worse than thieves.

Unable to resist the feeling, he turned his head to look back the way they'd come. The trench was empty as far as he could see. When he straightened, he saw Valix's wry amusement, no anxiety showing, though he could smell it. "Nothing here but us," she whispered.

He nodded. Despite her assurances, and the evidence of his own eyes, the feeling of being stalked grew again in the back of his head. It was a relief when Valix said, "They're coming out. Come on."

She scurried up the brick handholds. It took Sinch longer, balancing the apparatus atop his head, but he forgot the weight when he emerged into the stronger light of an alley and saw Valix at the end of the alley urging him forward.

The rest of the alley was deserted. He gathered the cloak around him, peering out of the space between the bottom of the fox head and the cloak's clasp. He still didn't feel convinced that he would pass for a fox.

Stepping out from the alley onto a wide street that paralleled the lake, it took him a moment to get his bearings. Even though there weren't a lot of foxes walking by, he still wouldn't have figured out that the low-backed open cart was Yilon's without Valix, Cal, and Mal's figures at its side. After that, it was all a matter of quickness and practice.

He walked slowly up behind the cart, looking for his opportunity. A pair of foxes walked by, after whom the space was clear. A paw out of the cloak, the satchel lifted and pulled under quickly, heavier than Sinch thought it would be, but not unmanageable. He probably would have been able to do it even if Yilon had not been expecting it.

He hesitated only a moment, finding it difficult to be so close to Yilon and yet not say anything. He leaned forward, and the tip of the dead fox's nose came within a hair of Yilon's ear. Sinch jumped back, stumbling, almost directly into the path of a slender vixen. She sniffed at him and kept walking.

Bad, very bad, he scolded himself. She noticed, she'll remember. Without waiting to see if Yilon had reacted, he turned and walked quickly away from the cart, away from the alley where Valix and the others would be waiting.

Chapter 7: Unpleasant Truths

"Gone?" Corwin stared as though Yilon had just told him the castle itself was no longer there. "What do you mean, gone? Why did you have it with you in the first place?"

"I didn't trust Maxon." Yilon was having a hard time acting as distraught as he knew he should be. His tail kept starting to wag despite his best efforts.

"Didn't trust...so you brought..." Corwin's paw flew to his muzzle, his ears flattening. "And it was mice. Oh, Teeth and Tail, this is bad. Very bad."

"How do you know it was mice?" Yilon's fur started to prickle. "Those were just beggars."

"You don't know this town yet," Corwin said. "They never come begging here this early in the morning. If they're about before noon, it's with a purpose." He moaned softly, then stopped when he saw the driver looking back at them. "Back to the castle," he snapped. "Now."

While the cart turned, Corwin leaned closer to Yilon. "Let me handle them, when we get back," he said.

The rest of the short ride passed in silence. Yilon didn't trust himself to say anything, and Corwin was not inclined to talk. As soon as they pulled up in front of the castle gate, though, he jumped out with surprising agility and called to one of the guards to run in and summon Lady Dewanne and Velkan.

The other guard looked bemused. "Is it lunchtime already, sir?" Corwin ignored the remark, gesturing to Yilon to follow him as he strode into the grounds.

It took Velkan several minutes to arrive. They convened in the dining hall, where Min and two other foxes brought them cups of a dark wine and then left. When they'd closed the door behind them, Corwin launched into the story of the theft. He'd only gotten halfway through it, even without his usual verbosity, when Maxon burst into the room, his vest askew over his tunic, fur sticking up between his ears.

"What's going on, my lady? Why is the governor here? Nobody told me there would be a meeting today."

"This was not planned, Maxon," Lady Dewanne said. "We are dealing with something of a crisis."

He looked around the table. "What crisis?" His eyes came to rest on Yilon. "What's he done now?" His breath came in pants, and he'd no sooner gotten that last sentence out than he broke out into a coughing fit.

"Calm yourself, please," Lady Dewanne said. "We are just hearing about it from Corwin."

"I didn't do anything," Yilon said, bristling.

Maxon's eyes narrowed. "You lost it, didn't you?"

Corwin and Lady Dewanne looked at each other. "The fewer who know, the better," Corwin said.

"Maxon knows many secrets," Lady Dewanne said. "His advice may be useful." To the steward, she gestured to a chair. "Please, have a seat."

Corwin looked dubious, but finished his story, after restating the beginning for Maxon's benefit. When he reached the discovery of the theft, Maxon jumped to his feet, glaring at Yilon. "I knew it!" he said, and then added, "your *lordship*."

"Sit down, Maxon," Lady Dewanne said. She and Velkan had not so much as gasped when the news was imparted. "There will be ample time to apportion blame. For now, the unfortunate incident cannot be reversed; therefore, it must be remedied. Velkan, Corwin, your thoughts?"

Yilon noticed that Velkan deferred to Corwin, but the older fox shook his head. "I am past the age of making decisions of import." He settled back into his chair with a heavy sigh. "I no longer feel the pulse of Dewanne, only those near to me."

"You do yourself too little credit," Velkan said briskly. "I would welcome your counsel, and ask no more of you than that. I will bear the weight of the decision, along with my lord and lady here."

"He's no lord now, nor shall he ever be," Maxon said.

"Maxon, have you any advice for us?" Lady Dewanne made a quick gesture with her paw to Corwin. An apology, Yilon thought, for usurping his speech. He acknowledged the gesture and turned, as the others did, to the steward.

"Advice? I have advice for you." He pointed at Yilon, who tried to look affronted. "Send the heir back to Divalia and find someone more suitable, who will treat the history of Dewanne with respect."

Listen to him, Yilon pleaded silently, while at the same time attempting to keep up his wounded expression.

"He was treating it with respect," Corwin said. "He wanted to keep it safe on his person. His only crime was in not being vigilant enough."

"His crime was trusting mice. Mark my words, that mouse that came with him from Divalia is behind this."

Yilon squirmed, the glow of his plan's success shadowed by this new twist. "Leave him out of it," he said.

Maxon cleared his throat to say something else, but Lady Dewanne cut him off. "I said, there will be time for blame later. We know how many different parties might have an interest in the crown."

"Yes, your ladyship," he said, though his eyes remained mutinous.

"Do you have advice?" she repeated.

"Yes." He glared at Yilon. "Send him home and then send twenty guards to scour the Warren until the crown is found."

"We'll not repeat Kishin's mistake," Velkan said.

"Mayhap Kishin had the right idea," Maxon shot back.

"We will not consider a revival of Kishin's ideas, Canis bless him," Lady Dewanne said.

Maxon turned to her. "Simply because he executed them poorly—"

"That's enough, Maxon." Lady Dewanne pointed to the door. "You may go."

The steward shut his jaw with a click. He looked around the table, letting his eyes rest on Yilon, then got up slowly and walked to the door. With one final look back at all of them, he left.

Lady Dewanne sighed. "He feels the weight of more responsibility. Especially since..."

"Nevertheless." Velkan turned toward the door, stroking his whiskers, and then returned to the meeting. "What is the disposition of the nobility, Corwin?"

"Ah, a question I can answer. I'm sorry to say that there is a still considerable amount of unrest. Each family resents, to one extent or another, the naming of an heir from Divalia. They will accept him, in time, but this incident, as you put it, will not be a help."

"I am certain it will not," Lady Dewanne said. "Velkan, your thoughts?"

"Do not move hastily." He leaned back in his chair. "Be sure of our facts and then strike cleanly and efficiently."

"So you don't blame the mice?" Yilon sat up.

Velkan favored him with a cool look. "Your story is insufficient to assign blame, except in your own carelessness."

Yilon folded his ears down. Lady Dewanne tapped the table with a claw. "Corwin?"

"My lady." He bowed toward her. "I know Velkan has only improved his judgment since I recommended him. I would not dream of questioning him."

"So you agree ." She inclined her head as Corwin nodded. "Very well, then. I know that you are retired, but if I might beg your help in this one matter, I would be most grateful."

"My lady," Corwin said, "of me you may ask anything and I would gladly give it."

"Then work with Velkan and your contacts. Find out what there is to know. The crown must be recovered, but it is best to avoid raising an alarm for as long as we can avoid it."

"Yes, my lady. And what shall we do should the Confirmation day arrive and the crown still be missing?"

"Let us continue to ponder that," she said, almost lightly. "Oh, I believe we should give more attention to the matter of Dinah. Can you discover whether she has returned yet?"

Velkan nodded. "I will have it seen to."

Corwin leaned forward. "Dinah was missing?"

"I fancied it simply a rebellious act from a young vixen. But now, I fear..." She stroked her whiskers.

"Yes," Corwin said. "Or perhaps the two incidents are related in another way. What if she was the figure Yilon saw? What if she is working with the mice?"

Yilon stared at the polished metal table, not wanting to give himself away. He hadn't identified the scent, but from the touch on his ear, he was sure the "fox" in the cloak had been Sinch.

"It's possible," Lady Dewanne said. "It would surprise me."

"And me," Corwin said. "But we have been surprised before."

Yilon raised his head in time to meet the eyes of Velkan. The governor raised his eyebrows very slightly. Yilon looked away, around the old stone arches supporting the ceiling of the dining hall, at the portraits of foxes gazing back down at him from the walls. They held the same reproach in their eyes. He looked down at the table.

"When we find Dinah, we can ask her," Lady Dewanne said. "Now, leave me with Yilon. I would have some words with him."

She looked steadily at him. Yilon fidgeted as Corwin and Velkan rose, bowed, and made their way out of the room. When the door had closed behind them, Lady Dewanne relaxed in her seat, shaking her head. Yilon curled his tail under his chair and waited for her to speak. He couldn't have said why he felt the stab of guilt now, of all times. Perhaps it was the way she sagged when she relaxed, or perhaps it was the lack of accusation in her eyes. He felt an urge to speak, but held his tongue, waiting for her.

"I will not send you away," she said finally.

His ears snapped back before he could help himself. Puzzlement clouded her eyes, even when he brought them up again, quickly, so he said, "But I can't be king without the crown."

"You can be Regent," she said. "You will be Regent, when I'm gone, until the Confirmation can take place."

"But I lost the crown," he said.

"It was stolen."

He pointed at the door. "They don't think I'm fit to rule."

Her voice grew sharper. She sat straight up in her chair. "They do not have the privilege of making that decision."

"Do you think I'm fit to rule?"

She waved off his question. "You are the heir. You are the ruler, no matter what."

"Even without the crown?"

"We will find the crown," she said. "You will render every assistance to Velkan to expedite its retrieval."

"What can I tell him?" Yilon slumped back in his chair. "Corwin was there, too."

"You were closer to the crown." Lady Dewanne leaned forward. "You may have noticed details. Velkan is very good at analyzing situations. Whereas Corwin's strength is in analyzing people."

"So he said." Yilon folded his arms.

She held his eyes. Hers were light blue, but steady and hard. "If I were not more sure that your father has instilled in you the good sense and wisdom he possesses, I would be very curious about your role in the convenient disappearance of the symbol of a land you care little for and do not seem at all interested in ruling, by a group of the same species as your traveling companion from Divalia."

Heat pricked at his fur. He couldn't believe he was that transparent. It had been a good plan! All he could do was seize on the part of her statement he could confirm, so that he could deny the rest. "How do you expect me to be excited about ruling here? I have no friends here, no family."

"Do you miss your family so much?"

He lowered his ears. "It's not like Vinton."

"Which, if I am not mistaken, already has an heir in your older brother."

"Yes," he grumbled, running his claws along the table edge.

"Listen to me," she said, with such force that he jerked his head up. "We do not always get to choose our destinies. For you to reject this land would be inconsequential in another time. In this time, you are needed.

Your birth and inheritance were arranged in advance by a wise lord who foresaw this need. Corwin thinks you will make a good ruler, and perhaps it is best that you have no emotional ties to Dewanne. But you will not abdicate this duty, and you will not leave this land leaderless and adrift. I will not allow it. Nor will your father."

It registered with him that that was the second time she'd mentioned his father as though Lord Dewanne were still alive. Or as though she knew the truth. "My...my father is dead," he said softly.

"Oh, no, Yilon. My nose may not be as sharp as it was when I was young, but I lived with my dear Sheffin for twenty years. I am as certain that you are not truly his son as you are."

"Then..." He sat up. "You're not sending me home?"

"As much as Maxon would like me to, no."

His ears folded back. "Does he know, too?"

"I have not asked. But he, too, knew Sheffin well. I would not be surprised."

Yilon rubbed his fingers along the surface of the table. "He hates me."

"He will not be the last." She said it almost lightly. "People hate lords for many reasons, some good, some not. Most good, I am sorry to say."

"If you'd had cubs, I wouldn't even be here," Yilon muttered, but regretted it instantly as Lady Dewanne's ears flattened, her eyes lowering. "But there have to be others who could assume the title, too" he said, trying to recover. "There are five noble families. None of them has the right bloodline?"

Her ears remained down as she answered. "There are five noble cubs in your generation. It will be six in three months when Llarina Durenin delivers. Three are male, all under the age of seven. They have not yet even been Sung in the church. There were three male cubs older than you, from eighteen years up to thirty. To a one, they left Dewanne to seek their fortunes elsewhere once it became known that Sheffin did not look favorably on any of them. Only one unmarried female cub of age remains. She is fifteen and of excellent character."

"What's wrong with her? A lady can hold the title, can't she?"

"Of course." She lifted her muzzle, showing a brief flash of amusement. "However, it becomes more difficult when it is impossible to locate her. Dinah is the one who's gone missing."

"Oh." Yilon's head sank.

"And also, by the way, your betrothed."

Chapter 8: Balinni's Price

This was the part of the plan that Sinch was most worried about, but he'd always been rather good at improvising. It took him very little time to find a sleepy, run-down side street, and not much longer to find a house that smelled empty. Around the back way, hidden from other eyes, he found a loose back door and let himself inside, down into the basement. A pile of disused sacks of rotting leather made a perfect hiding place. He made sure none of the satchel's newer leather was showing, then let himself out of the house.

As he slipped around the back, his whiskers tingled. There'd been no sound, nor scent he could detect, but something didn't feel right to him. He paused, looking around the chest-high metal railing and the small yard full of weeds. The smell of the weeds was strong, as was the rotting smell of the leather on his paws, but there was nothing else other than the reek of the disguise he was wearing. Nerves, he scolded himself as he hurried back to the alley.

Back on the main street, the crowd of foxes obscured any other scent he might have picked up. He dodged back and forth, slowing only when he saw a short tod stare at him inquisitively. It took him a second to figure out that what was making him stand out was that none of the other foxes were moving as quickly through the crowd. He slowed, keeping his hood down as he made his way behind the castle to a secluded area where he could safely get rid of the disguise.

When it was safely in its sack again, he leaned against the stone wall and breathed deeply, working his neck in a circle to loosen it. The breeze from the city carried the scent of foxes, as it did everywhere in Dewanne except for the Warren. He put it to his back and walked out from the shadow of the castle, around a small cluster of shrubs and down the dirt slope to the southern edge of the Warren.

Two bored guards lifted their muzzles as he came into view, ears perking up. "Bit late for garbage collection," the first said, sniffing the air.

"Sorry," Sinch said, and then added, "sir," to be extra-cautious.

They waited for more explanation, but when he didn't talk, the second guard's ears drifted back to a bored position. The first narrowed his eyes. "You'll hafta pay a late tax."

Sinch's heart beat faster. The last thing he wanted was to get involved in a confrontation. "Sir?"

"Aw, leave it," the second guard said. "What, you want to get a couple old bones? He don't got nothin'."

"I don't have anything, sir," Sinch said.

"Shut up," the second guard told him.

The first guard's ears had slipped back to their bored position. He picked his teeth with a claw, showing off the long row of sharp yellow points. "G'wan, then," he told Sinch, and waved him through.

"Thank you, sir," Sinch said, scurrying past.

"Shut up," the second guard called after him, punctuating the order with a yawn.

He picked his way around a pile of broken straw chairs, squeezed through a narrow gap between two houses that left his fur damp and trailing spiderwebs, and scrambled up a ladder of table legs to the second floor window of his room in Miss Chakray's house. He didn't mean to stop there, just to use it as a shortcut to get across the street to Balinni's, but as he crossed the floor, his eyes came to rest on his loose floorboard. Could he bribe Balinni to forget about the crown? Especially considering he didn't know what it was?

It was something to keep in mind. Best not to take the money with him, in case something bad happened. But not a bad idea. Everyone had a price, and he suspected he had more money than some foxes in this town did, let alone any of the mice. He ran down the stairs and through the common area, out into the street and across to Balinni's.

Valix showed him into the inner room without even asking him to wait. "You missed the meeting."

"I thought there was someone after me. I had to just come back here." He was relieved to see her accept his rehearsed excuse.

"Well, it was nice work," she said. "I wouldn't have noticed it myself if I hadn't been looking. What was it?"

"Ask him," Sinch jerked his head toward the office as he followed her inside.

She grumbled. "Sinch to see you," she announced.

Balinni looked up from behind the table he'd been eating at earlier that day. When he saw Sinch, he pushed the papers aside to make room for the sack. "Leave us," he said to Valix.

Sinch placed the disguise carefully on the table. Balinni opened the sack, reached in to touch each part of it, then placed it on the floor. "How did it go?"

"Excellent." Sinch waved a paw toward the disguise. "It worked perfectly."

"Kishin is a reliable favorite." Balinni beamed paternally at the sack. "So, show me the haul."

Courage. Confidence. Sinch breathed in. "I hid it."

The scarred mouse's eyebrows rose. "How interesting." He folded his paws on the table. "Am I to assume that you expect something further from us than providing the personnel and the means to act on the information you had obtained?"

"I've, er, developed sort of an attachment to it." Sinch breathed in, willing his heart to slow. "I was wondering if I might just buy it from you."

Balinni laughed. "Are you, now? Well, if you might get your paws on ten gold Royals, we might be able to begin having a discussion."

"Ten?" Sinch stood straighter. "I was thinking it was worth more like two."

Balinni spread his paws. "I've no way to judge that, so I'm left to rely on what I know of the Dewanne treasury. Which is—no offense—rather more than you do, I'll wager." He grinned. "I will wager, too, if you like."

Sinch's heart sank. He forced himself to look Balinni in the eye. "What if I could get five?"

"Five is better than two," Balinni said. "But nine is better than five."

"I don't think I could get more than six."

"I don't know that my curiosity could be put off for six."

Sinch sighed. "I really can't get more than six."

Balinni studied him. "All right," he said. "If you can get six, I'll deal with my curiosity somehow. Six gold is a nice haul, even if I have to give one to the other four. So what will you leave me until you return with the six?"

Sinch hadn't expected him to give in so quickly. "Leave you? I don't..." He looked down at his plain tunic and trousers. "I don't have anything to leave you."

"Not your dagger?"

The one Yilon had gotten him. He swallowed. "I'd rather not be defenseless."

Balinni's smile was too perfect, too calm. "Of course you wouldn't. But what else do you have?"

"Nothing." Sinch let his paw rest at his waist, on the hilt of the knife hidden under his tunic. He remembered Yilon's smile as he'd handed it to him. "All right," he said. "I'll leave the knife with you."

"Well, it's not worth six gold." Balinni leaned back, looking smug.

Sinch gaped at him. "But..."

"I just wanted to see if you'd part with it."

"It's from the Divalia armory!"

The scar on Balinni's eyebrow lowered. "Now, that is interesting. But it's still not worth six gold."

"You..."

Balinni shook his head. "I am a business owner," he said. "I'm afraid this doesn't strike me as a very sound business deal without something left behind."

"But I don't have anything else." Sinch was beginning to wonder whether he would be allowed to leave unharmed, even with the insurance of the crown.

Balinni seemed to read his mind. "Ah, then I can't allow you to leave me."

The room grew much smaller. "How am I going to get the money if I can't leave here?"

"Well, I meant figuratively. Valix!" he called behind Sinch.

Sinch turned as Valix sauntered back into the room. "Yes, sir?"

Balinni gestured toward Sinch. "Our new friend here is lonely in this new town. See to it that he doesn't lack for company until he's ready to come back here."

"Yes, sir." She said it languidly, the verbal equivalent of a shrug. Sinch stared at her, inhaling the vague overtones of rotten vegetables and unwashed clothing.

"Now you've got her company, you no longer need mine." Balinni didn't even waste a gesture dismissing them. He just pulled one of the papers back to the table and bent over it.

Chapter 9: The Strad House

"She's my what?"

Lady Dewanne smiled. "Dinah is the vixen intended to become your Lady. It will be quite good for the province. Her family, the Falavis, have not been part of the lordship for many decades."

"And she's the only one who could be Lord—Lady—in my place?"

"Yes."

"And she's gone."

"Yes."

Yilon sank his head into his paws. "But you said, at first— "

"She is wilful and has misbehaved in the past. However, in light of recent events, it is possible that someone attempting to solidify their claim to the lordship might have kidnapped her in order to marry her and install themselves as the lord."

"But wait," Yilon said. "I thought all someone needed was the crown."

"No," Lady Dewanne said. "Noble blood is also necessary. In this day and age, many foxes can claim a portion of noble blood, but a fox married to Dinah would have a much stronger position."

"Oh."

"In any case," the elder vixen said, leaning forward, "I simply wanted to advise you that rendering any assistance you can in the search for the crown would be very..."

"Welcome?"

"I was going to say, prudent." She let the barest trace of a smile touch her lips. "As I have said, you will not be sent back to Divalia, and if you are not the Lord in a few days' time, your position here in Dewanne will be extremely tenuous."

"You can't keep me here," Yilon said.

"In point of fact," the vixen said, "it would be remarkably easy to do so." She rose from the table. "Velkan will be conducting his operations from his house, the first one on the right as you enter the plaza. I strongly suggest you find him there and place yourself at his disposal."

She strode out of the room, leaving Yilon at the table with his paws folded over the stone in front of him. He watched the door close behind her and then got up, slowly.

He needed to find Sinch and get the crown back. Maxon's fevered talk about the mice worried him, even though Lady Dewanne and Corwin had dismissed it, and he'd proven his point about his unsuitability as much as he could. It sounded like his only chance was to find someone else just as qualified for the lordship to take his place, and his options on that score were limited to Dinah. Which meant that he had to find her.

At least this was a concrete course of action he could take. He could go to Velkan, in accordance with Lady Dewanne's wishes, or orders, and participate in the dual searches as best he could. With his own agenda, but nobody else need know that until the crown and Dinah were found. Then, hopefully she would be happy to take his place, for the good of Dewanne.

Min was waiting for him outside the door. "Your luncheon is ready, sir. Will you be taking it in your room?"

Yilon's stomach growled. "Yes, I'll..." He spotted a flash of movement by the front door: Maxon. The door opened and then shut. The steward was probably going to Velkan's house as well. "I'll be back in a moment for it."

"I'll keep it ready for you, sir."

"Don't call me sir," he said. "Remember?"

"Sorry." Min ducked his head, his ears folding back.

"I'm going to keep reminding you," Yilon said.

"I'll try to remember."

"All right. I'm just going to Velkan's. I'll be right back."

But when he got to the front of the castle and looked outside, the steward was not walking across the plaza toward the governor's house. Instead, Yilon saw just a quick glimpse of his blue vest and bushy red tail as he disappeared behind it.

The plaza was moderately busy, foxes stopping to talk, crossing slowly or quickly, but none looking specifically at him. He made his decision in a moment, and hurried around the back of the governor's house to peer around the corner.

Maxon's blue vest, fortunately, stood out among the small crowd of foxes in the narrower street behind the gardens of the governor's house. Yilon made sure Maxon wasn't looking back and then stepped into the crowd, making his way around other foxes, staying several yards back but always keeping his eye on the steward.

He managed to follow Maxon through the bustling Market Street, starting from the end farthest from the lake. The steward didn't make it up to where the clothing stores were; he ducked into a quiet side street just opposite a bakery whose aromas made Yilon's stomach rumble again. Yilon couldn't see a name for the side street, but he didn't have time to look.

On the quieter street, he had to stay further back. Fortunately, he wasn't wearing any of the bright, distinctive clothes he'd picked out that morning, so there wasn't much chance that Maxon would recognize him, or notice that he was being followed.

Yilon had no sooner thought that than the steward did look back, right at him. Yilon couldn't stop himself from flinching, but he did at least pretend to be hurrying to catch up to a couple walking ahead of him, the only foxes between him and the steward. Maxon didn't appear to have noticed anything; he carried on his way and turned down another wide street.

Here, it was easier for Yilon to follow. Maxon had turned right, away from the lake again. Yilon moved behind clumps of foxes, catching the distinctive blue of the steward's vest ahead of him, until the steward stopped to talk to a vixen out in front of a public-house. Yilon's ears pricked up. He sidled closer, trying to get close enough to hear what they were saying. It was only when he was within a few feet of them that he realized that the fox in the blue vest wasn't the steward.

Panicked, he spun around, looking all through the crowd. There, another blue vest. He hurried to follow, hoping he hadn't lost Maxon. Not that he had a wide experience of the steward's behavior, but he couldn't imagine what business Maxon would have in the middle of the day this far from the palace. The farther he went, the more suspicious Yilon grew.

The next street Maxon, if it were him, led him down certainly did not look like a place where a castle steward would have business. Red brick facades crumbled on either side, rather than the grey stone used nearer the castle. Laundry hung from windows, dirt accumulated in the corners around the stairs that led up or down from the street, and the foxes who walked here wore darker, dirtier clothing. For the first time, Yilon felt that he did stand out in the crowd. He wished he had a cloak he could draw around himself.

Fortunately, the blue-vested fox did not look back, perhaps thinking himself beyond the places where anyone would know him. He strode along the right-hand side of the street, stopped at a house three doors from the end, and called through the curtained doorway. Someone inside challenged him; he answered, and the curtain was pulled aside. As he entered, Yilon saw his muzzle in profile. It was definitely Maxon.

Yilon hung back while the steward entered the old brick building, then walked up casually once the curtain over the doorway had fallen again. The building didn't stand out on the block: its red brick and grey cornerstones were covered in a film of grime. The name "Strad" was engraved on the stone over the doorway, but other than that, he couldn't find any distinguishing marks. All the buildings on that side looked like residences, pressed so closely together there was only a body's width between them, many with names engraved over the door.

He lingered outside the curtain, hoping to catch some snatch of conversation, but nothing came to him. Despite his casual stance, several of the foxes who passed by gave him curious glances, and when one started shuffling toward him, he thought it was best that he leave. As though he'd just gotten bored, he pushed off from the wall and sauntered toward the bent shape, giving it an acknowledging nod. The cloak it wore was more patches than material, and he couldn't tell whether the rank odor emanated from the figure or from the sack slung over its back. It wasto be a combination of rancid food and oily musk, so perhaps it was both. Nonetheless, he respectfully did not swerve away as he passed.

A bony arm shot out from the cloak and gripped him around the wrist. Startled, he tried to pull away, but the figure yanked him back. "What are you doing here?" a raspy vixen's voice demanded. The hood of the cloak tilted to one side, sliding far enough that he could see the gleam of one brown eye. "What are you up to, boy?"

"I'm of age." Yilon struggled to free his wrist, to no avail. The vixen held him as tightly as a noose. "Let go."

"When I've got satisfaction." She shook his arm. "Who are you?"

"I'm your lord," he said, desperately.

"Lord?!" She screeched it, pulling him closer. Two foxes at the end of the street turned to look. She pulled his arm down until her muzzle was inches from his. He could tell now that her breath was definitely a major contributor to the odor.

"Let me go!" he cried.

She inspected him and then released his wrist, turning away. "Pfagh," she said. "You're no lord. I know the lord. I *know* the lord. He won't forget me. He'll come for us."

Yilon stared at her, backpedaling quickly. She'd stopped walking and now simply stood in the middle of the street talking to herself. Two foxes walking toward him from the other direction gave her a wide berth. She seemed to have forgotten all about him. He'd heard about crazies from Sinch, but in the small town of Vinton, he'd never seen any, nor had he encountered any in Divalia.

As he watched, the curtain to the Strad building moved. A tall, thin fox stepped out onto the landing, then trotted down the stairs. "Oh, Mother," he said. "Come on in. Who's been—"

He looked familiar, but the old vixen's powerful odor drowned out his scent. Yilon, trying to place him, didn't move quickly enough. The fox stared at him and then barked sharply, "Hey! Kites!" He ran back into the house.

Kites? The remark didn't make any sense until another fox, a short, thin one wearing a plain tunic and black trousers, stepped out of the Strad building and scanned the street, eyes narrowed, until he saw Yilon.

Yilon only saw Kites, if that was the short fox's name, leap down the staircase before he turned and ran. He had about twenty yards' start on the other, but by the time he rounded the corner back onto the wide street and glanced behind him, Kites had closed the gap by more than half. On the more crowded street, Yilon dodged between foxes as quickly as he could while trying not to attract attention, staying close to the right side of the street. He hoped his pursuer wouldn't assault him in public, and maybe he could lose himself in the crowd by the time he got to the end of the street.

Halfway down the street, he glanced back again. In the mass of tunics and red fur, he couldn't see Kites specifically anywhere behind him. He was already panting, so he slowed down, still trotting more quickly than the foxes around him, but not knifing between them. The street where he had to turn left was just ahead. He took a few steps toward it.

A paw grasped his arm. He turned to see Kites, the other fox's muzzle right at his eye level set in a broad smile. "Why don't we come along this way," he said. At Yilon's hesitation, the other moved his right paw just enough to show the knife blade hidden in it. "Keep quiet, or you'll end up with this between the ribs."

Yilon flattened his ears, looking around desperately to see if anyone was looking in their direction. A tall fox met his eyes, but ignored Yilon's attempt to silently call for help, walking on by. Kites pulled harder, half-dragging Yilon back into the nearest alley on that side. "Hey," Yilon said, lifting a paw, but before he could get any more words out, or attract any more attention, Kites flashed the blade at him.

A concerned vixen took a step toward them. "Tell her it's okay," Kites hissed.

Yilon forced a smile and shook his head at her. "I'm fine," he said, and allowed himself to be dragged into the alley. His mind worked furiously in the few seconds it took for him to be extracted from the crowd. No doubt this Kites fox was well-versed in knife use, and at close quarters, Yilon wouldn't have much chance if he started a fight. However, Kites hadn't knifed him immediately, which meant that Yilon had something he wanted. He would have to figure out what that was and stall as long as he could.

Until what? Nobody knew where he was. His only hope was that the circumstances would change, that he would see a better opportunity to escape later.

"Just walk nicely," Kites said. There were still foxes in the alley, one of whom gave them a curious glance before passing by. Yilon wished he were Corwin. Everyone would know him, everyone would want to stop and say hi. Nobody in this town knew who he was.

Kites dragged him into a narrow space between two buildings. Yilon felt the pressure of the knife slide inside his vest, pricking his tunic. "Now, lordling," Kites hissed, "suppose you tell me what you were doing down there?"

"Just...just out for a walk," Yilon panted.

The knife pressed in closer, through the tunic, and into the fur below. Yilon sucked in his stomach as much as he could. "Looked to me like you were out for a spy," Kites said. "Standing around on the street there." The point of the knife grazed Yilon's stomach. "Who sent you down there?"

"I...I can't tell you." That was the information he was after, then. As long as Yilon didn't tell him, he'd be safe. Or at least alive.

The pressure against his stomach became a sharp pain. He sucked in his stomach even more, hissing. Kites's eye gleamed. "We have other sources," he said. "It'll just be quicker if you tell me. But you know, we're not in that much of a hurry. In fact," he said, working his paw, bringing a stab of fresh pain with each movement, "I'd quite enjoy it if you didn't tell me right away."

"Who...who's "we"?" Yilon gasped.

"You should be more curious about your world." Kites withdrew the knife. Yilon's relief was short-lived; the other fox's paw moved to a different point on his stomach and pressed in. Yilon flattened himself against the wall as best he could, but he couldn't escape the knife point. He tried to move to the side, but as he did, Kites pushed harder, causing an intense burst of pain that made Yilon cry out. "We certainly know about you, lordling, you and your mouse friend. It's a good job you got rid of him. Saved us the trouble."

Desperate, Yilon pushed at Kites, but the other fox swept his arm aside with ease and pressed him hard into the wall with his shoulder. "If you don't tell me now," Kites said, "I can come up with other places to stick the knife." He grabbed Yilon's paw and pressed the knife point to it. "Now: who told you where our house is?"

"Lady Dewanne!" Yilon cried the first name that came into his head. Warmth leaked into his fur from the two wounds in his stomach.

Kites withdrew the knife, but didn't let go of Yilon's paw or move away from the wall. "That's a very interesting answer," he said. "It's almost certainly a lie." He looked past Yilon to the alley. "I happen to know that she's the one person who would—"

There was a thud, and Kites's head jerked forward. Something clattered to the ground. The pressure holding Yilon to the wall slackened, then vanished as Kites sank to his knees with a cry. He clutched his head, dropping his knife to the stone.

Yilon stared down at him, then to his left, to the shadows that hid the junction of the two buildings. A shape emerged from it, hurrying toward him.

"Sorry," a vixen's voice said. Her muzzle came into the light: a slender, light-colored face below two determined amber eyes. Large dark brown ears flicked all around, but her eyes stayed on the still-moaning Kites. "Took me a little while to get around behind you. Do you have a weapon?"

"Who are you?" Yilon stared at her. She wore a nondescript brown jerkin, with no tunic underneath, and trews rather than a skirt. In fact, were he unable to smell her, he would not have known she was female, even with the silver necklace that swung free as she picked up the fallen dagger and a large stone from the ground.

She shoved the stone into a pouch at her waist and straightened. Her eyes flicked to his midsection, where he could feel more wet warmth leaking. "I said, do you have a weapon?"

"No." Yilon watched, mesmerized.

"At least that excuses your pathetic lack of resistance." She turned away from him and brandished the dagger she'd picked up at Kites. "Give me one reason not to cut you open right now."

He lifted his muzzle, his eyes focusing on the vixen. A smear of blood stained the fur over his right eye. "You," he snarled, and staggered to his feet, lunging at her.

She raised her arm, sidestepping him. As he lurched past her, she plunged her knife into his throat.

Kites gurgled, falling hard to the flagstones. Yilon found himself unable to look away from the shuddering body, even as the smell of urine reached his nostrils. The vixen, similarly fascinated, remained frozen until the neck of the prone fox was soaked in red and the body's twitching had subsided. Then she swiveled her head and ears up. "No, don't help," she said, with some sarcasm. "I can take care of myself." Her voice sounded higher, faster than before.

Yilon gaped at her. "Come on," she said, and grabbed his paw.

As violently as Kites had, she dragged him out into the alley, but away from the side street. "Keep your paw on the wounds," she said, looking from right to left. "I don't know if any more of them are out there."

"I didn't see any," Yilon said. He pressed a paw to the wetness on his stomach, the one on the right that hurt more.

"You didn't see me," she snapped. "This way, across the street. Act normal. Hurry. Before too long, you're going to reek of blood."

He could already smell it all over himself. Quietly, he hurried behind her through a thin crowd of meandering foxes, across a paved street to an alley on the other side that was barely larger than the one where Yilon had been cornered. He hesitated at the entrance, but the vixen was already halfway along it to the daylight on the other side, so he padded in after her.

They emerged into a small twisted street, angled upward. The vixen padded to the right, following the street and then turning left, then right again, climbing up each time, onto another small street only four houses long on either side. Each house was tall and elegant, of grey stone with colorful designs over the doors and windows. On the left hand side of the street, one window stood open, an elderly fox leaning on the sill looking out. He followed their progress down the street, but didn't say anything as the vixen walked up to the house opposite.

She paused, her paw on the handle of the door, staring down at it and not at Yilon. A door, Yilon noticed, not a curtain. "He needed killing," she said, ears flat.

"I'm not arguing," Yilon said.

That must have been the right thing to say, because a moment later she opened the door. He touched the wood grain as he followed her inside. She pointed to a staircase that swept along the curve of the right wall. "All the way to the top," she said. "I will collect Colian and I'll be up in a moment."

She had a paw on the door handle at the back of the room before he thought to call out, "Hey." She turned. "What's your name?"

She gave him a long look, then shook her head. And then she was gone.

Yilon stared after her, then up at the stairs. The first step didn't hurt much, but by the time he reached the third floor, his stomach was aching and his legs were sore. He was glad to reach the empty bed that lay beyond the door at the top.

Chapter 10: Valix

"Cozy place," Valix said when they'd returned to Sinch's room. She sat in the corner of a wall near the door, arms draped across her knees.

"It's home. For now." Sinch's mind was racing. He wouldn't be able to get word back to Yilon, let alone retrieve the crown, until he got rid of Valix. Which would be easier in a public place. "Is there a good place to go to get something to eat?"

She tilted her head. "You asking me to lunch?"

"Er..." Sinch flicked his ears. "I thought you had to follow me everywhere."

"Aye, well." She shrugged. "Difference between following you to lunch and being asked to lunch."

He put on a smile. "If we're to be manacled together, might as well enjoy it."

She rose to her feet. "Suppose." She squinted at him. "Don't get ideas."

He opened his paws to show they were empty. "About what?"

"About me. Or running off. Balinni may be a creepy old bastard, but he's my boss."

"He is creepy, isn't he?" Sinch gestured for her to precede him out the door, but she grinned and shook her head. So he walked out ahead of her, and waited for her in the stairwell. "Do you love that head as much as he does?"

"What, Kishin?" Valix snorted. "It's a useful disguise. Balinni's old enough to remember when it was harder for us to do jobs in the city. Go left out the street and through the alley there."

With the sun high, the streets were less crowded. In the bright light of day, the detritus in the street looked less formidable, and more like the alley behind his home in Divalia when they couldn't afford to pay the garbage-haulers for a month. Except that the whole Warren was littered with debris, and the mice clambered over it as if it were nothing but pebbles.

Valix directed him down a wide street, the first he'd found in the Warren in which he could stretch his arms out to either side and not brush stone or brick. Despite the open space, the mice kept to the walls, avoiding the open street center, and Sinch followed them, diverting around grimy puddles and piles of broken reed and straw chairs when necessary. "Do people just throw their furniture in the street when they're done with it?" he murmured.

"How much furniture do you need? Turn in here," Valix said, at a narrow alley between a crumbling brick building and a rough stone edifice.

In this alley, Sinch could barely move without touching the building to either side, even with his shoulders hunched together. He wondered what would happen if another mouse were to come in the other direction, but perhaps because of the time of day, or because the residents of the Warren knew to travel this alley only in one direction, they did not meet anyone else.

When they emerged into a crooked little street on the other side of the alley, Sinch caught the scents of vegetables and spices on the air. Valix gestured in the direction of the breeze and said, "There, you can smell it now, eh?"

"Mmm." He stopped at a puddle large enough to be a moat, and turned to look back at Valix.

She grinned. "Get yer feet wet, princeling."

He rolled his eyes and stepped deliberately in the water, unable to keep from flinching at the chill and slime of it. A weight landed on his back, pushing him forward and nearly toppling him over. He felt arms around his neck, and then they were on the other side and Valix dropped off of him. "Thanks for the ride," she said. "I hate getting my feet wet." She stuck her muzzle forward, daring him to challenge her.

Sinch just laughed. "So that's why you wanted me to go ahead," he said.

Valix pulled her head back and studied him. "Aren't you the pleasant one," she said, and waved ahead of them. "It's around that corner. Climb up to the second floor."

The rough stone building at the corner, held together without mortar, buzzed with sound through the high-up windows. If there were a street-level door, it was buried beneath piles of reed and stone fragments. Around the corner, though, a pile of stones led up to a ledge on the building opposite, from which Sinch saw they could jump to the large open window.

He'd made far longer and more dangerous leaps than that, but he couldn't tell whether Valix was impressed when she landed beside him on the window ledge. Too late, he realized he could have jumped inside and lost himself in the crowd of mice below. But he didn't know whether there was an exit below, and besides, in the thick aroma of vegetables and broth, he was quite hungry.

They dropped to the floor, in an area cleared for just that purpose. Valix steered him past the long stone benches filled with mice slurping out of little bowls to the back corner of the room. A stooped mouse in a grey woolen shawl was ladling soup to a line of mice. "Best soup in town," Valix whispered to him.

The mice in front of them were all handing over small copper coins in exchange for the soup. Sinch dug in his pockets, but Valix put a paw on his arm as he did. He looked back, but she didn't say anything, just nudged him forward. When he got to the front of the line, the server held out her paw.

"Hello, Shaimin," Valix said.

Shaimin turned her head just slightly. "Afternoon, miss," she said. "This young'un with you?"

"Aye," Valix said.

"Right." The old mouse handed Sinch a bowl of soup, then ladled out another one for Valix. That ended the transaction; she turned to the small mouse who'd stepped up behind Valix and took his copper, preparing his bowl of soup.

It wasn't easy to find two seats close together. Sinch stood in the center of the room, looking, while Valix walked directly to the landing area and stood near a bench, over a mouse in a patched tunic, who got up immediately. The other mice scooted to either side, leaving two spots for them. Sinch sat next to her on the stone, looking around at the lowered heads of the mice around them, and the resentful looks from those further away. None was dressed as well as Valix. Most wore patched clothes, and some wore no shirt at all.

Valix sat and lifted the bowl to her muzzle, unconcerned by the surrounding looks. Everyone around them was doing the same, and there were no spoons around, so Sinch followed suit. The soup was full of noodles and vegetables, a little bland, but pretty good, and he said so to Valix.

"Told you," she said, slurping enthusiastically.

He lowered his voice, conscious of the mice around them, who'd inched away from them anyway. "So, you're pretty important here."

"Balinni is," she said.

The mouse on Sinch's other side muttered something under her breath, something that sounded like, "Trouble."

"How many mice work for him?" Sinch asked.

Valix paused in her slurping. "Enough," she said, and her eyes passed over him to look at the mouse beside him, who looked away immediately, then stood and left. "Don't worry," she said. "You pull this off, you'll be in just as good."

Over his bowl, he tried to see if there were some way he could escape. The thought crossed his mind that he could use the sympathy of the other mice to keep Valix restrained if he could somehow communicate that he was a prisoner. The problem was that they were not just antipathetic, but also afraid. So he finished his soup when she did, and stood with her.

"Outhouse is down the street," she said. "I need to go too."

He would've thought that the perfect opportunity to get away, except that when they'd made it to the front of the line and the exiting mouse was holding the outhouse door for Valix, she dragged Sinch into the outhouse with her. He barely had time to sputter, "What—" before they were inside, the door closed.

"Well," she said, undoing her trousers, "can't very well trust you to just stand around, and I can't hold it in all day."

"But I—you—" He slapped a paw over his eyes as she shoved her pants down and twisted to face away from her.

"I'll be quick, then you can go." She sounded amused. "I can leave you in here alone if you want. There's only one other way out of here and even if it led anywhere, I don't think you have the balls to take it."

He did ask her to leave when she was done, and as they walked away from the outhouse, he saw the looks the line of mice gave her, the same looks she'd gotten at the soup tables. "So are you and Balinni the toughs of the town?" he asked.

"What's that supposed to mean?"

Sinch crossed to an alley, noticing that the paths Valix guided him to were remarkably free of debris. "In Divalia, there were toughs, guys who smuggled big shipments of food and drink, guys who knew where you could get stuff. I always knew when one of them was around because people would act differently around them. But it wasn't like this, it was more just like...like some difficult job they did. Like the guys who come to pick up the rags, or clean out the cesspools."

Valix eyed the puddle they were walking around, and nodded. "That's us, yeah."

"But we weren't..." Sinch searched for the words. "We didn't hate the toughs. They just did another job."

"Well," Valix said, "you weren't a bunch of lily-livered fox-lovers."

Sinch blinked. He resisted the urge to say, "No, just me," and instead said, "So they don't think you should be stealing from the city?"

Valix shook her head. "The foxes provide for us," she said in a mocking, sing-songy voice, then dropped back to normal. "They don't care about Kishin trying to burn down their homes."

"Maybe they just think it's possible to live in peace."

"They're idiots." Valix gestured for him to go through the door of Miss Chakray's boarding-house. He had made it halfway through the common room when Miss Chakray accosted him, a bundle under her arm.

"You," she said, "must leave."

Sinch took a step back. "Wha—why?"

The landlady pointed a diminutive finger over his shoulder. "Her! You bring her into this house? I am a good mouse. Me and my tenants, we don't want trouble."

Valix stepped up beside him. "You think you will be better off without us?"

Miss Chakray drew herself up to her full height, almost to Sinch's chest. "If you stay here, my other customers leave. Then what will I do? Will you pay for all the rooms? No, you must go. Here, I have brought down your things. Go, go now. I will not ask you to pay for the room."

"But my..."

"Come on," Valix said. "I know a place we can go."

"Yes, good," Miss Chakray said. "Thank you for not making trouble."

Sinch was torn. He didn't want to make a big deal about the money under the floorboards in front of everyone, but he had very little with him. He was going to have to figure out how to more than double the money he had if he were going to buy the crown from Balinni—or, more accurately, buy his freedom. If he could only get back to Yilon, he was sure Yilon could help him, but with Valix attached to his side, that wasn't going to work.

He'd wait until night. She'd have to sleep sometime. So he followed her through the Warren, toward the mountains, deep into the twisting maze of buildings until he was no longer sure he could find his way out on his own. Here in the heart of the Warren, the older buildings loomed closer together, some built so close together that another building had been erected atop them both. Valix walked below these overpasses, unconcerned, but Sinch couldn't help scurrying under them, especially the second one, which was sagging in the middle and looked as though a stray gust of wind might send it crashing to the ground.

They passed stalls selling bread, but none that smelled of baking. Sinch felt no heat from them, which made him wonder where the loaves came from. The public-houses he could see into were dark and miserable, none with a cheery fire. It was next to one of these that Valix pushed aside a thick sackcloth curtain and ushered Sinch down an uneven flight of stone stairs, calling, "It's me," as she descended behind him.

Nobody answered, but she told Sinch as she followed him in through the second doorway on the right, "They listen for steps on the stairs. Here's where I stay when I'm on a job in the Warren."

Sinch crossed the room and leaned against the opposite wall, waiting for his eyes to adjust. Valix stood in the doorway, and if they'd stretched out their arms, their fingers would be just inches from touching. The whole room smelled of damp, of old cheese and stale bread. Sinch looked around for the food, but the only furniture in the room was a small rusted metal table and a reed chair, both bare. "Do you not sleep when you're on jobs?"

Valix grinned. She hopped onto the table and scrambled up onto a stone ledge that Sinch had taken for the ceiling. Her head poked down to look at him. "Bed's up here." The odor of cheese was stronger now. It took Sinch a moment to see that she was chewing. "Want a piece?"

He shook his head. "So...you do jobs in the Warren?"

She swallowed. "I go where the jobs are."

"I thought you just robbed the foxes."

Her head disappeared. A moment later, she jumped down to the table. "So where are you going to get this money?" she asked, stepping to the chair and then to the floor.

"I need to see—someone."

"How do you know someone in this place, stranger?"

Sinch folded his arms. "That's my business."

Valix plopped down in the chair. "Suppose I don't care, as long as they have the money. Sooner we get the money, sooner I can get back to work."

"Isn't this 'work'?"

She grinned at him. "Not particularly fun work. No challenge."

He didn't have a response to that, and she didn't have much else to say. In the quiet, he thought about the toughs he'd known in the past, and that led him to another, more dangerous idea about how to escape.

"In Divalia," Sinch said, "My—the toughs were afraid of the assassins. Do you have assassins here?"

Valix tilted her head. "Who were the toughs in Divalia? Your... what?"

Sinch's paw dropped to his waist, brushing the knife. "My circle."

"Circle of...?"

He didn't know why he felt reluctant to admit it to her. "Thieves."

"Oh ho." She leaned forward. "Kicked out? Stole something from one of the elders?"

He shook his head. "Just came out here for the adventure."

She laughed. "Fine. Don't tell me."

"So is there someone here Balinni's afraid of?"

Her expression unfocused for a moment. "Shadows," she said pensively.

Sinch waited, but she didn't say anything more. He searched for another topic, since that one had led to a dead end. "What do you do for fun here in the Warren?"

Valix focused her attention on him. "We go collect money to pay off our debts."

"Other than that."

She looked up to the bed. "You're here by yourself, right? No attachments?"

Sinch lifted his paw. "Uh," he said, "well..."

She laughed. "Don't worry, I don't sleep with people I'm supposed to be watching. Besides which, I'm married." She held up the paw with the silver wristband.

"Oh." Sinch leaned back on his elbows, wondering how he would ever manage to get away from her.

Chapter 11: Colian and Corwin

Yilon found his eyes drifting shut, even with the bright afternoon light illuminating the plain white walls. The scents in the room were old, and the foxes who'd left them had been old, too. A grandparents' bedroom, somewhere the aging foxes could lie and watch the city outside through the several windows. The bed was the only furniture, though, and the sheets had been cleaned.

He lifted his tunic, feeling his wounds with a paw. He'd never been in a fight that was more than a scuffle, never faced a knife blade in anything that wasn't a practice. He could still feel the cold metal of the blade against his fur, even with his paw right on top of the wound to tell him there was nothing there.

There had been, though. Kites and his knife had been too real, the threat genuine. He would've killed Yilon in the alley, had been intending to. Yilon wasn't even sure Kites cared about his information as much as he was enjoying toying with him. If these were the sort of people Maxon associated with, then there would definitely be some changes in the castle once he was Confirmed.

The thought of the missing crown temporarily diverted his mind from his near-death. He would have to go back and find Velkan, tell him what he'd observed. He hoped Corwin would be there, too. Of all the court of Dewanne, it was the former governor he felt the most confidence in. He would have to tell them about Maxon's journey, and about the attack.

His fingers brushed the deeper wound again. He moved them to the other one, which was less painful. He would have to tell them about his rescue as well, the mysterious vixen. He saw again the knife stuck in Kites's throat, the spreading pool of red, the frozen tableau of the three of them in the alley with Kites's body the only thing moving. He shuddered. If anything could have been designed to make him want to leave Dewanne even more, it could hardly have succeeded better than that afternoon's events had.

The scent of another fox came to him, young and male, but he didn't hear anyone on the stairs. In fact, the first thing he heard was a voice saying, "Cold?"

The voice was as light as the owner's tread must be, to have gotten into the room so silently. Yilon opened his eyes to the cheerful smile of a short, slim fox in a plain white tunic. "No, I'm fine," he said.

"You were shivering. I'm Colian. I understand you were in a bit of a tussle." He set down the bowl he was carrying and the small black packet and came to the side of the bed. "You're still breathing, so it can't be too bad. Let's just have a look."

"It didn't go in far," Yilon said, wanting for some reason to reassure Colian.

"Far enough." Colian lifted Yilon's paw gently, rolling his tunic back to expose his stomach. "If it gets past the fur, it's too far, I say. And he did get you twice."

"Is it bad?" Yilon craned his neck up, but couldn't see past his rolled-up tunic.

"Worse than once." Colian turned his head briefly, green eye winking. "Don't worry, sir. In a moment you will be feeling just fine. Lie back and trust me."

Yilon found that easy to do. He stared at the ceiling while Colian hummed to himself, taking some items from his bag. Yilon felt the cool dab of a wet cloth around the first wound, then the second, and then a tugging at his bloodstained fur. "Now, I'm going to shave just a bit of the fur around the wounds. Don't worry, it grows back quickly. I don't see any scars, so I'm going to guess you haven't had anything like this happen before?"

"No." Yilon shook his head. "First knife fight."

"Any knife fight you walk away from is a good one." Yilon felt the cool metal of the blade against his skin again, and couldn't help flinching. Colian stopped immediately. "Everything all right?"

"Yes. Sorry. Go ahead." He steeled himself. The next time the blade touched him, he was ready for it.

"That's good. Almost done here. Now the other one. This'll be quick. And...there." He smiled down. "Now, I don't think these are quite big enough to warrant wrapping a big ugly bandage around your midsection. Believe me, that'd be almost more trouble than it would prevent. But on the other paw, we can't just leave these wounds open." While he talked, he bent back to his bag and dabbed another cloth in the bowl.

"I'm just going to clean them out here, though I suspect they're not too bad. Your tunic looks quite clean. Well, the parts that aren't bloody. You'll have to get a new one." Yilon felt the cool wetness directly on his skin, making him shiver. That wasn't the only reaction the intimate touch was stirring in him. He thanked Canis that the wounds weren't lower. "But if you're brave, I can sew up the wounds. It'll only take one or two stitches on each one, and it won't hurt much more than it already does. What do you say? Trust my needlework?"

He only hoped Colian wasn't looking.

He rested a paw on Yilon's lower abdomen, green eyes sparkling in the light. Yilon smiled. "Go ahead," he said. "I can take it."

"I suspected you might." Colian brought his other paw up to show the needle and thread he was already holding. "Just relax, and I'll talk you through it. I'm no chirurgeon, but I've worked with one and I've sewn before. I've even tended to Lady Dewanne. Not with needle and thread, of course. But I could have." He lowered his head and blew softly on the nearer wound, stirring Yilon's sheath again.

The arousal lasted only until Colian pinched the wound, bringing the edges together. The sharp pain made Yilon grit his teeth, but it wasn't as bad as he'd felt earlier. A pinprick, then another, and the strange sensation of thread sliding through his skin. "Easy," Colian murmured. "This is nothing, right? You've had a great thick knife stuck in you, what's a tiny little needle?" Another set of pricks, another slide of thread, and tightening as Colian pulled the wound gently shut. The fox lowered his muzzle and bit off the end of the thread, his breath warm on Yilon's stomach.

"That wasn't so bad, was it?"

"No," Yilon breathed. "You're good."

Colian inclined his head. "My very great thanks, noble sir. Good enough to allow me one more?"

"Please." Yilon could feel the difference between the two wounds already, the open one raw at the edges, the sewn one merely aching. And somehow, the presence of the young male so near his sheath was still having an effect on him. Wonderful, he thought. He tried to will the response away, but thinking about it only made it worse.

"Do you think you can turn around for me? I can lean over you, but I'd prefer not." Colian held up the needle and thread.

Yilon nodded. He sat up in bed, swung his legs off, and lay back down with his head where his feet had been. As he did, he was aware of his erection pressing up against his trousers, and he only hoped Colian wasn't looking. His ears flushed.

"There we go. This'll be over before you know it." Once again, the fox blew on Yilon's fur, this one closer to his hips. His tail twitched.

The sewing was even quicker on this side, or perhaps it just seemed so. And perhaps it only seemed that Colian's nose lingered when he bent to bite off the thread. But when the fox straightened and said, "All done. Let's just clean it off one more time," his paw rested below Yilon's navel, just above the waist of his trousers while he picked up his damp cloth.

And when he'd finished dabbing at the wounds, brushing the fur back over them with gentle strokes of his fingers, he stood over Yilon. Wiping his paws clean, he tilted his muzzle, still with the same warm smile. "There. All clean and ready for just about anything. Speaking of which," he said when Yilon didn't answer, "your scent tells me there's one thing in particular you might be ready for right about now. I'm happy to assist you with that, if you like." He wriggled his fingers.

Yilon's ears flushed. "Oh," he said, "no, I..."

Colian glanced back at the entrance. "Don't worry," he said. "We can afford real doors here. We won't be disturbed."

"Not worried about that," Yilon mumbled. "I just can't."

"Oh, I'm sorry." The nurse's muzzle became serious immediately. "Are you sure? Because it smells like..."

"I don't want to," Yilon said, louder.

Colian held both paws up. "All right. No offense meant. I'm not to everyone's liking, I know that. Some people think I talk too much."

"It's nothing to do with you," Yilon said. "Can we not talk about it?"

Colian bowed his head. "I deeply regret any offense I might have given." His tone was serious, but when he raised his head, his muzzle held the same smile. "So how are you enjoying our weather recently? Autumn's truly arrived. Though I wager we'll get a warm spell before too long. We always do, before the winter comes."

Yilon propped himself up on his elbows, taking a better look at Colian. The small fox's green eyes reminded him of Sinch. Not the color, but the brightness, the way they always sparkled as if he were smiling. His ears always pointed straight up, and even his whiskers had a jaunty arch to them. "Do you know anything about the fox who attacked me?"

Colian shook his head. "I didn't even know it was a fox until just this moment. Don't you know anything about him?"

"Not much. His name." Yilon hesitated before saying it. "Kites."

He was afraid Colian would react, would say something wildly improbable like, "that's my brother." But the nurse didn't, just shrugged and said, "There are many foxes in the city I don't know, despite what my demeanor might suggest to you."

"I didn't think that about you," Yilon said.

Colian waved a paw, dismissing the remark, but Yilon heard his tail wagging. His sheath throbbed again, and he thought that maybe it wouldn't be so bad to take Colian up on his offer. Just with the paws, wrapping around his sheath and—

No. He sat up, sending a quick jolt through his stitched wounds. "Careful, sir," Colian said, reaching out but stopping just short of touching Yilon.

Reflexively, Yilon put a paw to his stomach. The stitches held, the only dampness under his fingers the cool of water. He regretted for a moment the distance he'd put between himself and the nurse. "So I can go?"

"I have no orders to keep you here, and no wish to hold you longer than needed." Colian's eyes drifted down. "But if you don't mind waiting, I would be happy to see if there is a spare tunic in the house."

Yilon followed the nurse's glance to the bloodstains. "That would be very much appreciated," he said.

"Done." Colian dropped the wet cloth into his bag and picked it up. "I will be back in a moment." He had disappeared down the stairs before Yilon realized that Colian had never even asked him his name.

When the fox reappeared, he was no more curious. He handed a neatly folded tunic to Yilon and gave him another wink. "I'll leave you in privacy to dress. Should we not meet again, it has been a pleasure to make your acquaintance."

"Thank you, Colian." Yilon put the tunic next to him on the bed. He would have to get back to Velkan and Corwin soon, but for the moment he was in a relative sort of peace. He pulled his tunic off by the window, looking down at the city streets. Fox after fox, in pairs and trios or all alone, strolling or hurrying on errands. None wearing a blue vest. He watched a young vixen running from one shop to another, never coming out with anything. She wrung her paws and disappeared around the corner. He watched a couple arguing, until the tod cuffed the vixen across the muzzle. She dropped her head and followed him, tail dragging.

Across the street, the afternoon sun cast a long shadow across the roof of the building. Yilon barely glanced at it, until a gust of wind blew a handkerchief up from the street. Then he noticed the shadow on the roof. Though it was no different at first glance from any of the other shadows on the other buildings, his eyes kept returning to it once he'd noticed it. His fur prickled. He became convinced that someone was hiding in the shadows, watching him.

No matter how much he stared, nothing moved in the shadow. He was being silly, still jumpy from his run-in with Kites. And thinking of that, he needed to get back to tell Velkan and Corwin about Maxon and Kites, and maybe his mysterious rescuer. He took one last long look at the shadow on the roof, then turned and pulled on the clean tunic.

Colian had estimated his size well; the tunic was large, but it still fit. Yilon made sure he had all his things with him, and descended the stairs.

On his way down to the ground floor, he caught voices. Colian: "... don't want him to see you, why did you even bring him here?"

And then the vixen, answering. "I wasn't thinking. I'd just been through..."

Silence. Then Colian, again. "Take a little time."

"Is he still there?"

"I haven't heard him leave, but he must have."

Another pause. Then the vixen said, "Go make sure."

Yilon hurried down the rest of the stairs. He reached the front door just as he heard the click of the latch behind him. His paws fumbled at the handle, yanked the door open finally. He pushed through it and outside, not waiting to see whether Colian had seen him leave.

Now it was simply a question of finding his way back. The elderly fox who'd watched him from the window as they'd entered was gone, the street mostly empty. For a moment, he couldn't connect this deserted street to the one he'd seen from the bedroom, until he realized that they were different streets. The bedroom must have looked out over the back of the house. Perking his ears in that direction, he heard the bustle of activity he'd been expecting. He retraced his path as best he could, using the setting sun as his guide, and soon came to Market Street, from which he found his way to Velkan's mansion easily.

The wood grain of the mansion door reminded him of the dark wood in the house he'd just left. The entrance was different, though; this one double the width with a much more ornate frame. Stone foxes with gold eyes guarded the corners, their tails meeting over the center of the lintel. To either side, a stone fox stood looking outward, each brandishing a sword. All four foxes bore elaborately detailed cloth armor. Over the center of the door, a small shield bore the crest of Dewanne.

He was about to knock when the door opened out, nearly knocking him over. Corwin was saying to someone behind him, "...and come find me if there's any news. One missing is one thing, but two—Yilon! Dear boy."

He threw his arms around Yilon. "Did you get lost on the way here? I sent someone to look for you—twice, you know how it is sometimes—and they finally reported that you weren't anywhere in the castle. So then I thought you might have gone to one of the alehouses, since you hadn't eaten any lunch. But Min couldn't find you in any of those. And then we started to worry, and I was just about to go look for you myself."

The fox behind him, a plump servant dressed in a frilled tunic and wearing a gold bracelet, tilted his muzzle. "I thought you said you were going back to your—"

"Ahem," Corwin said. "In any case, no need for that now. Thank you, Kevil."

Kevil bowed and retreated back into the mansion. "Listen," Yilon said, lowering his voice. "I was coming over here and I saw Maxon leaving. I followed him through the city."

"Maxon?" Corwin said.

"Yes?" The steward stepped into the doorway from inside the mansion. He narrowed his eyes, looking down at Yilon. "Ah, there you are."

He was wearing a green vest. Not blue—green. But he'd definitely been wearing a blue vest when he left the castle. Hadn't he? And did his cold look mean he'd talked with Lady Dewanne, had confirmed with her that Yilon was not, in fact, related by blood to the land of Dewanne? "Have you been here all afternoon?" Yilon asked, stupidly.

"Most of it," Maxon replied. "I have been arranging the search for the crown. Have you any new information to add?"

"I haven't remembered anything more about the theft," Yilon said. "Maybe..." He hesitated. Did he want to confront Maxon now about his wandering? If not for the vest, and the possibility that Maxon might expose his heritage, he might have. Both the steward and Corwin were staring at him. "Maybe if I talk to Corwin, we can remember something critical."

Corwin nodded. "Of course. Shall we?"

"Actually," Yilon said, "I still haven't had lunch. And my stomach is killing me."

He wasn't just being facetious; besides being hungry, his wounds were still aching, and the walk hadn't helped. He followed Corwin without complaint across the plaza to a small public house on the west side, where they found a vacant table in the corner of the restaurant. Corwin ordered a plate of cold roast fowl with bread on the side and two tankards of wine.

Yilon took a gulp of the wine as soon as it arrived. The sharp warmth settled in his stomach, spreading slowly through him as the taste faded from his tongue. Corwin, sipping more demurely, folded his arms on the table and leaned forward. "So," he said, "what details did you remember that you wanted to discuss?"

Yilon shook his head. "I just wanted to get away from Maxon. Was he really there all afternoon? Did you see him?"

"I was in with Velkan after we left. Maxon came in...maybe half an hour ago? But he said he'd been organizing the search. Why?"

"I followed him down past Market Street, to a big house that just said "Strad" over it. Do you know it?"

Corwin shook his head. "Except for Dun Hill, the far east side is terribly unfashionable. The less time you spend there, the better. Are you quite sure Maxon went there?"

"Yes. Well..." Yilon hesitated. "Was he wearing a blue vest this morning?"

"Now that you mention it, I believe he was." Corwin flicked his ears. "I've no idea why he would have changed to that old green thing he had on just now."

"So it was him. I was following the blue vest. I lost him once, but then found him again. He went into this house, and then...then someone else came out of it and chased me. And when he caught me, he attacked me. He wanted to know what I was doing there."

"Attacked you?" Corwin's eyes widened. He half-rose from the table. "Are you hurt at all? We need to get you to a chirurgeon."

Yilon shook his head. "Just scratches, and they've been tended to. I'm fine."

"This Confirmation cannot come quickly enough." Corwin's muzzle took on a determined set as he sat back down. "I have never seen things this bad in the city. Never in all my days. Guards everywhere, and still." His ears were still up. "You must not wander alone in the city, especially over on the east side. There are many dangers here that you are not aware of. Thank Canis you were not hurt more. But you said you were attended to?"

Yilon nodded. "I had..."

He paused as the owner came back up to their table, putting down the plate of cold roast fowl and warm bread. Corwin thanked the elderly fox, who leaned down and whispered that he'd given them the best cut of the fowl.

Yilon's first bite was good, tender and well-seasoned, even without sauce, and the bread was crunchy and slightly sour. He devoured several bites before continuing, having thought about how to tell Corwin about the mysterious vixen. Needing help to be rescued was embarrassing enough, but to have been rescued by a vixen was worse. "I had some help getting away," he said. "He was a nurse, too, and he cleaned the wounds at his place. They aren't serious."

"Oh ho." That mollified Corwin's concern over Yilon's injuries. "Was he cute? That would explain why you were gone for so long."

"No." Yilon folded his ears back. "I mean, I guess he was. But nothing happened."

Corwin chewed a piece of bread, watching Yilon thoughtfully. "I do hope I haven't put you off with all those stories about nobility being discovered in terribly salacious but wonderfully pleasurable activities. There is a good deal of depravity in this town, and it would be nearly criminal for you not to enjoy at least some of it."

"It's not you," Yilon muttered, filling his muzzle with meat that now had lost its zest.

"Don't tell me you've already lost your desires, not at your young age. Please." He placed a paw to his heart. "There are only so many tragedies these old eyes can witness. I beg of you not to add to them."

"It's not that." Yilon chewed a piece of bread as loudly as he could.

"You're not married, I know that. But you did bring a friend all the way across Tephos...someone closer than a friend?"

Yilon took another piece of fowl and chewed silently. Corwin sat back, drumming his fingers on the table. The silence stretched on and on until the older fox came to a decision. "Listen," he said, leaning over the table again and tapping on the stone tabletop beside the plate. "Would it help you to know that Marco Buleva had many mistresses, late in his life? Or that Belix Durenin, the head of that house, sleeps with a common tailor girl because his wife only wants to sleep with other ladies now she's borne him an heir? Or that— "

"That's okay," Yilon said. His ears felt flush. "That has nothing to do with me."

"The point is," Corwin said, "it's in the vulpine nature. It's nothing to be ashamed of. Just be discreet. You don't even have to be completely discreet, just enough that you're not a public embarrassment. You can have a night with a cute male nurse. You can have him come to the castle whenever you want. Would you like to know how many young tods spent the night in the governor's mansion on my watch?"

"No!" Yilon snapped. "I'm not going to be like that."

Corwin frowned. "My dear, if Canis made you to prefer males, there isn't much you can do about that. I'm distressed that you would even want to."

"It's not about liking males." Yilon said. "In my position, I can't be with a male. I have to marry and have an heir, and I have to be a good father to my heir."

"But nothing says you cannot enjoy yourself and be a good father all at the same time."

Yilon saw his father and Streak again. "I'm not going to be like that."

"Like what? Happy?"

"Being a lord isn't about being happy. It's about duty, and service."

Corwin rubbed his whiskers back along his muzzle, held them there, then let them spring free. "Yes, it is," he said. "But the weight of all that duty and service can be a fearsome burden. What merchant or farmer would begrudge his ruler some pleasure to ease that burden? In many cases, it is the very weight of the duty that drives these rulers to the extremes they seek. King Barris? Adequate king. Not extraordinary. He did not do very much, save promote some dreary fashions. He had no lovers, from what I hear tell in the palace. The Lord Dewanne before the late Lord Dewanne's predecessor, whose given name was Talil, was faithful to his wife throughout his reign, as best I have been able to ascertain. He was a terrible tyrant, taxing farmers and passing loads of unnecessary regulations on trade that his successor had to reverse."

"But he was honorable," Yilon growled.

"To his wife, yes. But honor means many different things, dear boy, many things indeed. If your people suffer but your wife is happy, is that honor? If you are faithful but your wife is miserable, is that honor?"

"What about Sheffin? Lord Dewanne? He was faithful, you said."

Corwin looked sharply at him. "Yes, he was. He was a good ruler."

So the former governor hadn't been made privy to Sheffin's one betrayal. "Canis teaches us to care for our pack."

Corwin nodded, holding up a paw. "And Fox has always held that one's family comes first. I know all this. But your pack will soon be the city of Dewanne."

"*And* my family."

"Of course. But—"

"Just because I have multiple obligations doesn't mean I can neglect one of them. That's the price of being a lord, isn't it?"

Corwin sighed. "Yes, you're right, you're right. And honesty compels me to admit that there have been good Lords, faithful and true. But if you can come to an arrangement with your wife—and Dinah may be headstrong, but she is a sensible vixen as well—then what's the harm?"

"What if," Yilon said tightly, "my wife agrees to the arrangement because she feels she has no other choice? What if she chooses to live in sadness rather than make my—rather than make me unhappy?"

The other fox's eyes studied his. "Then that is very noble of her. Very noble indeed. But it is not your burden to bear. Do you understand, Yilon? You will have enough burdens of your own without taking on those of your family."

The owner interrupted, coming to clear their empty plate and to ask if there would be anything else. Corwin shook his head, tipped three coins into the proffered paw, and emptied his tankard. "We should be getting back," he said. "Unless there is something else about the crown?"

Yilon opened his muzzle, then closed it again. Slowly, he shook his head.

Corwin looked around the house. At mid-afternoon, there were not many others in the room, and none within two tables. "Nothing to do with your friend the mouse?"

The sun had dropped to the point that it was coming through the window just over Corwin's ears, into Yilon's eyes. He squinted and dropped his muzzle slightly. "I haven't seen him since we arrived at the castle," he said, squirming a little at the lie.

Corwin inclined his head forward, bringing the sun back into Yilon's eyes. "Whatever may have happened is of little consequence if the crown gets returned," he said. "The stresses in this place—goodness, it's as bad as Minerva Lightly's corset, if not quite as likely to explode. Losing the crown is a serious issue for many more reasons than your particular future."

Yilon raised a paw to shield his eyes. "Why? What difference does it make who holds the lordship? It's not like there's some evil killer out there waiting to get his paws on the crown."

"Isn't there?" Corwin's expression was shockingly serious. "Let us assume that Dinah could be found. She has shown even less interest than you in ruling Dewanne. She'd prefer to be living in the hills, or perhaps leaving the valley altogether, like Delia—our current Lady. You at least have been raised with loyalty and honor, however much we might disagree on the exact application of those words. A neglectful Lord or Lady is worse than none at all, because the people expect a certain level of attention when there is a Lord in the castle. Now, when there is none, we are resigned to a small period of unsettlement." He glanced out the window. "Not this bad. Not this bad," he murmured almost to himself.

"But she's from here," Yilon pointed out. "She knows..."

"Yes, yes. But she is also missing. So let us assume that you are sent away in disgrace for losing the crown—this is what you wanted, my whiskers tell me, no? And Dinah manages to avoid her responsibilities. There are no clear choices after that. Sheffin had a bastard son, but he left here at about your age and hasn't been heard from since. Delia's sister died bearing a male son, with a clubfoot. He blames the mice for his disfigurement and his mother's death, and is currently under "observation" for killing one in the plaza right out here seven years ago. Tyle Durenin is five; Lady Dewanne would have to remain as Regent for another ten years. Dinah's sister Porti is younger still. Or another regent could be appointed, but that would be a long and contentious process as well."

"But it would be resolved eventually," Yilon said.

Corwin ticked off points on the fingers of one paw. "The longer the period of unrest, the worse our situation is. We are so far from the capital that our trade is always as tenuous as Chali Fortson's cookery. Any small disruption could be disastrous. Sheffin's illness and your distance from Dewanne have allowed thieves to operate more openly, not to mention the shadows. Then there is the point I mentioned before, about expanding the role of Dewanne. None but you are qualified to do that. There are always tensions between us and the mice, which you are admirably and uniquely suited to mediate."

He stopped at Yilon's exaggerated sigh, but left his fingers up, pointing directly at Yilon's muzzle. In the silence, Yilon could hear murmurs outside the open window as foxes and couples walked by it. He filed away the curious mention of "shadows" to ask about later, voicing the more urgent question first. "Have there been any good Lords who didn't want to be lord?"

Corwin smiled. He reached out and took Yilon's paw, clasping it tightly. "Only all of them, dear boy. Only all of them."

Yilon took a deep breath. "Sinch might know some more," he said. "He'll probably come to the castle tonight looking for me. I'll ask him then. If he knows...I promise I'll get the crown back."

"Wonderful." Corwin's ears perked up. "Then all this ugliness will be behind us, where it belongs."

"At least you will be able to tell this story to the next young lord to come into town."

Corwin laughed. "I should live so long. No, I will be happy to use it to lure the young tods who already know all my other stories to my parlor one more time. And for that, I thank you."

They rose and walked to the door. "Speaking of which," Corwin said, "you never did tell me the name of this adorable young nurse who saved your life."

"Oh." Yilon blinked into the sun. He turned to Corwin. "His name was Colian."

Corwin whirled, grabbing Yilon's shoulders. "Colian?" he said sharply. "You're sure?"

"Yes." Yilon frowned, his ears swiveling back. He squinted up at the former governor. "That's what he said."

"Where—" Corwin said, and then pushed Yilon back, not hard. His head came up, looking from side to side.

Yilon tried to follow him. "What?"

Something was poking him in the shoulder. He looked down and saw the end of a quarrel, slick with blood, protruding from the right side of Corwin's chest.

Chapter 12: Into the Shadows

By Sinch's reckoning, he'd been pretending to snore for three hours before he heard the rhythm of Valix's breathing settle. He peered down from the upper bunk to her shadowy shape on the floor. He gauged the distance from the edge of the bed to the hallway just beyond her body. The trick would not be clearing her; the trick would be landing silently. He knew how to land on the balls of his feet so his claws didn't hit stone. He knew how to minimize his impact to reduce the percussive sound. He'd practiced it many times. He'd just never used it in quite so critical a situation.

If there was one thing he'd learned, it was that nothing got easier for thinking about it too much. He got to the edge of the bed, gathered himself, and leapt.

His landing in the corridor didn't sound loud to him. He waited just a moment, but Valix didn't stir. Her breathing remained even. He padded back up the stairs and out to the street, which was busier now, much busier. This must have been difficult for Valix, staying awake while the sun was up, when most of their people were sleeping. No doubt that was why she'd fallen asleep so soundly, when she finally had.

Still, he didn't trust her. He stood just to the right of the doorway, waiting. When Valix didn't emerge after several minutes, he slid out into the crowd.

He felt like a stranger in the Warren. Now that the moon was up, the mice were more animated. Cheerful, even. They talked to each other as they passed on the street, with familiar waves and chirps of greeting. Only Sinch was silent, jostling through them, crowding over obstacles and through puddles with them.

First he stopped at Miss Chakray's house, though it took him the better part of an hour to get back to a familiar area from which he could find it. He climbed the pile of debris to the window that had been his. He listened, but no noise came from inside. Carefully, he climbed through, pausing to make sure the room was empty. He twitched his whiskers and sniffed, but the strongest scent was his own. Quickly, he dropped to the floor, prised up the loose board, and reached inside for his money and tools.

He hadn't realized he was holding his breath until he felt the weight of the small pouch. He exhaled, fastened the pouch at his waist, and crept back out the window.

Someone happened to be crossing the pile of debris as Sinch emerged. He started, nearly falling down in his surprise. "Sorry," the other mumbled, and scurried down the other side. Sinch descended his side with similar quickness, his nose twitching. For a moment, he'd worried that Valix was following him, peering in at the window to take his money from him, or that Balinni was having the room watched. But though he glanced back at the building and the barricade, nobody climbed back over it to follow him. Nothing ever got easier from thinking about it, he reminded himself, and hurried on to the outskirts of the city.

From there, it was easier to make his way to the castle. The mice on the outskirts of the Warren went about their business more quietly, the crowds more sparse and skittish, as though the castle now visible to the east were watching them. Certainly some vulpine guards were; Sinch heard their footsteps crunch across the dirt. They were easy enough to slip around behind for one practiced at moving quietly. It was before he even reached them, though, that Sinch's whiskers began to tingle, making him look back several times. Once he thought he saw a shadow slide behind a building, but the next time, there was nothing there. To be sure, he cut around and doubled back, then went around a building in the opposite direction, hiding for a full five minutes before making his way forward again. He waited for a patrol to pass, and when he padded quietly behind them, the tingling in his whiskers subsided. It didn't return as he hurried across the scrub grass, all the way up to the castle wall.

With one more check to make sure nobody was watching, Sinch made his way up the stone wall, holding on to the cracks in the stone with slender fingers. He reached Yilon's bedroom window and pulled himself to the sill. The window was closed.

Sinch cupped his paw against the glass, trying to see past the reflection of the moon. He scratched gently at the window frame. No sound or movement came from inside. He waited, looking down nervously at the grounds, then scratched again.

Nothing. Yilon wasn't there. Sinch took a worried moment to wonder where the fox might be, if not in his own bedroom (in someone else's?), before making his way back down the wall. He pressed himself against the stone, listening and sniffing the wind. No movement. The guards around the Warren were all that were deemed necessary, he supposed.

He allowed his mind to wander back to Yilon as his feet took him to the outer wall and the unguarded door. He would have to come back the next night, and if Yilon still weren't there, he'd have to get a message to him somehow. Sinch felt sure he could get into the castle if he really needed to. After all, they did silly things like leave the service door in the wall unguarded.

The moment he stepped through it, he was tackled to the ground. His left arm was twisted behind his back, its leverage used to press him down. He struggled only until he heard Valix's voice. "Keep still, you idiot."

Her scent filtered down to him through his own surprise and fear. He relaxed. "What are you doing here?"

"Idiot," she snarled again. "If I had known you were coming here, I would have tied you to the bed. Do you have any idea what you're doing?"

"How did you find me?"

He tried to twist around to look her in the face, but she prevented him. "So you know someone in the castle? Or you were just hoping to rob the treasury? No, you were at an upper window. So you know someone. The new lord?"

"If I'd wanted to tell you, I'd have invited you along," Sinch said.

At that, she did turn him over, though she remained straddling him. "Well, I'm along now." He set his muzzle stubbornly, turning over the possible lies he could tell her. "Oh, come," she said. "If I were Balinni, I would have a knife in your kidneys already, gold or no gold. I don't say you can trust me, but...it doesn't look like you have much of a choice."

"You work for Balinni," Sinch said.

Valix laughed softly. "I take 'im sweet cakes on Rekindling, too, but that don't mean I tell him everything."

Sinch furrowed his eyebrows. "Rekindling?"

"Summer festival. Don't you celebrate it in Divahhhlia?"

"No." He sighed. "Yes, I was going to try to get gold from someone I know in the castle."

"But he's not there."

"No."

She sat back on his hips, the pressure of her rear rubbing his sheath. "Then what now?"

Whether or not he could trust her, her expression looked sincere enough. He wanted to trust her, wanted to have someone else to confide in. Perhaps it wouldn't hurt to confide partially in her, and it would get her off him. "Wait another night? I don't really have another plan."

"Tchah. Balinni won't wait another night." She leaned closer. "If you don't come back with the money by noon tomorrow, I'm supposed to torture you to find out where you stashed the thing."

She said it so amiably that he thought at first he'd heard her wrong. "Torture?"

"You know, extreme pain to compel the release of information? I don't think you'd need extreme pain, though. Probably just a little." She tilted her muzzle. "Maybe just the threat."

The pressure on his sheath took on a different character. "All right," he said. "Get off."

From behind Valix, downwind, the clatter of a small pebble across the ground. Both their heads shot up, ears perked. "Rodenta's—" Valix started, springing off Sinch, but before she could finish either the action or the oath, a tall shape had grabbed her by the neck and lifted her bodily into the air.

Sinch scrambled back as the weight was lifted from him. "What luck," said a familiar voice, and then a cough. The scent hit him all in a rush.

"Maxon?"

The fox laughed, softly. "Yes, I remember you, too. It is lucky. I was just looking for you."

"*He's* your friend?" Valix squeaked, struggling.

Maxon looked at her as if just remembering he were holding her. "Quiet," he said, and threw her against the wall.

Sinch heard the crack of her skull, saw her slump to the ground. He started toward her, but Maxon held up a paw. "Ah-ah," he said. "Do not concern yourself with her. The guards will find her in the morning. In fact," he stroked his whiskers, "it might be best to ensure her body is still here in the morning."

"No!" Sinch cried, scrambling to his feet. "Don't you touch her."

"Tsk." The steward's smile gleamed in the moonlight as brightly as the blade of the knife in his paw. "And here I thought it was the lord-to-be you loved."

Sinch kept his eye on the knife. "Don't touch her," he repeated.

"So." Maxon eyed him. "We both want something from each other. Very well." He bent and picked up Valix, slinging her over his shoulder with surprising ease considering his slender frame. "Take me to the crown. If I have it in my paws before sunup, you and she will go free. If not, well, I will manage some way to explain a dead mouse in the city." He grinned again. "It won't be the first time."

Sinch's insides were ice cold. "What makes you think I know where the crown is?"

"For Canis's sake," Maxon said. "We may be provincial, but we are not stupid. How would a group of mice know that the lordling had taken the crown from me and was carrying it about the city? How would any mouse know, except for one?"

Sinch sighed. "It's in the Warren," he said.

Maxon shook his head. "Possible, but doubtful. In that case, you will have to get it yourself and bring it back, and I will take our guest here to the castle dungeon." He readjusted Valix's weight on his shoulder and held up the paw with the silver bracelet on it. "That looks too pretty for a mouse. Stolen, of course. Charged with theft, trespassing...she'll spend the rest of her life there. Such as it is. So which will it be?"

Of course Maxon wouldn't be tricked into the Warren. Sinch's shoulders slumped. "I'll take you to it."

Maxon made him walk ten feet ahead, so it was hard to keep an eye on Valix, but Sinch kept turning around to try. Even when the steward snapped, "Keep your eyes forward," Sinch snuck glances back whenever they rounded a corner.

He deliberately took a more circuitous route, partly to give Valix time to recover, partly because Maxon kept steering him down smaller, quieter streets. "We're going in circles," Maxon growled.

"I've only been there once," Sinch said. "The streets all look the same." He scanned the expressions of the few foxes they passed for any hint of sympathy, but they all looked away as soon as they came close to meeting his eyes, and he soon stopped hoping. Down alleys, he saw quick, furtive movements and recognized the scents of other mice, but they never even came close enough for him to see their faces. Help from them was even less likely.

"Why don't you just tell me where it is?"

"I don't remember the name," Sinch said truthfully. He was certain it wasn't the next street he turned down, though he thought it might be the one beyond. He would have to start from the site of the robbery to be absolutely sure, especially in the dark. But he walked with confidence. The city couldn't be so large he wouldn't find the street soon. And he only needed to stall Maxon until Valix woke.

The next time he looked back, the street was empty. He was about to turn back when movement in the shadows behind Maxon caught his eye. "One more look behind..." the steward warned, but whatever had been moving had stopped. Sinch's whiskers tingled again. He was about to turn forward when he thought he saw the briefest flick of Valix's ear.

He pointed behind them. "Thought I saw someone. Following us."

Maxon studied him. He held out a paw. "Stay." Then he turned his head quickly back. In that second, Valix stirred and moaned.

The steward glanced back to make sure Sinch was still ten feet away, then shrugged Valix off his shoulder. "Time to keep her asleep," he said, shooting a nasty smile Sinch's way. "If I have to do this much more often, all my promises may come to naught, you know. We'd better get the crown soon."

He hefted her, preparing to slam her against the nearest stone wall. Sinch dropped to a crouch, grabbed his knife, and in the moment before Maxon thrust Valix forward, threw it as hard as he could.

It struck the steward in the leg, just above the knee. The fox howled in pain and dropped Valix, crumpling to the ground. Sinch sprang forward, grabbing her paw.

They were still close enough that Maxon could swipe at them, but the steward hadn't quite processed what was going on. Valix staggered to her feet, stumbling after Sinch, at which Maxon did grab her leg. "Come on!" Sinch urged, tugging her.

Valix had a paw to her head, still looking woozy. She kicked weakly at the steward, but failed to dislodge him. The fox, grimacing, reached down to the knife in his leg.

Sinch stomped on Maxon's arm. The steward didn't howl this time, just growled and swiped at Sinch. He skipped aside and kicked out one more time, catching the fox in the shoulder and knocking him backwards. He grabbed Valix again and pulled her away, throwing her arm over his shoulder. "Come on!"

She was getting her senses back, enough to trot after him. Behind them, he heard the steward struggling to his feet. "Stop them!" the fox yelled in a high voice. "Thieves! They're getting away!"

Valix shook her head. "Did you steal something from him?"

"Just you. Do you know anywhere to hide?" No foxes had appeared yet, but with Maxon continuing to scream for help behind them, it wouldn't be long before—

There, ahead of them, footsteps. Sinch scanned the street frantically. There were two small storefronts next to them, and a closed residence across. Curtains stretched taut across the entrances, but Sinch didn't have his knife any more, and the one closest to him showed metal bars behind the curtains anyway.

"Corner," Valix said. "Around there, there's an alley to the left."

A fox appeared at the corner. Maxon screamed behind them. "Thieves!" He broke into a coughing fit. Sinch hoped it was as painful as it sounded.

They kept moving toward the fox ahead of them. He was tall and muscular enough that he stood his ground as they approached. "Hold on there," he said.

Sinch didn't have any sort of plan other than to get around him, somehow get around to the left, and find the alley Valix was talking about.

But as he got closer, he saw the flick of the fox's ears, a gesture he recognized from his friendship with Yilon. He stood taller. "Out of our way," he said, and reached for the empty knife sheath at his waist, looking as menacing as he could.

The fox took a step back. "Don't try anything," he said, but his voice wavered.

"Stop them!" Maxon shrieked.

Valix pushed away from him, standing upright. "Get out, redtail," she snarled.

"In the name of Lord Dewanne, stop them!" Maxon was getting closer, his wounded leg dragging on the flagstones.

The fox in front of them had his tail between his legs. "Just stop," he said.

Valix turned to Sinch. "Stick him like you did the other," she said.

Maxon's voice was a scant ten feet behind them. "Right," Sinch said. He grabbed at the empty knife belt.

The fox backed away another two steps. "I don't have a weapon," he said.

"They're unarmed!" screamed Maxon, but Valix and Sinch were already on their way around the corner. More foxes were approaching down the street, but they were keeping their distance.

"There it is." Valix hurried ahead of him, still weaving, to the dark crevice between the buildings. Sinch kept up, more slowly, making threatening jabs at the foxes watching them. Maxon rounded the corner, limping their way fast.

"I hope there's somewhere in there for us to hide," muttered Sinch as he followed her into the shadows.

"Leave that to me," Valix's voice floated back to him. There was a small clatter of metal as she appeared to lift up part of the flagstones. "Down in there."

She was holding a metal grate. Sinch hesitated at the smell of filth, faint though it was. "Hurry," she snapped.

He could hear the foxes behind them, seconds from the alley. He stepped forward and dropped into the darkness.

He only fell for the span of one heartbeat before his paws slapped down on the damp stone. Above him, the grate clanged back into place. "Out of the way," hissed Valix.

"I'm clear," he said, stepping to one side.

She landed beside him. When he started to say something, she said, "Shh," and looked up.

Through the holes in the grate, they could see the stars. Then a shape blotted out the light. "They went down there," Maxon's voice said. "I heard the grate."

Only muttering answered that. "Well?" he said. "Go down and get them."

"That's the sewer," someone else said.

"Aye, so it is," Maxon snarled. "And those are mice who attacked a member of the court. Who have valuable information that the Lord needs."

"He's closer to them than we are, now." There was scattered laughter.

"I order you to go down there. In the name of your Lord and ruler!"

"Our Lord died last month," another voice answered. "Go down yourself."

"Come back here!" Maxon yelled. "The court of Dewanne..."

"When there's a new Lord, he can tell us to go in the sewer," a voice called, faintly.

Maxon stomped around on the grate. The gleam of his eye appeared at the opening a moment later. "I can see you down there," he hissed. "I'll get you, never fear."

He coughed once and then was gone, revealing the bright pinpoints of the stars again. Sinch found a wall near him and leaned against it, exhaling. "How's your head?"

"Feels like someone slammed it into a stone wall," Valix said. "It'll heal."

"At least we can rest here for a while." Sinch couldn't see any dark patches in her head fur, but his examination was made difficult because she kept turning her head from side to side, ears perked. "You look okay."

"Well," she said, "this might be safe. If we're lucky."

Sinch felt a paw grip the back of his neck at the same time as a shadowy paw descended to clutch Valix's. Both of them jumped, but the paws held them fast. A cold female voice floated down to them. "Let us assume, for the moment, that you are not."

Chapter 13: "Not the Shadows"

Corwin's knees weakened, but his paws kept their grip on Yilon's shoulders, pulling him down. "Dear boy," he gasped. He took in a rattling breath. "Dear boy," he repeated. "Not...the shadows."

Yilon dropped to his knees, just as something split the air over his head and clattered against the wall of the public house behind. "Help!" he called. "Help!"

Foxes were already beginning to gather, and at the sight of the quarrel tail sticking out of Corwin's back, a vixen screamed. Paws pulled Yilon to one side, lowering Corwin to the ground on his side. Yilon couldn't tell if the older fox were still breathing. "Get a chirurgeon," he said.

"There's one near here," someone answered. "I'll go."

Other voices crowded the air with questions. "What happened?" "Who did this?"

Yilon shook his head and pointed up. "There, somewhere. Don't know." There was a line of buildings whose roofs looked down on the street with a perfect shooting angle. From where he was, near the street, they were now above the sun, so he could see their stark silhouettes against the sunset. Nothing moved up there. If the shooter had been on the roof, he was now gone.

Another paw landed on Yilon's shoulder. He looked up at a green vest. "You need to be away from here, now," Maxon said after a sharp cough. His eyes were narrowed, his ears down, but he wasn't looking around as though worried about the attacker. He looked angry, as if he were personally aggrieved that this attack had occurred in his city.

"But Corwin..."

"They're already fetching the chirurgeon," Maxon said. "There's no more you can do."

The tod who'd said he would go was returning now, a disheveled fox in a plain white tunic in tow. "What's this?" the chirurgeon was saying. "Shot? In the street? Again?"

Yilon watched long enough to see the fox kneel next to Corwin, touch the quarrel, and elicit a low groan from the injured fox, and then he followed Maxon away from the public house, back to the plaza. But when Maxon tried to guide him away from the governor's mansion, he resisted. "I'm not following you," he said.

"My lord," Maxon said, "there has just been an attempt on your life. The castle is most likely the safest place for you."

"I have to tell Velkan about the attack." Yilon stared stubbornly at the steward.

Maxon growled. "I can certainly relay the information. My primary concern at this moment is your safety."

"You weren't there!"

"And what information do you have from your presence there that I did not see, arriving moments later?"

Yilon opened his mouth to say, "the last thing Corwin said," but then snapped his muzzle shut, not only because he didn't want to tell Maxon what Corwin had said, but because he was now wondering something else. "Why *did* you arrive moments later?"

"You had been gone quite a while. Corwin's presence was requested."

He sounded believable enough, and now he was looking around the plaza at all the foxes walking by, up at the rooftops. "I'm going with you to the mansion," Yilon said. "We will send for Min from the castle and he will accompany me as my bodyguard. Will that soothe your fears?"

Maxon stifled a cough. "I suppose it will have to. Get inside the mansion now, then. My lord."

"But Min..."

"I will fetch Min. You will find Velkan in the great room to the left. Stay away from the windows." Maxon nearly pushed him through the front door.

He stepped into a marble-floored foyer, lined with tapestries and illuminated with the reddish light of sunset through a skylight. The place smelled mostly of the violet and red flowers placed around near the windows. Below it was the ever-present undertone of fox, but the floral scent was strong enough to mask the identities.

To the left, below a fresco of Canis bestowing a blessing on a fox, a large double door stood closed. Yilon was intercepted on his way to them by an elderly fox in green livery, who announced him to Velkan and then informed him that he was welcome.

The long room into which he was shown appeared to be a banquet hall, with windows at regular intervals all down the right hand wall. Facing them, more tapestries hung depicting scenes from the Book of Gaia: Canis creating His companions, Canis leading His pack, Canis blessing the First Foxes. Above the long table, two chandeliers that were intricate structures of glass were in the process of being lit by two servants on ladders. Below them, at the far end of the table, Velkan looked up from a large piece of parchment, Lady Dewanne at his side. Yilon barely saw any of them, the image of the bloody quarrel in Corwin's chest swimming before him.

Lady Dewanne spoke first. "There you are," she said. "Corwin went to look for you."

Hearing his name brought Yilon back to reality. "He—he's been shot." Yilon walked slowly toward them, tail curled back around his legs. He pushed away the thought that Corwin might even now be dying, or dead. If he didn't think about it, it wouldn't be real.

Lady Dewanne's ears shot up. Beside her, Velkan's did too, his jaw dropping. The servants stopped lighting the chandeliers and looked down. The only sound was the click of Yilon's claws on the marble floor. Velkan said, in a short, clipped voice, "What?"

"We were leaving the public house and he was shot with a crossbow. From a rooftop, I think." Yilon reached Lady Dewanne's side, opposite the windows. On the parchment, the city of Dewanne was laid out, with small markers near the Warren and at the spot where the crown had been stolen. Yilon's ears flushed. To distract his attention, he pointed to the approximate spot on the map where the public house was. "Here." But he couldn't keep his eyes from the marker of the spot of the theft, so close to where his finger's claw rested.

"Is he...?" Lady Dewanne's eyes were wide, one paw at her muzzle.

Yilon squeezed his eyes shut briefly. Sixteen years without seeing a fox stabbed, and then twice in one day, he thought. "He was alive when I left." He pointed to his upper chest. "It came through here."

"From a rooftop?" Velkan said.

Yilon moved his paw around to the spot over his shoulder, between his shoulder blade and spine. "It came in around here."

"Might not be fatal," Velkan observed. The governor touched the same spot on his own upper chest. "Where did they take him?"

"A chirurgeon came to tend to him," Yilon said. "Maxon dragged me away after that."

"Maxon?" Lady Dewanne said with a start.

"Another public shooting," Velkan said. "From a rooftop. It might be time again." His paw lingered over a point on the map. "My lady?"

"I wanted to mention about Maxon," Yilon said, but at that moment the liveried servant entered the room and announced that the steward had returned.

"Your servant is waiting outside, my lord," he told Yilon as he strode briskly past the ladders to join them. "And this message arrived for you today." He handed over a folded parchment.

Yilon saw the seal of the steward of Divalia. He stepped back from the table and broke it, unfolding the parchment. Velkan told Maxon briefly what they had been discussing, while Yilon read the words.

Yilon,

According to palace records, the only person to arrive from Dewanne in the past two weeks was the steward Maxon, with his driver. No merchant wagons were registered at the gates. It is possible that a single rider might have entered the city and given a false destination, or been hidden in another wagon, but that is beyond the limits of my information. I can safely say that no legitimate traveler arrived from Dewanne with the exception of those noted above.

Your obedient servant,

Jinna

"News of your family?" Maxon said.

Yilon re-folded the parchment and tucked it in with his coins. "The answer to a question." He stepped back to the table.

Lady Dewanne looked across at Maxon, started to ask him something, but then turned to Yilon and said, "Velkan's opinion is that the Shadows are taking advantage of the period of transition. This second attack would seem to bear out his theory." He could hear the proper noun in the way she said "Shadows," and her voice was colder, more distant. As she finished, her eyes dropped to the map.

Velkan nodded. "They've been mostly quiet during my term as governor. I know in the past there was need for corrective measures against them from time to time." He rubbed his whiskers. "It almost feels that they have a grudge against Corwin."

Lady Dewanne was still staring down at the map. Her voice was soft. "But of all of us, he was the one to argue most strongly against the use of violence. And why begin acting out today of all days?"

"Because the new lord has arrived," Velkan said. "They want to show him their power. That's why we need to respond quickly and decisively."

"I don't like it," Lady Dewanne said. "Corwin would not want..." Her voice trailed off.

"There is no other explanation," Maxon said, tightly. "If they are attempting to flex their muscles, we need to put a stop to it."

Yilon had to force himself to ask the question, hating his ignorance in this grave discussion. "Er...what are the Shadows?"

All three of them turned to him, then looked around at each other. Velkan said, "My Lady, perhaps..."

Lady Dewanne nodded. "The Shadows are a group of...we assume they are mice, but those are only the ones we've caught. They live in the sewers under the city. It's usually too much trouble to go flush them out except on extraordinary occasions. Besides, they always come back soon after."

"The sewers?"

"Yes, we have sewers here," Maxon said. "Just like in Divalia."

"Except that you have people living in them," Yilon said.

"You think Divalia does not?"

"Please," Velkan said. "My lady, may I go begin preparations?"

Yilon looked away from Maxon's smug expression. "Corwin said something about shadows to me."

All three of them turned to him. "When?" Maxon said.

"After he got shot." Yilon closed his eyes. "He said, "Not Shadows.""

The room fell silent. The servants, finished with their lighting, remained at the top of their ladders. "Are you certain?" Velkan asked.

"How could he have known?" Maxon said.

Lady Dewanne spread her paws. "Perhaps he saw his attacker."

"He was shot in the back," Maxon reminded her.

"But he was facing the public house," Yilon recalled. "He could have seen the reflection in the glass, perhaps."

"He'd just been shot in the chest," Velkan said. "I doubt he was exercising all his powers of perception."

"I knew he would not want this," Lady Dewanne mused, looking again at the map. "Where did you say they took him?"

"Incic took charge of him," Maxon said. "But Corwin was not conscious when they moved him. It is unlikely that he has regained consciousness by now. If..."

He let the unspoken alternative hang in the air. The servants descended from the ladders, heads bowed, and left the room at Velkan's dismissal. "Well," the governor said, "if we delay, we lose our chance to act. If it is the Shadows, as we all assume it is, then they may become impossible to control."

"What do they do?" Yilon asked.

"If we don't act now," Velkan said grimly, "whatever they want. And besides, we do not know for how much longer the guard will remain true."

That brought Lady Dewanne's slender muzzle up. Her eyes hardened. "Yes," she said. "Velkan, assemble the guard. Do it quietly. You know the procedures." To Yilon, she explained, "They have spies all over the city. We never know when they're watching."

His fur prickled. "Would they be on rooftops?"

"Almost certainly," Maxon said.

"I think...I think one was watching me."

"When?" Velkan looked down at the map. "And where?"

Yilon stared at the map, trying to retrace his steps. Maxon tapped the table. "It doesn't make much difference where," he said. "There's only four places to enter the sewers, and we have to enter all four at the same time. And for that to happen, we need to assemble the guard now, especially if we're to do it in secret."

Velkan nodded. "Can you assemble the captains of the guard?"

"Of course." Maxon turned to leave, then met Yilon's eyes. Yilon saw again the steward slinking through the back streets of Dewanne, cutting through crowds, entering the Strad house from which Kites had come. He had to tell Lady Dewanne about Strad and about Kites, but that would mean leaving Maxon free to do whatever he wanted.

"I'm going with you," he said.

To his surprise, Maxon smiled. "That is an excellent idea," he said. "It will give you a chance to get acquainted with the guard, and for them to get to know you."

"All right," Yilon said. Velkan was already looking at his map again. Lady Dewanne was rubbing her muzzle, also staring at the parchment, though it didn't look like she was seeing it..

"We'll return here in one hour if we need to change plans," Maxon said.

"And in the meantime," Yilon said on the way out, "you can tell me more about the Shadows."

Chapter 14: No Fox Is Friend

Their unseen captors had climbed down the walls, and now pushed Sinch and Valix forward. "We're just here hiding," Sinch said.

"From a fox," Valix added. "Sinch threw a knife at him."

Her captor laughed, sharply. "That is the only reason you are not already dead."

"You saw us?" Sinch tried to twist around to look at the person behind him, but he got a smack on the ear and a shove forward.

"Of course they saw us," Valix hissed. "Let me do the talking."

The passage was dark and cold, but not so dark that Sinch couldn't see the wide ridges in the floor, dimly grey against the darker space between them. The one time his foot slipped into that darker area, it landed in cold, slimy water. He was careful not to lose his footing again.

The mice behind them—they sounded like mice, and their paws were as small as mice's—pushed them around corners, down small side tunnels, back around corners, until Sinch had lost all sense of direction. Several times, they passed below a grate through which Sinch saw the moon or stars, but they had moved on before he had time for more than a quick glance. Further confusing him were the smells of filth and waste, though they weren't as bad as he'd smelled in Divalia's underground.

And yet, for a city so much smaller, the sewers were wide enough for two mice to walk abreast. Dark alcoves in the walls made Sinch's whiskers twitch, until he became convinced that in every one, a pair of eyes watched them pass. By the time they arrived in a wider passage and were pushed roughly back against the walls of the sewer, Sinch would not have been surprised to see a whole parade of mice trailing behind them, watching.

Only their two captors stepped around to face them. Behind them, a small light shone, enough to throw them into silhouette and the rest of the tunnel into darkness. Sinch only gradually became aware of three other mice standing at the edge of the light, from further down the tunnel. They presented an eerie sight, in the darkness of the sewer. All five had fur of solid black, so deep and impenetrable that the only thing Sinch could see of them at first was the gleam of their eyes. He couldn't tell whether they were even wearing clothing until one stepped closer to him, inspecting him up and down, and then Sinch could see the collar of a tight black shirt around the mouse's neck.

"Frost. Go and get Whisper," the mouse who'd been holding Sinch said.

The one who'd stepped close to them turned, his ears up. "You need more than intruders to bother Whisper," he said. His breath stank of something familiar, but in the miasma of other odors, Sinch couldn't quite place it.

"If these were just intruders, I would be telling you about their quick deaths instead of holding them against the wall," the first mouse growled. "Go."

"Dagger, you go. I'm eating." One of the other two newcomers hurried back into the wide passage. As the mouse with the breath—Frost?—stepped back, Sinch saw what he was holding in the paw he'd kept behind his back: it was a small bone with clumps of meat clinging to it. The mouse grinned at him and then, very deliberately, tore off a chunk of meat with his teeth and chewed it noisily.

Sinch's stomach lurched. He hadn't been able to place the smell of meat because it was a mouse's breath, but the evidence of his eyes was impossible to ignore. And now he recognized it as the faint smell he'd caught that morning in the passage beneath the guards along the trench. He brought a paw to his muzzle, desperately willing himself not to retch. Out of the corner of his eye, he saw Valix's wide eyes and similar struggle.

Sinch's captor turned her attention from him to Frost. "If I'd wanted Dagger, I would've told Dagger to go."

Frost turned. "*I* wanted Dagger to go."

The two stared at each other. Sinch's captor remained stoic, and it was Frost who blinked first. Without any more words, he turned and walked away, chewing on his bone. The darkness swallowed him up as if he'd never existed.

Sinch snuck a look at Valix again. He could hear her rapid breathing and caught the fear in her scent. Her eyes stared straight ahead. He reached over to take her paw to calm her, but it was cold when he touched it, and she didn't clasp back immediately. He held it nevertheless, and then she did squeeze back.

The three mice remaining near them had stepped back to form a semicircle. Their two original captors, without taking their eyes from Sinch and Valix, produced short black daggers from somewhere and began tossing them back and forth, throwing and catching in unison. The third mouse padded down the tunnel, returning a moment later with a hunk of meat. The fat on it gleamed white in the darkness. Sinch felt his stomach lurch again.

It seemed to him that the moments dragged on, one after the other, but the mouse eating his meat had only gotten halfway through it when two shapes materialized out of the gloom at the end of the tunnel. Sinch wouldn't have been able to tell Dagger apart from the other three, but he knew in a moment which one was Whisper.

Whisper carried himself upright, striding through the darkness so that Dagger had to hurry to keep up. Broader in the shoulders than any of the other mice, he nonetheless walked with quick, silent grace through the semicircle to face Sinch and Valix. After a moment's scrutiny, he turned to their two captors, who appeared shorter in his presence. "Well?"

"He can throw," Sinch's captor said. "He stuck a fox."

Whisper turned back to Sinch. "Give him a dagger."

Sinch couldn't believe what he'd heard. Before he'd had time to completely process it, his captor had held out one of the black daggers he'd been throwing.

"Take it," Valix hissed under her breath.

Sinch reached out. His fingers closed around the handle, and it was not snatched back from him. When he held it in his paw, he could tell how precise the balance was. Though it was lighter than the knife he'd taken from Divalia and thrown at Maxon, he knew immediately that it would fly true, and he suspected that the blade was sharper than the other had been.

Whisper stepped back to the fringe of the lit circle. "Throw at me," he commanded, palm flat against his chest. "Right here."

The others all watched. Clearly it was some kind of ritual. But what if Sinch hit him? If he killed their leader, they would fall on him and Valix, for sure. But if he failed, they would think him weak and would likely kill him anyway.

Nobody spoke. Whisper watched him with bright eyes. The others, and Valix, watched him with widened eyes. He thought of Yilon, what the fox would do in this situation, what the fox would advise him to do.

"Make me proud," he thought Yilon might say. Well, if throwing a knife at a mouse in the dark was what they wanted to see, then he would do his best, and if they killed him afterwards, at least he would die proud. He flipped the knife around in his paw, testing its balance, and then swept his arm around in a smooth motion and let it go.

Whisper's arm moved in a blur. Sinch didn't even see the path of the black knife; he only heard the clatter as it struck the stone of the sewer wall and fell.

Sinch let out his breath in a long exhale. "Wow." he said, without thinking. "That's amazing."

Whisper bent to pick up the knife. He tossed it to Sinch, handle-first, an easy throw that practically settled into his paw of its own accord. "Keep it," he said. "Those who know how to use it are rare. Do you want to learn our ways and join us?"

"Join you?" Sinch looked at Valix, to get some sort of hint about who these mice were, or at least what she thought about the invitation, but she was just staring at him. He turned back to Whisper, who had drawn his own knife and was playing with it between his fingers. "Who...are you?"

The black mouse showed the faintest hint of a smile. "We are the Shadows," he said. "We are the opposition to the light. We live in the darkness and watch the city. We strike where others dare not."

"That sounds okay, I guess," Sinch said. He turned the black knife over in his paws, feeling more confident with it. "I mean, thank you. That's very nice of you. What do I have to do besides throw a knife?"

Beside him, Valix made a choking noise. Whisper ignored her. "You have already demonstrated your willingness to fight the Fox."

"Oh," Sinch said. "Well, just one fox, really. He hates us anyway."

"No," Whisper said, showing the first sign of impatience. "*The* Fox. The power in the society of Dewanne that oppresses the mice, that keeps them in the Warren, that takes their money and their lives, that treats them like cattle. The power that is in *all* foxes, that is what we fight against. Even though some," and here he looked at Valix, "do not respect our way."

Valix didn't look like someone who didn't respect Whisper. She looked like someone who was terrified of him. "Oh," Sinch said. "I don't hate *all* foxes. Do I have to?"

The mood turned cold. "All foxes are complicit in the oppression of mice," Whisper recited. The other black mice murmured, "all foxes."

Sinch retreated until the cold stone pressed into his back. "Some foxes are good. I have a good friend who's a fox."

Whisper and the other mice all leaned forward, their eyes narrowing. Valix's muzzle lost the rictus of fear, but the panic that replaced it wasn't much different. "What are you doing?" she hissed. "Why would you—"

"No fox is friend to a mouse," Whisper intoned. "No mouse is friend to a fox."

"He's not from here," Valix said. "He doesn't know the foxes here."

She succeeded in drawing their attention to her. "Who was the mouse with you this morning?" Whisper said abruptly.

"What?"

"The mouse with you, wearing your disguise. The one who took the crown from the cart."

Valix turned to Sinch. "The *crown*?"

He spread his paws. Whisper sounded irritated. "You did not know what you were stealing?" His eyes slid to Sinch. "But you did?"

Sinch opened his muzzle. "Of course he didn't," Valix snapped quickly. "He's new in town. We wouldn't take him on a job of...of that importance."

"Why would you undertake a job of such importance, and then be so careless with the goal? Who organized the job?" Whisper demanded.

"I can't—" Valix said, and then stood straighter. "It was our job," she said. "It's nothing to do with you."

The mouse who'd been Sinch's captor said, "Everything that takes place here has to do with us. You should know that."

"This was—" Valix stopped at a rushing murmur, like water hurrying along the tunnel. All the mice turned to listen, the black mice for only a second before melting away into darkness. Sinch and Valix found themselves alone in the circle of light.

"What's going on?" Sinch said.

"I don't—" Valix twisted around, and then her eyes went wide. She slumped to the ground.

Behind her, a black shadow watched her fall. "Foxes in the tunnels," a cold female voice said, as it pulled a black knife from her back. "Here because of your job this morning. This will make sure they find you."

Sinch thrust forward with his knife, but his blade cut empty air. Laughter remained behind.

He crouched next to Valix and touched her shoulder. She wasn't moving, but it was hard to tell if she were breathing. He hesitated before putting his paw in front of her muzzle. The rushing sound in the tunnels was growing louder, so he couldn't hear any small noises she might be making, and the slight breeze over his fingers concealed any faint breath. He moved them closer, finally felt warmth, and exhaled.

The rushing sound resolved into footsteps, many of them. Sinch lifted his muzzle and sniffed the air, but still could not smell anything but the filth of the sewer. "Help!" he called. "Help!"

For the longest time, all he heard were faint echoes of laughter, and footsteps growing louder and louder. It occurred to him that he might want to get to a hiding place, but he didn't know any, and he couldn't leave Valix behind. So he waited, straining for some sign through the darkness, some motion of air across his whiskers or some flicker in the gloom, a scent carried through the fetid breeze. All the while, he kept his paw by Valix's muzzle, clinging to the reassuring warmth of her breath.

He smelled them before he saw or heard them, sharp musk cutting through the sewer smell. "Help!" he called again, but crouched at the ready anyway, in case they shot on sight. The first fox to penetrate the circle of light held a crossbow at the ready, but he didn't fire it. He was dressed in the guards' familiar grey uniform with green trim on the shoulders and a crest on the chest.

"Who are you? What are you doing down here?" he demanded in a whisper. Another joined him, wielding a sword, and another. The third one went on down the tunnel while the first two remained behind.

"She's injured," Sinch said. "We need to get her to help, fast."

"What are you doing here?" the fox demanded again.

"Please!" Sinch said. "They stabbed her. Please help."

The two foxes looked at each other uncertainly. The second whispered something to the first that Sinch couldn't hear. The first nodded. "I know, but the captain said he didn't want anything living left behind."

"We can't just shoot them," the second said. "They're not..."

They both stared at Sinch and Valix. "Get the captain," the first said finally.

"I don't know where he is." They were still whispering, hissing at each other. "I hate this place."

"I can get us to an exit," Sinch said. "Just please hurry."

The foxes exchanged looks again. "We'll get you to the nearest exit," the second one said. "But you carry her. Back this way."

While Sinch was trying to gather Valix up in his arms, the two soldiers held a hurried conference that resulted in the sword wielder leading the way while the other walked behind Sinch, crossbow held high. Sinch knew he should feel reassured at having been rescued, but he kept hearing Whisper's confident assertion that "no fox is friend to a mouse," and couldn't stop looking behind him at the fox with the crossbow.

Their progress was considerably slower and rougher than it had been with the mice as their captors. Sinch slipped more than once, his balance much more difficult with Valix's weight to account for. Even so, he felt he had the beginnings of understanding about how to navigate the tunnels.

The foxes did not. They kept stopping to check the walls; only the fourth time did Sinch realize that they were checking scent marks on the walls. Clever, he thought, and something the mice wouldn't be able to comprehend or use. After that, though their progress was slow, he trusted the foxes to lead him and focused on not dropping Valix.

Several times they passed below grates, but the foxes didn't stop. Sinch briefly thought he might suggest leaving via one of them, but he wouldn't be able to scale the wall with Valix in his arms, and the foxes weremoving more confidently now. Indeed, after several twists and turns, they came out into a tunnel that was at least twenty feet wide, and the scent of foxes in clean, open air overwhelmed him.

The tunnel was full of soldiers, coming and going, all in the same grey and green uniforms. Besides the tunnel they were emerging from, at least three more led away from the wide space, but most of the comings and goings were to the large exit at the far end. Though soldiers were posted at the entrances to each smaller tunnel, they did not appear particularly tense; the two Sinch passed laughed and jeered at him, unsheathed swords hanging loosely in their paws.

He stumbled forward, whiskers twitching as he raised his head to get a better sense of the space. As a result, he nearly tripped over a pile of dead black mice, four or five of them. He pulled Valix more tightly to his chest and followed close behind the soldier who'd found them, who was moving quickly now, scanning the crowd ahead.

The fox's ears perked up and he raised a paw, hurrying so that Sinch almost had to run to keep up. "Captain!"

A tall fox with grey at the tips of his ears turned. "Dellis," he said, and then his gaze sharpened as he caught sight of Sinch. "What's this?"

"Prisoners," Dellis panted. "We found them in the tunnel. It looks like they—the Shadows—caught them."

"Please," Sinch said. "She's hurt very badly."

The captain shrugged. "We have casualties of our own," he said, and only then did Sinch notice that the foxes leaving the tunnel were carrying stretchers between them. "What were you doing in the sewers?"

"She might die," Sinch said. He couldn't stop staring at the growing patch of red on her back. The smell of fox was stronger than the scent of blood, but he could tell it would not be for long.

The captain's muzzle twisted. He looked away. "You can take her back to the Warren, but leave your name and where we can find you. We'll want you to come back tomorrow to report on any information you have about the Shadows."

"We won't make it back to the Warren!" Sinch cried. "Please, you have to—you can't just—" He heard Whisper's voice again, and his words died in his throat.

"You don't think we'll waste our own chirurgeon's time on a mouse, do you?" The captain waved a paw. "Dellis, escort them out."

"Yes, sir." Dellis gestured with his head for Sinch to follow him.

"Where's Yilon?" Sinch said desperately.

He stepped into a room full of foxes.

The captain's muzzle snapped back to face him. "What business is it of yours?"

"He's my..." Sinch swallowed the word 'friend.' "He's my lord too. I...I demand you take me to him."

"You...demand?" The captain's smile showed his sharp canines. He leaned down until his nose was almost touching Sinch's. "Do you, now?"

If it hadn't been for the weight of Valix in his arms, Sinch would have backed away. "If he won't see me, then I'll...I'll go quietly. Otherwise I'm going to start shouting for him."

"You make a sound and we'll run you through," the captain snarled. "Then your friend won't get any help, will she?"

"No," Sinch said, and now he remembered Maxon's words, about another dead mouse to explain. "You don't have to take me to him. Just tell me where he is. Is he here?"

The captain shook his head, straightening up. "I've better things to be concerned with," he said. "You're not worth dirtying my sword over. He's here, just outside the entrance there. Go, before I change my mind."

"Should I escort them, sir?" Dellis asked.

"Don't waste your time. Get back in that tunnel!" The captain turned and barked orders at another nearby fox, dismissing both Sinch and Dellis, who looked not at all happy with that turn of events.

Sinch hurried forward, dodging soldiers, stumbling over the floor. He emerged into a wide ditch with dirt walls, though the ground beneath his feet remained stone. The ditch itself looked deserted, but as he cast from side to side, he sensed the huge mass of a building looming over him to his right, and he turned in time to see the stairs leading up to it.

His arms ached, and the stairs were built for foxes, so by the time he reached the top, he had to lean against the door frame to catch his breath. Valix stirred, giving a low moan that filled Sinch with a sense of urgency. He shouldered past the heavy curtain, into a small anteroom that his whiskers told him was barely ten feet across. The glow of firelight around the curtain at the other end obscured the rest of the room. Taking a breath, he pushed through that curtain as well.

For the second time that night, he stepped into a room full of foxes. Where the tunnel had been filled with soldiers, the lobby of this building had been transformed into a sort of makeshift military headquarters. The only foxes in guards' uniforms were posted immediately inside the entrance, two raising their swords at him as soon as he entered, while two more stood to either side with crossbows leveled in his direction. The rest of the foxes wore decorated tunics and robes, and overall smelled much cleaner.

"State your business!" one of the sword-bearers barked.

Sinch looked around the room for Yilon. To his left, under a sign reading "Dewanne Sewer Authority," three large braziers cast a flickering light over the room. Opposite them, along the right wall, three groups of foxes conferred, the nearer two groups all standing, the third seated around a table. He didn't see Yilon at first glance in any of them.

The fox nearest him jabbed his sword at Sinch. "I said, state your business," he said, louder. The nearest group of foxes turned, ears perked curiously.

"I need to see Yilon," Sinch said. "I need...she's hurt, she's dying." He tried to lift Valix toward the foxes, but his arms were too weak.

One of the foxes in the nearest group wore a green vest. He coughed as he turned, and as he and Sinch recognized each other, a smile grew across his muzzle. "Soldier!" Maxon said, limping in their direction. "I'll take care of this."

"No!" Sinch stepped back, toward the curtain. "Yilon!" he called.

"The lord-in-waiting is not here," Maxon said. "Why don't we step outside and I'll make sure your friend gets the treatment she *requires*."

Sinch dodged around him, or tried to. He slipped on the slick marble floor, his legs flying out from under him. Valix landed on his stomach, and the black dagger he'd gotten from the Shadows clattered across the floor.

Maxon kicked it away, eyes, glittering, and reached down. He cleared his throat. "Soldier, help me escort these intruders outside."

All the foxes had turned to look at Sinch now. At the far end of the hall, he spotted a white tunic rising from the far side of the table. Relief flooded him at the sight of the familiar muzzle, a relief so strong he nearly collapsed from the lifting of the weight on him. "Yilon!" he called. "Yilon!"

His friend stepped around the table. Maxon moved to block his view. "Outside, now!" he hissed.

Sinch didn't move. Maxon growled an oath and turned, his ears folding down when he saw Yilon walking in their direction. "Oh," he said, in a much smoother tone, "the lord is here. I had thought he'd left."

"You don't fool me," Sinch said in a voice pitched only for the steward's ears. "I know you."

"So you may think," Maxon said, "but your friend the lord needs my help to rule. So I would advise you to keep your thoughts to yourself." He stepped aside.

Yilon stopped some ten feet away. He looked at Valix, then at his friend. "Sinch?"

Chapter 15: Secrets Revealed

Sinch looked terrible. Covered in grime, clothes torn, eyes wide, and shivering, though the room was warm. But as bad as he looked, the mouse huddled next to him on the floor looked worse. She smelled of blood, though Yilon couldn't see where she was hurt. Her breathing came in quick, shallow pants, and though her eyes were closed, her eyelids fluttered in the firelight. He couldn't tell whether she was as grimy as Sinch, because her clothing was the same greyish-brown as the dirt that encrusted it.

But despite all that, Sinch's smile and bright eyes were unmistakable. "Yilon," he said. "You're here."

Yilon padded closer, dropping to one knee beside him. "I'm here," he said. "What...what in Canis's name happened to you?"

Sinch shook his head, pointing at his companion. "Later," he said. "We have to get her help."

"I don't know." Yilon touched her shoulder. "She might be beyond help."

"No!" Sinch lurched upright. The nearest soldier barked out a warning, jumping between them, but Yilon brushed him aside. The soldier looked mutinous for a moment, until Yilon glared at him. He lowered his ears and stepped back.

"Min!" he called, raising a paw. To Sinch, he said, "I know where there's a nurse nearby. We'll take her there. If there's anything he can do..."

Sinch's eyes glistened. "I knew," he said, and then just reached a paw out. Yilon held it and squeezed.

Min hurried up behind him. He stopped dead behind Yilon. "What... er, is this your lordship's friend?" He dropped his voice to a whisper for the last word.

In public, and especially in front of soldiers, it was best that Min keep using the honorific. Yilon indicated the other mouse. "We need to get this one out of here," he said.

"She has information about the Shadows," Sinch said.

Yilon stared at him. He started to ask what Sinch had been doing in the last day, that he'd been covered in grime and had acquired a companion who had been grievously wounded, and now appeared to have information about the Shadows. "We're taking care of the Shadows," he said. "But we will take her. Min, can you carry her?"

"I...yes. My lord." The fox knelt and gathered the mouse into his arms with a gentleness that belied his clipped tone. His expression softened. "Where are we going?"

Sinch scrambled to his feet. The soldiers around them drew back, staring at Min and Yilon, confusion in their eyes and flattened ears. Maxon, at their fore, said, "My lord...this is a mouse."

"I am aware of that," Yilon said coldly.

Maxon drew him to the side. "If you ever hope to lead these soldiers, you will not abandon this battle for the sake of a mouse. The wounded one—you don't even know it."

Yilon swept the soldiers with his eyes. None looked back. "I have to do this," he said loudly. "We can and will punish those who have done us wrong. But she is no Shadow."

He returned to Min's side. Maxon followed. "Your safety..."

"Is not in question. Thank you," Yilon said. "I will have Min with me, and I trust my life to him." Min looked startled, then beamed in pleasure. Behind Maxon, the soldiers' ears rose, slowly. They knew Min, and trusted him. "Come, follow me. Maxon, I will return soon."

They descended the stairs and turned away from the sewer. Yilon thanked Canis silently for the moon that night. He wasn't familiar enough with Dewanne to know his way without landmarks, but he now knew the hill, and he could make his way there along the wider streets until he found the one he knew. Sinch remained a few paces behind him; his breathing was labored and he was limping, but he did not complain.

"You could've been killed," Yilon said, when he couldn't hold it in any longer. Sinch didn't respond. Bloody memories from that day stained Yilon's thoughts. "The Shadows don't just fight foxes. They've killed mice, too. Left bodies in the streets for the guards to find."

"I know." Sinch's small voice made Yilon regret his tone immediately. He wanted to ask what Sinch was doing down there, but Min's presence kept the question down. Instead, he asked Min about his second most pressing concern. "I thought the soldiers were starting to trust me," he said. "Was this a mistake?"

Min hesitated. "It might have been," he said. "But your—you spoke from your heart and you spoke to them directly. They will respect that. I believe that they will give you another chance."

"As long as Maxon isn't poisoning them against me."

"He has not spoken against you in my presence," Min said.

Sinch spoke up, his breathing labored. "He's clever enough not to."

"That's true," Yilon said. "I don't trust him. He's got some other motive and I don't know what it is. He was..." He hesitated. Min was watching him attentively as they walked. He trusted Min, though, didn't he? "I followed him to a house on the east side, where I was attacked. Later, he denied being there."

Min's eyes narrowed. "I have not been listening closely. From now on, I will."

They rounded a corner, and there was the door and the building. Yilon ran up and pounded on the door. "Colian!" he called. "Colian, please, we need your help!"

The street remained silent. Yilon pounded on the door again. Sinch and Min stood behind him, their postures tense. Yilon had just raised his fist to strike the door a third time when it cracked open. He saw through the narrow gap, not Colian, but the vixen who'd rescued him.

Her fur was all unkempt, but her ears were perked straight up and she was frowning. "What do you mean, calling on Colian—*you*?" The door slammed abruptly.

Yilon recovered his composure quickly. He struck the door and yelled, "We need help! We have a wounded..." He had learned enough to avoid the word "mouse." "She's going to die!" he yelled.

Behind him, he heard a voice call, "Keep it down. Some folks want to sleep!"

He could sense her behind the door. He raised his arm to knock again, but Sinch reached up to stop him. He put his muzzle to the door. "Please," he said. "Have mercy."

Yilon heard a slow sigh. They remained perfectly still, as though the least movement might tip her decision in the wrong direction. Her claws scratched the other side of the door in a slow, pensive rhythm, and finally, it opened.

"Come in," she hissed. "Colian's on the second floor. Just...just go."

Yilon bowed to her and pointed out the stairs to the others. The vixen shut the door behind them and stood with her back to it, watching. She wore nothing but a nightshirt, which was at least more feminine than the jerkin and pants, and her eyes still bore the crust of sleep about them. But there was a grace and beauty to her, even in this rumpled state, that made Yilon pause. He couldn't reconcile this picture of her with the vixen who'd coldly stabbed a fox in the throat.

"Our very great thanks to you," he said. "I hope we will not be disturbing you for very long."

She shook her head. "I knew I shouldn't have helped you."

He frowned. "I...but you saved my life."

"Yes, I had to do that, I know. But I could have just knocked him out and left." Now she looked annoyed. "If you weren't so helpless..."

"He took me by surprise," Yilon said.

"Even a cub learns to defend himself. You don't even carry a knife. What kind of noble goes through life not learning any fighting skills?"

"I shoot a short bow," he said hotly. "Very well, in fact."

She yawned. "That's wonderful. When you can fit a short bow in a pouch at your waist, I will be impressed." She glanced at his crotch. "Other than the one you've already got. But I'm guessing that doesn't shoot as far."

"Better than throwing rocks," he retorted. "And you didn't carry a knife either. You had to..." He fell silent. She looked down at her paws, then folded her arms and just stared at the floor.

"Anyway," he said, by way of apology, "I guess it doesn't apply to you, right? You're not a noble, so even throwing rocks is pretty impressive. You knocked him right out, too."

"Hah," she said, and then scorn gave way to disbelief. "Wait. You..."

"You did." He tried as hard as he could to be complimentary. "I mean, I've thrown rocks before, but never got...I never could...what?"

She'd started to laugh, a high, clear sound that echoed in the dark stillness of the building's tall lobby. Her shoulders relaxed back against the door, and she clutched her sides. "Hoo hoo hoo! You really don't know! How could you not? Did you..." Her laughter subsided to a chuckle. "Did you not tell anyone about our little misadventure?"

"I told people," he said. "I told Corwin, but then he got shot."

Her smile vanished as though cut. "What? Corwin's shot? Is he...?"

"I don't know." Yilon spread his paws. "They took him to a chirurgeon. The last I heard, he was still alive, but he wasn't awake."

"Who shot him?"

"I don't know. They say the Shadows did, that's why we were there tonight..." His voice trailed off, realizing he probably shouldn't be sharing military secrets, but then, it wasn't really a secret, not now. "But he said "not Shadows" right before he collapsed."

"How was he shot?" She'd stepped toward him, her eyes intense.

"We were just outside a pub," he said. "In fact, I was just talking about..."

She brushed his story aside. "What was he shot with?"

"Oh. Crossbow quarrel. You can tell because they're thicker and heavier than a shortbow arrow, but shorter than a longbow—"

"He's right." She rubbed her muzzle, turning away. "But what if the Shadows used a captured crossbow to make it look like it wasn't them?"

"That's what Maxon said, too." Yilon felt he was losing his status in the conversation. "But how do you know Corwin?"

The vixen shot him a scornful look. "He's my Pack-father," she said. "Didn't he ever talk about me?"

"He might have," Yilon said. "It's hard to say without knowing your name."

She sniffed. "I can't believe you haven't figured it out. I'm Dinah."

Chapter 16: Sinch in Despair

By the time Sinch and Min got to the second floor, a short, slim fox had emerged into the small hallway. He was pushing his arms into a tunic that was the only piece of clothing he wore, but he'd clearly taken in the situation. "In there," he said, gesturing to the door nearest them. "There's a mat."

Sinch opened the door into a tiny, musty room. To the left, a low sleeping-mat sat against the wall. Under the window, a worn leather case and a pile of cotton rags sat on a set of shelves. While Min set Valix down on the mat, the fox walked to the shelves. He handed Sinch two of the cotton rags.

"Get her clothes off. It's a wound, right? She's not vomiting blood? I definitely smell blood." His nose wrinkled.

Sinch shook his head. "She was stabbed. In the back."

"Good. Take those, press them to the wound to staunch the bleeding. I'll take a look. Not sure how much else there will be for us to do except make her comfortable." He sighed. "I'm not a chirurgeon," he said, almost under his breath.

"Will we need one?" Sinch knelt beside Valix, working at her clothes.

The nurse talked over Sinch's head, to Min. "I'll know more in a few minutes. There's one a few blocks from here. I don't know if we can wake him up."

"If he is needed, I'll go," Min said.

The room was quiet except for the sound of Valix's clothes tearing as Sinch tried to get them off quickly. Light flared from a candle, and then the nurse knelt beside Sinch and said, "Very well. Let me have a look." He handed Sinch the candle, lifting the now-red cotton from the wound. "Hold it there. Don't let the wax drip."

Sinch held the candle as steadily as he could while the fox examined Valix's bare back. He pushed the fur aside gently, directing Sinch to bring the candle closer. Valix moaned as the fox probed at the wound.

"Your fingers are clean, right?" Sinch said nervously.

The fox looked at him briefly, then turned back to the wound. "Move it over here. Careful with the wax."

Sinch held the candle almost directly over the fox's head as he peered down into the wound. The nurse probed with his claws, sniffed them, watched the flow of blood for another moment, then replaced the cotton rag and took the candle. "Hold that there," he instructed, as he stood.

"Will we need the chirurgeon?" Sinch asked, his voice shaking.

"He wouldn't get here in time." The fox's voice was tired.

Sinch's heart pounded. He curled his tail more tightly around his legs. "So she's..." His voice broke into a squeak. He pressed on the cotton cloth.

"Maybe." The fox brought a small pot out that smelled strongly of pennyroyal. "Let me rub this on the wound. Then...if she makes it through the night..."

Sinch didn't ask him to finish. He lifted the cotton and let the fox's fingers spread salve on the wound and fur below. He felt like the bleeding had subsided, and when the fox gave him a clean cotton rag to press to it, he thought the red didn't spread as quickly as it had.

"I'll bring some water," the nurse said. "If she wakes, she'll be thirsty. You'll be thirsty too."

He left Min and Sinch alone in the room. Min began to move toward the door, and Sinch realized that he didn't want to be left alone. More, he ached to tell Yilon what he'd been going through, to have the fox put his arms around him and tell him he'd be okay, that they would be eating together and practicing together and exploring the streets of Dewanne just as they had in Divalia, or even that they would be returning to Divalia together any day now. He wanted to hear about life in the palace, how Yilon had come to know where a nurse lived, and who was the vixen who'd welcomed them in, and how he had come to be at the sewer with the soldiers sent in to kill the Shadows. Most of all, he wanted to lie down in bed and press up against the fox, feeling the rise and fall of his breathing, the warm pulse of his sheath, the strength in his casual embrace.

"Please," Sinch said as Min reached the door. "Can you...can you hold this? Just for a moment. I need..."

Min stopped, then nodded. "I need to go too, but I can wait. Go ahead."

He knelt beside Valix and held the cotton rag in place. Sinch stood, giving him a downward perspective on the fox's ears and muzzle. It was so much like looking at Yilon, in the dim light, and yet the scent was so different, that his head spun. He shook it to regain his composure. "Thank you," he said, bowing clumsily, and left the room.

At the top of the stairs, he paused. Yilon and the vixen were still talking, below, and it sounded rather spirited. He crept down one stair, then paused, torn between courtesy and need. He took one more step down, and then the vixen's voice saying, "marriage" stopped him dead.

The silence following it seemed to last for hours. Yilon said, "Of course I want to marry you."

Sinch retreated up the stairs and leaned against the wall. Their voices faded back to murmurs. His heart pounded against his ribcage. Yilon was getting married. No doubt that vixen was a noble vixen, the marriage arranged for the throne of Dewanne. He wasn't going to have time for Sinch, not to explore Dewanne, not to return to Divalia, not once he got married.

Don't be silly, his mind told him. He wouldn't just abandon you like that. But his heart was talking louder. The stress of the day, from the theft in the morning to the running around the Warren to being captured by Maxon to being captured by the Shadows...he'd only been in Dewanne one day, and already he'd made many more enemies than friends, and deadly enemies to boot. And the only people he could even remotely count as his friends were planning marriages to strange vixens, and dying in the room down the hall.

The air felt suffocatingly warm. He smelled the nurse again, moments before the fox emerged from an open doorway at the other end of the hall. He bore a ceramic pitcher in both paws, walking carefully with it, and he stopped when he saw Sinch. "Are you all right?" he said, and held out the pitcher. "Here, drink."

By reflex, Sinch took it. The nurse tipped the pitcher toward his muzzle, enough for Sinch to lap at the water. It was cool and fresh, and to his surprise, it did actually make him feel better. The nurse was looking at him with concern. "You were with her when she got stabbed?" Sinch nodded. "And you weren't hurt? You aren't the one who stabbed her, are you?"

"No!" Sinch jerked back against the wall. Water splashed on the floor.

"Okay, easy, easy." For the first time, Sinch saw him smile. "Listen, you did great, you know? Got her here all the way from...somewhere, and she's not gone yet. She's got a chance, and it's because of you."

"Because of Yilon," Sinch mumbled. "He brought us here."

The nurse didn't respond. When Sinch looked up, he met sympathetic eyes. "Why don't we go back in there with her, and you can tell me what happened. Maybe it'll help me figure out how to treat her."

Sinch followed him back into the room, where he took over holding the cloth for Min. The nurse opened the window and then sat cross-legged on the floor beside him. "My name's Colian," he said.

"I thought it might be, after Yilon was yelling it. I'm Sinch." His breathing came more easily. The breeze in the room definitely helped. "I came here with Yilon from Divalia. We were best friends there."

"Ahh." Colian's ears flicked. "That explains it. How long have you known each other?"

"Two years." Sinch rested his other paw on Valix's shoulder. It reassured him to feel the warmth. "He came to Divalia then. I was a castle crow, and he was new in town. I showed him the city, and he got me into the castle."

Colian nodded, his eyes soft gleams in the darkness. Sinch went on. "He's the heir of Dewanne. I don't know if you know that. But he is. So we came out here, with the steward who hates me, but I think he just hates all mice. And they wouldn't let me in the palace, so I went to the Warren. That's where I met Valix."

"And where did she get stabbed?"

"In the sewer. By the Shadows." Sinch groped for a way to get a handle on his story. "Maxon—the steward—chased us there. I was trying to get back to the palace to see Yilon, and he caught us there." He told Colian about Maxon throwing Valix against the wall, carrying her through Dewanne, and their escape, omitting both the reason Maxon was holding them and the knife he'd thrown at the steward.

"You've had quite a day," Colian said. His quiet assurance reminded Sinch of Yilon. "I've lived here my whole life and I don't think I know anyone who's been chased from the castle into the sewer and had a friend stabbed on their first day. Trust me, Dewanne has much to offer that is quite enjoyable, as opposed to the experiences you have unfortunately had. The Shadows normally don't trouble us, I can assure you, not unless you've done something to upset them, which it's rather difficult to do unless you're trying, and most of us are rather more well-brought-up than to try."

Sinch felt the knot in his chest loosen further. He managed at least an attempt at a smile. Colian's return smile reminded him of Yilon's. "It's been a weird day," he admitted.

"Sounds like it," Yilon said behind him.

Chapter 17: A Question of Trust

Yilon gaped at the vixen. "*You're* Dinah? But you're supposed to have been kidnapped! You went missing..."

"And here I am." She gestured to the open space above them. "Everyone thinks I'm either in some hideous part of town or run away to the countryside, I'm sure, unless they believed that ridiculous ransom note. At least, nobody has thought to look here. Sometimes I'm not even sure my family remembers we own this building."

Yilon pressed his fingers to his forehead. "You're not at all like I pictured you."

"You weren't picturing me in my nightshirt?"

"No," he said. "More like...in a nice parlor, with all your relatives standing around making me uncomfortable." If he blocked out the nightshirt, and just focused on her muzzle, he could construct that picture still. She had a confident, easy bearing, and now that he knew to look for it, even in the dim light, he could see the care that had been taken with her grooming. Nevertheless, she couldn't have been more different from the noble vixens he'd known in Divalia.

"That's what I ran away from," she said. "Mostly. But also...you."

"Me? I only just got here." He shifted his weight back and forth. "And if you were running away, why were you following me?"

She made an exasperated "tchah," and rolled her eyes. "I've been promised to the new lord ever since I was twelve. I wasn't running from you, I was running from him. Who turned out to be you."

"That still doesn't explain why you were in the alley."

"I was curious," she snapped. "I don't like running. Only I didn't really have much choice, you see? If I were here to greet you, you'd know who I was, and then there'd be all this planning and promising and ladies-in-waiting and dresses more complicated than a Delford puzzle-box..." She sighed. "And now you know me, you'll be telling everyone where I am. It'll start anyway, all these preparations leading up to marriage. If you want."

She was looking at him with an uncertain look, afraid of rejection, no doubt. Yilon said, stiffly, "Of course I want to marry you."

"You don't seem very excited about it, is all," she said. "You haven't been ogling me in my nightshirt."

"I wondered why you weren't going in to change."

"It's because you weren't ogling me." She straightened the nightshirt, pulling it over certain curves deliberately. Yilon tried his best to look interested. "But I should change. I want to go see Corwin."

"I'll go with you," Yilon said. "But I need to check on my friend."

"Yes, who was the injured mouse?"

He looked up toward the second floor. "I don't know. But she's important to my friend."

"Your friend...the fox? Or the other mouse."

"The other mouse." He told her about Sinch, quietly and succinctly, about their arrival from Divalia and his being barred from the castle. Her expression changed from interest to respect as he concluded his story with Sinch's arrival at the sewer building.

"Friends with a mouse," she said, and then walked past him, tail swaying. "That should get people upset at you."

"It has already." Yilon saw Maxon's furious expression again. "But I don't care. Anyway, it won't matter too much longer anyway."

She shot a curious look over her shoulder, but only said, "I'll be changed in a short time. It's so much easier without maidservants."

He watched her walk through the door at the back of the lobby, and then started up the stairs himself. As he turned into the hallway, he heard Sinch's voice talking about what had happened to him that day. He leaned quietly against the door to listen. As Sinch talked, Yilon's heart ached for him, and he felt a cold anger at Maxon. After the steward had convinced him that he was acting in the country's best interests, to hear about his brutal behavior toward the mice was like a cold slap in the face. At the same time, he couldn't escape the ultimate blame for Sinch's predicament. He was the one who'd convinced the mouse to come to Dewanne. He was responsible for him.

Colian's eyes flicked up, so he knew the nurse had seen him, and he'd assumed Sinch would have smelled him, but the mouse's start when he spoke told otherwise. Sinch started to get up, then remembered he was holding a cloth to the other mouse's wound and sat back down. For some reason, he was reluctant to meet Yilon's eyes.

Yilon stepped into the room. "What's her name?"

"Valix," Sinch said, and then he twitched, as if he'd done something wrong. "I met her in the Warren."

Yilon wondered if she'd been one of the mice at the cart that morning, but he'd not gotten a good enough scent then to remember it now. He yawned. "Dinah wants to go see Corwin," he said. "I thought I would accompany her."

"Aren't you tired?" Sinch asked.

Yilon shook his head. "I napped before going down to the sewer. Velkan thought we might be up all night with the operation, and it was important that we be alert. But if you need to rest, wait here, and I'll come back for you."

"You don't have to," Sinch mumbled.

"Do you have a place in the Warren? Somewhere I could meet you?"

Colian perked his ears at that. "Oh, sir," he said, "I would strongly advise against your planning any kind of expedition into the Warren. The sewers are one thing, technically they are owned by the city, you know, but the Warren is another matter altogether. For a fox to enter the Warren is a declaration either of war or of suicide."

To Yilon's surprise, Sinch nodded. "I'll wait here," he said, sounding very tired.

"Oh. I thought you might come along."

The mouse shook his head slowly. "I'll be here," he said. "You go ahead."

Yilon shifted from one hind paw to the other. "Can I...can I talk to you, then? Before we leave?"

Sinch raised his head, facing Colian, who nodded and reached out to take the cloth. "The top floor room is empty," the fox said.

"Thank you." Yilon raised a paw as Sinch rose slowly to his feet. He led the way up the stairs to the bedroom where he'd lain not twelve hours before. It was dark, but he could see just enough to find the window. When he opened it, moonlight flooded into the room. He breathed in the fresh night air and then turned to Sinch, who was still wringing his paws in the doorway.

"Are you all right?" Yilon said. Sinch nodded, but didn't look at him. Yilon crossed the room and put his paws on Sinch's shoulders. "Are you really?"

Sinch pressed against him, trembling, head pressed into his shoulder. "I miss you," he sniffled. "I hate it here."

Yilon wrapped him in a hug and pulled him gently back into the room. He wanted to say, "It'll get better." He wanted to say, "I'll take care of you." He wanted to say, "Let's go home." Instead, he said, "It's been hard for me too. We just need a little time."

"Can you sneak me into the castle? Just to spend the nights. I'll walk around during the day. I just can't...I can't stay there at night."

Yilon stroked Sinch's ears. "I'll...I'll do what I can," he said. "I'll tell you one thing: I'm going to get rid of Maxon as soon as I can. How he treated you...I should have listened to my instincts back at the inn. He's no good."

"He's just like all the other foxes," Sinch said, dully. "Except you."

"I'll change things." Yilon wished he felt as much confidence as he was trying to project. "I just need time."

"Yesterday, you wanted to leave," Sinch said. "Now you want to stay and change things again. And you're going to—" He stopped and pulled away from Yilon, crossing his arms and leaning against the bed.

"What's the matter?"

"Nothing," Sinch said, but even as Yilon opened his muzzle to tell him that he knew that was a lie, the mouse sighed. "You're going to marry that vixen."

"Dinah? No, we're...we're supposed to get married, but I don't think she's very interested either."

"But you're going to because you have to," Sinch said. "And you know you have to."

Yilon couldn't think of anything to respond with. He looked out the window at the ghostly landscape of rooftops. The city seemed unreal to him, as if this were Sinch's old room upstairs from his mother's house and the window just a painting he'd hung there. If not for the smell wafting in from the city, he might almost be able to convince himself of that.

"It's all right," Sinch said quietly. "You do have to. I didn't mean what I said. I'll stay here with you."

"I wanted to go back home," Yilon whispered, conscious of the people downstairs. "I thought the plan would work. But they...things are bad here, and they need someone. There's all kinds of crime going on—robberies, murders—if I don't step in, it could get a lot worse."

"Does it have to be you?"

"Maybe I can leave it to Dinah, I don't know, but it's not going to be easy."

Sinch matched his whisper. "So you need the crown back."

Yilon nodded. "It's caused too many problems. That whole raid on the sewer—" He grimaced.

A commotion from the second floor interrupted them. Colian and Min appeared to be arguing. As Yilon stopped to listen, ears turning back toward the door, the argument died down. A moment later they heard the click of claws on the stairs. He and Sinch faced the door, as Min appeared in the doorway. He held something in one paw, which gleamed as he stepped into the room and brought it from his shadow up into the moonlight. "Do either of you recognize this?"

Sinch gasped a moment before Yilon did. Min was holding his knife.

"Where did you get that?" Yilon said.

"It was thrown into the second floor window." Min held it by the handle, loosely, as though it were filthy. And perhaps it was; Yilon could smell grime from a few feet away. "What is it?"

"It's a message," Sinch said hoarsely. He reached out for it. "They're through with me."

"It looks like a threat." Min handed the knife to him gingerly.

"Maybe." Sinch cleaned it on his trousers as best he could and then stuck it back into his belt.

Yilon shook his head. "You mean they found the knife where Maxon threw it away...and followed you here and saw you through the window and threw the knife in after you?" He spun toward the open window, and in a moment had crossed the room and closed it, plunging the room into darkness. "They're out there watching us, aren't they?"

"If they had wanted to kill one of us, they would have," Min said. "Assuming we are talking about the Shadows. If they want revenge for tonight, it is not with myself or Colian." He paused. "But they will want revenge. They exact their own justice. So do we, when there is no lord to mediate our fights."

"They wanted me to join them," Sinch said in a whisper. He turned the knife over in his paws, staring at it.

The revelation shocked Yilon even before he saw Min's horrified expression. "They what?"

Sinch snapped his head up, looked at both the foxes, and shrank back. "I didn't!" he said. "I didn't ask...Valix took me there. They saw me throw this and told me I should join them, but I couldn't, I couldn't." He held Yilon's gaze. "I just couldn't."

"We shouldn't stay here." Min was also staring at Yilon, eyes gleaming in the dim room. "If the Shadows are watching, we're in danger."

"You're not in danger," Sinch said. "They don't want you. They want her. Or me."

Yilon put a paw to his eyes, trying to think more clearly. "How could they want you? You've only been here a day."

"They tried to kill her for...for something, I don't know what. I was protecting her."

You just met her, Yilon wanted to say, but looking back on his own day, it seemed weeks ago that he and Sinch were lying in his bed in the castle, let alone in the inns on the way to Dewanne. "You should come with me and Dinah. You could be in danger here."

Sinch shook his head. "I'd just make more trouble for you. I'm safe here."

"You're not safe," Yilon protested, and then, his eyes adjusting to the darkness, saw Min signaling discreetly to him. He looked at the closed window, then at the door, the real wooden door. "All right. Stay here, but don't go near open windows. I'll make sure Colian doesn't let anyone in." He took two steps toward the mouse, but the scent of blood stopped him. It was not fresh; it took him a moment to realize that it must be coming from the knife. He also heard Min's breathing, and became uncomfortably aware of the fox watching him. So he put one paw on Sinch's shoulder. "I'll be back. I promise. Just wait here."

"Okay." Sinch's voice sounded very small, very resigned. Yilon had to stop himself from hugging the mouse again, in front of Min. There'll be time for that when I get back, he told himself. Part of him wanted to stay with Sinch, but part of him also needed to check on Corwin. Besides that, his dream of returning to Divalia, so easily faded by the events of the day, had gained strength after meeting Sinch and the clearly competent Dinah. If he spent more time with her, perhaps he could convince her to assume the lordship, leaving him free to go.

For that, he would need the crown, and for the crown, he would need Sinch. But Sinch wasn't in any shape to go get it right now, and it didn't look like he would leave the other mouse even if he were. He might, if Yilon asked. But that was precisely why Yilon did not want to ask. They were in a new, strange place, and the new bonds they made here would be important to their well-being, if they weren't able to return. So he just patted Sinch's shoulder and repeated, "I'll be back."

On the stairs, Min said softly, "I don't know whether you noticed, but he was almost falling asleep on his feet. Best to let him get rest. If he keeps the windows closed...if the Shadows have delivered their message and have no further interest in him...then he should be safe for your return."

Yilon nodded, wondering why he hadn't noticed Sinch's fatigue. "Will you stay here, too? I don't think we'll be gone long—an hour perhaps."

"If you wish me to stay, I will stay."

They'd reached the second floor. Yilon nodded. "Please do."

Min turned to face him on the second floor landing. "Be careful, sir," he said. "Dewanne at night is not always the safest of places."

Yilon nodded toward the ground floor. "I'll be with Dinah," he said. "She's got a sling."

"Indeed. That's why I am not arguing to accompany you." Despite Min's smile, his ears were low and his eyes half-lidded. Yilon realized there was probably another reason Min wasn't arguing to come along.

"Get some rest," he said. "I'll come find you when I get back."

Dinah was waiting by the door, dressed in the same clothes he'd first seen her in: the brown jerkin and trews. At least, they appeared to be the same, but there was no trace of blood on them that he could smell when he got closer. If she were wearing the necklace, it was hidden inside the jerkin. She watched him descend. "Not bringing your shortbow?"

He reached the bottom of the stairs and lifted an eyebrow. "Am I going to need it?"

She shrugged. "You never know. There might be some bad people a hundred feet away."

"I'll take that chance." He gestured to the door. "After you."

He let her lead, although he was pretty sure he could find his way at least back to the plaza. From there, Maxon had told him the way to the chirurgeon's business; Corwin would be there until he could be moved, and then—if that happened—he would be taken home. But they didn't know when that would be. Yilon wasn't sure the chirurgeon would be awake at this hour, but Dinah said they would have a nurse tending to him night and day.

"Which reminds me," Yilon said, frowning, "why do you have Colian with you? Does he tend to you?"

"He's been with me since I was eight," she replied. "I broke my arm twice, and my parents decided that if I were going to have a personal servant, it might as well be a trained nurse."

It was odd, Yilon thought, that her parents would provide a male nurse for a female cub, but perhaps he'd been the only one available. Dewanne was not a large city; unlike Divalia, he supposed there might not be enough nurses for every position, let alone one suited to be a personal escort for a headstrong cub. "He's a good nurse."

"Of course he is," she scoffed. "My parents wouldn't get just any nurse. Corwin recommended him. He's good with wormwood." She drew out the last word sarcastically.

"Is that something young vixens need?" Yilon said, the word reminding him of Madame Colet's whispered request to Corwin in the tailor's shop.

Dinah snorted. "Most of them, around here." She turned around the edge of town toward the back of the castle.

"I thought the plaza was that way," he said, pointing back toward Market Street.

"If you want to walk along the more trafficked streets, it is." She didn't wait to see whether he was following her. After a moment, he did.

They were certainly conspicuous, nearly alone on the moonlit street. Yilon read the signs on the storefronts they passed: Royal Apothecary, Fur Trim and Restoration, Metallurge. The stores boasted more glass on the fronts, and the few that did not have wooden doors sported elaborately patterned curtains. Leaning closer to examine the repeating fox pattern on one he particularly liked, he noticed metal bars behind it.

"Why don't more people have metal doors?" he asked Dinah as she hurried around the corner, checking for other pedestrians before proceeding.

She shook her head. "A metal door? What purpose would that serve?"

"If wood is scarce..."

"Metal doesn't make good doors, I guess. I don't know. I never really thought about it. That's my family's house."

She waved a paw casually up to the left, where a three-story mansion loomed over the street they were walking down. It was wider than the two stores and one house it stood behind, with small towers on either side and three cupolas in the middle. On the center one, Yilon could see a silver emblem shining under the moon, though he couldn't quite make out the design beyond a large stylized 'F'. "You grew up there?"

"No. I *grew up* out there." She gestured higher, to the mountains behind the house. "In there, I'm still a cub."

"I know the feeling," Yilon said. "They didn't think you'd be fit to rule."

Dinah shot him a narrow, calculating look. "Is that what they said about you?"

His ears folded back, feeling warm. "No. But I didn't run away when I had to do something I didn't want to."

"Hmph." That stopped her for only a moment. "What didn't you want to do? Come all the way out here to the edge of the country?"

"Wrong edge," he murmured half to himself, then said to her, "Have you ever been out of Dewanne?"

"I've seen the things that come here from the capital, the fashions my mother cooes over, the woodworking and weapons. It's nothing we couldn't do here. Why do we need anyone from outside the valley?"

"One of the only things I liked about the capital," he said, "was that there were people there from all over. You could get all kinds of different foods, clothes, rugs—anything you liked."

"I don't even need to live in the city," she said. "I could survive in the mountains if I had to."

"I remember. That's where everyone's looking for you."

"If they're looking at all." She peeked around another corner, then hurried around it.

Yilon ran to catch up, finding himself at the side wall of the castle, the one his bedroom faced. "Why wouldn't they be?"

"It doesn't matter anyway," she said. "There's no use staying hidden now, and once we see Corwin, he'll tell everyone I'm fine. Then I'll go to your Confirmation and we'll get married and that'll be that."

"There may not be a Confirmation. I sort of lost the crown."

She stopped dead, just before the plaza. "You *what?*"

He told her briefly about the theft that morning, as if it had been a completely unexpected occurrence in which Sinch had not been involved. She shook her head. "You had it out with you? In public? You aren't fit to rule."

"Well, that's what I said."

She'd turned to the plaza again, and now stopped. "You don't want to become Lord Dewanne, do you?"

"Do you want to be Lady Dewanne?" he countered.

"You first."

He sighed. "I didn't, but now I don't know. It's all so complicated. I don't want to do it, but there doesn't seem to be anyone else who can. It's nothing against Dewanne," he said. "It's a decent place."

"It's not that nice," she said. "You've only been here a day or two. I probably wouldn't want to stay here if I'd seen the capital."

"You just said you don't need anything from the capital."

He grinned at the flattening of her ears. "Doesn't mean I don't want to go," she said in a low voice.

"It's not the capital," he said. "I miss Vinton."

She glanced at the plaza, then rested against the wall. "Okay. What's Vinton?"

He told her about the mountains, the mountain goats and the berries, the way the sun hit the river in spring, and the walks he took with his mother to see the marketplace, the leaves in fall, the flowers in spring, the fruits in summer. Then he felt the need to apologize, again. "It's not that it's better than Dewanne. It's just where I grew up."

She responded with a surprising lack of sarcasm. "Sounds nice," she said. "I can see why you'd want to go back there. No Shadows, no fighting, no...Kites."

"Is that why don't you want to stay here?"

"I just don't want to be...locked into what they think I should be."

She took out her sling and played with it, stretching the fabric between her paws.

Yilon watched her, his ears lowering slowly. He sighed. "Well, if you don't want to do it, then I guess I have to, don't I?"

"We could both run away," Dinah said. "They'd think we were kidnapped, or that the Shadows got us. We could go to Vinton and live there. It sounds better than here."

Yilon shook his head. "We—I have responsibility, a duty."

"You're not from here," she pointed out. "You only have an assigned duty, because Lord Dewanne died without his own heir."

"It's still my duty."

She shrugged, turned on her heel, and marched into the plaza. He considered just letting her go, going back for Sinch and the crown, but then he recalled that he wanted to check on Corwin as well. It would be silly to have come this far and not go across the plaza to see him. So he followed Dinah, at a short distance, along the shadowed edge of the plaza. She had just reached the far side when a shadow reached out and grabbed her. She yelped and then vanished into the darkness.

Yilon froze, unable to believe what he'd just seen, and then ran to the spot where she'd vanished. He stood there, swiveling his head, straining his ears in all directions. Her scent was in the air, and another scent that was naggingly familiar. He heard breathing behind him, then a soft clearing of the throat. He whipped around.

"You shouldn't be here." The familiar voice came from a silhouette in the doorway of the large building. "Neither of you."

"Maxon," Yilon growled, "what have you done with Dinah?"

"I'm right here," her voice came to him from the shadow. "Don't be so dramatic."

"Get away from him," Yilon said. "He's dangerous."

"I'm flattered you think so," the steward said. "I should point out that if I wanted to harm either of you, your loud progress across the square would have afforded me several opportunities. In fact, I am here to protect you both."

"From what? Innocent mice?" Yilon stepped into the doorway, letting his eyes adjust to the darkness. He saw the white of the underside of Maxon's muzzle.

"You must both return across the plaza. It's not safe to go further. Corwin is resting but has not regained consciousness."

"How did you know we're going to see him?" Dinah spoke up. She had edged closer to Yilon; he felt the brush of her tail against his leg.

"I did not know you would both be here. I guessed that after tonight's operation, Yilon would come back, and I'm not the only one to guess that. Which is why you are in danger." He said it patiently, as though explaining it to children.

"Sinch told me what you did," Yilon said quietly.

The steward didn't look away from him, but Dinah was the first to speak. "What? What did he do?"

"I acted in the best interests of the court of Dewanne," Maxon began.

"Oh, don't give me that 'court of Dewanne' excuse," Yilon said. "How were those mice threatening the court of Dewanne?"

"They were withholding information," Maxon snapped, "and you will note I did not harm your friend. He did not extend the same courtesy to me. Should you become Lord Dewanne, I hope you will consider both sides of a story before making your judgment."

""Should" I become Lord Dewanne?" Yilon stepped closer to the steward, keeping himself from looking at Dinah. "Who else might become Lord?"

"Earlier today, you would not have cared, as long as it wasn't you," Maxon said. "Does this mean you have had a change of heart?"

"Yes," Yilon said fiercely, because he wanted Maxon to be wrong.

"In the last five minutes?" Dinah said.

"I told you, I have a duty." Yilon kept his eyes on Maxon, now able to see the steward's frown. "One that this fox keeps trying to stop me from doing."

"You young whelp," Maxon growled. "You will have to learn who to trust and who not to trust if you wish to be Lord. And why do you now wish to be Lord? What has changed today?"

"What difference would it make to you?" Yilon shot back.

"What harm can it do to tell him?" Dinah said.

"It's...he attacked a mouse earlier tonight, and almost killed her! I don't trust anyone who would do that."

"It's. A. Mouse." Maxon enunciated each word.

"He stabbed her? Really?"

"No. But he slammed her against the wall."

"There are hundreds of common gutter trash just like that one," Maxon said.

Yilon stepped back. "See?"

Dinah shook her head. "I don't agree with his attitude, but...you should still talk to him. He's not the only one who feels that way."

"That doesn't make it right."

"Why do you think it was so easy to convince Velkan to clean out the sewers?" Maxon pointed out.

"That's different." The plaza looked as bright as if morning were coming. "Those are...criminals, killers."

"And your friend's companion, what is her line of honest trade?" Maxon sneered.

"That doesn't make it right." Yilon felt the force of his argument fading. "What you did..."

"Creatures who live by force understand only force," Maxon said. "Speaking of which, might I suggest that this discussion would be far better suited to an indoor room during the daytime?"

"We came here to see Corwin," Yilon said.

Maxon sighed. "You cannot see him tonight. Need I say that again?"

"Really," Dinah said, "what motivation would he have to stop us from seeing Corwin?"

"I don't know. What motivation would he have to protect us?"

"As I believe I have mentioned in the past," Maxon said with a cough, "I serve the court of Dewanne. It is not currently in the court's best interest to have two potential rulers of the province be injured or killed."

"And how do you know there is danger?"

The scents in the small space changed slightly while Yilon waited for his answer. Dinah's, after an initial spike of fear, had calmed down. Maxon's, initially calm, now acquired an overtone of fear or desperation. Outside, the plaza remained quiet, but Yilon could now see how their progress would have been obvious to anyone watching, despite the precautions Dinah had taken. He still was not sure whether Maxon meant them harm in the long run, and it frustrated him that he couldn't figure out the steward's motivations.

"You have to decide whether or not to trust me," Maxon said finally.

Across the plaza, two foxes hurried on some errand. Yilon watched them go, knowing he couldn't be seen. "What do you think?" he asked Dinah.

"I trust him," she said, "but then I don't have a friend whose friend is dying in my house."

He knew that Maxon's eyes were as inscrutable in bright daylight as they would be in the darkness, but he returned to them nevertheless. The steward returned his steady gaze. Everything Maxon had said made sense, and even if he wouldn't reveal how he knew the danger Yilon was in, there were things Yilon wouldn't tell him either.

He didn't trust Maxon. But the fact that the steward was letting him make the decision meant that in this case, he just might be telling the truth. "All right," he began to say, but then Dinah grabbed his arm and shushed him, pointing.

On the other side of the square, a shadow was moving from one building to the next. If not for the darkness in their hiding place, Yilon would not have been able to see it at all. As it was, the best he could tell was that it was a fox, though the white of its tailtip was darkened.

"Now, *he* knows how to move inconspicuously," Maxon whispered, but just as he said that, the figure stopped moving.

"What's he doing?" Yilon whispered back. Conscious of his own tail tip, he curled it behind him, away from the street.

"Waiting for you," Maxon said grimly.

"How do you know that?" Dinah kept her voice soft as well. "He could be a thief, or after someone else."

"Thieves just walk around at night?" Yilon had not even thought to question Maxon's statement.

Maxon and Dinah exchanged glances. "More than we would like," Maxon said. "A situation that has only arisen in the past year, since Lord Dewanne's illness, and one we hope the new Lord will address."

"I used to be able to walk up to the hills alone at night," Dinah said.

Maxon pushed them both back, deep into the recesses of the alcove. "Wait here," he said. "I'll try to get him away. Don't move until I come back for you."

"Don't be foolish," Yilon said. "How do you know he won't kill you?"

"I told you," Maxon said. "He's not here for me."

"And how do you know that?"

Maxon put a finger to his muzzle and slid out of the alcove, padding around to the northward side of the square.

Yilon and Dinah watched the opposite side of the square, straining their eyes to see any further movement in the shadows. Nothing stirred until Maxon approached, and then they heard the low murmur of voices. A silhouette detached itself from the dark recess and resolved into a black-clad fox, walking alongside Maxon as the steward headed south, toward the castle.

"Maybe he was right," Yilon said. He settled back against the wall, facing Dinah.

Dinah flicked her ears. "Or maybe he just told the thief that he was under arrest and to come with him."

"Have you known him long?"

"Maxon? No. Receptions at the castle, and twice last year when my parents were finalizing this whole engagement."

Her muzzle, still mostly shadowed, turned away from his. He let his paw drop to his side, brushing his tail back and forth. "They barely talked to me about the engagement," he said. "Mostly they talked to me about becoming the lord. But not even very much of that."

"Sounds familiar," she said. "Nobody cares what we think. They just know what they want us to be."

Yilon let that thought guide his musings. "What do you want to be?"

"Free," she replied immediately, as though it were a problem she'd already solved. "No obligations. No duties."

"No responsibility?"

"Responsibility is okay. Duty is what other people tell you to do. Responsibility is what your heart tells you to do." She tapped her chest.

"You think it's that easy?"

"Don't you?" She turned toward him. "What does your heart tell you to do?"

He almost laughed. Here he was, sitting in a dark alcove in a still-strange town with a vixen he'd known for half a day, talking about his heart. "I don't know. I love Vinton. I love...those people."

"Dewanne isn't so different," she said.

"Like you said, there's no Warren there," he reminded her. "No tension, no Shadows."

She inclined her head. "So why not stay here, and work to make it as pleasant as Vinton?"

The thought struck him, bright as the moon. Could he? "Are you trying to talk me into taking the title now?"

She chuckled, softly. "Better you than me."

"Even though if I take the title, we're to be married?"

"Well," she said, "first I convince you to take the title, and then I convince you not to marry me."

Now he did laugh. "I don't know. I don't have much experience handling..." He looked across the square. "How long does it take to clear the path for us?"

"Maxon's very thorough," she said. "He and Velkan basically ran the province the last two years."

"Not very well, if there are thieves all over the place."

"My mother says Lady Dewanne wouldn't let them do all the things they wanted to."

Yilon peered out into the square again. It was completely empty. "Like what?"

"Oh, they wanted to go back into the Warren. My mother says that was a disaster when Kishin did it, but they thought they could do it more effectively."

"Kill all the mice," Yilon muttered. "Probably wishes he could do them all personally, like Valix..." He stared into the emptiness of the plaza, replaying the conversation in his head. His fur prickled. "Does Maxon know about all the houses your family owns?"

"He might," Dinah said. "Like I told you, he's very...oh. But he can't know..."

"We told him," Yilon said, turning to her. "We told him that Sinch's friend is at your house."

They stared at each other for only another second before running out of the alcove. "What if they're still waiting for us?" Dinah said.

"He's after Sinch," Yilon barked back. "Which way?"

"This is fastest." The deserted streets echoed with their footsteps. Dinah took him past Market Street and up a steep hill. The sling bounced against her waist as they ran. "He wouldn't go to that house first. He'd go to the big one."

"Let's hope so."

"Can your friend take care of himself?"

Yilon felt again the tight embrace, Sinch clinging to him in the top room. "Normally, I'd say yes. But he was tired, and under a great deal of strain today. Does Colian fight?"

She panted laughter. "Only with fur tangles."

He recognized the path she was taking several streets away. Any pleasure he might have in the familiarity he was acquiring with the town was lost in the urgency to make sure Sinch was safe. His paws were sore, but he didn't let up. "Around here, right? Then right at the end of this block?"

"Yes." He thought to leave her behind, but even as he sped up, she kept pace with him. They passed two startled foxes without pausing, but saw no other life until the familiar three-story house came into view.

Yilon reached the door first. He threw it open, leapt for the first stair, and pounded up. Colian came out onto the second floor landing just as Yilon ran by. "Good Gaia," he said. "Did you forget something terribly important?"

By the time he finished talking, Yilon was most of the way to the third floor, covering two steps at a time. He shoved open the door to the bedroom and ran inside. Sinch's smell was strong in the room, but not strong enough. Even before he reached the bed and pressed his paws to the still-warm sheets, he knew the mouse was gone.

Dinah had stopped at the second floor landing, talking to Colian there. Both foxes looked up as Yilon descended, reading the answer in his flattened ears before even beginning the question. He stood two steps above them. "Did anyone come in?" he asked Colian.

The nurse shook his head. "No. I heard the door open, then heard Min talking."

"Min! Where is he?" Yilon looked past Colian.

"I don't know, that's what I was starting to tell you. By the time I had settled our patient enough that I could leave, Min had gone. I supposed your friend was still sleeping, but I confess I didn't check."

"So she's still here?" Yilon gestured toward the second floor room.

"Yes, and just a few moments ago, her fever appeared to break. At least, she is much cooler to the touch. I would not celebrate her recovery just yet, but I believe she will live to see another sunrise."

"That's only three hours," Dinah pointed out. "Not much confidence."

Yilon sagged back against the wall. "If only she were awake," he said, "she might know something about where Sinch is taking Maxon."

Colian's ears perked. "Did I not mention? She woke up when her fever broke. She's awake now."

Chapter 18: The Deed Is Done

The fog of sleep lifted slowly from Sinch. He was aware of voices arguing outside, and for a moment thought his mother and sisters were arguing again. But the voices were lower-pitched, with longer nasal tones, and as he struggled awake, he recognized them as foxes. "Yilon?" he murmured.

He must have been tired. Usually he came awake quickly. He sat up in the bed and shook his head to try to clear it. The voices were getting closer, and now he heard one say, "Sir, you should not..." and the other respond, "Leave me alone! This is important business."

Something about that second voice spurred him out of the bed, to throw the window open. He could hear claws on the stairs now, an irregular footstep. Someone limping up to the third floor.

He connected the limp to the voice, and then he was awake, scrabbling desperately at the window sill to pull himself up and through. Halfway through, he reached around to the other side to see if there were a ledge he could cling to, but nothing was within arm's reach. No help for it, he thought. He pushed himself the rest of the way through, swung around, and pulled the shutters closed as best he could with one paw while hanging by the other.

"Where is he?" Maxon's voice demanded. "I can smell him." Sinch lowered himself all the way down, and, thank Rodenta, his hind paws felt brick below them. Softly, he let himself drop, just as the shutters rattled. The other fox, whom Sinch thought was Min, said, "We're three floors up. You think he jumped to his death?"

"I'll have to use the other one," Maxon said, and then the shutters closed. Sinch heard the snick of the latch.

He wasn't in Maxon's clutches, but it was hard to see any other benefits of his situation. He saw that the ledge he was standing on ran all the way around the building, never coming closer than five feet from the adjacent one on this side, and that one was only two stories tall, so it would be at least a six or seven-foot drop to that roof. He could probably make the leap, but what then? If he followed the ledge around the front of the building, he'd be visible to the street, so he edged carefully around the back.

This side of the building, shielded from moonlight, was darker. No other method of escape suggested itself here, not even another building five feet away: the back of the building faced onto an open patio with an outhouse whose odor nearly completely overwhelmed a small garden. But the ledge circled the house, and there were no windows on this side to expose him, so he continued around, only once nearly losing his balance when a brick he grabbed shifted under his paw. Fortunately, the temperate air was mostly still, so there were no gusts of wind to be careful of.

As he approached the corner, he became aware of another scent. More accurately, it was the absence of a smell, as if the breeze had been generated out of nothing. His whiskers tingled. Down in the sewers, it had been hard to notice that the Shadows masked their scent. Up here, where few smells reached the third story, the curious sharpness of the masking agent was easier to notice. He crept to the corner and cautiously peered around.

The ledge, as far as he could see, was empty all the way to the street. On this side, though, the roof sloped downward at a sharper angle. Clearly, any room on this side of the third floor was no more than a storage area. The edge of the roof was a very climbable three feet above the ledge, should Sinch see a need to get up there. He saw no sign of any Shadow on this side of the building, even after careful perusal of the deepest dark patches, but that didn't stop the tingling in his whiskers. When he looked across at the adjacent building on this side, which was three stories tall, he saw several dark spaces that could hide a Shadow.

His paw slid to his waist. The reassuring hardness of his knife fit nicely into his fingers. If there were a Shadow over there, it meant they were still watching Valix, no matter what their message to Sinch had been. That could mean she was still in danger. And it was still his fault.

Running footsteps echoed in the street, getting closer. Sinch perked his ear until he heard them getting closer, and then he craned his neck around the corner to see. The first fox was visible for only a fraction of a second, but he was sure it was Yilon. The one following him was the vixen. Was she chasing him? Hard to tell, but she was very close behind him. He heard the door swing open and then shut. Slowly, he worked one hind paw around the corner of the building.

A piece of the shadow across the way came hurtling toward him. If he hadn't caught the motion out of the corner of his eye, he might have fallen. The shape landed on the ledge, seeming to stick to the building, and a black-furred muzzle grinned at him. "Thought it was you."

Sinch thought his heart would break through the brick it was pounding against. "Dagger?"

"Hah. I am The Frost That Bites The Tail. And it doesn't matter how well you creep around walls. Whisper isn't going to let you in. Fox-lover."

"You're monsters."

"What are you doing here?"

"Shh." He pointed downward. "We were going to finish the job, as revenge. But there's a noble in there I don't recognize, and a vixen who's a noble too. That'd be good retaliation for tonight's raid, don't you think?"

A chill spread through Sinch's body. Frost was watching him keenly, and though the black mouse affected nonchalance as best one could while clinging to a brick wall three stories up, Sinch didn't miss the right paw held ready near the waist. He wished he could reach for his knife, but that would be too obvious at this point, and he wasn't certain enough of his balance. He knew a few things he could do without the knife, though he had never practiced fighting high above the ground. "Why do you have to retaliate?" he said. "If you retaliate, they'll just retaliate back, won't they?"

"You don't know anything about it," Frost said. "They expect us to fight back. What would you have us do, let them walk all over us?"

"If you'd just let them alone..."

"No fox is friend to no mouse," Frost recited. "But you don't believe that, do you? You'd get on your knees and suck their sheath if one of them asked, wouldn't you? Bend over and let yourself be used, and ask for more? Anything with a red coat. Just like all the other little plant-eaters."

Sinch opened his mouth to protest, but Frost went on. "You want us to stop fighting, to stop stirring up trouble. You don't want any part of what we do. But without us, things would be worse. Without us, the Warren would be a charred pile of rubble and you and your friends would all be living in holes in the mountains, tithing all your goods to the blood-coats and living off scrub grass. We are the shadow they fear. We are the reason they respect mice."

"You're monsters," Sinch said without thinking.

Frost's eyes glittered. "Monsters, perhaps. At least we fight for our dignity, and for yours."

"Rodenta teaches us to kill only as a last resort," Sinch said desperately.

The other mouse grinned widely at that. "We have very different teachers."

The motion of his arm was so fast, Sinch didn't evade it completely. The black dagger caught his tunic, nicked the skin beneath. Jerking away, he nearly lost his balance on the ledge, scrabbling at the brick with his fingers for any sort of hold. The rough stone caught on his pads, helping him regain his balance as Frost lunged at him again. This time, Sinch was ready, balancing on his toes as he hurried away from the corner as fast as he dared.

Frost didn't pursue him. Maybe gone was as good as dead, if Sinch left him alone. But as much as Sinch wanted to flee this nightmare, he couldn't. He thought of Yilon inside the house, of the black dagger coming through the window, and he steeled his resolve.

When he made it back to the corner, Frost was nowhere on the third story ledge. Sinch crouched as low as he could, almost lying down so that he could lower his head to look down to the second story. A flash of motion swept past his eye, and he felt a sting in his ear. He jerked his head back up, clinging to the rough stone.

So Frost was on the second story, getting into position outside the window where Yilon was. What now? He thought back to his training. What would your opponent expect you to do? Do the opposite. As if it were that easy. The only thing he could imagine Frost expecting him to do was run away. But if not, then what? He was clearly prepared for Sinch to drop down and attack him. But what if...what if...

Sinch retreated along the ledge, looking for the loose piece of brick. He found it and worked it loose, then crept carefully back until he was at the corner again, lying flat on the ledge. He listened carefully, but couldn't hear any activity from below. What he did hear was Yilon's voice: "How did you and Sinch find yourselves among the Shadows?"

Hearing Yilon flooded Sinch with panic. That meant he was near the window, and within range of Frost. If the window on that side was where he remembered it, just opposite the third floor room, and if Frost was somewhere near it, even now lifting his black dagger...

He swung his arm down and let the brick fly, in an arc parallel to the wall of the building. He heard a soft thud and then a scrabbling against brick. Quickly, he looked down and saw Frost standing dazed on the second-floor ledge, just regaining his balance. Sinch scampered as quickly as he could along the ledge on his level until he judged he was past Frost, then swung down.

He seemed to fall through air for an eternity. He spent most of it trying not to think about how far down the ground was. His hind paws found the ledge; his body automatically pressed forward against the wall until his weight was centered over brick and not empty air. It only took two or three seconds for him to turn his head toward Frost, but that was enough time for the black mouse to swing his knife, catching Sinch in a long gash on his unprotected right arm.

Pain flared across the arm, but didn't incapacitate it. Sinch struck reflexively upward, knocking Frost's arm away from his. His fingers closed around cloth. He pulled hard away from the wall, using the motion to press himself against it and secure his balance, even as he felt Frost's weight shift in his paw. He turned his head to look.

The other mouse tottered on the edge, flailing to regain his footing. Sinch's paw had caught his tunic at the black sleeve, twisted it so he couldn't bring his arm up to grab back. The Shadow's weight pulled more heavily as he groped for purchase with his free paw. Sinch thought of Yilon, and let go.

"You'll die for this," Frost hissed, swiping in his direction, but whether it was to pull himself back or to pull Sinch with him, his paws clutched only empty air.

Sinch shrank back against the wall, his eyes wide. He watched Frost topple away from him, the black shape disappearing slowly, slowly, into the darkness. An eternity later, a dull noise came from the street below, the thick impact of a body and the snap of bones breaking. Then there was only Sinch's heartbeat and the light from the window. If not for the pain in his arm, it would have been hard to believe Frost had ever been there.

Sinch had never killed before. Even when captured by Maxon, the most dangerous situation he'd ever been in, he hadn't even thought to throw his knife at the fox's head or chest. The silence from the street below unnerved him, so that he had to hold his paws to prevent them from shaking. Breathe, he told himself, remembering the words he'd learned back in Divalia: *You made your choice and the deed is done. Take a moment to make sure there was no other way it could have ended. If you acted with a clear conscience, make your peace.* He'd hoped never to have to kill anyone, had only known one other thief in Divalia who had, but he'd known someday he might. Yilon talked about fighting and war so casually, about defeating enemies and hitting targets and doing what must be done, surely he would not be standing on a narrow ledge after saving Sinch's life, worrying about consequences. Surely he would have long since made his peace.

Still, it took ages for Sinch's heart to return to its normal pace, and in all that time, no more sounds came from below. He couldn't bring himself to look over the edge—for fear of losing his balance, he told himself. The window, barely three feet over from him, was now closed. It astonished him that nobody had come to see what was going on outside.

But nobody did. Finally, he slid himself over to the window, and peered in through the crack. Valix was sitting there, talking to Yilon and the vixen, with Colian standing by. Their nearness excited Sinch, filling him with relief as warm as a hot mead. He drew his knife, lifted the latch, and pushed himself through the window.

Chapter 19: Recovering

The mouse whose name was Valix shrank back against the wall when the foxes all entered the room. It took some soothing on Colian's part to assure her that she wouldn't be harmed, especially since Yilon could see that she was still in tremendous pain. Colian gave her some herbs, which she looked at doubtfully until Dinah pointed out that if they wanted to kill her, there were plenty of quicker and more pleasurable ways of going about it than feeding her a small quantity of poisonous herbs. Yilon thought this was going too far, but it did convince Valix to chew the plant.

By that time, Yilon was reasonably sure that she had been one of the mice who'd distracted them during the theft of the crown, scent or no scent. He'd guessed that she and Sinch had gone to the sewers to hide or retrieve it, but he didn't dare say anything about the crown, and she stuck to her story that Maxon had knocked her unconscious, she'd woken in the middle of Dewanne, she and Sinch had escaped from Maxon when he wasn't looking (she refused to admit to any knowledge about the knife Sinch had thrown, even when Yilon told her they knew about it), and she'd led Sinch to a sewer grate which they'd jumped into to escape.

Yilon asked twice if she were looking for something in the sewer, but she just shook her head and said, "I told you the truth." That was when they all heard something outside that sounded like a whisper. Yilon, remembering the threat of the Shadows, hurried to the wall next to the window where they were all now looking. Dinah and Colian simply nodded as he closed the shutter, but Valix visibly relaxed.

"Do you remember anything that might help us figure out what Maxon was doing with you and why he was after Sinch?" Yilon asked, sitting next to her.

She flinched, but he didn't move, though he did carefully curl his tail away from her. "No," she said. "He just said he wanted us to show him something, but then he knocked me out and didn't tell me what. And I don't think Sinch knew either. He said he was just stalling 'til I woke up."

Which might or might not be true. Yilon had spent a good deal of time with Sinch and his family, and Valix reminded him of them: stubbornly loyal to family and friends, not deceitful for the sake of deceiving. He suspected that if she were lying at all, she would be lying to protect Sinch. Which made him feel warm, that Sinch had made himself that close a friend in so short a time.

"I'm Sinch's friend too," he told her. "I came here with him from Divalia."

She had just opened her mouth to reply when the shutter crashed open and a small shape came hurtling through the window.

Yilon leapt to his feet on the bed. Colian jumped for the door. Valix jerked back and then let out a squeak of pain. And Dinah moved fastest, pinning the body down before it had stopped moving, one paw across its throat, the other raised in threat, teeth bared. "Who are you?" she barked.

"It's me!" squeaked the shape.

"Sinch!" Yilon jumped from the bed and pushed Dinah aside, though she was already sitting back. "You're bleeding."

"What?" Sinch looked genuinely startled. Yilon touched his arm, where the cloth of his tunic was stained red. "Oh, that. That's nothing, just a scratch. I'm fine." He wrapped both his arms around Yilon's chest.

Yilon heard Corwin saying, "Just don't be a public embarrassment." It took him a moment to decide that Dinah, Colian, and Valix were not enough to constitute a public, and then he hugged Sinch back. "How did it happen?"

Colian was already kneeling, parting the cloth and looking at the arm. "This is more than a scratch," he said. "Come over to the bed and sit down. I'll bind it."

"And Valix, you're awake." Sinch looked as though he might cry. "How are you feeling?"

She grimaced. "Like someone stabbed me in the back. It's better than it was, but it still hurts when I move."

"You shouldn't be moving," Colian said, lifting Sinch's tunic off. "An inch or two to either side, and you'd be incapable of movement. Or speech. Or thought, for that matter. Your body has probably not been through anything this violent before in your life. You need to relax."

"You're the ones who had me sit up."

"Sitting is fine," he said, reaching into his bag and pulling out the long razor. "But sit perfectly still. All this looking around and jumping is not going to help."

"I didn't arrange for Sinch to come barreling through the window like the Lost Cave Miner."

Sinch held his arm out while Colian shaved the fur around the wound. "What's the Lost Cave Miner?"

"Old fairy tale," Dinah said. "What happened to your arm?"

Sinch turned toward Yilon, his ears flattening. "I had to do it," he said. "I didn't have a choice."

Yilon's mind turned immediately to Maxon's mysterious absence. His neck prickled. "Did what?"

"He was going to kill you." Sinch leaned forward.

Colian muttered an oath under his breath and pulled the mouse back. "Sit still, unless you want a matching slice above this one."

"Who was? Maxon?"

Sinch shook his head. "Frost. The Shadow."

This time, Dinah sprang to the window, holding it shut while she fumbled at the latch. Sinch's entry had knocked it somewhat askew, but not broken it, and with some fiddling, she managed to get it into place. Valix, meanwhile, had jumped again and was now staring at Sinch as best she could through eyes teary with pain. "You...killed..."

Sinch winced, though that could have been from Colian swabbing at the now-visible angry red gash with a cloth. "I didn't have a choice."

"A Shadow?" Dinah was gaping at him.

Yilon looked around the room, finally figuring out what Sinch meant. His skin crawled at the thought of the assassins outside, focused on him. He dropped to his knees so he could look Sinch in the eye. "Why did he want to kill me?"

Valix shook her head. "Oh, you're in trouble. You need to get away, back to the Warren, or further. They're going to get you now."

"Revenge for tonight," Sinch said. "But I don't think they know who you are."

"They can't get him," Dinah said to Valix. "He killed the Shadow."

"Why would they want to kill me if they don't know who I am?"

"They work in pairs," Valix said, just as Sinch told Yilon, "You look important."

In the ensuing silence, Colian held a clean cloth out to Sinch. "Bite down on this," he said. "I'm going to sew up the wound."

Yilon and Sinch stared at each other. "So they're after both of us now," Yilon said. Sinch's muzzle screwed up in pain around the cloth as Colian drew the needle through his skin, quickly and efficiently.

"Looks that way," Valix said, perhaps emboldened by the weight given to her words. "Say, no offense meant, your noblenesses, but is there another room you could go attract Shadows to?"

Yilon stood. "We'll go to the top room."

"I was kidding. The other won't do anything right now. He'll come back with a partner, but probably not tonight."

"How do you know so much about them?" Dinah still had a paw on the window. Her voice was higher than normal, her eyes a bit wide.

"I grew up hearing about them," Valix said. "How did you manage to kill one?"

"He's good," Yilon said, because Sinch was still holding the cloth clenched between his teeth.

"They're better," Valix said.

Colian tied off the thread and dabbed something else over the wound. He took the cloth gently back from Sinch. "Done," he said.

Sinch raised his ears and looked determined to show it didn't hurt. He looked right at Yilon. "I threw a rock at him from the third floor. Then I jumped down and he swung at me. I grabbed his arm and pushed him. He fell."

"Are you sure?" Dinah's voice still sounded high-pitched. Colian turned his ears toward her, pausing in his ministrations of Sinch's arm.

"Yeah," Valix said. "If you didn't poke the dead body..."

"He didn't move," Sinch said. "I didn't hear anything."

"You should've stuck a knife in his throat," Yilon said. "Then there'd be no doubt."

He'd hoped to reassure Dinah, remind her that she was capable of dealing with enemies, and break the tension in the room, but the remark had the complete opposite effect. Her ears flattened to her head and her eyes widened further, showing whites. Her tail, already down, curled between her legs.

Valix, looking at Sinch rather than Dinah, started to say, "Hah. Only way he'd do that is..." She got no further before Dinah bolted from the room.

Colian sighed. He got to his feet, giving Yilon a reproachful look. "She didn't enjoy that," he said, and left the room after her, leaving Yilon alone with the two mice.

"I didn't..." Yilon started after the nurse, then stopped. He spread his paws, facing Sinch. "I didn't know."

"Know what?" Sinch asked.

Briefly, Yilon told them about Kites. Valix said, "Nobody likes killing. When it comes to it."

"Have you ever killed anyone?" Yilon asked.

She shook her head. "Hope I never do. That's for the Shadows to do." They all looked at the window. "Maybe you would have made a good one," she said to Sinch. "You do throw a good knife."

He shook his head. "They hate foxes," he said.

"Ah." She settled back on the bed with a grimace. "So this is the friend you were hoping to get money from."

"You need money?" Yilon asked, and Sinch, with some reluctance, told him what had happened with Balinni, wrapping up the story quickly as Colian led Dinah back into the room.

Her ears were down. Nobody talked until she said, "I'm sorry." She took a deep breath and then let it out. "I'll be okay now."

Sinch moved before anybody else, walking over to her. "I never killed anyone before either," he said. "You have to remember that you made the right choice. There was nothing else you could have done, right?"

"I said, I'll be okay." Dinah was trying her best not to look at the mouse even though he was right in front of her.

"It's kind of you to say so," Colian said.

He touched her arm gently, brown fingers resting just at the border where her russet fur shaded into dark brown. "You have to make peace," he said. "You can't change what happened. You have to learn from it."

"So," she said, sounding forcibly courteous. "You're Yilon's friend from Divalia."

"More than friends," Valix said.

Yilon could have strangled her. The situation with Dinah and the lordship was confused enough without introducing Sinch into the mix. But Dinah, strangely, perked up at that comment and looked over the mouse's head at Yilon. "Is that true?"

Now Sinch was looking back at him, and Yilon couldn't lie in front of him, no matter how little he wanted to tell the truth. "In a manner of speaking," he said.

"But that's wonderful." Dinah clapped her paws together.

Yilon stared at her. "I really don't understand females," he muttered.

"You don't want to marry me!" Dinah said. "I don't know why you didn't mention it before. So you'll be a lord, and we won't have to get married."

"I can't..." Yilon gestured vaguely toward Sinch. "He's a mouse."

"That doesn't matter," Dinah said. Colian gave her a reproachful look, but didn't speak.

"And anyway, I have to get married. I have to have a legitimate heir."

She waved at the floor and ceiling. "This house came into my family because my great-grandmother was the mistress of the Lord. He gave her this house and they stayed together for twelve years, until he died. And she kept the house after that. Just build a house on the edge of the Warren."

Valix was shaking her head. Yilon said, "That's not what I mean."

"Oh, I thought you were in favor of mice," she said. "It doesn't matter, really. It'd be easier with someone like Colian, whatever you like."

"While the young lord is attractive," Colian said, smiling, "I fear he does not feel the same for me."

"I said someone like you," Dinah said. "It doesn't have to be you."

"I see." Colian's smile didn't fade. "My pardon. I thought I detected another attempt on your part to remedy the cold loneliness of my existence."

"I need to have a legitimate heir," Yilon said again. The room, with the shutters closed, felt stuffy to him. He paced back and forth. "If I don't marry you, I'll have to marry someone else."

"Lady Dewanne never had an heir," Dinah said.

"And look at what that's done to the city!"

Dinah stared back at him. "They brought you here. You can just bring someone else in. Do it sooner."

"I don't want to be here!" Yilon cried. "I don't want to drag some other poor cub out of his home to this city just because I don't *want* to have a wife and family."

"Lord Dewanne did." Dinah shrugged. "Lords do all sorts of things."

"They didn't have a choice," Yilon said. "Lady Dewanne couldn't have cubs."

Colian said, "Who told you that?"

"That's ridiculous," Dinah said. "She had two cubs that died."

"I heard one," Valix said.

"She said she wasn't favored by Canis," Yilon said.

"If she couldn't have cubs, he would have taken another wife."

"Not right away," Yilon said.

"You can't wait forever. 'Steeth, it's been drilled into my head: have an heir within three years, have an heir within three years. Colian, what did she tell you?" Dinah asked.

"Now, would you have me tell her about the conditions I've treated you for?" Colian said with a smile.

"*I* don't care." Dinah's fangs showed over her lower lip.

"Look," Yilon said, "I have to get the crown back first. Then we can worry about all the rest."

"That's all very well," Dinah said. "Who knows where the crown is now?"

The stuffy room became very quiet. Sinch and Valix looked at the floor. "Let me worry about that," Yilon said.

Dinah folded her arms. Yilon found that he wanted badly to tell her, to enlist her as a partner in the retrieval of the crown. Was there anything she could offer? He searched for any excuse to tell her, and while he was thinking, she gave him the perfect opening. "You're going by yourself? Out there into the city where the Shadows are trying to kill you?"

"Not just them," he said.

Dinah tilted her muzzle. "Right. Maxon's mysterious 'assassins.' You don't think that was all a story designed to keep us out of the way?"

"No. He stopped us before we told him where the mice were."

"*You* told him?" Valix said. "Well, thank you. I thought the Shadows were the only ones who'd stabbed me in the back tonight."

"Not on purpose," Yilon snapped.

"Regardless," Dinah said, "you'll need some protection and a guide. You're new in town and there are assassins after you. And Min isn't back yet."

"Where did he go?" Yilon asked it rhetorically, but Colian inclined his head, lifting his shoulders in a small shrug.

"He said something about using "the other one,"" Sinch said. "Maxon did. When he was up in that room." Valix and the foxes all turned to stare at him. "I was outside," he said.

"Who's the other one? And why would he take Min with him?" Yilon looked around the room.

Sinch whispered something to Valix that Yilon didn't catch. The other mouse shook her head. "The only fox he ever talked to was named Dewry," she said.

"Who?"

"My...boss," she said. "He mentioned a fox named Dewry, but he knew him before I was born, I think. He said there weren't any good foxes around since Dewry left."

Dinah frowned. "That name sounds familiar."

"Regardless," Yilon said, "I can't figure why Min would go along with him and not wait for me."

"Maybe he didn't go along," Sinch said.

"Then where did he—" Yilon stopped, his head lifting. "I told him I didn't trust Maxon."

"You think he would have followed him?" Dinah tapped her fingers on her arm.

"I've only known him a couple days." Yilon flicked his ears. "But yes, it's possible. Wouldn't we have met them on our way in?"

"Not if they went the other way, down to the east side," Dinah said.

"Where that Strad building is," Yilon said.

They were all silent for a moment. "He's a trained soldier," Yilon said. "He can take care of himself."

"You don't know those people," Dinah said. "Is he expecting to run into someone like Kites?"

"Are there more?" Yilon saw the answer in Dinah's flattened ears. "If he's in danger, we have to go help him. But we don't have time for that and the other errand," he said. "It's almost light. There will be people around."

"At least the Shadows won't be as active," Valix said.

"Aren't they always around?" Dinah said. "That's what I was told."

Valix shrugged. "That's what they like people to believe. Sometimes they are, sometimes they aren't. They like to know what's going on, and most times things go on during the day." She yawned.

Yilon rubbed his fingers along his tunic. "Sinch, can you go by yourself?"

Sinch nodded. "It's probably faster and safer."

Valix snorted. "You'd be safer with me."

"You are not going anywhere for at least two days," Colian said. "Maybe more."

"I can't stay here," Valix said. "I need to be back to...the Warren by morning."

Colian shook his head. "Absolutely not."

"Once I get back, I'll go for you," Sinch said.

Valix snorted again. "I'm sure that will help. What are you going to tell him? That I'm stabbed and lying in a building somewhere in the Heights, but he shouldn't worry, I'll be back in a week?"

Sinch's ears fell. "No."

"Look," Yilon said, "we'll worry about that in the morning. Right now we need to find Min and the crown."

"It is morning," Valix pointed out, but Yilon was already moving toward the door, Dinah behind him.

"I'm coming with you," she told him when he turned around, before he had a chance to say anything. "I know how to get there, and besides, without me, you're liable to fall in a hole, or on someone's dagger."

He thought about it for a moment and then nodded, once. "All right. Let's get going, then. Colian, if Min comes back, have him wait here. We'll come back here before we do anything else."

"Be careful," Colian said. "I'll be here."

"Sinch," Yilon said. The mouse sat up, meeting his eyes, though his ears stayed down. "I'll meet you back here." Sinch nodded, but didn't say anything. Yilon raised his paw and followed Dinah down the stairs.

They turned right on the street outside. A fox was passing, but not one either of them recognized. "I think it's down this way," Yilon said.

"By here is faster," Dinah said, and started walking.

Yilon hurried after her. "Do you know who lives in the Strad house?"

"Yes," she said, in such a grim tone that for the moment, Yilon held his questions and just walked beside her in the slowly lightening street.

Chapter 20: Loss

Sinch watched Yilon leave, his thoughts chaotic and restless. He didn't even realize he was still staring at the door until Valix said, "You sure have the worst luck."

"Me?" He saw, unexpectedly, sympathy behind her wry grin.

"Not so good to have it so bad for a fox. Not around here. Isn't that so, sawbones?"

"I'm not a chirurgeon," Colian said. "Nor am I a judge. It would be rather easier for you to make an arrangement were you a fox, but Dinah, if she does eventually agree to marry, will be quite willing to come to an agreement, I'm sure. Even if she may find the situation slightly..."

"Disgusting?" Valix said.

"Unusual." Colian grinned. "We are not all Kishins, Miss Lightfingers."

"*I* think it's disgusting," Valix muttered.

"It doesn't matter," Sinch said. "He's not going to want to come to an arrangement. He's...you heard him, with his duty and honor. He's a noble fox, a really...a wonderful person."

"All right," Valix said. "Well, if I can't go anywhere, then you'd better get going. I'll think of something you can say to Ba—er, my boss."

Sinch nodded. "And keep to the back alleys," she continued. "It's getting busier out there."

"Thanks." He got up and bowed to Colian. "Thank you, too, for your assistance."

Colian raised a paw. "Don't come back needing more."

Sinch plodded down the stairs. Though he could see the rosy touch of dawn in the sky, he couldn't make himself move much faster. After all, he reasoned, he had to be careful, not only of the Shadows, but also of the foxes on the street, who would no doubt be somewhat disturbed to see a mouse walking boldly through their streets in the morning. But even as he crept along the sides of buildings, from alcove to doorway, he didn't give his surroundings more than a cursory look.

There were a few foxes on the street, but he managed to avoid them easily enough, even though these streets were clean and clear of debris. It helped that they were servants hurrying on errands, not paying much attention to their surroundings either. The only foxes on the flagstone streets who weren't servants were a well-dressed couple, talking softly to each other, too absorbed to take any notice of him.

He turned after they'd passed and watched them. Maybe I should go back to Divalia, he thought. It would make the most sense. The Shadows were after him, the steward hated him, and even on the off chance that Balinni would believe that he had not murdered Valix, there was little hope of protection there. Even if Yilon were to become Lord Dewanne, he wouldn't have enough pull to counter all of that trouble. Things would just keep going wrong.

But every time he pictured himself traveling back to Divalia, he felt his heart constrict. Everything would be right there, he could go back to his family and his life, but it would still be wrong. He couldn't explain it, couldn't do anything about it except do anything he could to stay. And that meant getting the crown back.

The sky was definitely growing lighter. In Divalia, he'd learned to be inconspicuous by keeping his head down and walking determinedly, but not too quickly or too slowly. The problem here was that a mouse on the streets in this part of the city would stand out no matter how quickly he was traveling. At least, that's what he thought until he turned into one of the side alleys and saw what was unmistakably a mouse hurrying away from him, a large sack slung over its shoulder.

Curious, he followed. As the mouse reached another set of houses, he or she stopped to rummage through the small bins left outside the back gate of each one. From each, the mouse drew a piece of cloth: an old tunic, a piece of curtain, a scarf. The cloth was added to the sack, and the mouse scurried on to the next house. At that bin, he saw Sinch (it was definitely a he, Sinch was close enough to smell) and snarled. "I got this street," he said. "Clear off."

Sinch put up his paws. "I'm not after clothes."

"Oh." The mouse relaxed. "Chikka's already been through. No metal left. Scroungin' for food?"

Sinch shook his head. "I'm...on an errand."

That put the mouse on his guard again. "Well, don't hang around me. I don't need trouble. I make an honest living." He shut the bin, obviously finding nothing in it, and moved on.

Did they all just assume any errand was a dishonest one? "I'm new in town," Sinch said. "Do...are there a lot of mice around this area in the morning?"

"New?" The mouse stared at him. "Why in darkness would you come here?"

Sinch sighed. "Doesn't matter," he said. "Good luck."

"Go back where you came from!" the mouse called after him.

Now that he was looking, he saw mice everywhere in the alleys, picking through bins, rolling wheelbarrows, pushing large barrels that stank of waste on large carts. Once he saw one slip out of a back yard, look around furtively, and scamper away. There'd been no mice around in the daytime, so if he were to pose as one of the scavengers, he'd have only a little time to do it. Even knowing that, he couldn't make himself go too quickly, his conflicting feelings like molasses around his feet. If Yilon were with him, it would be easier, he thought. A fox could provide an excuse for a mouse, even if they had to play at him being a captive, or being chased through the street. No: if he were being chased, someone might help, like that fox there, dressed in a plain tunic but obviously on his way to the bakery at the corner.

Sinch's stomach growled at the aroma of fresh bread coming from the back of the small store. He considered for a moment stopping to snatch a loaf, more to save the time it would require to explain his presence than because he didn't want to pay. But he turned away and down another small alley, patting his stomach. When he got back with the crown, there would be breakfast.

None of the streets here were familiar, but he had drawn a rough map of the city in his head, and he knew he was getting closer. At the first turn onto a street he recognized, he saw something out of the corner of his eye, and his whiskers tingled again. He spun around, but saw nobody on the rooftops, no movement in the crevices of the buildings behind him. The openness of these streets, even the alleys, worked to his benefit now; it would be harder for someone to follow him unnoticed. After a long look, he returned to his mission.

It took him only a few more minutes to find his hiding place, and his whiskers didn't tingle again the whole time. The door he'd used before—that morning? Had it really been less than a day ago?—was still ajar. He let himself in and crept down to the basement.

The whole structure smelt of mildew and decay. The rotting bags in the dark basement, more than he'd remembered there being, overwhelmed him with their pungent odor. With little light coming through the grimy windows, he would have to rely on the smell of the newer leather to find the satchel holding the crown. He remembered approximately where he'd hidden it and sniffed around. Maddeningly, the smell had diffused over the course of the day, probably carried by the damp decay, and so he had to stick his paw into and around a number of the slimy, moldering sacks.

His heart beat faster. It had been on this side of the room, in this corner, he was sure of it. Had he come down a different way and become disoriented? He could dimly see the outline of another staircase. Maybe he'd used that one, which would put the bag...over on this side. He hurried to that corner, but the smell of leather was nonexistent there, and the other stairs, when he got closer, proved to be simply a pile of crumbling bricks stacked in a tiered arrangement.

He returned to his original site, where he began throwing bags aside. He could definitely smell the leather of the crown's satchel, and a faint trace of the fox aroma that had been on the costume. Most of the old bags came apart in his paws, and the ones that didn't were empty. At the bottom, the leather was slimy with mold, but he pulled at it anyway, until his fingers touched the cold dirt floor of the cellar. Enough light trickled in through the window by now to let him see quite plainly what his nose had been telling him for the last half hour, almost since he'd arrived.

The bag was not there. The crown was gone.

Chapter 21: Inside the House

Yilon followed Dinah along the broad streets of the heights to where they grew narrower and dingier, windows streaked rather than shining, brick crumbling, stickiness on the flagstones under his paws. He saw shadows in every corner he looked, so after startling for the fourth time, he stopped looking, worrying more about tripping on missing stones.

Ahead of him, Dinah was focused and tense, judging by the curl in her tail and the constant flicking of her ears. He didn't disturb her with any more questions until they reached a street he recognized, though he wasn't sure whether it was because it was the first street he'd been on before or if it was simply now light enough for him to make out the familiar pattern of the houses on it. Dinah turned before he would have, though.

"Isn't it up that way?" He pointed.

She followed his finger. "If you want to walk in the front door," she said.

"There's a back door?"

She nodded. "Come on."

They walked up a narrow passage between houses, around a yard and up a neglected grassy patch that had once been a park. When they cut back down between another row of houses, Dinah stopped him and pointed, across two back porches. "There."

"Wouldn't Maxon go out the front?"

"We can see the street from here." She nodded the other way, down along the house they were standing behind. "One of us should keep watch this way, the other there."

"Why don't I just go down to the corner? I can hide behind that house and see more of the street."

She shrugged indecisively, and he realized then that she had little better idea of what they were doing than he did. "Well," he said, "are we looking for Min, or waiting to follow Maxon?"

"I'm guessing both. If we find Min, he'll probably be following Maxon, won't he?"

Yilon nodded. Since she was watching the back yard, he kept an eye on the street. More foxes were moving back and forth, but it was now light enough that he could see that none of them was Maxon. "How do you know the house?"

“Shh,” she said, indicating the house they were near.

He lowered his voice. “Okay. How do you know the house?”

She sighed. “Leave it.”

He wanted to, but curiosity burned brighter. “If there’s anything that would help me figure out what’s going on...”

“No.”

After that, he kept quiet. The sun crept closer to rising, brushing the bricks and flagstones in brightening reddish light. The morning was already warmer than the previous day; perhaps this was the late summer Corwin had talked about. Yilon watched the foxes pass on the street, but still did not see Maxon, although one of them looked familiar. He was rubbing his paws together, but his muzzle was down and mostly hidden by a cloak, so Yilon couldn’t say what was familiar about him. The feeling nagged at him, until he forgot it not five minutes later.

“There he is,” he hissed, grabbing Dinah’s arm. Maxon had just appeared on the street, walking slowly with his head down. The clothes, the gait—it was definitely him.

Dinah followed Yilon down to the street. Both of them scanned the area, but saw no sign of Min. “He’s got to be around here somewhere.”

“Maybe he didn’t follow Maxon. Maybe he went looking for you.”

Yilon looked back at the Strad house. “One of us should check there. Just in case.”

“One of us has to follow Maxon.” Her ears were flat, her eyes wide as she followed his gaze back to the house.

“Can you do that?” He didn’t like the idea of going into the house, but she clearly was terrified to. “I’ll go into the house, check around quickly, and we’ll meet back at your place where Colian is.”

She bit her lip. “All right.” She stared, trying to work out something in her head. “Listen. There’s bad people in that house. There’s...”

He nodded. “I know. That’s where Kites came from. Go, you’ll lose Maxon.”

Unexpectedly, her paw reached out and squeezed his. “Be careful.”

“You too.”

He watched her slip away into the street behind Maxon, waited until they’d both turned a corner to creep back up the gap and around to the back door of the house.

The whole area behind the houses was silent and still. If they’d posted guards, Yilon didn’t see any. He crept closer, wishing Sinch were with him. It wasn’t just that the mouse knew more about sneaking around than he and Dinah combined; it was that their adventures were always fun. Of course, they'd never had an adventure with stakes quite this high. The image of the knife in Kites' throat flashed before him again before he was able to banish it.

There was a jog in the wall of the house which created a small corner. Yilon padded into it and flattened himself against the old brick, nose filled with the smell of dirt and ancient stone, ears perked to catch any conversation. Sinch would be able to climb up and crack the window open, but Yilon didn't trust himself to be able to do it both silently and without falling.

Of course, the night they'd met, Sinch had still been learning. Yilon had only been in Divalia a few weeks. He'd been walking around the gardens at dusk, trying desperately to banish the gnawing ache of homesickness in his gut, and had not seen Sinch until the mouse had tumbled to the ground right in front of him.

"I'm new here," Yilon had said, "but aren't you not supposed to do that?"

Sinch had tried to scramble away, but Yilon, sensing a kindred spirit, had laughed and told him to relax. He'd taken Sinch down to dinner, amused that the mouse was so nervous (though he only learned the full reason later), and feeling happy that he was able to both help someone else and flaunt the rules of the palace. Sinch had relaxed by the end of the night, helped along by some of the palace's mead, and had promised to come back later.

Yilon supposed that the ache of homesickness was what had brought that particular memory to his mind. His groin tingled at the memory of the night they'd both finally admitted they found each other attractive—he, at least, had been feeling it from that first night. It had been a nice couple years, he thought, and it was nice that there were a lot of mice here. Sinch could find a place to live, a nice mouse to devote himself to, and the two of them could remain friends. He would have them over to the palace—old rules cast aside by then—and their cubs would grow up together. It was the best he could hope for.

He fidgeted against the wall, realizing he had not been listening carefully. More and more foxes were walking down the street out in front, and some were talking. The rattle of a carriage sounded in the distance. Yilon sighed and edged further along the wall, toward the back of the house, under a different window.

Another fox walked through the alley behind the houses, so Yilon adopted a casual pose as though he were waiting for someone. The fox glanced at him but didn't stop.

It occurred to him that if Min had been following Maxon and had stayed to listen to the house, he was probably somewhere around the house, maybe around the other side. Nothing was happening inside the house here, anyway. He waited a little longer, to make sure nobody else was coming along the alley, and then moved around the back porch.

He strolled past, as slowly as he could while remaining nonchalant. Two stairs led up to a stone porch that was littered with old leaves and some dirt accumulated against the stone railing. In the center of the porch, cracked stone defined a doorway in which hung a heavy curtain. The breeze that barely moved the curtain, blowing toward the house, was no help in detecting any scents that might have lingered on the porch. On the other side of the house, he glanced at the back windows once, then turned the corner and walked toward the street. As soon as he was out of sight of the porch, he crept back against the wall again and perked an ear.

He still heard no sounds, but now he could smell the breeze coming past the back porch. It took a few seconds to sort out the combination of scents that tickled his nostrils. One was more familiar than the rest. "Min," he breathed.

He edged back along the wall, peering around the corner to the back. Still, nothing moved there, and no sound came from inside the—

The house's silence was broken by a muffled cry. "Help!"

Yilon snapped his head around. It was Min's voice, without a doubt. He padded back to the window in time to hear a thump, and then another cry. This one was followed by silence and then, after a span of four or five breathless heartbeats, a high-pitched giggle.

If he'd harbored any doubts about going inside, they were gone in that moment. He ran to the back porch, pushed the heavy curtain aside, and charged in.

He found himself in a tiny anteroom in front of another curtain, this one tied down. The giggling came from inside once more. Yilon pushed at the curtain, but it was tied at the corners. He attacked the knots, undoing them as quickly as he could, and wishing Sinch and his knife were there to help, trying to ignore the thick smells coming from inside the house, hoping that the sour smell of blood was old. "Come on," he muttered, pulling at the twisted pieces of rope. As soon as he got two knots undone, he had enough room to push past the curtain.

To his surprise, he emerged into a large room as nicely furnished as any in the governor's or Dinah's house. Carpets lined the floor and walls, with bell pulls hanging between the wall tapestries, and several fine wooden cabinets around the room bore candlesticks, two small mirrors, books, and what looked like a collection of grooming tools on their smooth tops. The sight was so at odds with the filthy exterior that Yilon had to stop for a moment, staring around to make sure he wasn't dreaming. And yet the smell matched perfectly: decay and rot and blood.

Two doorways led off to the right, one to the left, and one straight ahead. He crept cautiously toward the near doorway on his right, his fur prickling at sounds of movement and the smell of blood, growing stronger. A foot from the door, his ears caught a soft, tuneless humming. He paused, his insides turning cold at the emotionless, distant sound.

The nearest bell pull caught his eye. This rope was smoother than he'd ever seen, although it had numerous loose fibers sticking out of it. An odd, disquieting smell came from it, drawing him closer to examine it in the half-light of the room.

It didn't look be woven or braided. He peered more closely, lifted a finger to touch it—

—and jumped back, revolted. The thing was a tail, a mouse's tail.

Yilon stared at it, then looked wildly around the room. All the "bell pulls" were mouse tails, not hooked up to anything, just hanging as trophys. He staggered against the nearest cabinet, making it rattle as the grooming tools jumped. Reaching down to settle them, he saw that there were two silver pairs of scissors; the rest were vicious-looking knives, curved and straight, serrated and slender. And there was a space on the top of the cabinet where two more of the gleaming blades might have rested.

Min isn't a mouse, he told himself, but the memory of Kites poking the knives into his stomach came back to him. The house was still silent; now not even the sound of movement or humming coming from the room to the right. He crept back toward it and was just about to look around the corner when a scratchy voice echoed through the large room.

"What are you doing here?"

He spun around to see an old vixen. Her smell reached him in the same moment, through the miasma of the room: she was the one who'd accosted him on the street. She shuffled toward him, glaring. "Come to steal, have ya?" Her voice raised. "Thief! Thief!"

"No!" he hissed. He glanced at the curtain he'd come in by. He could probably duck out, be outside in a moment. But Min was still in here.

His whiskers twitched at movement behind him. A light paw fell on his shoulder and spun him around. He only briefly saw a fox his height grinning at him as happily as if he were a long-lost relative. The white shine of the grin, the one long canine tooth he could see, that image was what stuck in his head as the fox's arm whipped around and something struck the side of his head. Pain flashed, stars exploded in his field of vision, and then blackness.

Chapter 22: Sinch's Resolve

Sinch rocked back and forth in the cellar. He kept staring at the place where the crown should have been. This was it, this was his ultimate failure. Yilon had trusted him to take the crown and hold it safely until needed, and he had failed. Someone had followed him, had come into the cellar and had not wasted any energy rooting through the decaying sacks. Whoever it was had gone directly for the crown, able to sniff it out, knowing exactly what they were looking for. And he had been careless, had let himself be followed. Maybe it was Balinni, negotiating over price, all the while laughing inside at the stupid mouse from the capital who thought himself so smart.

There had to be carriages leaving for Divalia every day. He had enough money that he could find passage on one. At worst, he could buy food and walk down the pass. Maybe he would freeze to death. He kicked at one of the sacks. The prospect of returning to Divalia felt no more attractive now than it had earlier. The empty leather bags only gave him extra motivation; they didn't reduce the pain of the decision.

But there was nothing else he could do. He'd lost the crown; Yilon would never trust him with anything again.

The bag tore into pieces under one more kick. It hadn't taken him long: Not only his life in Dewanne, but his friendship with Yilon, all of it in tatters. At least when he returned to Divalia, his family would be there, his friends among the thieves. He could go back to stealing trinkets, sneaking into the palace to catch glimpses of the life the nobles lived.

That was what he was meant for, wasn't it? He didn't belong with the nobility like Yilon, nor with the mice here. He ran back through the list of enemies he'd made in two short days: Balinni, Maxon, the Shadows...

And there he paused. He'd made an enemy of the Shadows, but he'd fought back. He'd protected Yilon by killing one of them. He'd gotten away from Maxon, throwing a knife that had gone exactly where he'd aimed it. He'd even thought he'd gotten the better of Balinni, until this moment, getting Valix to come at least partly around to his side after hiding the crown.

He aimed a kick at another of the bags, sending it flying into pieces across the room. His paws clenched into fists, he stalked back and forth across the cellar, grabbing pieces of old leather and tearing them. He had his knife, he had his legs, he had his wits. The gash on his arm barely hurt him anymore. If he wanted to protect Yilon, he still could. But he would have to get the crown back.

Blood flushed his ears, pumping through him. He shut out the smells of the cellar, squeezing his eyes shut to think. It was Balinni, he was sure of it. The bastard had had one of the other mice follow him—not Valix, she would have told him (wouldn't she?)—and that other mouse had taken the crown. So he would have to go confront him. He would confront him, and he would not be afraid, and he would get the crown back.

The decision felt good. It was scary, for sure. But he reminded himself of what he'd done under pressure. Why not, then, take the same initiative now? It helped that he had no more appealing choice.

He fingered the knife at his waist. If he went back to Valix, he could get some token or word to assure Balinni that she was all right, and perhaps use her as leverage to get the crown back. Of course, if he were going to do that, he didn't really need a word or token at all. The mere fact of his presence without her would force Balinni to listen to him. If he could make it to the Warren without being stopped.

One more time, he looked around the cellar, at the wreckage of the sacks he'd torn apart. The leather might not be valuable, in its rotten state, but it didn't look any worse than some things he'd seen mice scavenging. Carrying an armful would give him camouflage moving through Dewanne on his way to the Warren. Nobody was likely to look twice at a mouse carrying a load of something that smelled that bad.

He ripped two more bags apart, hurriedly and without much difficulty—they almost came apart at the touch of his paws. With an armful of leather, holding his breath as best he could, he made his way back up the stairs and peered through the tattered curtain. He had to wait until a few foxes passed by for the street to be clear, and then he stepped out, hunched over his load as though protecting it, even though it smelled terrible and had spiders crawling over it. Twice he had to stop to shake them off his paws, but even when he did that, the foxes in the street ignored him.

He made his way easily back to the trench they'd used to cross the plaza, this time walking right past the guards, keeping his head down. Now, when he passed the dark, forbidding holes the filth drained into, he moved quickly past them, knowing what else was down there and why Valix had insisted on silence. Two other mice with lighter loads passed him, just as quiet, tails curled tightly around themselves as they half-ran. Sinch wanted to go faster now that he was mostly under cover, but he didn't want to lose his footing and fall, and he needed to keep his load at least until he reached the Warren.

Mice stood at the top of the trench, dumping their barrels of filth in. Two who noticed him waited until he'd passed. He nodded acknowledgment to them, dodged the shower of filth from the less polite ones, and hurried on. The trench led around the plaza, along the west side, to a narrow set of stairs at the edge of the Warren. Sinch climbed up, surprised at how relieved he felt to see the familiar ramshackle buildings and grimy streets. At the first narrow street that led deeper into the maze of buildings, he dumped the rotting scraps of leather on the first barricade he came to and hurried around it. He turned a corner and stopped.

The huge pile of detritus he'd had to clamber over was gone, now spread into two long piles. Was this the right street? He took two steps down it, uncertain, then strode forward. He would have to trust his sense of direction. After all, piles of garbage could move around—and apparently did. The next street he turned onto was also rearranged; only the large puddle of water was exactly where it had been, now larger.

With more confidence, he joined the stream of mice navigating the obstacles and made his way deeper into the Warren. Nobody stopped him, nobody attacked him, and within half an hour he was standing outside Balinni's house.

Cal and Mal were on duty when he walked in. "Hey, been waiting for you," one of them said.

"All day yesterday," the other said, standing.

"Waited for you and Valix."

"Boss said you wouldn't come back with the money."

"He said Valix would come back with your corpse."

"All right," Sinch said. "I need to see Ba—the boss, right now."

The first one—Sinch decided to call him Cal—laughed. "Boss is busy."

"Important meeting," his brother said.

"No disturb."

"He'll want to talk to me," Sinch said, "if he wants to see Valix alive again."

That shut them up. They looked at each other, back at Sinch, then back at each other.

"You go tell him."

"You go."

"What if he's lying?" Mal indicated Sinch.

"His problem."

"You know the boss."

They turned to Sinch and said, in unison, "Are you lying?"

Here was the first test of his new resolution. What would Valix do in this situation? How would Whisper handle it? For Yilon, he breathed, for Yilon I can be like them.

He drew his knife in one fluid motion and backed Mal up to the wall, placing the blade to his throat. He turned to Cal, who was just getting to his feet. "Go disturb him," he said. "Or I'll throw your brother's head in there first. You think that will disturb him?"

His heart was racing, energy coursing through him. All the anger, all the frustration of the previous day was trembling in his arm. Mal must have been able to feel the knife twitching against his throat, because he called in a high-pitched voice, "Go! Go!"

Cal stared at Sinch and then bolted through the doorway inside. His high, scared voice was broken by the low, measured tones of Balinni, and when Cal spoke again, he was a little less scared. Sinch kept the pressure of the knife to Mal's throat, the other's wide, scared eyes staring into his own. He felt an urge to apologize, to tell Mal that he had nothing against him personally, it was Balinni he wanted to have under the blade of his knife, but then it occurred to him that it was likely either Mal or Cal who'd followed him, who'd told Balinni where the crown was, and that gave fresh life to his anger.

Certainly, if Mal knew anything about the crown, he wasn't revealing it in his expression. So perhaps it had been Cal who'd followed him, or else Mal was just overwhelmed by the terror of being threatened in his own house.

"Let him go," Cal said from the doorway.

"Can I go in?" Sinch said without moving.

"Yes, yes." Cal stepped forward, then stopped, one arm half-raised as though trying to pull his brother to safety from a distance.

Sinch dropped his arm. He felt Mal sag against the wall in relief, but didn't see it, already shouldering past Cal and into the inner chamber.

It had been only a day ago that he'd sat on the other side of this desk, intimidated by Balinni, wanting desperately to help Yilon without giving away the game he was playing. Now, Balinni was almost pathetic to him compared to the Shadows, compared to the soldiers in the sewers.

"The boss" must not have been in a real meeting, or else the others had left through the back door, because he was alone behind the desk. The package that contained "Kishin" was sitting on one edge of his desk, the rest littered with papers and an ink pot. He looked up at Sinch, ears perked in interest, eyes slightly narrowed. "I admit," he said, "I did not figure you for the temperament of a fighter. I'd rather thought you were a thinker."

He shrugged, but Sinch saw the twitching of his whiskers and knew the affected disinterest for what it was. "Apparently I was mistaken on both counts. Where is Valix?"

Sinch put both paws on the desk, one still holding his knife, and leaned close. "Where is my prize?" A sharp scent tickled his nose, but he ignored it.

Clearly, that was not even within the realm of possible remarks Balinni had considered. The mouse's eyes widened, then creased in annoyance. "It's safe. I assume you are proposing a trade?"

"You filthy lying rodent!" A tall figure sprang into the room from the back door, seizing Balinni by the shoulder and throwing him to the ground. "You said you didn't know where it was!"

"I...thought you'd left..." came the feeble response from the ground. Sinch backed up two steps, holding his knife at the ready. The figure was a gaunt fox, wearing a cloak whose hood was thrown back over his shoulders.

"Thank Canis I didn't. Clearly His paw held me here to see your treachery." The fox kicked the chair out of the way and drew a slender knife from his belt, holding it point down over the prone mouse. "I should dispatch you here and now."

"No!" Sinch said impulsively, more out of a desire to see no more killing than to specifically spare Balinni.

The fox shot him a venomous look, and Sinch felt a bolt of recognition—the same muzzle looking at him from over a crossbow for two weeks, on the trip from Divalia. "I'll deal with you presently," the fox said.

"You're our guard!" Sinch burst out.

"And you're the pretender's sex toy." He looked down at Balinni's gasp. "Oh, you didn't know that? Well, when you make a practice of lying to others, you can hardly expect them to tell you the whole truth. Yes, this fierce puppet over here bedded down with the pretender lord every night on our journey out here. And he still has more dignity than you." The fox kicked out, eliciting a muffled cry. "He begs for your life. Well, you may yet have some use."

"Who are you?" Sinch demanded.

"Oh, we'll come to that presently." The fox faced Sinch across the desk. "Balinni told me that you were behind the theft of the crown, but that he didn't know where it was at the moment. He didn't tell me that right *away*." He kicked out again.

"He had me followed!" Sinch said. "I went back to find it and it's gone. He has it somewhere."

He wouldn't have thought the fox's eyes could narrow further, but they did. "Is this true?" he said, with a sharp glare at the mouse on the floor.

"No, no!" Balinni cried feebly. Sinch felt a moment of pity, and then fear at what this fox might represent that had reduced Balinni to such a pathetic state. He quelled the fear. For the moment, the fox was respecting him, at least to his face, and if he were to show any sign of weakness...

"Then what happened to it?" he yelled across the desk.

"I don't know!" Balinni called. "Ow!" The fox had kicked him again.

"Who else could have followed me?" Sinch found himself getting angrier at the frustration of being so close without getting his answer.

The fox had turned back toward him. Their eyes met as they both realized the answer at the same time. "You little fool," the fox snarled. "You've given the crown of Dewanne to the Shadows."

Sinch's arm sagged, the knife point almost touching the table. "I didn't give it to them."

The fox pointed his knife at Sinch. It gleamed in the light. "You come in here, new in town, try to steal the crown. You have no idea how things work here, no idea what you've set in motion. No matter how fortuitous your ignorance may have been—"

"Balinni set it all up," Sinch said.

"And you turned it on its ear." The fox shrugged, his muzzle curling upward in a humorless smile. "Then you are going to have to go retrieve it from them."

Sinch forced his knife to stay level with the fox's. "I can't."

"You have very little choice."

"They hate me."

The fox laughed. "You have barely been in town for two days. What could you possibly have done to incur their wrath?"

"I killed one of them."

The room grew so silent that he could hear Mal or Cal in the other room saying, "Did he just say he killed a Shadow?"

Sinch kept his own expression neutral, watching the fox's eyes widen, the smile vanish. His ears kept perfectly still, and now Sinch could see the grey edging up their black sides. "Surprised him from behind, no doubt," he shrugged. "I do not think—"

"We were on a second-story ledge," Sinch said. "He cut me in the arm. I threw him to the street." He pointed to his bandage, his confidence increasing with the respect he saw in the fox's eyes.

"Then you should have no fear to go back there and demand the crown from them."

Sinch looked steadily at him. He could detect the bravado in the fox's voice. "What's your name?"

"I don't owe you anything," the fox said.

Sinch shrugged. "I can walk out that door right now," he said. "And it won't be too much trouble to find out who you are."

The fox sneered. "You're going to ask Maxon? Who tried to leave you behind at the inn? I'm certain he'll be anxious to answer your questions. Or you could ask this pathetic wretch on the floor. But he wouldn't dare answer."

Sinch studied the fox's narrow, fierce muzzle. He knew Balinni, so he must have lived in Dewanne and then left to go to Divalia. And Maxon had brought him back.

He said there weren't any good foxes around since Dewry left.

"Maybe he's already told me...Dewry."

The fox's jaw snapped shut. He stared at Sinch. "What else did he tell you?" he demanded.

Sinch did his best to hide his inward glee. "Why don't you ask him?"

"He would have told me," Dewry said to himself, rubbing his muzzle. "But who else would have known? Did this lying thief tell you after all?" He kicked Balinni again.

"Please," the mouse's ragged voice came from behind the desk. "I didn't tell him anything. I wouldn't betray our trust."

"You'd betray our trust for a bowl of hot soup," Dewry sneered. "I've never held any illusions about that."

"No, no," Balinni protested.

Dewry had already turned back to Sinch. He drove his knife point into the table and spread his paws. "Very well," he said. "Then I will tell you this: if you do not bring the crown back here by sunup tomorrow, I will kill your little pretender lordling. Ah, yes, that's gotten to you, hasn't it?"

He looked impassively at Sinch's knife, which had moved to within inches of his muzzle. It was trembling despite Sinch's efforts to hold it still. "You want to be careful," he said, rage and fear pushing his newfound confidence to dangerous highs. "I killed the Shadow for threatening Yilon. I'd bet you don't have nearly as many friends."

Dewry laughed, pushing the knife away with a careless paw. He picked up his own and sheathed it. "Enough to make sure that your lordling will not survive if I'm killed, even without poor Kites. No, I would say it is in your best interests to keep me alive for the moment." He gathered his cloak around himself and lowered his ears so he could flip his hood over them. "I have more friends in this town than you have in the world, little sextoy.

Never, never forget that. I will see you tomorrow morning. If I see you before then, it will not go well for you."

Before Sinch could reply, the fox had swept out of the back doorway, hunched over until he was nearly a mouse's height. Sinch stared at the empty doorway, lowering his knife to the table slowly.

"Is he...is he gone?" Balinni said from the floor.

Sinch walked around the desk and poked his head out of the back door. He looked onto an alley that was narrow even by the standards of the Warren, barely wide enough for a mouse to walk with his shoulders squared. There was no place for anyone to hide, and the alley was empty in both directions. "He's gone," he said, coming back into the office.

Balinni was pulling himself up by the edge of his desk. He avoided Sinch's eye as he dusted himself off, picked up his chair, and seated himself behind his desk again. Sinch remained standing, with his dagger out, playing with its balance in his paw. "So," Balinni said, as though the interruption had never happened, "what have you done with Valix?"

Sinch looked down at the scarred muzzle, as composed as it had been when it was telling him that his knife wasn't worth six gold, that Valix would be his shadow. "Do you have any way to negotiate with the Shadows?"

Balinni flicked his ears back. "One doesn't hold this position without having certain connections."

"Good. How can we..."

The mouse laughed, shortly. "Why do you assume that my connections would be put at your disposal?"

"Because you want to see Valix alive again."

Balinni smiled. "So she is alive. Why didn't you tell me you're sleeping with the lord-to-be?"

"He may not be the lord if we can't recover the crown," Sinch pointed out. "And if we do, then whoever helped me recover it might earn quite a bit of favor."

The scarred mouse's ears flicked forward, but his expression remained neutral. "The Shadows do not negotiate."

"You just said..." Sinch sputtered.

Balinni spread his paws. "I said I had connections. The Shadows work on their own. They despise us for weak, ineffectual creatures. We despise them for their savage natures. But they fill a necessary role. They force the foxes to respect us."

"Meanwhile, you live off of them."

"Of course," Balinni said. "We all live off of the foxes one way or another, but they live off of us as well. They," he gestured outside his office, "collect the refuse, the discards, and make a life from it. In return they provide labor and service."

"And you simply take nice things from them. From the foxes."

"To deliver to the rest of our people," Balinni said. "We pass along luxuries that improve their lives."

Sinch sat down, still playing with his knife. "They don't seem to appreciate you."

Balinni waved a paw. "There are a few hard-headed fools who would prefer to live in squalor than take the remotest chance of offending the foxes. They remember Kishin only as a tragedy, not as a triumph."

"Triumph?" Sinch raised his eyebrows.

"They could have razed the Warren. We fought them off! A few mice died, but it could have been so much worse! And Kishin didn't live out the year."

"You killed him?"

Balinni looked annoyed. "We certainly were instrumental in his downfall."

"How so?"

"We haven't time to review all of that," Balinni said. "I believe you have a crown to retrieve."

"So how can you help me?"

Balinni pulled out a parchment and unrolled it on the desk. "This is a map of the entrances to the sewers, the ones that are usually patrolled and the ones that aren't. Once you get in there, it's up to you."

Sinch studied the parchment. He was pleasantly surprised to find that through his adventures of the past day, he was familiar enough with Dewanne—at least, the east side—to find one or two of the marked entrances. While looking at them, he studied the rest of the map of the city, locating both Dinah's house and the entrance Valix had led him to when they were fleeing Maxon. "What can you tell me about Dewry?"

He had made the mistake of not looking up when he asked the question. At Balinni's silence, he did, and saw the scarred mouse trying to hide his fear. "He wouldn't want me to say anything."

"Why does he want to kill Yilon?"

Balinni paused, looking into the distance, fighting to make a decision. At length, he said, "You'd best be on your way. Please...please don't hurt Valix."

Sinch stood. "She's safe. She was hurt, but she's recovering. I'm sure she'll come back as soon as she can."

The scarred mouse nodded. "Thank you," he said. "And good luck."

Sinch sheathed his knife, and glanced at the package on the edge of the desk. "Can I take 'Kishin'?"

Balinni hesitated, placing a protective paw on the package. Sinch leaned over. "It's my best chance to settle things with Dewry."

The scarred mouse set his jaw. He raised his eyes to Sinch's and pushed the package across the desk, scattering papers. "Bring him back safely."

Sinch couldn't tell whether Balinni was more concerned about the costume than he'd been about Valix. He tucked the bundle under his arm. "If I'm not here when Dewry arrives tomorrow, try to keep him here. I will be here if I can."

"Rodenta be with you," Balinni said.

Sinch walked out past Cal and Mal, who were gaping at him openly. He paused in the doorway and turned back. "Can either of you fight?" he said.

They looked at each other, then shook their heads simultaneously. "Of course not," he said, and walked back out into the Warren.

He had it in his head that he might be able to track Dewry by the fox's smell, but though it remained strong in the small alley behind the house, he lost it in the tangle of smells in the busier streets. So he turned his steps toward the trench. With the sun halfway up the sky, the refuse in it smelled even worse, but at least it was deserted. He ducked into the same small tunnel, beneath the guard post, and opened the sack.

To his surprise, he found the costume less objectionable this time. The smell of fox was just as strong, but he avoided looking into the glassy eyes and instead pulled the cloak over the head almost immediately, letting only the nose show. That was how Dewry had covered himself; even in disguise, foxes would want their noses exposed to sniff out any possible threat.

With the head secured on his shoulders and the cloak firmly around him, Sinch ascended the stairs on the city side, glancing back to make sure the guards were not in view. A short wall separated the west side of the city from the Warren, but it came up only to his chest, and even in the disguise, Sinch would have little trouble hopping over it if he needed to, on the way back. He walked along the dirt road that the mice had called "Uphill Way" even though it sloped gently downward. Few other walkers joined him on the road; the mice in Dewanne were either at their hidden service jobs or had already come home. He walked until he felt flagstones under his feet and smelled the warm, fresh odors of bread and porridge, and then marched along the street toward the plaza.

The first thing he had to do was make sure Yilon was safe. Dewry's speech had set a gnawing nut of worry in his gut that only the fox's smiling muzzle would dispel. The smells of food reminded him how long it had been since he and Valix had shared that soup, back in the Warren an age ago, but he didn't feel quite confident enough in his disguise to attempt to buy anything. Hopefully Dinah would have food at her house.

The thought of a breakfast of porridge with Yilon in the new, bright day set his paws moving quickly across the plaza. He kept to the side nearest the lake, opposite the castle, but he couldn't help glancing over at the castle as he walked. The plaza was not crowded, and what foxes there were moved deliberately, strolling in the shadows of the old stone buildings and their rooftop crests. And then, as he was about to move beyond the plaza and along the lakeside road, he took one more look toward the castle and stopped so abruptly that the fox walking behind him brushed the cloak and muttered "Your pardon" as he swept by.

Sinch stared along the facades of four buildings, to where a cloaked, hooded figure stood at the corner of the building nearest the castle. He felt as though he were looking into a mirror at the other, as still as he himself was. There were other cloaked foxes in Dewanne, some of which he had seen while walking through the west side, but he felt sure that this was Dewry.

The fox's head turned, and now Sinch could feel the weight of his gaze. He hurried onward, nearly stepping on a fox's tail in his haste to get out of sight. But the image of the cloaked fox would not leave his mind. Dewry, meeting someone outside the castle? He knew he should go immediately back to Yilon, but he had to know more. He turned right down the first street and wove his way through the thicker crowd of shoppers, the heat of the morning already suffusing the street with the smell of a hundred foxes over the smells of the fabrics they'd come to shop for.

Sinch made his way to the end of the street and there turned right again, cautiously, looking for Dewry. The cloaked fox was not where Sinch had seen him last, but after a moment of panic, Sinch spotted him, closer, walking in his direction along with another fox. Sinch moved around, but Dewry's companion's muzzle was in shadow, and foxes kept walking between them. Then they stepped into a patch of sunlight, and Sinch felt no surprise at all as he recognized Maxon.

The two of them had their muzzles close together, and though Sinch couldn't see Dewry's expression, his ears were perked up while Maxon's were back. The steward frowned and said something, then flicked an ear to listen for Dewry's answer.

He had to hear what they were saying. Heart pounding, paw on the hilt of his knife, he moved closer, passing them and then circling around

He had to hear what they were saying.

behind. He cupped his free paw to one ear, and fortunately his cloak helped focus the sound of their whispers so that he could at least catch some of the conversation, as long as he stayed directly behind them.

When he passed them, the steward was saying, "...tell where we might be overheard. This is safest." Sinch didn't hear Dewry's response; by the time he was behind them, Maxon was speaking again. "...get a message to me and meet somewhere else. Don't come up here again."

Dewry's response included something about "my way," probably telling Maxon it was on his way back. The steward dismissed this and asked something, to which Dewry said, "...didn't know anything," and then the word "sextoy" came loudly back to Sinch. His ears flushed and flattened, so that he missed the next thing Dewry said, but it ended with "he'll do it, all right," and a laugh.

"Don't be so sure," Maxon said. He lowered his voice, so that the only words Sinch caught were as he was finishing: "...than you might think."

"I didn't need Kites." Dewry's voice was sharp.

Maxon murmured something else, to which Dewry responded, "He found it?"

"Shh." The steward hushed him, and the next few exchanges were inaudible. Sinch had just begun to creep closer when Dewry stopped in his tracks. Sinch turned quickly and looked in the nearest store window.

"How could you let that happen?" Dewry cried. Another fox, passing nearby, flicked his ears but kept walking. Both Dewry and Maxon looked at him and lowered their heads again.

"Did not have any choice in the matter," Maxon said. He put an arm around the other fox and urged him forward. "Come on. It's best you not go back there just yet."

Sinch hurried to catch up. Dewry was saying, "...kill him no matter what happens."

"Moderate your voice," Maxon said sternly. Sinch lost most of the rest of his sentence, until he finished by saying, "...if he should die."

"Ha." Dewry now seemed less worried about keeping the conversation secret. "What could anyone do?"

"Put a stop to you." Maxon sounded quite irritated.

"You wouldn't," Dewry said. "You've been too much help, invested too much."

Maxon's response, whatever it was, made Dewry stop cold and shove the steward angrily away from him. Maxon stared back at Dewry, but Sinch's movements had placed him, too, directly in the steward's line of sight. He felt the stillness of both of them and hurried to move around

Dewry, ducking into the nearest store. Behind him, Maxon called, "Ho! You there, in the cloak!"

Sinch didn't stop. He had made his way into a sweets store, where a middle-aged fox leaned on his stone counter. "Morning, sir," he said. "What can I interest you in?"

Sinch gestured behind him, staying as far from the counter as he could. "My friends would like a sample," he said, trying to keep his voice low. "Outhouse?"

"Certainly." The fox reached under his counter and came up holding a tray. Maxon was already at the door of the store. "Right back there."

"My thanks." Sinch bobbed the fake head and hurried to the back of the store. Behind him, he heard Maxon telling the storekeeper that he was *not* interested in samples. He pushed the back door open and rushed into the sunlight.

The outhouse stood down the street, a communal one that Sinch could smell from fifty feet away. Traffic was sparser here in the street behind the shops, as most foxes were either hurrying toward the outhouse or away from it. It occurred to Sinch, belatedly, that he might have been better off remaining on the better-trafficked main thoroughfare, but it was too late for that now. He hurried toward the outhouse, looking around for any other foxes with cloaks to confuse pursuit, but there weren't even any with covered heads. The warmth of the morning was already enough to keep cloaks and hats in wardrobes; Sinch was panting in the heavy cloak under the disguise.

He had no way of seeing where Maxon was behind him. All he could do was keep moving ahead as fast as he could. The costume was heavy on his shoulders, but he couldn't take it off. Running through the crowd as a mouse would be even worse. Fortunately, he knew Maxon probably couldn't run very fast.

He jogged around one fox and light flooded his eyes. The hood of the cloak had fallen back, exposing him to the sun and exposing "Kishin" to everyone around him. He cast wildly around for a place to hide while he replaced the hood, but just as he'd spotted a shadowy corner and moved in that direction, he found himself face to face with an elderly vixen.

The cloak hid his face from her, but she wasn't looking down. She was looking straight ahead, into the glass eyes of the dead fox head. He moved out of her way as fast as he could, but a moment later he heard a piercing scream, and the bustle of heightened activity behind him.

As he ran, screams trailed behind him as "Kishin" fixed each fox with a dead stare and then moved on. Sinch would have to disassemble the whole costume, without someone to help him simply fix the hood. He couldn't reach up there by himself. The shadowy corner he'd spotted just didn't have enough cover. He stumbled on past it, staring at the street beyond. Angry yells punctuated the screaming now, the noise behind him loud. And there, ahead of him...

At the top of a small rise, a building with a round cupola, over which rose the five-pointed symbol of Canis. A church! It was a church of Canis, but it was still a church, still a sanctuary.

A paw grabbed at his cloak from behind. He pulled away from it, almost losing his balance in the process. His momentum carried him into a building, with a jarring thump, but somehow his legs kept him driving forward. Another paw grabbed at his cloak, pulling the fabric tight against his paws. He lost his grip on the cloak and felt it slip away, pulling the harness and the fox head with it.

They teetered unsteadily atop his head and shoulders. He tried to steady himself, but was moving forward too quickly. The straps threatened to pull him over backwards. There was nothing he could do but slide his arms out of them and jump forward.

"A mouse!" someone shouted.

"By Canis's fur..." The fox sounded about to be sick. More screams, higher-pitched now, chased Sinch up the hill. Unencumbered, Sinch sprinted forward. No paws touched him before he reached the church door. He turned as he pulled it open.

A small band of six foxes ran up the street toward the church. Behind them, a crowd had gathered around the disassembled "Kishin." Further back, at the base of the street, Maxon, holding his leg, hobbled forward. His eyes blazed at Sinch, but whatever he was yelling was lost in the noise of the crowd. Sinch gave the steward a cheerful wave, and slipped inside the church.

The noise died down almost immediately, and disappeared altogether when the door swung shut. They would probably come in very soon. He padded quickly along the inside wall, looking up.

This church was smaller than any he'd been in back in Divalia, but still larger than a house. The fading frescoes around the upper tier of windows, depicting Canis as a fox, were a good thirty feet over his head, with the top of the dome, inset with the five-pointed star of Canis, another thirty feet over that. There were seats for perhaps fifty foxes, facing a single altar with a small silver circle of Gaia over top of a prominent silver symbol of Canis. The proportions bothered him a little, but only in the back of his head. To either side of the rows of seats, a small chapel was set into the wall. Sinch headed toward the chapel to the right, praying it would be empty. Coming around the side of it, he saw nobody on the bench, nobody reading the large book on the altar. He ducked around the corner and flattened himself against the wall just as the door of the church opened again.

"Spread out," someone said. "Get to the back door first."

Behind the altar which held the book, a worn curtain covered the back of the altar. Sinch looked down at the open book, which was thinner than the book of Gaia he was familiar with. Words on the page caught his eye: "...with all that ye do. For the cub steps in the path of the mother, and the shadow of the father falls across the path of the cub..." He didn't have time to read more. Someone was coming along the aisle outside, slowly, no doubt looking down all the pews.

If this church were like the ones in Divalia...he offered up a short prayer to Rodenta and pushed aside the curtain at the back of the alcove. There was just enough space between it and the wall for him to fit and pull the curtain back across. But he wouldn't be able to hide here, not if people searched the church. They would come into the alcove and smell him.

He felt a moment of panic at the solid-looking stone wall and floor, and then remembered a lesson from his training. His paws skimmed the stones all along the wall as quietly as he could, looking for loose mortar between them. Behind him, he could hear foxes moving through the church, respectful but determined. They would be here at the chapel within a few minutes.

One of the stones shifted under his paw, a large one at waist level. He pushed and met resistance, but when he worked his fingers around the edge of the stone, it pivoted toward him with a scraping noise that echoed in the small chapel. And there in the space behind it was a narrow stair, leading down.

He climbed in quickly, head first. The inside of the stone, filthy with dirt and spiderwebs, had a crude handle carved into it that allowed him to pull it closed. He padded as quietly as he could down the stairs. He'd bought himself a few minutes, maybe more, depending on how assiduously the foxes searched and how common the knowledge of this passage was. All churches in Divalia had a crypt, the entrance concealed to varying degrees, many of them forgotten except by thieves. In the old Rodenta churches, bodies were stored in crypts to keep them safe from predators, but he hadn't been sure a church of Canis would also have one. This one felt as though it hadn't been trodden in several lifetimes.

The only problem was, he was trapped in here. According to Balinni's map, there was not an entrance from the church into the sewer, and most crypts only had the one entrance. They often had places to hide, even if people did remember them. One thief, Sinch heard, had hidden three whole days in a crypt while the priest himself searched nearby without finding him, the ancient stones and the smell of mold hiding him completely.

Sinch made his way down the stone stairs into the chill of the cellar by feel. At the base of the stairs, his paws met a cold dirt floor. He put his paw out to touch the stone wall, and walked along with his paw against the stone. A few feet from the stairs, the wall disappeared. His paw plunged into the space beyond and encountered bones. He jerked it back and stood perfectly still, listening for noise from above and absorbing the smell of must and mold while his eyes strained to adjust to the pitch darkness.

The bones meant that the gap in the wall was a mensa, a shelf built to put bodies to rest. Likely there were three: one at ground level, one at waist level, and one above his head, reserved for the most important burials. So this had been a functional crypt, unlike some of the ones in Divalia that were only ever used to store wine. Nobody had followed him down here, so probably the current residents had forgotten about it, since the Panbestian Church favored burials in churchyards and sacred ground rather than in underground rooms. He wondered how long it had been since anyone had been down here. There were no fresh smells of any sort, not foxes, not mice, not even wild mice. His paws found reliefs on the walls, and he spent a moment tracing them, trying to puzzle out the pattern in his head.

It would be nice to have a little more light to see the carvings. And to see whether there was another exit. Hesitantly, he walked along the wall again, but this time, when the wall went away, he didn't probe the empty spaces. As much as his whiskers twitched at the thought of what these foxes might have been buried with, valuables that wouldn't be missed by anyone, his first priority was to get out and find Yilon.

There were no other stairs. By the time he'd made a complete circuit of the crypt and investigated the crumbling columns in the center, he thought the foxes searching the church would have given up. He hoped so. Just pushing the stone aside to check would make enough noise to give him away, if anyone were within earshot.

He placed his paw on the stone. One more minute, he told himself. Just one more.

He told himself that ten more times, and then finally pushed the stone as gently as he could. By working it slowly back and forth, he moved it as quietly as possible until he had a crack he could put his ear to.

The church was silent, empty of footsteps. He heard the low murmur of prayer, but no other sounds. Slowly, he worked the stone out, listened again for any disturbance, and then crept out. The curtain was still stretched across the space at the back of the alcove. Checking his surroundings at every turn, he made his way out of the church.

Chapter 23: Shredded

Yilon dreamed of standing under Menroc Falls in Vinton, but the falls had been suspended. As he looked, the cliff gave a low, shuddering groan and the water started falling. He couldn't move. It cascaded over his face, dripping into his ears and eyes.

"Come on, get up."

Water hit Yilon full in the face again, pouring into the ear that wasn't squashed to the floor. He shook his head and sputtered, slowly becoming aware of the world around him: bright light piercing his eyelids, a throbbing pain on the side of his head, the smell of foxes and the acrid tang of blood, and a soft nasal whistle in front of him, as of a fox with a stuffy nose breathing quickly.

The high-pitched voice spoke again. "Didn't hit you *that* hard. Delicate little thing. Not like him." The wheezing grew louder. The voice came from right in front of him next. "Come on, eyes open. Look at me. That's what you want. That's why you broke in."

Yilon lay on his side on the floor, his arms behind his back. When he tried to push himself upright, he found he couldn't pull his wrists apart. His ankles, too, were fastened together with thick rope. His tail was kinked painfully beneath him, but he couldn't manage to work it free.

He looked up at a short fox crouched next to him with a stone pitcher casually resting in one paw. The black fur of his lower forearms glistened wetly in the light as he set the pitcher on the floor. "There we are," he said, and stood. One of his ears was partly missing, and his smile looked crooked.

Yilon blinked water from his eyes and flicked his ears. The water in them gave the world a faraway sound, as though someone else were speaking through the fox from far away. "Where...who are you?" he said through a mouth that felt stiff and sticky. Maybe the smell of blood was just from his own muzzle. He could taste it, now that he moved his tongue around.

"Silver Strad. Shreds." The fox was about Yilon's height. He wore a simple dark brown tunic fastened with a strap around the waist, and a dirty pair of short trousers that had once been white. With his right paw, he held a silver dagger, and it was the spatters of red all up and down the blade and handle that drew Yilon's eyes. As he watched, a drop hanging from the point of the blade quivered and fell to the floor.

"Where's Min?" Yilon demanded, with considerably more bravery than he felt.

Shreds waved the knife. "I didn't ask his name. If you're talking about the other thief who was skulking around, hee hee, he's just over there."

Yilon couldn't make himself turn over to look where Shreds was pointing. The fox's scent was strong and acrid up close, and nauseating in combination with the sour blood smell. The air in the room, stuffy and warm, made it hard to breathe. "If you've hurt him," he said, even though it was an inane thing to say to the bloody knife.

"Hee hee," Shreds said, "Hurt him? No, no, we've been playing, hee hee, greenstones. He lost." He swung the knife back and forth. "I had a brother," he continued. "We used to play greenstones." His crooked ear flicked.

"When is your brother coming back?" screeched a voice from the hallway.

Shreds turned his head. "Shut up, Gran!"

"Where is Stewell?" she yelled. "There's thieves about!"

"I know, Gran! I've got one in here now!"

The old vixen came shuffling into the room, carrying her tail in her arms and chewing at its tip. She eyed Yilon, and pointed a bony finger at him. "He said the lord was coming."

Shreds pushed her quickly back. "Gran, hee hee, you're not to come in here." But she'd already looked over to the other corner of the room. She drew in a breath and started to scream.

"Oh," Shreds said, and pushed harder. He turned to look over his shoulder at Yilon. "Don't you, hee hee, go anywhere."

Yilon watched them leave for the hallway, and struggled to free his wrists the moment Shreds was out of view. From the hallway, he heard the old vixen asking for Stewell again, her voice high and querulous. Shreds's responses were impatient and snappish, moving further down the hall.

Disturbed though he might be, he tied knots well. Yilon managed to get a little play, moving his wrists an inch or so apart. After that, the ropes held fast.

His ankles were a bit looser, but not much. As he struggled, he rolled onto his back, and his head turned toward the other side of the room. His eyes focused despite himself, and his struggles stopped.

Against the wall under the window, he could see the long, red tail of a fox, its white tip smeared with brown dirt and blood. The fox it had been attached to lay sprawled on the opposite side of the room, next to an overturned chair. The white wall and stone floor around him were smeared with his blood, and one of his arms was bent at an unnatural angle. He wore a guard's uniform that had been...Yilon couldn't help thinking the word... shredded. "Min," he hissed.

Min didn't move. Yilon tried again, more loudly. "Min!"

"Hm," came a high voice behind him. "I'm not sure he can hear you. Maybe there's, hee hee, something wrong with his ear."

Yilon looked up in time to see Shreds saunter across the room. He bent over the fox and pulled up the head by one of the ears. Min, if it was him, still did not move or react. With a quick motion, he slashed the knife across its base and turned around, swinging the severed ear in one paw, the knife in the other. "Here," he said, kneeling down next to Yilon and holding the thing up to his muzzle. "Why don't you take a look?"

The triangular piece of flesh hung inches from Yilon's nose, reeking of blood and death, but under it, he could smell Min, and that clenched a fist around Yilon's stomach. He gulped and then convulsed, turning onto his side and spewing the contents of his stomach onto the floor.

"Oh, hee hee," Shreds said. "There's something wrong with your stomach. Let's, hee hee, let's have a look, shall we?"

He dropped the ear and pushed Yilon onto his back. With an easy gesture, he slipped the knife up the front of Yilon's tunic. The cloth parted with a rip, falling away from his stomach. He cast about for something, anything to say to stall the lunatic. "What happened to him?"

A peevish look flashed across the fox's muzzle. His mutilated ear flattened. "He kicked me," he said. "We were having a nice conversation, hee hee, he wouldn't even miss his tail, and then he kicked me." He rubbed his side with the paw that wasn't holding the knife, and then looked down. "Oh, see, this is the problem, hee hee, did my brother make these holes? They're too small, and they're all patched up."

"Your...brother?"

"I had a brother," Shreds said, picking at the stitches with the point of his knife. "I *had* a brother."

"Kites?" Yilon tried to edge away from the knife, but Shreds pressed it harder against him.

"You killed him, that's what he told me, said not to tell Gran, but she doesn't even know about Father, why would I tell her? You killed him."

"He was going to kill me!" Yilon said. "He was stabbing me in the stomach!" He knew there was no reasoning with Shreds, but the longer and louder he talked, the better the chance that someone might hear him, that Dinah might come looking for him. From the position of the sun, he couldn't have been unconscious for long.

"Wasn't going to kill you, no, no." Shreds had pulled the stitches out of one wound. He ran the knife across the bare, shaved skin, and then slid the point into the wound again. "Just wanted to know how you got here." He stared straight into Yilon's eyes, and giggled. "*I'm* going to kill you."

He made as if to plunge the knife down. Yilon jerked back and winced as the point tore the edge of the wound. "Hee hee," Shreds said. "Don't worry. I won't kill you right away. We have time to play a little."

"I didn't kill him!" Yilon said. "And he would have killed me!"

"He just wanted to play!" Shreds wasn't giggling now, and too late, Yilon realized that he might have made a mistake in talking more about Kites. "He just wanted to play!"

"I don't know how he died!" Yilon yelled.

"This is how we play," Shreds said. He grabbed Yilon's tail, and started chanting, "Line up the mice, five to a row, take off their tails and swing them below." With a jerk, he pulled the tail out from under Yilon and raised his knife.

"I'm not a mouse!"

"Line up the mice, four to a row, take off their feet and see how they go," Shreds sang. He pulled Yilon's tail straight out. Pain flared at the base. Yilon pulled against the grip, but Shreds held him in place. He lowered his knife and ran it along Yilon's tail, parting the fur. When he found a space between the bones, he pressed the knife down.

At the sharp pain, Yilon swung both his legs up and kicked Shreds as hard as he could. He caught the fox in the shoulder and sent him hard against the wall. Using the momentum, he got up to his knees and threw himself against the stunned Shreds, with no real idea of what he was going to do other than keep attacking, keep him off balance. The knife grazed his hip and then fell clattering to the stone floor. For a wild moment, Yilon thought he would be able to knock the other unconscious. He slammed against him again, his bound paws scrabbling at the floor for the knife.

Then teeth sank into his shoulder. Classic mistake; he could hear his instructor saying, "Never bite in a fight, because that gives your enemy leverage on your head." He tried to swing his shoulder around, to bang Shreds's head into the wall, but his body twisted awkwardly and he only managed a light tap against the stone.

Shreds did open his jaw, but only because his paws had gotten hold of Yilon's torso. He threw Yilon to one side, sending the young fox roughly onto his stomach. Yilon's jaw smacked the hard stone; spots danced before his eyes as he struggled to get to his knees again. A moment later, Shreds was on his back, forcing him to the ground.

"Hee, hee," he panted in Yilon's ear. "I like, hee hee, a bit of a, of a fight. It makes, makes the trophies, hee hee, *so* much more meaningful."

"Let me go," Yilon said, as calmly as he could. "I'll reward you. Money, land..."

Shreds was moving around to straddle his hips. His paw yanked Yilon's tail up. As he settled himself, Yilon felt the uncomfortable hardness of the other's arousal. "Don't," he said, squirming as hard as he could. Shreds pressed down harder, holding his tail up.

"Only two rewards I want," he said. "One is this." His paw yanked Yilon's tail painfully.

Yilon gritted his teeth, waiting for Shreds to tell him the other. Finally, he realized that Shreds was waiting for him to ask. He resisted, until his tail was yanked again, the pain more intense, and he feared Shreds would just take it off. "What's the other?" He prayed it had nothing to do with the hard sheath rubbing into his thigh.

Shreds leaned over. His hot breath came in Yilon's left ear. "I want my brother back," he said. Before Yilon could respond, Shreds sank his teeth into the ear. He pulled, and then a cough sounded, out in the hallway.

Both foxes froze. Shreds started to move first, until something struck his head. Yilon felt the impact through the teeth in his ear before they released, and the weight atop him toppled slowly to one side.

"Dear Canis," someone breathed behind him in a tone that was almost a prayer.

"I told you," a sharp female voice said.

"Dinah!" Yilon called.

He heard a scuffle. "Let me go," she growled, nearby.

"You can't just..." He coughed, again, and Yilon recognized Maxon.

"I already did the other one," she said. "It'll be a better world without them both."

"*You* did?"

"Excuse me," he called, "but could someone untie me?"

"Stay away from him," Maxon said sternly. Paws worked at the knots around Yilon's wrists, and then his ankles. He turned himself over, stretching his arms and wincing at the bite in his shoulder. Maxon had taken the ropes he'd pulled from Yilon and was binding the unconscious Shreds the same way. Dinah stood by the door, pointedly facing away from Min, but when Yilon sat up, she walked around Maxon to his side.

"Are you okay?"

"My tail hurts," he said, "but it's still attached. And he bit my shoulder. And my ear."

"You're bleeding here, again." She pointed to his stomach.

He looked down. "He ripped out the stiches."

Dinah shook her head. "Colian has never been as busy as he was this night."

"What are you doing in this house?" Maxon demanded.

Yilon lifted his chin. "I came in to find...to find Min. He called for help."

Maxon shook his muzzle. His ears sagged, the sunlight highlighting the grey fur on them and on the top of his muzzle. "You came in here to rescue a guard?"

"*My* guard," Yilon said. "He was here...because of me." The weight of that truth bowed his head. If he hadn't involved Min in this...if he'd kept Min with him, or given him orders to remain behind...

Though Dinah and Maxon were facing the back of the room, where Min lay, neither of them looked in that direction. Maxon straightened and held out a paw to Yilon. "Let's get out of this room," he said. "There are some things I need to say to you."

Yilon didn't reach out his paw. Maxon met his eyes. "My lord," he added.

His eyes were steady and calm, a hard brown, but his head was bowed in respect. Yilon lifted his arm and grasped the steward's paw.

"Shall we return to the house?" Maxon asked.

Yilon shook his head. "I think I would rather sit down for a bit before walking back, if you don't mind." He bunched up part of his tunic and pressed it to the wound in his abdomen. "I'm not bleeding that much, but I don't feel too steady."

Maxon led them to a sitting room that, thankfully, smelled only of age and decay. Yilon brushed spiders from a padded chair and sat gingerly, while Maxon and Dinah pulled their chairs up to a small table. "What about the old vixen?" Yilon asked, pulling the halves of his tunic around him.

"She's closed in her room," Maxon said. "Silver must have done that. Before we leave, I'll find you a new tunic. I think you're Silver's size."

Yilon shuddered. "I'll go naked before I wear something of his. He's insane."

"He wasn't always," Maxon said. "Losing his brother...Dewry should never have told him about that."

"You didn't know them," Dinah said. "They were always like that." She got up from the chair and walked to the door, then the window.

Maxon cleared his throat. "He is worse now than he was two days ago. Fair?"

"Did you see the tails in the hallway?" Yilon couldn't stop himself from saying.

"Yes, but..." Maxon stopped himself, nodded his head gravely. "It is a fair point. But this is not the time for local justice. When we leave here, I will call a guard, and he will be taken to prison."

"Should we even be here now?" Yilon looked around. "What if someone else comes back?"

"The only other person who would come here is Dewry, and he will be gone at least another hour. Long enough for me to say what I need to say. I would prefer not to put this off." He coughed.

"Who's Dewry?" Yilon rubbed his shoulder. The bites didn't feel deep.

Maxon took a breath and let it out without coughing. "He is Sheffin's—the late Lord Dewanne's—son."

Chapter 24: Maxon's Story

Yilon stared at Maxon. "That's impossible."

Maxon shook his head. "Lord Dewanne was fifty-eight years old when he died. Dewry turns forty next month."

Dinah, who had stopped her pacing around the room at Maxon's announcement, now began again. "That's why I didn't know him."

"He has spent the last twenty years or so in Divalia," Maxon said. "But let me go back to the beginning. I believe we have time, and it is important..." He coughed. "I want you to hear the story."

"Go on," Yilon said, and Dinah sat down again as well.

Maxon took a breath. "I was twelve when Lord Dewanne selected me to be his personal servant. My father was a miner; he died in a collapse of the mines. The mice who were supposed to have built the constructs..." He shook his head. "I joined the guard, to support my family. Lord Dewanne—he was not the lord then, just the heir, so he was in charge of the guard—he saw that I was not old enough to be a useful guardsman, but rather than dismiss me, he took me into his service. I was close to his age, only four years younger."

"He was my age then," Yilon murmured.

Maxon inclined his head. "As captain of the guard, Sheffin spent a good deal of time out in the city. His father wanted him to get to know the people of Dewanne he would one day govern. That is how he met Kayley."

When neither Yilon nor Dinah reacted to the name, Maxon pointed toward the adjacent room. "Kayley is the old vixen in the next room. Dewry's mother."

"Oh," Yilon said.

Maxon nodded. "She was different then, of course. Younger, vibrant, energetic. Sheffin visited her many times, telling only me where he was going so that I could make excuses for him if needed. And then one day, he came back and told me she was going to have a cub. 'If it's male,' he said, 'he'll be my heir.'

"His father would have nothing of it, of course. Kayley was beautiful, but she was common, and a match had already been arranged with Delia. That's Lady Dewanne. She's of a noble family, and their cubs would have been..." He shrugged.

"Was she unable to have cubs?" Dinah leaned forward.

Maxon did not answer immediately. "Lady Dewanne's private affairs are not mine to discuss," he said finally. "Kayley, now, she was determined to have her cub. She believed that he would one day rule Dewanne. Sheffin's father wanted her to not have the cub. Sheffin tried to convince her to take the cub elsewhere once he was born..."

"But she had to have been in season," Dinah cried. "How did he not know she was in season?"

Maxon's ears lowered. "He did not know. She entered early, I believe, or perhaps he was in love with her and thought that if he made out to have been tricked, his father would relent. In any case, his father was unsympathetic, and Kayley's cub therefore fatherless."

"But not as far as she thought," Yilon said.

Maxon inclined his head. "Indeed. As Dewry grew up, she told him he would be lord one day. I got to know him well, for whenever Lord Dewanne wished to send her money or food, I was the one tasked to take it. He would not trust anyone else. And when Dewry turned ten, Lord Dewanne sent him to Divalia to be tutored with the other noble children."

Yilon thought of Sinch, who hadn't even had that benefit. "Even though he wasn't officially the heir?"

"Even so. When he reached adulthood, Dewry returned here and joined the guard. Lord Dewanne had been married to Delia for..." He counted in his head. "Nine years? Perhaps ten. There were stirrings and rumors, because they had not yet produced a cub. But they lived in Divalia and visited rarely, and Corwin managed the city well. When Dewry joined the guard, though...he served faithfully for two or three years, and then rumors about his parentage began to slip out. He denied them, but in a clever way that suggested he was merely forbidden to tell the truth.

"Soon after he turned twenty, though," Maxon's eyes narrowed. "There was an attack on the palace. A burning arrow was shot into the chambers next to Lord and Lady Dewanne's. Nobody was hurt," he said quickly, to Dinah's gasp. "A young fox deserted the guard the next day. Everyone assumed it was him. He knew Dewry, it turned out." He stared past them. "I never believed Dewry had anything to do with it."

"But he had friends who would murder for him?" Dinah said, her voice high and loud. "Even if that's true, that's just as dangerous."

Maxon rubbed his muzzle. "Lady Dewanne thought the same. She insisted that Dewry leave Dewanne. The only other place he knew was Divalia. So, at the behest of his father, I gave him a mount from the palace stables, a small purse of money, and the names of several tradespeople in Divalia where he could apply for work as a guard, or learn a trade.

"I did not hear from him for many years. Sometimes gifts would arrive at the castle, addressed to me, with no signature. Glass goblets, a package of sweetened grain, a cask of mead. I guessed they were from him, and I was happy to think he was doing well. I did not consider that he had no training other than soldiery, that the gifts were far beyond a soldier's means.

"When Lord Dewanne passed, I had my orders to fetch you. But I had promised to serve the court of Dewanne, and I had always thought that Lord Dewanne would have wanted his son to take the throne. I had no way of contacting him, but he had heard of the lord's passing and wrote to me, eagerly asking whether he could return, giving me an address where a return message would find him. After meeting with your family," he inclined his head toward Yilon, "I met him at that address and talked to him for several hours. He was so desperate to return, so full of plans for Dewanne, it was clear he had been following the political situation from afar as best he could."

He paused and looked to the window, away from Yilon. "I did not learn until later that he was spying on you and had already tried to kill you."

"That was him?" Yilon found he could not muster much surprise.

Maxon nodded. "He had heard of your arrival in Divalia. When Lord Dewanne took ill, he wrote to ask if he could come home. His mother told him that you had been designated his heir."

"His mother? Her?" Yilon pointed at the other room.

Maxon coughed into his paw, a prolonged fit. "Yes," he said. "The noble families were told. Word spread through the city."

"But she's..."

"She has not always been so," Maxon said sharply.

The room fell silent. "All right," Yilon said, after exchanging glances with Dinah. "So he was spying on me and shooting arrows at me. Then what?"

"Then..." Maxon looked down at his paws. "He promised he would make no more attempts against you, if I brought him back to Dewanne."

"So you bought him a mount, or something?" Yilon leaned forward when Maxon didn't answer. "You had to. Nobody else came with us, except... the *guard*? He was the guard?" Maxon nodded, slowly. "The fox who tried to *assassinate* me?"

He'd half-risen from his chair. A sharp pain in his stomach stopped him. He sat again, wincing.

"He promised," Maxon said, "and he kept his promise."

"I'm starting to see the pattern here," Yilon said. "You wanted him to assume the lordship. You never thought much of me. You knew..." He stopped himself, aware of Dinah's presence.

The steward opened his jaw, and then shut it with a click. His eyes met Yilon's, and in that look, Yilon saw that he was right, that Maxon had guessed the truth of his parentage. Slowly, Maxon nodded. "You have the right of it. I admit it. I serve the court of Dewanne, and I was determined that this land should have the best ruler."

"You didn't know me," Yilon said.

"Nor did I know what Dewry had become," Maxon shot back. "But I always believed that Lord Dewanne wanted him to be named the successor. It was Lady Dewanne who hated him, who banished him, who insisted on appointing...another family's son to the succession."

"Why?" Dinah put in.

"I have not asked," Maxon said stiffly. "But I believe she resented Kayley, and wished her son to be forever relegated to obscurity, if not poverty."

"No, I mean...why did Lord Dewanne not cast her aside? Take another bride?"

"If Sheffin had one failing, it was too much affection, too much devotion," Maxon said with the same stiff posture.

Yilon stood, and winced again as the motion pulled at his wounds. "And we're all paying for that failing," he said. "I need to ask you one question."

Maxon looked up without rising. He nodded. "We may not share all the same values. But I have come to respect your courage and your dedication. Dewry has surrounded himself with criminals and lunatics, and he has not stopped trying to achieve his ends through violence. I have made my decision. The best interests of the court of Dewanne will be served with you as their lord."

"Oh," Yilon said.

Maxon's muzzle curved into a slight smile, the first Yilon had seen in a long time. The steward cleared his throat. "I do hope to bring some influence to bear on you on the question of the mice. That lies in the future, however."

"Thank you," Yilon said. "But I was just going to ask what arrangements we can make for Min. When you call the guard, can you ask them to bring him to his home, or to wherever they take guards killed in the line of duty?"

"Of course." Maxon pushed his chair back and stood. "I will go now. You will return to the house in the Heights?"

Yilon looked at Dinah, who nodded. "Colian is there," she said. "Yilon needs to be bandaged up. Again."

Yilon pressed his paw to his abdomen. "It's nothing," he said.

Maxon's gaze traveled from Yilon's stomach up to his ear. "My lord," he said, "My role in this...you might have been killed. Once you have safely assumed the lordship, I will tender my resignation."

Merely an hour ago, Yilon would have liked nothing more. Now, he hesitated. "We shall see about that when the time comes," he said. "In the meantime, let's get the crown back, and anything you can do to stop Dewry would be most welcome."

Maxon hesitated. "I would...I would like to send him back to Divalia. For the memory of my old lord."

"He's tried to kill me," Yilon pointed out. "At least twice."

"Only because he saw an opportunity. When the opportunity is gone, he will not trouble you again."

Yilon didn't believe that for a moment, but he didn't have time to argue. "We will deal with that when the time comes," he repeated. He turned to leave, and then stopped, his paw on the table. "When you stopped us at the plaza," he said, "was it Dewry waiting for us?"

"Yes."

"And who shot Corwin?"

Maxon looked directly at him. "I don't know. It might have been Silver."

"Or it might have been Dewry."

"It might."

Yilon suspected that Maxon knew that it was, that it was his affection for the bastard that kept the whole truth from them. But again, he decided not to press the issue. He would deal with Dewry later. "Did you discover anything else about the location of the crown?"

"No. Dewry went to the Warren to talk to his connections there." The steward's mouth curled downward.

"Find out what you can," Yilon said. "Dinah and I will go back to the Heights and wait there."

Shreds had woken, when they returned to the hall. He spat curses at them, and when he saw Maxon, pleaded with him, but they ignored him, as they ignored the creaking shouts and dull thumps that came from behind the heavy fastened curtain. Maxon accompanied them out the front door.

Before leaving, Yilon took off his tunic and wrapped it around the bloody wounds of his stomach. He'd worried about attracting attention, but he needn't have. The crowd of foxes bustling back and forth along the street did not look twice at him. Many of them went bare-chested themselves in the oppressive heat, and those who didn't wore dirty, patched tunics that were barely more presentable than his. Dinah and Maxon attracted more attention than he did, envious glances and mutters to their tails.

At the end of the street, Dinah took two steps to the left, while Maxon started to the right. He stopped and bowed. "This is where I take my leave," he said. "The guard station is near Velkan's mansion, so I will stop there and brief him and Lady Dewanne. I will also find out about Corwin's health and will either come tell you myself or send for you."

Yilon inclined his head. "Thank you, Maxon."

"Rest well, my lord," the steward said, and walked off into the crowd.

Yilon and Dinah watched him go before climbing the shallow hill. As they crossed an invisible border into the Heights, Yilon became more aware of the stares of the well-dressed foxes at his bare chest. To keep himself from feeling self-conscious, he turned to Dinah. "How did you know to bring him back to the house?"

Her ears folded back. "I didn't, exactly. He caught me following him."

"Oh."

She shot him a look. "He's hard to follow! I got too close and he recognized me. He was going to take me to the governor's mansion, then I told him you were at the Strad house and we went back there."

Yilon tried to hold his tunic shut. "Well, you saved my life."

She didn't answer until they'd reached the end of that street and turned. "I knew them as cubs," she said. "I liked to hike up into the mountains, and so did they. I used to...I used to find some of the small creatures they'd tortured."

"That's why you killed Kites," he said.

"That, and he was going to kill you." But her ears stayed back. If there were any further history between her and the Strad foxes, she wasn't about to tell him now.

"Do you trust Maxon? I mean, do you think he's really come over to our side?"

That brought her ears back up. "He seemed really upset about your guard. And if he'd wanted to get rid of you, that was the perfect time. He only needed to leave you with...them."

Yilon nodded. "He told us we would have to decide whether or not to trust him."

"Although that was when we shouldn't have."

Yilon shook his head. "I don't know. I believe he didn't know where he stood at that time. He was saving us from Dewry."

"To go get the crown for himself." She slowed as they reached another hill. "Are you okay?"

Yilon nodded, holding his tunic closed with the paw he was pressing to his wound. It was sore, but not too bad. "I don't think he wanted to crown himself, though. He just wanted to decide who got to be crowned."

"He doesn't have that right."

"Just as long as he's on our side now." Yilon had fallen slightly behind her, plodding up the steep hill.

Dinah didn't look back, but her tail curled down as she said, "That doesn't mean he'll be on our side in the future."

"Two more days would do," Yilon said.

At the top of the hill, they reached the street on which Dinah's house stood. Rather than walking along it, Dinah turned to face Yilon. The passing foxes skirted them, some raising eyebrows at Yilon's undress, but none stopped. "Don't think I've changed my mind about marrying you just because I'm helping you."

Yilon shook his head. "Nor I you."

"It's just that you're so helpless."

"At least I managed to follow Maxon without being spotted."

She snorted at that, and then broke a smile. "You probably put him on his guard. Why don't you want to get married? I mean, apart from having your mouse on the side."

"Oh, I intend to be married," Yilon said. "I have to. It's—"

"Your duty, yes, I know. But you clearly don't want to."

He looked around and then down the street. "Can we continue this in the house?"

She followed his gaze. "Nobody here's listening. When you get to the house, Colian's going to take charge of you, and then I expect you'll sleep for a while."

"Well, let's walk, at least." Without waiting for an answer, he set off toward the house. She hurried to match his pace. "It is Sinch, if you want the truth," he said. "I can't...be with him anymore, after I'm married."

"Why ever not?"

"Because when you get married, you dedicate your life and love to one person. It's not fair to have someone on the side."

"So you'd expect your wife to be devoted totally to you, even though she may have no more feeling for you than you for her?"

His ear twinged when he flicked it. "That's how it works."

"'Steeth," she muttered. "Now I definitely don't want to marry you."

"I didn't make up the rules," he growled. "If you're gay, your life as a noble is destined to be unfulfilled."

They'd reached the door of her house. She held it for him. "Go see Colian and get your rest. I'll see you later."

He was on the stair when he heard the door close, and her voice below him say, "I have no intention of having an unfulfilled life."

He turned, but all he saw was her tail disappearing into the ground floor room.

Chapter 25: Sinch and Yilon

The sun had reached its zenith by the time Sinch found the house in the Heights again. He'd walked through the upper class neighborhood, ignoring the stares from the well-dressed foxes, avoiding guards when he saw them and hurrying away when he heard people calling them. He kept his eyes shaded against the sun and kept moving, looking up at the rooftops for shadows, and when he found the right door, with Yilon's scent on the doorstep, he pushed at the wood and let himself in.

The house was silent. He padded up to the second floor and looked in on Valix, but she was asleep with the window shuttered, and Colian wasn't watching her. Farther down the hall, the two remaining doors were shut.

The door to the third floor room was also shut, but he caught Yilon's scent on it, fresh, and he eased the door open.

Yilon lay on the bed on his side, facing away from the door. A bandage circled the base of his tail, and another was fastened to his ear. He wore no tunic, nor pants that Sinch could see, but a sheet draped over him hid everything below the waist. Sinch felt his heart skip as he closed the door behind him and hurried over to the bed side.

Two patches on Yilon's stomach were shaved and bandaged, but he had no other visible injuries. Sinch exhaled, and at the soft sound, Yilon opened one eye.

"Hi," Sinch whispered.

Yilon grunted and turned over onto his stomach, then rolled to the opposite side, pulling his tail across his body to hang off the far edge of the bed. Sinch noticed the slight wince as he pulled it. "What happened to your tail? And ear?"

"A few scratches. I got in a fight." Yilon patted the bed. "Can't really lie on my back. How are you?"

Though the bed was narrow, Yilon had made plenty of room. Sinch sat up on it and traced his fingers down Yilon's arm. "I found out where the crown is. I just have to go get it. Who did you fight with?"

Yilon nudged his muzzle against Sinch's arm and sighed, a sound that conveyed more than anything he said. "Just a thug. He was working with a fox who wants the lordship for himself."

"Dewry?"

The lazy mood was gone. Yilon jerked his head up. "How do you know that name? Did you run into Maxon?"

Sinch shuddered. "I wouldn't be here if I had. I met Dewry. He was threatening Valix's boss."

"You met him? You talked to him?" Sinch nodded. "What did he say? What did *you* say?"

"You've met him, too," Sinch said. "He was the—"

"Guard on our trip," Yilon finished. "Maxon told me."

"He told you? But I just saw him talking to Dewry."

"Don't worry about Maxon. He's on our side. For now."

"I'll still worry," Sinch said.

Yilon slipped an arm around his waist and pulled him closer. "Don't," he said. "Come here, tell me about it."

Sinch reached down to rub the unbandaged ear. "There's not much to tell," he said. "He was threatening Balinni. I stood up to him and he went away." The rush of accomplishment he'd felt after the meeting with Dewry came back in a faint echo.

Yilon arched an eyebrow, looking up. "Really?"

"Sure." Sinch grinned. "When I tell someone to go away, he goes away."

"I mean..." Yilon said, and then looked into Sinch's eyes. He grinned and rested his muzzle against Sinch's chest. "Can I stay?"

The previous feeling was nothing compared to the warmth in his chest now. Rather than try to talk, Sinch slid down the bed until he could lie flat next to Yilon. Careful of the bandages, he stroked a paw down the soft fur from the fox's ribs to his hips, finding as he moved under the blanket that Yilon was naked. Yilon's arm curled around him in turn, their muzzles a whisker apart at the head of the bed. "So," Sinch said, when he was sure his voice would remain steady, "I just have to go get the crown, and bring it back here."

Yilon licked his nose gently. His paw tugged at Sinch's tunic."Don't bring it here," he said. "Bring it to the palace. But wait until I'm there."

"Why?"

"If you present it to me...they won't be able to keep you out. That's a great service you've rendered the province. Even Maxon will have to acknowledge that. Tail and Teeth," he swore suddenly. "I never thought places this backward still existed."

Sinch wriggled out of his tunic and pulled it over his head before lying back down. "Could we maybe not talk about Maxon in bed?"

Yilon grinned. "What would you like to talk about?"

"I don't know that I want to talk," Sinch said. He pressed up closer, sighing in Yilon's embrace, feeling the strong beat of his heart. If he closed his eyes, there was nothing more to the world than that rhythm and the strong smell of fox in his nostrils. Yilon echoed his sigh, pulling him tight.

"Missed you," he murmured.

"Me too." Sinch tucked his muzzle under Yilon's chin and nuzzled the collarbone. "If I'd been around, maybe you wouldn't be so beat up." He allowed his fingers to trace the bandages on Yilon's abdomen. "Does it still hurt?"

"Nah," Yilon said, though he flinched at the touch. "Maybe a little tender."

Sinch inhaled, Yilon's fur tickling his nose. This was what he wanted, just this, right here. If they went home...but he'd already said that, in the depth of the night. Here in the daylight, that thought felt silly. Of course they couldn't go home. Yilon was the heir to the lordship here. He had duties and responsibilities, beyond any unspoken commitment he might feel to Sinch.

"Do you still want to go home?" Yilon whispered.

His claws scratched gently through Sinch's fur, as though he'd asked nothing more than what Sinch wanted for breakfast. Sinch's fingertips rested against Yilon's stomach. "I..." he said, and then shook his head. "Maybe later. Once you've been..."

"Mmm." Yilon nuzzled between Sinch's ears. "I wish I could take you to Vinton."

"I like the mountains here," Sinch said. "Makes me feel protected."

"Vinton's mountains are warmer."

Sinch drew ruffs of long, silky fur through his fingers. "Could we sit out on the terrace and drink chilled honey mead?"

"And eat goat cheese and spiced nuts."

Sinch closed his eyes against the lure of the vision and slid his paw further down. "I like fox nuts better," he said.

Yilon tensed, started to relax, and then said, "ow," softly.

Sinch moved his paw. "Don't tell me you're hurt there, too."

"No, no." Yilon kissed his ear. "I forgot and wagged my tail. You can put your paw back."

"You sure?" Sinch said.

"Mm-hmm."

"I wouldn't want to cause you any more pain."

Yilon took hold of Sinch's paw with his and pulled it toward his sheath. Sinch pulled back, and grinned when Yilon growled softly, "I'm fine."

"If you're absolutely sure."

By way of answer, Yilon pulled Sinch's paw again and placed it firmly on the warm and growing hardness between his legs. Sinch closed his eyes and snuggled against the fox, fingers traveling up and down. It seemed a lifetime since he'd held the familiar warmth in his paw, but he remembered every inch of it, every detail of Yilon's reactions. The little noise he made when Sinch's fingers found the tip of his shaft, the way he liked to put his nose next to Sinch's ear and exhale warmly into it (which also got Sinch rather hard), the kneading motion his paws made when he was trying just to focus on the light stroking.

As much as Sinch wanted his own pants off, he didn't want to disturb the flow of the moment. Besides, if he knew Yilon, there would be a set of paws working at his trousers in short order. So he just trailed his fingers up and down the growing shaft, curling around its warmth when it was long enough, feeling the shivers through the warm, thick fur pressed against him.

It had only been...three days? since the inn at Frontier, where they'd pressed into each other's mouths, hot and fast, and collapsed against each other in a warm haze afterwards, the way they always did. How much things could change, and yet still the core of who they were remained the same, no matter how many scrapes were bandaged on Yilon, nor how many enemies were waiting for Sinch when he left this haven. His own sheath throbbed as he stroked Yilon's erection, holding it more firmly, rubbing against the tip with every stroke and spreading the dampness there around.

Strong musk filled his nostrils, impelling his paw to stroke faster. Yilon made small whimpering sounds against him, hooking one bare leg over both Sinch's own. His fingers slid into Sinch's pants, rubbing his hips and tracing the line of his tail down his rear. Sinch worked his paw and braced himself, shivering a bit in delighted anticipation.

He knew something was wrong when he felt Yilon straining against him. He should have finished by this point, his knot should be full and tight. But Sinch kept his paw moving along the fox's trembling erection until he felt the shaft lose some of its tautness. Then he stopped and just held it.

"Keep going," Yilon panted. "I'm..."

Sinch nuzzled his neck. "It's okay," he said.

"No, really. Keep going."

Sinch did, but slowly, caressing up and down rather than pumping. "You're thinking of her, aren't you?"

Yilon snorted, then sagged back to the bed. "It's all so complicated."

Sinch traced a claw down his sheath, over the soft-furred sac, and back up the shaft. "Don't worry about all that," he said. "It's a long way away."

"I don't want to hurt you," Yilon said.

Sinch nuzzled his chest. "I've gotten wet before," he said, closing his paw around the fox's shaft again.

"Sinch..."

"Hush." Sinch started again, stroking up and down. "You're not married yet."

"But..."

"You're not even Lord Dewanne. You're just Yilon. And I'm Sinchon. And we're here together, and that's all." He squeezed a bit and flicked his thumb over Yilon's tip.

"Mmm." Yilon rested his head by Sinch's ear and exhaled softly, a breath that might have contained the words "love you" in a deep whisper, or might not, but Sinch felt their warmth regardless. He felt a pressure in his throat, and had to tell himself to calm down, not to be silly. He'd just told Yilon not to worry about the future, and here he was failing to follow his own advice. Clear your head, his teachers had told him, though in the context of very different activities than the one he was currently applying himself to. This is the moment, he told himself. Let the future be the future. And the pressure in his eyes subsided, though the warmth in his chest remained, and he moved with Yilon, his paw teasing and then stroking, the fox's length warm and hard and wonderful inside it, his knot now growing larger and tighter.

This time, when Yilon began to whimper, and Sinch felt the full hardness of the erection in his paw, there was no delay, no retreat from climax. His breath came in hot, whuffing pants against Sinch's ear, his paw squeezed Sinch's rear, and his back arched. Sinch kept his paw's strokes going even as Yilon groaned and strained, his body shaking, and wetness bloomed on Sinch's paw and stomach fur. "Huh...huh..." Yilon panted, his shaft spasming in Sinch's paw.

And then the moment was over, leaving behind the warmth and musk. Sinch pressed up against Yilon, bringing his paw to his muzzle to lick it clean as Yilon hugged him fiercely. "Ow," he said, releasing Sinch from the hug without moving away.

Sinch had to giggle. "Be careful!"

"Just pressed on my stomach here," Yilon said. "It's nothing. It's..." He took Sinch's ear in his lips, chewing playfully on it while Sinch squirmed happily. "It's your turn, is what it is."

"If you're tired," Sinch began, but Yilon pressed his shoulder against Sinch's muzzle, cutting off the words.

Chapter 26: Yilon and Sinch

Yilon was tired, his body drained after the tension and climax, but he had to return the favor for poor Sinch, after all the mouse had been through—after all they'd both been through. And as Sinch had said, this was now, and he wasn't married yet. So he pushed at Sinch's trousers, ignoring the little pains in his shoulder and abdomen, until he'd managed to get the pants mostly off. His own shaft was still dripping as he pushed Sinch onto his back, resting on his side next to the mouse and rubbing through his stomach fur.

Sinch was considerably dirtier than he was, and probably not just because he hadn't gotten cleaned twice by Colian. Even his stomach fur felt gritty and dusty. His hips shivered as Yilon's paw moved down to them, and again he tried to protest, and again Yilon silenced him. Dear Sinch, always trying to please him. No matter how often Yilon told him that he enjoyed getting him off, Sinch didn't quite seem to believe it.

He did enjoy it, though, liked playing with Sinch and feeling the pleasure coursing through the body next to him as if it were his own, breathing in the delightful scent of climax, curling up beside him afterwards. Enjoy it while you can, an inner voice warned again. Yilon ignored it. He brushed the back of his paw over Sinch's sheath, and then up the already-showing length resting on his stomach.

Sinch's arm, at his side, was resting in just the right spot for his paw to fall on Yilon's sheath. His fingers curled lightly around it, but just holding, not stroking, and the warmth was nice, so Yilon didn't protest. He brushed his finger pads across Sinch's sheath and then took the warm shaft in his paw, giving it a squeeze before starting to rub lightly up and down.

Originally, Yilon had thought he would take Sinch into his mouth, but the gritty, rough feel of the fur under his paw gave him pause. Sinch was fully hard already and his body shivering, so Yilon slowed his strokes, holding the slender erection firmly. The activity held his tiredness in abeyance, his fur tingling as though it were his sheath being rubbed and teased, as though his body were building to climax again through the glow of the one that had just passed.

So he took his time, lazily sliding his paw up and down the firm hardness, listening to Sinch's breathing get heavier. Through all of that, Sinch's fingers didn't tighten on Yilon's sheath. They just rested there,

Sinch pressed up close to him.

maintaining their warm connection. Yilon traced his claws down around his friend's sac, then back along the shaft before grasping it and stroking again, a little faster now. He'd almost forgotten how Sinch's smell changed while they were intimate, the familiar mousy scent, now covered with sewer overtones, becoming deeper, more rich. It wasn't the musky smell of his seed; that would come later. It was just Sinch, flooding Yilon's nostrils and filling his head.

Now the muskiness crept in, just as his fingers felt dampness at the tip of the shaft. He rubbed it as Sinch had rubbed his, thumb brushing across it, and now he got a squeak with each breath, next to his shoulder. He let the mouse's pleasure build slowly, looking down his muzzle at Sinch's closed eyes and parted lips. His tail wagged again, sending a spark of pain along his spine, but he suppressed any exclamation this time.

Sinch pressed up close to him, head turned to pant into Yilon's chest fur. Yilon nuzzled the soft ear, breathing in the scent of him, pressing close to feel the tension in Sinch's shoulder, listening to the rapid panting. Abruptly he lifted his torso, curling forward, and lifted Sinch's shaft with his paw. Before the mouse could make more than a move in response, Yilon had closed his lips around the tip of his shaft, lapping the salty fluid from it and then lowering his muzzle to suck firmly on it.

The scent of Sinch, the scent of his arousal, overwhelmed any residual smell of the sewer. Sinch's hips thrust up into his muzzle as he drew his tongue along the hot shaft, the taste getting stronger. Yilon closed his eyes and bobbed his muzzle up and down, letting his paw cup the base. Sinch had no knot, like he did, but he could tell from the mouse's shudders that he was close.

That was when Sinch's paw finally tightened around his sheath. Yilon grinned inwardly, listening to the rapid, jerky breaths. He pressed his tongue against the shaft as it began to spasm, warmth spilling across his tongue and the back of his throat. As he swallowed, he felt his own body suffuse with warmth, felt the jolt of pain again as his tail wagged, this time less sharp. He slid his other arm beneath Sinch's shoulders and pulled the mouse close to him as the slight frame jerked and then finally relaxed.

Yilon lifted his muzzle, licking the dripping shaft clean as he did and straightening without letting go his hold of the mouse's torso. Sinch murmured something into Yilon's chest fur, so softly that even Yilon's ears didn't catch the words, but it was two syllables, and it might very well have been, "Love you." Yilon squeezed the bony shoulder with a paw and let Sinch down to the bed, only Sinch didn't want to go down. He stayed pressed to Yilon, his paw remaining on Yilon's sheath even as Yilon's remained on his, until Yilon lay down on his side and rested his muzzle against the top of Sinch's head.

"We'll figure out something," he said, without any idea of what he was thinking.

"Mmm," Sinch said.

"When you bring the crown back," Yilon murmured. "They'll see. Even if..." *Even if we can't be together like this.* "Even if they don't want to."

Sinch nodded slowly, and yawned. Yilon yawned himself, and tried to think of what to say next, but he couldn't quite manage to focus on thinking about Sinch and Dinah and the lordship. His eyelids drooped. He felt Sinch slip into a regular rhythm of breathing and his own matched it. The last thing he remembered thinking before falling into sleep was how, even in the flush of climax, Sinch's body was nowhere near as warm as he remembered.

He woke to a dim room and an empty bed. His paw found only residual warmth as he moved it around sleepily. Sinch must have gone to check on Valix, he supposed. He yawned and stretched, pulling himself out of bed. His wounds were still sore, but felt better. "Nothing like a little rest," he murmured, slipping into his new tunic and trousers.

Valix was still asleep, alone in the second-floor room. Yilon sniffed the air, but caught only a faint trace of Sinch. The rest of the second floor was deserted as well.

From the stairway, he heard the murmurs of voices, and followed them to the ground floor. Colian and Dinah sat together in a room off the foyer, facing another fox. It wasn't until Yilon had entered the large parlor and greeted them that he recognized Maxon.

The steward inclined his head as Yilon sat, careful of his tail. "I presume we are all feeling more rested now."

"I know I am." Yilon looked at Dinah, his insides tensing. She gave him a quick nod.

"It will be my turn soon," Maxon said. "I wanted to let you know that I have arranged for a funeral for Min. It should be in four days, after your Confirmation."

"Thank you," Yilon said.

"And your wedding can be held anytime in the year after that."

Yilon met Dinah's eyes. She gave him a resigned sigh. "I haven't been able to talk him out of it."

"What if neither of us wants to get married?" Yilon said.

Maxon shrugged. "I'm certain we can locate a less well-qualified vixen for you, but Dinah is the best match for you and for the future of Dewanne. For the strength of the land, it would be very difficult for me to advise you to make a different match."

"But she doesn't want to marry me."

Maxon arched an eyebrow. "While I am in perfect sympathy," he said, "we are not always privileged to be given the life we want."

Yilon opened his mouth to snap a retort until he saw the faint curve upward at the corner of Maxon's muzzle. "I suppose," he said, "I'm not anyone's first choice. Speaking of which," he said, "what's going on with Dewry?"

The steward's ears flicked down. "He is on his way to Divalia. I arranged a carriage for him not two hours ago."

His tail twitched under his chair. Yilon made a show of relaxing as Dinah was doing. "Then we can stop worrying about that. How's Corwin doing?"

"He has not woken, but he hasn't joined the Pack." Maxon stood. "Colian, if I may have a word?"

"Of course." The nurse joined him.

Maxon bowed to Yilon and Dinah. "I will await you at Velkan's mansion for dinner," he said, and left, with Colian close behind.

"Dinner." Yilon put a paw to his stomach. "I'm starving."

"Maxon wanted us to talk," Dinah said.

Yilon settled back in his chair. "Does it have to be settled now?"

Dinah waved one paw. "He said that after a period of disorder like this, "the fewer things that are left unresolved, the better for Dewanne." I don't really know. But it's important to him."

The parlor they sat in had been painted in lavender and rose, with sconces in the shapes of large flowers from which candles protruded, unlit in the daylight. Though the room itself was clean, Yilon could smell the dust and disuse in the pink velvet fabric of the armchair as he rubbed it with one paw. Motes of dust rose into the light. "This doesn't look like a room you would pick out."

"It belonged to my great-aunt Balstrie. She came to live with us when I was three. She died when I was four." Dinah wrinkled her nose. "She loved the shape of flowers but hated the smell."

Yilon smiled. "I never met any of my mother's family. Nor my father's, I guess."

"Your father's a Lord, right? Wallen?"

"Vinton. South of here and far to the east. But it's also in a mountain valley."

Dinah looked at the shuttered window, at the sunlight streaming through the crack. Her eyes drifted closed. "You're going to accept the lordship."

"I have to. Too many people have sacrificed too much." He closed his eyes for a moment to banish the image of the fox's tail in the corner.

She tapped the arm of her chair, inhaled, exhaled. "I have a sister who's five. She'll make a good wife in nine or ten years, and you'll still be young then. You could have a decade of freedom before your duties take over your life."

"Duty takes over from the moment I take the title," Yilon said, but the possibility sparked hope in him. If he could be betrothed but put off the marriage, if he could have that extra set of years with Sinch...

"Not all duties."

But still, there was the problem of the foxes and the mice. Was it just dreaming to think that he and Sinch could have any time together with that looming over them? Would they even be able to enjoy that time, knowing it would eventually end?

More importantly, if he didn't believe that, then why had he told Sinch to deliver the crown himself? "I don't know what I want," he said, frustrated.

"Seems pretty clear to me," Dinah said.

"What, then?"

She raised an eyebrow. "You want your mouse friend."

"That's not all," he said.

"Well, you want to be lord, too. You know, if you didn't have this hangup about fidelity, it would all be easier."

"Of course," he shot back. "When you ignore the rules, the game becomes easier."

"Who said it's a game?"

"Everything's a game."

She laughed, shortly. "So what if it is? How do you win?"

He frowned. "What do you mean, win?"

"Just that." She tapped her chair arm. "If it's a game, there must be a way to win. So how do you win?"

"By..." He paused to think about that. "By following the rules, by being the best."

"Hmph." She turned back to the window. "It's not like I even want you in my bed."

"I know, you think I'm a city-raised weakling." He said it almost absently, still thinking about what she'd said about how to win.

"It's not that. It's that you're male. Haven't you figured that out yet?"

"Figured what out?" He lost his train of thought. "That you don't... wait. You're...?"

She nodded. "Just like you."

His muzzle hung open. "Can vixens *do* that?"

Dinah rolled her eyes. "Boys," she said. "Think the whole world revolves around your little short bows. Of course vixens can do that."

"How?"

"You wouldn't understand," she said.

He narrowed his eyes. "You don't even know."

"Why would I tell you?"

"Because I'm asking. You want to know how two boys do it? One takes hold of the other's—"

"Please," she said. "It doesn't take much imagination."

"So what do you—oh, the muzzles?" Yilon stuck his tongue out experimentally and rolled it into a tight cylinder.

"Don't be disgusting."

"I didn't bring it up," he pointed out. "So you'd be just as unhappy married to me."

"If you insisted that we had to be miserable together."

"I thought that's what marriage meant."

She snorted. "My parents love each other very much. They sleep in separate rooms only because Mommy kicks in her sleep."

Yilon rubbed his chin. "If we were to get married," he said, "what would make you happy?"

"Take me to Divalia," she said. "I know there are other females like me there."

He tilted his muzzle. "So you've never...with another vixen?"

"Well..."

He ducked his muzzle. "I hadn't done anything 'til I was fifteen either."

"You don't have to lie to make me feel better."

"I'm not. I just knew I didn't feel attracted to any females, even when they were in season. My mother..." He shuddered. His mother's seasons had ended after his tenth birthday, but while growing up he remembered them as terrifying, upsetting times when she sent him away to the care of the governor. The first time, he'd stolen back to her room to surprise her and had heard her screaming and sobbing even before he sniffed the heavy, nauseating scent in the air. He'd run back to Anton and had spent the next day crying in his room, not eating until he nearly felt faint from hunger.

"Well," Dinah said, "Nobody wants to see their parents in season." She stuck her tongue out.

Yilon thought about a city full of foxes, all going into heat at once. "The seasons here must be terrifying."

"Why do you think I spent every Kindling up in the hills?" She grinned toothily. "Was the mouse your first?"

"No."

She thought about that. "Was the first scary?"

"Pff." He shook his head. The memory of the jackhammer beating of his heart, the embarrassment of spurting all over the coyote's paw within seconds, was far away.

"This town is so backward," she said, and then her muzzle came back from the window and looked him up and down. "When is Sinch going to be back?"

He shook his head again. "Do you know where he went?"

She frowned. "Don't you know?"

"I woke up and he was gone. Did he tell you where he was going? It shouldn't be long now."

"We didn't see him," Dinah said. "Maxon told us the Shadows have the crown, so I guess he went back there."

It took a moment for her words to sink in, and then Yilon jumped out of his chair. "The Shadows? He went in there alone?"

Dinah stood, too. "I thought you knew."

"And we've been sitting here, talking about..." He started to pace, and then action crystallized in his mind and he raced for the door.

"You can't go after him," Dinah called. "You don't know where he went."

Yilon turned in front of the door to race up the stairs. "No," he said, "but I know someone who does."

Colian met him at the second floor landing, arms folded. "Absolutely not. She shouldn't even be talking, let alone moving." Behind him, Maxon met Yilon's eyes and moved to one side. Yilon pushed past Colian and into the room. Valix sat up, trying to hide her wince of pain.

"He'll die otherwise," Yilon said. "You owe him your life."

"That doesn't mean she has to sacrifice hers in addition to his," Colian said, coming up behind him. "I worked hard to save it! Doesn't she owe me anything?"

Valix met Yilon's eyes and nodded, slowly, once. "Can you rig up something to help me walk?"

"No time." Yilon held his arms out.

Chapter 27: Return to Shadows

Sinch dressed in silence. He couldn't stop himself from looking once more at Yilon before leaving, and having looked, he had to bend over and kiss the fox's nose. Then he ran for the door, heart beating as he closed it behind him. He ran down the stairs, expecting every moment to hear Yilon behind him.

At the second floor landing, with the house still silent, he padded to Valix's room, but she was still asleep. He walked down and eased the front door open, stepping out into the daylight. He stood there, blinking in the sun, holding the door open an inch, until some of the foxes passing stopped to stare at him, and then he let the door swing shut.

He still drew stares as he padded down the street. He turned the corner quickly and stuck close to the wall through three more intersections, but he was still aware of foxes' heads turning as he passed. By the time he turned down the dead end alley toward the sewer entrance, he felt the weight of eyes on his shoulders, and he had to turn around to make sure nobody was following him.

The grate shifted easily. Though foxes were passing along the street in front, nobody was in the dead end, and nobody watched him lower himself into the dark hole. His feet found a steady enough hold to brace himself while he pulled the grate back into place, and then a series of steps in the wall that allowed him to reach the sewer floor.

The smell was stronger and worse than his memory. The first two steps he took made his stomach lurch, so he stopped to acclimate, one paw pressed against the wall. After a short time, he felt steadier, and his stomach didn't protest when he walked forward.

The sewer was silent except for the echoing drips of water and a low, background rustling. He found the same steps he'd found earlier, which kept his footing sure and reasonably quiet. His problem now was that he had only a general idea of where he was going, and his sense of direction was no good down here in the darkness and the stench. Fortunately, the tunnels were more or less straight, so he made sure that when he turned in one direction, he turned the opposite way the next chance he got.

He passed a grate above him, and was tempted to climb up and open it to see where he was, but he didn't want to make more noise than he needed to. It only occurred to him a moment later that that grate might have been one of the guarded entrances. He wouldn't have smelled the guards, of course, but his whiskers hadn't tingled, and when he stopped, he didn't detect the curious absence of smell that he associated with the Shadows. Carefully, he moved forward.

It was around the next corner, with the grate out of sight, that his whiskers did tingle. He stopped immediately, his heart speeding up. He reached his paw out to touch the wall, and encountered instead fabric, warmth, and taut muscle.

Before he could react, his paw was seized and twisted behind his back, driving him to his knees. He slipped from the stones and plunged into the filthy water up to his waist. His free paw reached around his waist, trying to get to his dagger, but before he could, he was yanked up to his feet. He felt the weight of the dagger lifted from his belt. "Walk," a curt voice said.

"I need to see Whisper," Sinch said.

"You'll see Whisper if he wants to see you," the voice replied. It wasn't one Sinch recognized. But it sounded like he wasn't going to be killed right away, so he marched docilely along with the Shadow behind him. Maybe they didn't know about Frost yet. He only wished he still had his dagger.

After several turns, the sewers began to feel familiar. As disgusting as it was, Sinch realized that there were nuances to the smells. Here, he was detecting a slight fishy odor that hadn't been present elsewhere in the sewers. By smell, he thought, he would be able to learn his way through the whole sewer, and it struck him then that that was how the Shadows did it. Did the mice who cleared the garbage above dump it in a particular pattern that aided the mapping of the sewers? Or did the Shadows just take advantage of the patterns that already existed?

Time enough to worry about that later, he thought, if he were lucky. He needed to focus on how he was going to negotiate for the crown with a group of mice who hated him and didn't negotiate. Keeping to the path took a little concentration, leaving him mostly free to think about what he would say to Whisper.

When he was pushed into the open area, he was surprised to see that it was still mostly dark. He was pushed under the one guttering torch and held there with a dagger at his throat. The Shadow holding the dagger waved a paw to the blackness, which was met with soft rustling. And then he waited.

"It is you," a familiar voice said out of the darkness. "I had not believed you so stupid as to return."

"I came back for the crown," Sinch said. "I can explain why you should give it to me."

"We are not interested in your explanations," Whisper said, stepping to the edge of the light. "For the first time, we have true power over foxes."

"You have a chance to make peace," Sinch said.

"The only peace we will accept is the silence of foxes," Whisper said. "While we hold the crown, the foxes cannot confirm a lord. While there is no lord, the city will sink deeper and deeper into chaos. When there is no more law, we will come forth."

"But you can live with the foxes," Sinch said. "You can help each other."

"No fox is friend to a mouse," Whisper said.

"That's not true!" Sinch almost shouted.

The knife pressed closer to his throat. Whisper's tone of voice did not change. "We will not argue with you. You have not the knowledge that we do."

"There's more to life than your sewers!" The arguments had sounded much more rational in Sinch's head, when he wasn't shouting them to a shadowy figure.

"We are the Shadows," Whisper said, and now the other voices joined in. "We are the opposition to the light. We live in the darkness and watch the city. We strike where others dare not."

That reminded him about the attempt on Yilon's life. "You have a chance to make an alliance," he said. "If you return the crown to me, the new lord will look favorably on you."

"No fox—"

"You're wrong!" Sinch did yell now. "Why do you think I came down here to get the crown?"

The word "crown" resounded and died away, leaving Sinch in silence. He didn't dare swallow, but eventually he had to, his throat stinging against the knife. At length, Whisper said, "We do not care about your reasons." But there was hesitation in his voice.

"I want to bring it to the one who's meant to be the lord. He trusts me."

He thought they would repeat their "No fox is friend to no mouse" chant, but Whisper said, "You hope to elevate yourself by stealing the crown and returning it to him. You will not divert us from our ways."

"I'm not trying to!" He noticed, now, that something of a crowd had gathered on the side Whisper was on. He could hear the massed sound of their breathing.

"You talk of foxes and change, but this is not the way of the Shadows. We fight the Fox, and the Fox fights us."

"If you're not going to give me the crown," Sinch said, "you might as well kill me. There's no life for me here." The words were easier to say because he was honestly surprised they already hadn't.

"Your words are not those of an appeaser," Whisper said. He sounded curious, as though Sinch had green fur or a fox's long canine teeth.

"What does that mean?"

"You do not act as one who has thrown his lot in with the Fox," the Shadow went on. "Those mice fear us. They stay on the surface and do not venture into our world. You have come here twice and you have killed Frost."

"Oh," Sinch said. So they did know.

"By our law, that gives you the right to take his place. However, if you have thrown in your lot with the Fox, you are our enemy."

Take his place? "He was trying to kill Yilon."

"Our law demands some measure of retaliation whenever the Fox invades."

"Your law," Sinch said. He stared at the glittering black eyes of the mouse who was holding the knife to him. "What else does your law say?"

"Only the Shadows know the law."

Sinch sagged back against the wall. "At least stop trying to kill Yilon," he said. "He's new here, he doesn't know all the laws and customs and things. Just like I don't."

Whisper stepped forward. Sinch could see the reflection of the torch now in the shine of his black eyes. "That is why he is the target. He is significant without being critical, important without being intertwined in the land. The Fox will mourn his passing with the mind, not with the heart."

"That's ridiculous!" Sinch said, grasping at anything that might spare Yilon. "You're just afraid, and he's an easy target."

His throat stung again as the blade pressed into it. Whisper stared at him and then laughed, softly. There was no humor in the sound. "Do not question our ways. You are as much an outsider as he is."

"Exactly," Sinch said. "So why do you not suppose he could become your ally?"

"No fox is friend—" The voice was not Whisper's; it came from behind him, closer to the wall. Others tried to join in, but Whisper cut them off.

"That is not the way of things."

"Why do you find it so hard to have faith?"

"The Shadows have lived here for over ten generations. When the first mice came to the city, many generations before, they did not understand the world they were living in. They joined it, believing they could make it their own. They worked the mines and built their homes in the tradition of Rodenta. They were promised peace. They were promised happiness. And on Red Night, the Fox came and took it from them, leaving them destitute.

"Some went home. Most stayed. They built again, labored again, lived again. And whenever it suited him, the Fox took what he wanted from the mice. Any who resisted were slaughtered and left in the street as a warning to the others. Even the Church could not stop the injustice.

"It was a mouse named Shadow who took up arms. He used the underground city the Fox had built to dispose of waste, and made it his home. From out of the darkness he struck at the Fox, until the Fox understood that there would be repercussions for his actions.

"Shadow is the father of us all. We live with him in the darkness, we are the Shadows. For a mouse to walk in the light, he must cast a shadow; a mouse without a shadow walks in darkness.

"This is the truth. It has always been the truth."

"So what are you going to do with the crown?" Sinch asked. "Hold onto it forever? How do you think that helps you?"

He heard a soft hissing sound from the darkness to his left, and then the pressure on his throat vanished. The mouse who'd been holding the dagger to him dropped it with a clatter as he fell to the ground, clutching his hip. Sinch and Whisper looked down together at the green-and-grey-fletched arrow protruding from it.

"Don't move," a voice said from the darkness of the tunnels to his left. "I'm rather interested to hear the answer to that question myself."

"Yilon!" Sinch jumped toward the voice, then lunged for the fallen mouse's dagger. He needn't have bothered. Nobody else was moving.

"You okay, Sinch?"

"I'm fine." The paw he put to his throat came away sticky, but he didn't care. He felt like laughing and dancing. "You see?" he said to Whisper, who, incredibly, was still standing just inside the circle of light. "He came for me! Let's hear you say 'no fox is friend to no mouse' now!"

Whisper looked steadily at him, then turned his head toward Yilon's voice. "We will not willingly surrender the crown."

"That's okay," Yilon said. "As long as you give Sinch back."

Whisper stared. "What trickery is this?"

"The crown would make some things easier," Yilon said, "but as long as you're not going to chase down Dewry and give it to him, I don't think I much care what you do with it. But I only have one real friend, and if you hurt him, well, I have a bunch of arrows here. I can account for a lot of you before you get within knife range, and I don't think there are many of you left."

"We are legion," Whisper said, before Yilon cut him off.

"And I am sorry about that. I know you didn't steal the crown, and I know you didn't shoot Corwin. But I don't have the power to stop the raids on your home. Yet."

Whisper was silent, but behind him, Sinch heard other Shadows whispering, "Home? Our home?" He wanted to say something, but Yilon's words had moved him to the point that he didn't trust his voice any more.

Yilon said, "Well?"

"What good is the word of a fox?" Whisper mused aloud, as if to himself.

"What good is the word of a mouse?" Yilon responded. "I stand in your house, alone. I brought no soldiers, only a guide whom I left at the entrance."

"What did you do with the sentry at that entrance?" Whisper demanded.

"There was no sentry."

A voice spoke up, directly in front of Sinch in the darkness. He saw the grey of shadows shifting. "I'm...here, sir."

Whisper did not turn his head, just nodded. "We will discuss your punishment for leaving your post later, Shard."

"I shot once because I feared for my friend's life," Yilon said. "I did not strike to kill, or your comrade would be dead."

"He's a good shot," Sinch said.

"And I ask only that you let Sinch come with me, unharmed. I will leave and will not trouble you again, and I give you my word that we will not invade your home again for as long as I am Lord Dewanne."

"By what right do you claim dominion over mice?" Whisper said.

"By the ancient right of the lords of this land," Yilon said easily. "But dominion does not mean misery. I promise you that as well."

"You are but one fox," Whisper said.

"With your help," Yilon said, "we can bring peace to Dewanne."

"We were promised peace in the past," Whisper said.

Yilon's voice carried down the tunnels, firm and clear. "But not by me."

Whisper could have been an ebony statue of a mouse, for all that he moved. All the sewer was silent, as if holding its breath. Sinch couldn't take his eyes from the tall black mouse.

"Should you renege on your promise," Whisper said, deliberately, "our vengeance will be swift and terrible."

"I swear to you, by Canis and by Rodenta, that I will prove worthy of your trust."

Perhaps it was only the resonance in the tunnels, but Yilon's voice had grown deeper and more regal in just those few minutes. Sinch stood proudly, all his attention focused on his friend.

And so he was not prepared to react to the swift motion behind Whisper. By the time he had seen the flash of the dagger flying through the air and leapt back to his feet, it was too late to do anything about it. Whisper fell in slow motion, the dagger quivering behind his left shoulderblade, crumpling to the stone as though a crucial support had been withdrawn from him.

Sinch leapt toward Yilon, into the darkness, landing in a crouch. Another blade went flying just over his head, and then a short Shadow stepped into the light, standing over Whisper. "Fool," he said. "You would lead us all into damnation."

Sinch's heart sank. He lifted his knife, but hesitated: if he killed this assassin, would they turn against him and Yilon forever? Would it be worse if he let this Shadow assume the leadership? The assassin had turned to look in his direction, leaning slightly as he searched the darkness. Sinch remained perfectly still.

Even though he was staring directly into the torchlight, he nearly missed what happened next. Whisper rolled almost all the way onto his back, and the right arm that had been beneath his body came up in a blur of motion. The assassin made a funny half-jump, then leaned forward further and didn't stop leaning until he had pitched forward onto the ground. Sinch only briefly saw the black handle of Whisper's dagger sticking out of the bottom of the assassin's muzzle before he fell atop it.

Whisper got to his feet and pulled the dagger from his shoulder without wincing. He brandished it at the mice behind him. "Is there any other who questions my judgment?" he said.

"He's a *fox*," a female voice said in weak protest.

"He was not born here," Whisper said. "There may be worth to his promises. And we have all lost friends, or family, these last two days."

"That is our burden," a male voice said.

"And continues to be. But what if our burden were vigilance rather than vengeance? We will not stand down or leave our way of life, but neither will we continue to fight needlessly. For all those Shadows who sacrificed before us, for all those who stand ready, let us take this chance."

He drew a cloth from a pocket at his waist, rubbed the blade of the dagger on it, and then sheathed it. The other mice facing him murmured amongst themselves, but none stepped forward. “Very well,” Whisper said. “Light the torches, and let us see this foreign-born fox who claims dominion over the Shadows. Fox! You may lower your bow and step forward.”

Chapter 28: The Shadow's Tooth

Yilon swayed and almost fell when the tension left him. He was aware that this leader of the Shadows was trying to maintain status by giving him permission to come forward. In this case, he thought, it would not hurt to acknowledge the mouse's advantage in the sewer. But he couldn't resist a small rejoinder as he stepped forward. "I lowered my bow several minutes ago," he said, lifting it and slinging it across his back.

The leader stared through the darkness and then laughed. "You are indeed a strange one," he said as torches flared to life behind him. "You and your friend both."

Yilon smelled Sinch a moment before he saw him, the mouse a crouching shadow in the growing torchlight. Before he had time to say anything, Sinch had jumped from a crouch to wrapping his arms around Yilon, giving him a quick kiss on the muzzle and releasing him before Yilon could hug him back. "You're great," he whispered into Yilon's ear, padding around to walk behind him as he approached the leader. Yilon curled his tail around to the side to brush Sinch as they walked, not trusting himself to say anything to his friend this close to the Shadows.

The leader stood in front of a group of perhaps ten other mice, all painted black and wearing the same black robes he was. Yilon was not used to looking down on such a crowd of people. The leader was the tallest, and even his ears came up only to Yilon's muzzle. Still, his black eyes glittered with pride as he welcomed Yilon, arms folded across the chest of his black robes. "I am The Whisper Of Death In The Night," he said.

Yilon felt the need for something more formal than just his name. "I am Yilon, son of Volle Lord of Vinton, son of Lord Wiri of Vinton." The names of the lords of Vinton felt less and less relevant. "Appointed heir to the throne of Dewanne by Lord Sheffin of Dewanne."

That sent a murmur through the crowd of mice. Whisper raised a paw without looking behind him, and the mice fell silent.

Yilon studied Whisper even as Whisper studied him, waiting for the other to say the first words, partly deferring to his authority, and partly because he had no idea how to conduct the remainder of the meeting. At length, Whisper dropped his arms and turned to the mice behind him. "Ice and Edge, stay here. The rest of you, back to your posts."

The small crowd dispersed, except for two who stepped forward.

"Edge, you will retrieve our prize. Ice, bring us the Shadow's Tooth."

The last two Shadows moved off into the tunnels. Whisper spread his paws to Yilon, palms up. "There are no rituals to guide a meeting like this. I am turning our existing rituals to a new purpose."

"It's okay," Yilon said. "You can make up whatever you want. We will start a new ritual together." He put an arm around Sinch's shoulder. "I'm planning on doing a lot of that. Like bringing mice into the palace."

Whisper made a startled noise and then shut his jaw. It wasn't until the Shadow had composed himself and Yilon could see the white gleam of a smile in his black muzzle that he recognized the sound as a laugh. "You are ambitious indeed," he said. "Very well. The first ritual is the bonding of blood."

"Blood?" Sinch said.

Yilon hadn't heard the other Shadow return, but he was there behind Whisper, holding a small long box made of silver in intricate filigree shapes, sharp-toothed patterns that curled around gems that gleamed darkly red. Rather than open the box, Whisper glanced at it and then walked part of the way down the nearest tunnel.

"We do not reveal the Shadow's Tooth in light," he said over his shoulder. "Come."

Yilon glanced at Sinch and then walked to the edge of the circle of light. He could just see Whisper's outline. "Let's do this at the edge of light and dark," he said.

Whisper turned, tilted his muzzle. "Very well," he said after a moment's thought. "Ice?"

The Shadow behind him held out the box, its curves and gems flickering faintly with the distant torchlight. He lifted the lid and brought out a dagger that did not catch the torchlight. Yilon smelled tarnish and must as Ice held the dagger out, point up. It looked insubstantial, a ghost's tooth in the black sewer.

"Your arm," Whisper said. "We pierce the wrist, not the paw, not the fingers." He held out his own arm, the wrist over the knife point.

"Pierce?" Yilon said.

Whisper's eyes shone. Neither he nor ice made a sound. Yilon sighed and extended his left arm over Whisper's, paw pads down.

Whisper turned his arm over to grasp Yilon's forearm. "Take my arm," he said.

Yilon curled his fingers around the mouse's cold, bony arm. Their wrists lay flat against each other, immediately over the point of the shadow dagger.

"Now," Whisper nodded to Ice.

Yilon reached for Sinch's paw with his right, squeezing his eyes closed and bracing himself. He counted five beats of his heart before he felt a line of fire trace the inside of his wrist. Not through it; over it. He opened his eyes and saw Ice sliding the Tooth between his wrist and Whisper's, scoring the flesh on either side so that the blood would run together.

Whisper's smile looked remarkably smug. "It would hardly do for we, who live by our skill, to cripple our new initiates, would it? We merely bond our blood. The compact is made and witnessed."

"You had me fooled," Yilon said, releasing Whisper's arm as the Shadow released his. He drew it back and rubbed the painful line across it. "I wonder if I'm going to spend an hour in Dewanne without getting cut." When he lifted his arm to his muzzle, he smelled Whisper's blood and got the mouse's scent for the first time, a rich, clean scent that was hard to follow beneath his own vulpine musk.

"Now we celebrate our bond with the traditional meal," Whisper said. "You and me alone." His eyes fell on Sinch, standing behind Yilon. "Unless you have changed your mind."

Sinch bowed slightly, his paw remaining in Yilon's. "I am more inclined to do so now than I was an hour ago," he said. "But I think I will take more time to consider it."

"As you wish," Whisper said. He turned to Ice, who took the dagger and replaced it carefully in the box. "Put that away and bring some food." The Shadow bowed and stepped back into darkness.

Yilon had turned to look at Sinch, who met his eyes with a slight smile. It surprised him that Sinch would have turned down the Shadows twice, especially now that they had sealed an alliance. "I think you'd be the best of them," he said.

The mouse's smile broadened just a bit. He watched Whisper walk past them, toward the torches. "I already serve a lord," he said.

Yilon squeezed his paw, at a loss for words. "You don't have to serve me," he said, softly.

"I know I don't have to," Sinch said. He tugged at Yilon's paw. "Also, I don't feel like eating meat."

Yilon stared at the mouse's smile, which was now a grin. "Meat?"

"Can't you smell it on their breath?" Sinch waved his paw in front of his nose.

"I guess I didn't notice." Yilon curled his tail back around to brush Sinch's leg. "They eat meat?"

Sinch nodded. "That's probably what they're going to get."

Yilon lifted his nose, but couldn't smell anything beyond the rank filth of the tunnels. "Is it good meat, at least?"

"They live in a sewer," Sinch said. "What do you think?"

Yilon laughed, stopping himself as Whisper accepted a familiar-looking leather satchel from one of the Shadows that Yilon assumed was Edge, though he couldn't have picked him out of a crowd. And he wasn't focusing on the mouse; he was staring at the satchel as Whisper brought it closer to them.

It looked much the same as when he'd last seen it. A glistening smear of brown along the back hadn't been there two days before, but otherwise it was so familiar he couldn't believe it was real. But the weight as Whisper was carrying it looked right, and a moment later, even over the smell of the sewer, Yilon caught the scent of leather and metal. Whisper weighed it in his arms and then set it on a small ledge nearby as Ice walked up behind Yilon and Sinch with a small bowl whose reek of meat drove the leather smell out completely from Yilon's nostrils.

He couldn't even tell what kind of meat it was. Whisper took the bowl and sniffed it, then extended it forward. Yilon took a deeper sniff himself and suppressed his cough. It wasn't completely bad; he'd had meat that old in Vinton before, and in the dark, rank sewer, the smell wasn't too repulsive.

"This will not be as significant for you as for a new initiate, but it is significant for us. By sharing a meal, we are accepting you as an equal." His eyes narrowed. "This has never been done with a fox."

Yilon bowed his head. "I am honored."

Whisper picked a bone whose meat shone with fat, and held out the bowl again to Yilon. It felt like much less of an honor when his fingers were in the greasy bowl. He picked out the first lump they closed around.

Ice took the bowl back and disappeared. Whisper raised the hunk of meat to Yilon as though making a toast. "We welcome you to...the home of the Shadows," he said. "We share this food as we share our trust. You will stand as...by our side. You will be..." He paused. Yilon could see him working through the words of the ritual in his head.

The sight, strangely enough, made him relax. It made him realize that he was not the only one treading unfamiliar ground, making up promises. "I will be honored to be an ally of the Shadows," he said, lifting his lump of meat. "With this food, I seal the bond between the...between the world above and the world below."

Whisper raised his eyebrows and inclined his head approvingly. "Then let us eat."

The meat tasted about as bad as it smelled, but Yilon chewed and swallowed. It sat in his stomach as he watched Whisper do the same, and then chew on the bone, the crunching magnified in the small space. He brought the bone he was holding back to his mouth and bit down, feeling it crack between his teeth, the sweet marrow just touching his tongue. Sinch looked away, though he couldn't tell whether it was from him or from Whisper.

In the darkness behind the torchlight, he saw movement, and made out the shapes of two Shadows watching them—Ice and Edge, perhaps. But Whisper was putting the bowl down and reaching for the leather satchel.

"In the normal course of the ritual," he said, "here I would present you with a dagger. Instead, I think this will do." He held the satchel in both paws, against his stomach, and then held it out, not to Yilon, but to Sinch.

Yilon was about to protest, and then remembered something Maxon had told him. "Go ahead," he said to Sinch's look. "I'm not supposed to touch it before the Confirmation."

Sinch took the satchel and slid his head under the strap, curling an arm protectively around it. "Why not?"

"Tradition, I guess." Yilon looked around. "Besides, look what happened last time I tried to take charge of it."

"You touched it before and Corwin didn't say anything."

"Only the satchel. I think it's just the crown that matters."

Whisper cleared his throat. The rough noise reminded Yilon of Maxon, making him smile as he thought how horrified the steward would be at the comparison. "We will be watching," he said, "for your honor or betrayal."

Yilon nodded, cupping his ears forward. "I have grown accustomed to the feeling of being watched in this city. And I in turn will be listening to the shadows." He tried to think of something dramatic to say. "Because we all live in both light and shadow, and neither should be ignored."

Whisper paused to consider that, and then nodded curtly. "You can find your way out?"

"I believe so." Yilon hitched the bow across his back. "Should I return, it will be in peace."

"And, we trust, as the ruler of the city. Go with Gaia." Whisper raised both paws in front of him, cupped as though around a small sphere.

Yilon echoed the gesture. "Go with Gaia," he said, and turned to follow Sinch down the tunnel, into the darkness.

Chapter 29: Underground

Sinch could hardly believe the weight in his paws, the crown retrieved, Yilon against all odds alive and walking out of the sewer at his side. When they'd left Whisper behind, he said, "I can't believe you came here by yourself."

"I wasn't going to let someone else pay the price for my actions," Yilon said. "Not again."

Sinch couldn't see his expression, but his tone was sharp and determined. "That's the sort of thing a lord should say," he said.

They'd reached the near grate. Sinch felt rather than sensed the presence of the sentry, but didn't acknowledge him or her. He could see Yilon's muzzle now that the thin moonlight was falling on it, and he heard the slow exhale as Yilon sighed. "It's all about keeping promises," Yilon said. "Not just keeping promises, but making the right promises and then keeping them. And figuring out what the right promise is."

"You did great," Sinch said. "They hate foxes so much..."

"It was you," Yilon said. "You came for me, and I came for you. That's what convinced them."

He stopped talking to climb up the rough brick of the wall, which was lucky because Sinch found himself blinking back tears. He wiped his eyes and took a deep breath. It was the tension vanishing, he told himself. No more than that. No more than that. He touched the hilt of the dagger in his belt, and for a moment he was standing again in the palace in Divalia, in front of the armory.

"Coming?" Yilon said.

Sinch looked up at the white tip of Yilon's tail, almost glowing in the dim light under a layer of dust and streaks of grime, and at the long vulpine smile above it. He squared his shoulders, the weight of the satchel feeling like nothing at all as he climbed.

"You were impressive too," Yilon said, replacing the grate and looking around the deserted street. "Coming here all by yourself. You should've told me."

"I guess it's not just lords who have to keep promises." Sinch couldn't stop grinning.

A voice floated out from a small arched doorway, hidden in shadow. "I'll be damned to Dark."

Sinch saw the ropy end of a mouse's tail twitching along the pavement in front of it. He took a step closer and lifted his nose. "Valix?"

"Did you at least leave a few corpses behind for that?"

"What are you doing out of bed?"

Her arm came out into the light, pointing at Yilon. "He carried me out here."

"He what?"

Yilon had the grace to flatten his ears. "She was the only one who knew where you might have gone."

"She shouldn't be out of bed!" Sinch knew he should be acting more indignant, but the sacrifices that Yilon and now Valix had made warmed his chest and made his tail curl in on itself.

"It was boring in that bedroom anyway," Valix said. "I feel fine. Long as I don't move too much."

"Let's get you back there," Yilon said. He walked to her and picked her up gently, while Sinch watched, shaking his head.

"Can't believe you two," he muttered, falling in behind them. "Rodenta must be working overtime."

"*I* can't believe us," Valix said. "A fox walking around carrying a mouse, with another mouse behind him. You'll be lucky if the guard doesn't stop us."

"Let them," Yilon said.

They saw only two guards patrolling, two streets away. Yilon didn't look in their direction as they crossed. Sinch saw the garbage-collectors stopping to gawk at them, so he walked taller and held his muzzle up in the face of their incredulity.

"So," Valix said, "how did you get it away from them, anyway?"

Sinch told her of his argument with the Shadows, and Yilon's dramatic entrance. "Lucky shot," Yilon said, laughing, and then grinned down at Sinch. "But a definite win for me."

Sinch's sheath tingled. "I will not argue with that," he said.

"And then I just negotiated with them," Yilon said.

"I still can't believe they didn't kill you outright." Valix kept turning her head to look at them, though she winced every time she did.

"Stop moving," Yilon said. "I looked for the sentry like you told me, but didn't see him around. When I saw them threatening Sinch, I tried to figure out a way I could save him. Because if I killed one of them, they'd likely kill him."

"But that helped convince them, I think," Sinch said, "that he didn't kill them right away. And he'd come to save a mouse."

"They'd have a hard time believing that, all right," Valix said. She fiddled with her wristlet, turning it around her wrist.

"And I think Whisper...lost someone close to him...in the recent raid," Yilon said, panting as they climbed a hill toward the Heights. "Just the way he talked."

"Oh," Sinch said. "I didn't pick up on that."

"I might be wrong," Yilon said. "But he's certainly taking a chance, giving us the crown back."

"I'll say," Valix said. "What did you promise in return?"

"Alliance," Yilon said. "Peace."

"Hmph." Valix craned her neck to see Sinch. "You going to help with that? They like you."

"Going to try," Sinch said.

"You'd better come through, for all our sakes. That's all I have to say," Valix said, and indeed she stopped talking until they reached Dinah's house and the second floor bed.

Colian, fuming, chased them out of the room as soon as they'd laid her down. "If she never walks again, the blame rests on your heads," he called through the door. "She needs rest and peace and quiet, not being dragged around in the middle of the night to lie on filthy stones and Canis knows what else. Go save the world without her."

Sinch stopped on the landing. "Never walk again?" he said softly to Yilon. "Really?"

Yilon patted his shoulder. "I bet right now he's telling her he just said that to scare us."

"I hope so." Sinch trailed Yilon down the stairs, waiting while he went to wake Dinah. Sinch's paw brushed the leather of the satchel, hoping Valix would be okay. They'd needed her help, no doubt about that, but what if she never did recover from the injury? What if she became a cripple? She'd been the only real friend he'd made here in Dewanne. He paced back and forth at the bottom of the stairs until Yilon and a sleepy Dinah emerged.

"Sinch, you stay here," Yilon said. "The two of us are going to the governor's mansion. Colian said Maxon went back there, and we need to fetch Lady Dewanne and Velkan anyway."

"Can't we just sleep another hour?" Dinah complained. "It's still dark out."

"By the time we get everyone together, it'll be light." Yilon padded over to Sinch and hugged him. "You should be safe here. Hide in the third floor room and wait for us."

Sinch moved the satchel to his other shoulder and nodded. "But..."

Yilon had already started to walk back to Dinah. "What? You want to come with us?"

Sinch shook his head. "Just...people know about this place. Shadows, Maxon...and it'd be just me guarding it."

"They're all on our side now," Yilon said.

"I know, but still." Sinch perked up. "Wait. I know the place. Are there services in the church today?"

"Only Caniday and Gaiaday," Dinah said. "Why?"

"I found a hiding place there." Sinch patted the satchel. "It's closer to the palace, too."

"Castle," Yilon said. "They call it a castle here. It's still risky for you to walk with it by yourself, in daylight. Why don't you just wait in the church until we arrive?"

"They'll like that anyway," Dinah said. "The crown presented in the church and all. Although..." She looked at Sinch.

"They're going to have to get used to Sinch being around me," Yilon said firmly.

Dinah nodded. "Hopefully they'll be so happy about the crown they won't care, right? Still, maybe you don't want to start with the church."

Sinch was thinking the same thing, but he didn't know where else the crown would be safe. Yilon narrowed his eyes and grinned. "I just walked into the lair of the Shadows and survived. They can survive my friend in their church." He saw Sinch's objection and answered it before Sinch even had a chance to open his mouth. "I made a promise to you, too," he said.

And Sinch just nodded, because in that moment Yilon looked a foot taller, his ears straight up and brimming with confidence, and Sinch believed he could do anything he set his mind to, because he saw in his friend's eyes that he believed it, too. "All right," he said. "But if there's any trouble..."

"They'll deal with me."

Dinah smiled, her own ears perking up. "And me," she said. "You're right. They'll listen to us, for a change."

Even the "us" from Dinah couldn't dim Sinch's pride in what Yilon had accomplished. He walked a little behind Yilon, trying to imitate his confident, upright bearing past the few foxes they encountered. Behind them, in the east, dawn crept over the slopes of the mountains, outlining them with soft light. The mice in the alleys were making their final rounds; he saw fewer and fewer of them as they drew closer to the church, and as the dawn crept further and further up the sky.

"Nice," Yilon said, rounding a corner. He stopped for a moment to look down the street at the elegant building at the end of it. Sinch had been afraid he wouldn't recognize the church, in the darkness, but there was no mistaking it. In each of the windows that ringed the lower level, candles burned, and although they weren't facing the front of the church, Sinch could see now that the sign of Canis was glass, stained green, lit from inside and glowing, atop the warm windows below. Even to Sinch, about whom he was sure Canis cared nothing, the sign beckoned him in with the promise of safety.

"We'll walk you to the door," Yilon said, starting up the street. Dinah followed him, and Sinch followed her.

The church was not empty, it turned out. A fox knelt on one of the benches, head bowed. At the creak of the door, a tall fox in white robes with green trim paced over to them. Sinch watched him between Yilon and Dinah, watched his ears go back and his smile waver when he looked between them too, and saw Sinch.

"Sir," he said softly, approaching Yilon, "this is a church of Canis."

"My father," Yilon said, "I am to be the lord of Dewanne, and this... and Sinch is under my protection." He put a paw on Sinch's shoulder and stepped aside so the Cantor could see Sinch clearly. Sinch straightened his shoulders and tried to appear as harmless as he felt. "He requires a safe, quiet place for an hour, perhaps two, until I return with Lady Dewanne."

"Can't...can't I go with you?" Sinch didn't feel threatened in the church, but he didn't feel welcome.

Yilon glanced at the leather satchel. Sinch took his meaning immediately, that he didn't want to leave the crown unguarded. "I don't want to cause a scene at the castle. And I don't know Velkan's mansion. You'll be safe here. Won't he, my father?"

"Uh, well..." The Cantor looked from Sinch to Yilon. His ears had folded slightly back and Sinch could see the whites of his wide eyes.

"My father," Yilon said, "I know it is hard for you. I ask you to trust me."

"I'll stay in that chapel," Sinch said, pointing. "I just want some time alone. I won't take anything."

The Cantor looked pointedly at the leather satchel. His nose wrinkled. "It looks like you've already been busy," he said.

"He's holding something for me," Yilon said, his voice colder. "I will be responsible for any damage he causes."

"Shh!" The Cantor flicked his glance back to Yilon. "Don't let him hear you say that."

"I don't care," Yilon said, staring back. "I will also hold you responsible if he and his burden are not safely here when I return."

"This is not a storage area," the Cantor said. "And you are very young to be responsible for—"

"I am to be the lord of Dewanne." Yilon's voice was as icy as Sinch had ever heard it. "This mouse is under my protection, and I am asking to entrust him to yours."

As inspiring as it was to watch Yilon, Sinch couldn't bear to meet the Cantor's gaze. Looking around the church, he noticed that the praying fox's ears were swept back, also probably embarrassed or annoyed. Sinch felt less comfortable now than he had when the church was empty; the Cantor's musk was strong, reminding him that his goddess was nowhere around, and that the dim morning light was a carnivore's time. Though the symbol of Gaia was displayed above the altar, all of the symbols lit with candles were the star of Canis. Around the upper tier of windows, he could no longer see the fading frescoes he'd seen the previous day. In deeper darkness or better light, he would feel better.

The Cantor drew himself up. "I will accompany him to the chapel, and he will wait inside there until you return."

"That's fine," Sinch said hurriedly.

Yilon rested a paw on his shoulder. "I'll be back soon."

Sinch nodded and smiled, not wanting to display the affection he felt, here in front of the Cantor. He patted the leather satchel. "I'll be here."

He watched Yilon and Dinah leave, while the Cantor tapped his paw. When Sinch turned back, the Cantor swept away toward the chapel, the backward sweep of his ears the only indication that he cared whether Sinch was following him. Sinch did, at a distance, trying to soak up the calm of the church. Even in the carnivore's hour, even with the Cantor's attitude putting his nerves somewhat on edge, the idea that the church had been here for hundreds of years reassured him.

At the chapel, the Cantor waited without speaking while Sinch went inside, and then drew the curtain across. Here, in the smaller enclosed space, Sinch felt safer still. He took one step forward.

"Don't touch the book," the Cantor said curtly.

Sinch jumped at the words, then exhaled slowly. "Wasn't going to," he muttered, but now, perversely, he wanted to. Still, he refrained, though he did look to see if the page was still at the same place. The words were indistinct in the faint light, but he thought the illuminations were familiar. Something about the shadow of Canis on the cub. He didn't intend to linger long enough in the chapel for the sun to brighten the page for him. As soon as he heard the Cantor move away, he padded quietly to the back and around the curtain. The stone, looser this time, made less noise as he moved it aside. He pushed the satchel through the opening and then squeezed through himself.

On the other side, in the darkness, he listened for any activity. The heavy curtain dulled most of the sounds from the church; probably it also dulled the sound of the stone being moved. Rather than make more noise, he left the stone ajar. The Cantor wouldn't let anyone else into the chapel, and even if he did, they wouldn't look behind the curtain. Sinch picked up the satchel and crept down into the blackness of the crypt.

He walked around the stairs, feeling with his paw for a place to put the satchel down. The floor felt too grimy, and there were spiderwebs around too. But the mensas, when he touched them, were dry. There was one, partway along the wall, that had enough space for the satchel. He brushed it as clear of dust as he could, stifling sneezes, and then paced the distance from it to the stairs and back again, until he was sure he could find it easily. Then he placed the satchel on the ledge and sat beneath it, closing his eyes, intending to nap for an hour.

He'd just dozed off when something jerked him awake. Disoriented, he imagined for a moment that he was in the basement of the palace in Divalia, hiding overnight, and the kitchen boy had just come down to get flour for the morning's baking. But of course, that was ridiculous; the basement of the palace smelled like dried fruit, salted meat, and grain, not like spiderwebs and old bones. Silly dream, he thought, and then, just before he could completely relax, he thought he heard something, a scrape across stone.

Ears straining, he froze. The room was silent. But no; there it was again. A light click, someone with claws who hadn't been taught how to walk completely silently. Someone descending the stone stairs, trying not to be heard.

Sinch got slowly to his feet. He padded away from the satchel. Finding a support column, he put it between him and the stairs, peering around it to listen. He heard another click, and then one more, on the floor of the crypt. The fox was in the room with him. Two short sniffs, and then a low chuckle. "You know, I never made the connection. I had to go all the way to Divalia to learn about crypts beneath churches, and it never occurred to me to look for one here in the church where I grew up until I saw you run in here yesterday. They've forgotten about this. You probably figured that out. Very clever. Very clever. Almost as clever as a fox."

He recognized the voice, the same one he'd last heard in Balinni's office. The anger was gone, and in its place was a purr of smug satisfaction. "And now you're trapped. They don't build a second exit to these places.

Who would need it?" More sniffs. "You know you're trapped. I can smell it. You poor creatures, so dumb to the world. How can you know the richness that we do? We hear better, smell better, run faster. And still you think yourselves equals."

Dewry was moving around to Sinch's right. All of Sinch's nerves screamed at him to run, run! But he held his ground. If only the fox would move a little further, away from the stairs. "And you have the gall to touch the sacred crown. The gall! But Canis knows when injustice is being done. I'm here by His paw."

I'm sure you are, Sinch thought. Now just let His paw move you a little to the right. He stepped quietly around the pillar to his left, keeping it between him and Dewry. The fox had stopped talking, but his claws gave away his position as clearly as if he had been. He moved past the stair, past the ledge where Sinch had hidden the crown. He paused there, and Sinch heard another sniff. He tensed, prepared to leap at Dewry if he heard the scrape of leather on dusty stone that would signal that he'd found the satchel.

But Dewry was apparently still just sniffing for him. He moved again, closer to Sinch, and now Sinch had a clear path to the stairs. Dewry was perhaps fifteen feet from him, moving closer slowly. Sinch let him get a little further, and then he sprang across the crypt.

He couldn't hear anything over the sound of his own paws hitting the rock. He deliberately ran to the left of where he knew the stairs were, so that he could turn along the wall until he found them. When he made the turn, he heard Dewry's paws close behind. He jumped forward, and came down on the floor; he'd run too far to the left, overcompensating. But Dewry hadn't caught him yet. He jumped forward again.

His feet landed on the rounded corner of the first stair. He fell forward hard, but his paws were out to break his fall, so he suffered no immediate injury beyond scraped paw pads. Scrambling up the stairs even as he tried to regain his balance, he listened for Dewry behind him, but the fox was apparently taking his time so he wouldn't fall. Sinch panted, running up the stairs, and now he heard Dewry at the bottom of them.

His pounding heart urged him faster up the stairs, but he knew he was far enough ahead that he would make it now. His main concern was making sure Dewry followed him. Lead him out into the church, he thought. Don't let him stay down there with the satchel. If he turns around, you'll have to turn and fight.

And then, abruptly, there were no more stairs beneath his paws. He lurched forward and hit a stone wall, dust and spiderwebs sticking to the fur of his muzzle. Frantically, he felt for the opening in the wall, but where there had been a patch of grey, there was nothing but blackness.

"Ah, did I forget to mention I closed the stone leading down here?" Dewry was halfway up the stairs, advancing as he spoke. "How forgetful of me. I'm certain you can find it, given time. But I think you'll give me the crown first."

"It'll never be yours," Sinch said, and then immediately moved, in case Dewry used his voice to throw something at him. He cursed himself for a fool for not realizing that his best chance would have been to keep moving around down in the darkness until he had an opening to attack Dewry. He'd been herded up the stairs where Dewry could find him easily. Perhaps if he rushed the fox, he could knock him down the stairs—but then Sinch would fall, too, and Dewry might have a dagger out.

"It is mine." Dewry sounded peevish. "I just don't have my paws on it yet. But you'll help me with that." He'd stopped, almost at the top of the stairs. Sinch used the cover of his voice to draw his own dagger. His paws were trembling, with fear or anger or a combination of both.

"Do what you want to me," Sinch said. "Yilon will be back soon, and he knows about the crypt."

"Ah," Dewry said. "When your pretender lord comes back, well, I have a fellow with a crossbow just outside. If he doesn't see me come out with the crown before then, he'll shoot your master through the heart."

Sinch's heart stopped. "Liar," he said, ears cupped.

"Just as he shot Corwin." Dewry's voice had gotten sharper.

"You don't have any men left."

"Then you've nothing to worry about. Just stay where you are. I won't move. You'll come to me."

Oh, Rodenta, Sinch breathed. He was sure, sure Dewry was bluffing. Yilon had told him that the house was empty, that Kites and Shreds were gone. But he couldn't stop his fingers from tightening around the dagger. His mind formed a picture of the stairs, Dewry leaning against the wall on the right hand side. His head would be *there*, his chest would be *there*. A blind throw, in the dark? Whisper could do it, no doubt. But could Sinch? He would have to wait until Dewry spoke again.

But the fox seemed content to remain silent, having baited Sinch. Sinch crept to his right and stood upright. "What makes you think they'll let a coward like you be Lord of Dewanne?"

"I'm no coward," Dewry said sharply. Sinch ducked to his left and threw his dagger as hard as he could. He heard the soft impact and Dewry's yelled curse, and ran down the stairs as fast as he could.

As he passed the stair where Dewry stood, pain lanced through his side, just below his ribs. Momentum carried him forward, but he lost his balance halfway down the stairs and fell, landing with a sharp crack on the stone floor. He could hear Dewry gasping, making his way down the stairs, and he struggled to get to his feet, but only one of his arms was working, and his side throbbed, his fur soaking with warmth. He felt dizzy.

"You little piece of gutter trash," Dewry wheezed. He was at the base of the stairs. "Bastard!"

Sinch crawled away from him, toward the wall. There was a mensa there, clear of bones on one side. He pulled himself in with his one good arm, and found another hollow behind it, a small cavity that let him down below the floor. He landed on more bones and then lay still, breathing in dust and ancient fur, one paw pressed to his side.

Dewry stumbled down the stairs. "I know you're here!" he screamed, his voice echoing in the crypt, but sounding distant to Sinch. "I'll find you!" He reached into the mensa above Sinch, and then scattered the bones on the shelf above which Sinch lay. A piece of bone dropped onto Sinch's thigh, but he didn't move. A moment later, the sounds of searching had moved on. "I can smell you!" Dewry was shouting, but his voice was even more distant.

Sinch felt the darkness growing thicker around him, as if he'd fallen into an icy river and were sinking slowly. He pinched the wound in his side to keep himself awake, gasping at the pain as stars burst across his vision. *Not yet, not yet...*

Chapter 30: Brothers in Canis

Collecting Lady Dewanne and Maxon took forever. Velkan, informed that they were going to see the crown returned, yawned and said that he was sure it would all happen perfectly happily without his involvement and that after a night of raiding the Shadows and a night of cleaning up, he would rather have some sleep. Lady Dewanne was not in her chambers, but they found her in one of the lower rooms, staring out a window, holding a clear glass ornament in her paws.

"Have you been awake all night?" Maxon asked when they found her. The steward had not taken being awoken with very good humor.

"Most of it," she replied. She set the glass down on the table, where its curves caught the light, setting the green streak of color inside it to glowing softly. "Where are we going?"

"To get the crown." Yilon smiled.

She nodded, turning from the window and walking slowly after them out of the room. Her muzzle did lift as they walked out of the palace, looking up at the sky.

The sun had risen, but not yet cleared the mountains nor the thick blanket of low-lying clouds. Though the air was still warm, Maxon drew his cloak around himself and glared as they set off from the castle gates. "I presume that you are going to introduce us to a mouse, and that is why you did not bring him to the castle."

"It's your rule," Yilon said.

"No rule prevents mice from standing just outside the palace gates."

"I've been incautious with it once," Yilon said. "I didn't want to risk anything again. Sinch is in a safe place."

"Let him be, Maxon." Lady Dewanne sounded tired. "He wants to create an effect."

Maxon coughed. "He's creating an effect of making us sick."

"It's not winter yet. We're about to get a lord. Enjoy the weather."

"Easy for you," Maxon said, with another cough that Yilon was sure was exaggerated. "Come winter, you won't be here."

"I think it's nice," Dinah said, unexpectedly. "It feels like an old ritual of some sort, the recovery of the crown in the church."

Yilon tensed, waiting for a shocked reaction at a mouse in the church, but neither the steward nor the lady said anything. Good, he thought.

After Dinah's last comment, they fell silent, with Lady Dewanne and Maxon letting Yilon and Dinah lead them forward through the waking streets. Yilon recognized not only the landmark buildings, glowing in the early light, but also smaller houses and oddities like the break in the landing-stone outside the small grey stone building, the peculiar smell of the goat-cheese shop down that street. Perhaps this wouldn't be such a bad place to live. Dinah felt right at his side, a comrade-in-arms if not a lover, and they were going to join Sinch.

At the crossroads where they turned right, Yilon thought he saw a shadow on the roof, far ahead to the right. I haven't forgotten, Whisper, he said in his head. I'll make it right.

And then they came around a corner, the flagstones angling upward under their feet, the gleaming dome of the church and the five points of the star above it shining ahead of them, gathering the dull light struggling through the clouds and making it stronger.

Lady Dewanne greeted two foxes on their way up the street, but apart from that, none of them spoke. Maxon cleared his throat several times, while Yilon and Dinah were breathing hard. Only Lady Dewanne walked without any visible signs of stress. At the top of the hill, at the edge of the circle where the church stood, they paused to rest. Yilon looked up again at the roof, but the shadow was no longer there, or couldn't be seen from this angle. He knew they were still out there watching him, but he didn't feel threatened.

"Are we ready?" he asked the group.

"Yes," Maxon said, with a cough. "Let's get this over with, shall we?"

Lady Dewanne inclined her head. "Lead on."

Dinah smiled and stepped to his side. Together, they crossed the street to the front door of the church and opened the door.

The church was brighter, the western side painted with morning's glow, the eastern wall touched softly by reflections of that glow. Both the Cantor and the fox who'd been praying were gone; the church was empty. As the door eased shut behind Maxon, Yilon padded ahead of them, toward the chapel. He felt a twinge of annoyance at the Cantor for vanishing. After all, anyone could have gotten in to find Sinch and cause trouble.

The curtain across the chapel moved, and a fox came out. He looked like the Cantor at first: tall and thin, though his robes were so filthy it was impossible to tell if they'd once been white. He stopped when he saw Yilon, and then walked quickly down one of the pews.

"Hey!" Yilon said. The smell of mold and dust drifted across the air to him. The robes, he saw now, were not robes at all, but a loose tunic. The

"Keep your weapons down."

fox made his way halfway down a pew and then stopped to look at Yilon, turning so Yilon could now see the familiar leather satchel hanging from his right shoulder. It wasn't the Cantor. It was the guard from their journey, the thin fox who'd sat quietly atop the carriage with his crossbow.

Maxon's voice rang out through the church. "Dewry—"

"Quiet, traitor," the Cantor—the fox who wasn't the Cantor—said. "I've no more need of you."

"Where's Sinch?" Yilon reached across his back and grasped his short bow.

"Keep your weapons down," Dewry said sharply. He put down the satchel with a dull thud, and lifted a crossbow from the pew with his right paw. "This is a sacred place."

"How dare you!" Maxon said.

"What did you do with the Cantor?" Dinah stepped forward.

Dewry ignored them both. "It was most inconvenient of you to stop here. Had you stayed in the Heights, none of this would be necessary, and you could bury your little sex toy wherever you liked."

"Where is he?" Yilon shouted.

Dewry's ears flicked at the ringing echoes. "He's defiling the bones of my ancestors. That's fine. There will be plenty of time to find his body later." He reached down to pat the satchel. "I have what I need."

Yilon stared at the chapel, at the curtain hiding it from the rest of the church. Had it moved again? Was it wishful thinking? He ached to run over and look, but he couldn't make himself do it. The disappointment if it were empty would be too much to bear. And if it weren't, what would he do? He started to walk back toward the entrance, away from the chapel and the altar. "You're lying," he said, though he couldn't imagine Sinch giving up the satchel while he was still alive. His eyes flicked to the silver star atop the altar. *Please, please, let him be alive.*

Dewry followed him with the crossbow. He was holding it awkwardly in his right arm, and now that Yilon looked at him, he saw the left hanging limply at his side. Halfway down the upper arm, a large dark reddish blot spread across the grimy white fabric. Good for Sinch, he thought fiercely. He scored a mark. He gauged the range of the crossbow, trying to estimate how much Dewry's wounded arm changed things. From where he was, it would be a difficult shot with only the one arm for balance. But if Dewry had shot Corwin from the roof, he could certainly shoot Yilon from across a church, wounded arm or no.

"Dewry," Lady Dewanne said. "You are not the heir."

"I have the crown," he said. "You can't stop me any more."

She stepped forward from the door, down the center aisle. If she'd been distant on the way to the church, she was fully present now. "You've no idea what your father wanted."

"You're the one who had me sent away," Dewry snapped.

"It was easier for you to accept that, wasn't it?" Lady Dewanne said, so softly that Yilon wasn't sure Dewry would be able to hear her.

But he did. "It's the truth! That's what he told me!" He kept the crossbow trained on Yilon, moving along the pew, trying to get closer. Yilon moved in the same direction, away from the chapel, trying not to look in that direction to see whether the curtain had moved again, lest he draw Dewry's attention to it.

"That's what Maxon told you," Lady Dewanne said. "Sheffin did not want to hurt you."

"He wanted me to be Lord!" Dewry said. "He loved me!"

Lady Dewanne stepped forward, even with Yilon, blocking him. She rested her paws on the back of the rearmost pew. "In his way, yes."

Yilon stopped, not wanting to step behind her. Dewry still held the crossbow on him, but he'd stopped moving, now sneering at Lady Dewanne. "He wouldn't let you have cubs of your own. That's why you had to get this unwanted second from some other fox family."

Yilon hadn't expected Lady Dewanne to smile. "You poor thing," she said. "You thought that was his decision?"

For the first time, the crossbow dipped. Dewry's eyes widened, his ears flattening. They came back up almost immediately. "It was, of course it was. Don't be ridiculous. He had me. Why would he...?"

"Canis mark my words," Lady Dewanne said, splaying her paw over her heart.

"Ha." The crossbow swung slightly in her direction, then returned to Yilon. Dewry's left arm twitched, and Yilon caught his wince of pain. "You're the one who wanted a cub. You wanted to get rid of me, put me out of the picture forever."

Lady Dewanne didn't say anything, but she held Dewry's eyes, and after a moment, his ears flattened again. "That wasn't me."

"It was never *proven* to be you. And yet," she said, with a graceful wave at the crossbow.

"I'm not going to kill *you* now," he said. "*You* have no claim to the lordship." As if she'd reminded him of his mission, he started moving toward the center aisle again. Yilon judged the distance, and which way Dewry might miss. He could perhaps dodge the crossbow if he timed it just right. But Dewry was closer now, and it would be a tricky thing.

"I chose not to have cubs," Lady Dewanne said, her voice ringing through the church, "because I was terrified you would try to kill them as well."

Dewry stopped again, at the center aisle, and stared. Lady Dewanne went on. "And your father agreed with me."

"I wouldn't..." Dewry shook his head. "He had to know..." He looked to the steward, ears flattened, eyes widening. "I would have stepped aside. For my brothers, of course I would. Maxon. Maxon! Tell her."

Maxon stepped forward, past Lady Dewanne. "Do not do this," he said.

Dewry's muzzle twisted. "Did she turn you against me, too?"

"You did that." Maxon took another step toward Dewry.

Yilon saw Dewry flinch. He tensed, ready to move quickly. The crossbow swung to point at Maxon, the deadly quarrel tip gleaming in the sunlight. "Stop there." Dewry shook his head, and then smiled again. "It doesn't matter. Doesn't matter." He lurched forward and swung the crossbow around, bringing it to bear on Yilon.

"He *is* your brother!" Maxon cried, stretching out a paw.

The word 'brother' echoed from the dome, dying away into silence. Yilon was only watching Dewry, but with the exception of Maxon, he felt all other eyes in the church on him. Maxon took another step forward. He was very close now, perhaps three steps away. Yilon wanted to shout at him to come back, that Dewry was clearly unhinged and might shoot him. "Your father," Maxon went on, "he made an arrangement..."

"He can't be," Dewry whispered.

"He is," Lady Dewanne said. "It was the only way Sheffin could have another son who would be safe from you."

"You said you would step aside for your brother." Maxon spoke firmly.

"Not him!" The crossbow trembled in his paw. "Not that mouse-loving, city-born, pampered..." His head twitched. In that moment, he looked uncannily like Shreds. Yilon gripped the stone back of the pew and prepared to move.

"Give me the crossbow," Maxon said calmly. "You can still go back to Divalia." He reached out.

"No!" Dewry's eyes blazed. "You're lying! All of you!" The crossbow came up so that Yilon caught a glimpse of the silver point, aimed directly at his eyes, but it was only a glimpse. He heard the thrum of the string, but his view was obscured by a grey blur. Maxon had leapt for Dewry at the moment the crossbow was fired.

Only the steward's coughs echoed in the church. Dewry had lowered the crossbow, but was making no attempt to draw it again, staring at Maxon as the steward staggered against the stone. Yilon leapt over the pew, running across the stone backs as Dinah paralleled him down the aisle. She reached Dewry a moment before he did.

Dewry brought the crossbow up instinctively. Dinah knocked it aside and bore him to the floor, just as Yilon dropped to the ground beside them. "I got him," Dinah growled, so Yilon knelt next to Maxon.

The steward had slumped against one of the pews, a paw curled around the quarrel that had pierced his chest. Yilon couldn't help but notice that it had struck him in almost the same place as Corwin had been hit, though at much closer range. "My lord," he whispered, and then coughed. Flecks of blood spattered his chest below the large, spreading red stain with the silver center.

"Shh." Yilon took his paw. The pads felt cold as ice.

Lady Dewanne knelt beside them. "Be at rest, dear friend," she said, her voice choked.

Maxon's eyes held Yilon's. The steward's jaw worked, but he made only guttural noises. His eyelids fluttered; he strained to keep them open.

"You have served the court of Dewanne well," Yilon said. "As well as anyone could have asked."

Maxon's ears lifted, and his muzzle curved into a satisfied smile. Then his eyes closed, and he made no more attempt to open them.

Yilon couldn't let go of the steward's paw. So many times in the past week (only a week?) he had been furious at Maxon, for his attitude, his treachery, his behavior toward Sinch and Valix. He'd only recently come to understand the steward even a little. Now he found himself wishing for more time.

"It was a good thing to say," Lady Dewanne said quietly to him.

Yilon couldn't look away from Maxon's expression, peaceful now. The paw he was holding grew stiff. "He told us a lot of his story, yesterday."

Gently, Lady Dewanne took Maxon's paw from Yilon. "He did not have an easy life, but he led it as well as he knew how. If he made mistakes, he did his best to atone for them."

Yilon nodded, numbly. His eyes came to rest on the crossbow quarrel, which brought his mind back to Dewry. He turned to see Dinah with one knee on Dewry's back, twisting one arm into the air. With one last glance at Maxon, Yilon stood, looking down at them.

"You should go call the guard," Lady Dewanne said, remaining crouched beside Maxon, her blue dress puddled on the floor.

"No," Dinah said, "you should help me get this bastard outside." She spit the epithet out, ears flat back against her head. "We don't need the guard to take care of him."

"There are laws," Lady Dewanne said. "And I am still Lady Regent."

"Yilon, give me a paw here." Dinah made as if to slide off of Dewry, who looked insensate.

The temptation was strong. He wanted to hurt this fox, for what he'd done to Corwin, Maxon, and Sinch. He wanted him to suffer as they were all suffering. But whatever they would do to him would not repair the damage he'd already done. His lessons had taught him that. "No," he said. "There will be judgment for him, but not today."

Dewry's ears flicked, but he made no other movement. Lady Dewanne stood and brushed her dress sleeve, her gaze resting on Yilon. "He is what he was raised to be," she said softly.

"He is what he is," Dinah said.

Lady Dewanne shook her head. "We sent him away from home and family. He knew his father only at a distance, and then not at all. Sheffin bore the guilt for his youthful lust all his life, and so did he." She gestured toward Dewry's prone form.

Yilon squeezed his eyes shut. Dinah's voice echoed sharply in the church. "I barely know my father."

"He's there for you, dear." Lady Dewanne's voice carried a touch of impatience. "Should you wish to know him better—"

"We neither of us knew our father." Yilon barely stopped himself from adding the plural. He stepped around to Dewry's head and looked down at the filthy fox. Cobwebs trailed from his ears, and his arms were more grey than black with all the dust on them. Yilon saw a piece of white fur clinging to Dewry's shoulder, and shuddered to think from where it might have come; he'd talked about the "bodies of his ancestors."

Dewry lifted his head slowly, wincing as Dinah twisted his arm further. He stared up at Yilon, his eyes not defiant, nor angry, but desperate. His ears were flat back against his skull. "Are you really my brother?"

Something in the harsh croak of his voice made Dinah's ears perk. She relaxed her grip, sitting back, allowing Dewry to turn onto his side, to see Yilon more clearly. Yilon saw Lady Dewanne's curt nod, but he didn't need her permission, nor her encouragement. "I am," he said.

Dewry closed his eyes. His chest heaved, and then his torso twisted, throwing Dinah off of him. Yilon and Lady Dewanne both took a step back, but Dewry made no move toward them. He craned his neck up toward the ceiling of the church, his muzzle opened, and out came a naked howl, wordless, anguished, that sent Yilon another step back with the force of it. The scream built on itself, echoing back from the corners of the church to join with itself, and it went on and on.

Yilon stood, as they all did, mesmerized. He didn't understand it fully, but he could almost see a dark haze in the air above Dewry, as if some malicious spirit were escaping through his scream, dissipating in the sacred air of the church.

When his breath ran out, Dewry panted hard, still staring at the roof. Then he collapsed to the ground, staring dully at nothing through glistening eyes.

The guard took him away while Yilon searched for Sinch. In the chapel, he found the Cantor, bound and gagged, a stole covering his head. "He asked me to come in here," he said, when Yilon released him, "and then he seized my arms."

Volle sniffed around the chapel. He could still smell Sinch, but the mouse was nowhere to be found. "My friend, the one I left here..."

"He was not here." The Cantor rubbed his wrists and looked fearfully at the curtain. "What...what happened?"

"He killed the court steward," Yilon said. His eyes came to rest on the book at the small altar, while the Cantor placed his splayed paw to his chest in the sign of Canis.

"Is that...who screamed?"

"No."

When Yilon didn't elaborate, the Cantor went on. "I remember him from childhood. A little older than I was. We were told not to make sport of him because he didn't have a father." He ducked his head. "Canis have mercy on his spirit. May his paws find the true path at last."

"The shadow of the father lies over the path of the cub," Yilon murmured, the verse familiar from his childhood as he read it from the book, just above his fingers.

"And yet," the Cantor went on, "it is the cub who chooses his path."

Yilon read the words in the book as the Cantor said them. He pushed aside the thoughts they stirred. "Where did my friend go?"

"I don't know. He did not leave the chapel."

Yilon frowned. "That's impossible." His eyes fell on the curtain at the back of the chapel, a decorative tapestry that he'd seen as a wall.

"I did hear the scraping of a large stone," the Cantor offered, but Yilon was already looking behind the tapestry. There, in the wall, a large stone some two feet across by a foot and a half high had swung out from the wall.

Mold and dust smells floated out on cold air, along with a whiff of blood.

"Merciful Alpha," the Cantor said behind him, but Yilon was already squeezing through the opening.

"Get me light," he called back. He couldn't believe how absolute the darkness was. He could smell the decay from below. *The bones of my ancestors*. This had to be where Sinch was.

The Cantor's head disappeared from the opening. Yilon explored the area with his paws. "Sinch?" he called, but his voice was swallowed by the darkness. "Sinch!"

Silence answered him. He couldn't wait for the Cantor. He edged forward slowly, until his hind paws found the edge of a staircase. Keeping his paws on the walls, he walked slowly down each step. The chill in the air crept into his fur.

The wall on the left gave way to an open space. Yilon groped at air, called, "Sinch?" again. The sound of his voice and the twitch of his whiskers told him there was a large room open beyond. The silence remained absolute, but now the smell of blood grew stronger. *If You love me*, he prayed. *Please, please, no...*

Down two more steps, and his toes encountered something soft. He recovered his balance and crouched on the stair. Now he recognized Sinch's scent, drowned out by blood and dust and bones and mold. His paw hovered in the air. If he touched Sinch and found him as stiff and cold as Maxon, what then? What would he do? He listened for breathing, for movement. Surely in the silence of the crypt, any noise would reach his ears.

But he could not hear anything over the sound of his own breathing, his own heartbeat. He lowered his paw slowly and met cold fur. A soft whine escaped him before he realized it. "Sinch?"

Light flickered at the top of the stair, enough for him to see Sinch. He was sprawled on the stair, one arm reaching for the step above. Below him, a trail glistening in the dust showed where he'd crawled from the floor up three steps before his strength had given out. Yilon couldn't see where he was hurt, but he wasn't conscious. There has to be a chance, he thought firmly, and wouldn't allow himself to believe otherwise.

He gathered Sinch in his arms. Slowly, mindful of his balance, he stood, and then climbed the stairs as quickly as he dared, moving his paws to feel for any sign of life. There, a pulse? No, it was gone now. Sinch stirred in his arms—or was it just the way Yilon was carrying him, a natural movement? My fault, my fault, my fault, sang voices in his head, and he couldn't argue with them. His breath came out in sharp whines until he reached the top of the stairs, looking past the lamp at the Cantor's bewildered muzzle.

"He's hurt," he said as the Cantor withdrew the lamp. "You have to take him to the guard, get him to a chirurgeon."

The Cantor's muzzle twisted at the sight of the mouse's head, thick with dust and cobwebs. "I..."

"He needs help!" Yilon cried. "Please!"

Calm settled over the other's muzzle. "Yes, of course," he said, and reached out his arms.

Through the opening, Yilon watched him carry Sinch's limp form out of the front of the chapel. He sat back heavily on the stone floor. He knew he would have to leave the crypt soon, but when he did, he would have to find out whether he had killed his best friend or merely caused a near-fatal wound. In the darkness, none of that had happened yet.

He tried to hate Dewry, but he couldn't. It would be too easy to blame him for everything, when in fact Yilon had been the one who'd left Sinch alone with the crown; Yilon had convinced him to steal the crown; Yilon had brought Sinch here in the first place, into this place where there was hatred and danger and death.

A muzzle appeared at the hole in the wall. He smelled a vixen's scent and thought it was Dinah. But her voice was Lady Dewanne's. "How curious," she said. "Are you planning to stay there for much longer?"

"Not much." Yilon curled his tail around his legs, taking hold of the end with a paw.

"Your friend is on his way to a chirurgeon," she said. When he didn't respond with more than a slow exhale, she continued. "Dewry is on his way to jail. Maxon is..."

It was her turn to let out a long, slow breath. Yilon stirred. "I know." No words felt adequate. "I'm sorry."

She seated herself on the other side, leaning against the wall and speaking through the opening. "It's not your spirit that bears the burden."

"I should have rushed him. He would have hurried the shot—Sinch wounded his other arm."

"And then you might be lying on the floor of the church. His spirit is with Canis, and though I am certain he would have liked to witness your Confirmation, he did not regret the manner of his passing."

Yilon buried his muzzle in his paws. "Is this what it's like? Every day, wishing you could change something you've done that hurt someone else?"

She did not immediately respond. He lifted his head and saw hers bowed, her eyes closed. "I can tell you," she said, "that a great deal of a Lord's time is spent attempting to right wrongs, and that in many cases those wrongs will be your own."

"How do you do it? When every decision you make might cost someone his life?"

"Not every decision has quite as much weight." She opened her eyes now. "And you must remember what Canis says: Though your Alpha mark the trail, still you must choose where to place your paws along it."

"He may compel you to follow, but you choose the manner of your following," Yilon recited.

"Precisely."

He flicked his ears. "Look how much damage I've caused in just three days. I don't trust myself to lead."

"Your father does."

He jerked his head all the way up. "My father? He just sent me out here, with no preparation. I was picked by Lord Dewanne years ago. Because of a lie."

Lady Dewanne did not act perturbed. "You were not named to succeed until two months ago."

"Not formally."

"Not at all."

Yilon frowned. "There was an agreement..."

"Yes. But part of the agreement was that your father would make the final recommendation, and Sheffin would make the final decision. Oh, it was well known that you were going to be considered. The noble families here have known for some time. But it was not until we received the letter from your father that Sheffin made the formal designation."

"Letter?" He squeezed his tail, staring at her.

"I have it back in my chambers. You may read it if you like."

"What did it say?" he whispered.

She smiled. "He told us how intelligent you were. That you had a marvelous aptitude for history, and that while your sense of diplomacy could perhaps use some development, he would be proud to hand over the rulership of Vinton to you, were you the first-born." She rubbed her whiskers. "We made the announcement the day after receiving the letter."

"So Dewry really thought it might be him."

She nodded, slowly. "He has held on, all these years, to his hatred of me and his love of his father. I am not sure he will ever be the same, after seeing with his own eyes the lengths to which his father was willing to go to keep the lordship from him."

"Is that what you meant by 'righting wrongs'?" Yilon said. "His loving Kayley, giving Dewry hope all those years...stopping you from having your own cubs?"

She remained silent. "I'm sorry," he said. "I don't mean to speak ill of Sheffin."

"He loved too much," she said. "He could not bear to put one he loved aside, even when that one took advantage of his love. Of all the mistakes a lord can make, that is not such a bad one."

"He tried to make my mother betray her husband."

"None would have needed to know, in his mind. He did not want to hurt your father." She rested a paw on the opening. Grey hairs speckled the brown fur of her long, delicate fingers, and two narrow silver bracelets clinked against the stone. "Which brings us back to you."

Yilon still didn't move, though the chill of the stone was creeping into him further and further. "Give me a minute." He was trying to understand what it meant, that letter from his father. His first bitter thought was, why couldn't he have sent Volyan out here if he liked me more? But things didn't work that way. And so here he was, sitting on a cold stone floor in a crypt on the other side of the country from everything he thought of as home. He'd never wanted anything more in that moment than he wanted his mother's presence near him, a warm cup of milk, and a sleep unencumbered by worry or responsibility next to a healthy, happy Sinch.

Dinah's voice came through to him, followed a moment later by her muzzle as Lady Dewanne withdrew. "Sinch is going to be okay," she said, encouragingly. "They've got him on the way to the chirurgeon."

That just reminded him of the feel of the limp body in his arms. "I'll be out in a minute," he said.

She looked away, up at Lady Dewanne, probably. "We're counting on you."

"Who?" He couldn't think of anyone who wouldn't be better off without him, but he couldn't bring himself to say it.

"Me. Lady Dewanne. All of the city." She paused. "The Shadows."

The Shadows. He looked up and around at the darkness. But for the lack of water and filthy odor, this place was dark enough to be the sewer. He thought of his promise to Whisper, and how proud Sinch had been of him afterwards. If he did nothing else for his friend, that would be a fitting legacy. Atoning for past mistakes, Keshin's and Shadow's and countless foxes and mice. And, not least among them, his own.

He breathed in the cold air once more, flicked his ears to the palpable silence, and then rocked forward to his knees. "All right," he said. "I'm coming."

Chapter 31: Confirmation

The muted light of morning streamed into Yilon's chambers. The heat had broken; the clouds that filled the sky now bathed the city in a gentle rain. He held his arms out, waiting for the young fox to finish fastening his garments. He had tied and re-tied the fastenings on the back of the doublet three times, each time following it with, "I'm sorry, my lord," in progressively higher and more nervous tones. His name was Raffi, and he had been appointed by Maxon to be Yilon's servant after Min's death, one of the last acts the steward had ever made.

"It's okay," Yilon said, though his arms were starting to ache and the wide belt rubbed his stomach wounds, even through the soft chemise he wore under the doublet. "Just relax."

"There." Raffi stood back. "I think it is all done now." His tail relaxed, uncurling from around his leg, and then he jumped at a knock on the door. He stared at Yilon.

Yilon lowered his arms and smiled gently. "Answer it?"

"Oh!" Raffi ran to the door and opened it.

Caffin walked in, dressed in a more formal footservant's uniform than Yilon had seen before. He bowed. "My lord," he said, "the ladies are waiting for you."

"I'll be there in a moment." He couldn't help contrasting Raffi's nervous eagerness to please to Min's more confident and capable manner. "Are we done, Raffi?"

"Yes, my Lord. Almost, my Lord. There is this chain...if I may..."

Though Raffi was two years younger than Yilon, he was nearly a foot taller. Yilon didn't even have to duck for his servant to loop the silver chain around his neck and fasten it. It tugged at the fur on the back of his neck.

"My Lord?" Caffin hesitated at Yilon's nod. He ducked his head. "Forgive me the presumption, but...is it true what they're saying?"

"About what?" Yilon already knew.

"In the church, yesterday...they say that after he killed Maxon, and threatened you," Caffin briefly pressed his fingers to his chest in a quick approximation of the sign of Canis, "Canis descended from the sky and struck his senses from him. They say he's lost all reason."

Yilon lifted one of the links from his chest and turned over the finger-sized circle so that the star of Canis inside it caught the sun. He let it fall again as Raffi came around to the front, brushing fur from the green fabric of the doublet. "Yes," he said. "That's about right."

Raffi stared at him, wide-eyed, and then remembered what he was doing. "There," the young servant said, finishing with the doublet. "Let me just..." He straightened the chain, let it fall, straightened it again. When he reached for it a third time, Yilon raised a paw.

"We're ready. Lead on, Caffin."

For most of that morning, Yilon had been trying to forget the events of the previous day, up to the time when he'd crawled out of the crypt, past the bewildered workers who were just arriving to decorate the church. He'd made Lady Dewanne take him to the chirurgeon Incic, where he'd sat in the small, private waiting room pacing back and forth until Incic himself came out to tell him that he'd done all he could and they would have to see if Sinch would make it through the night. Yilon had wanted to stay, but Lady Dewanne had reminded him that he needed to attend the ceremony Maxon had died to make possible, and that guilt drove him back to the castle. After a nearly completely silent dinner, he'd retired early to his room and slept fitfully until young Raffi had woken him.

They approached the office. From inside, Yilon heard the voices of Dinah and Lady Dewanne stop when Caffin knocked at the door. "Come," Lady Dewanne said.

"The Heir to see you," Caffin announced. Yilon stepped through as Caffin held the door for him. Raffi tried to follow, but Caffin took him firmly by the wrist and pulled him back.

"Caffin," Lady Dewanne said, "Please bring our other guests up when they are ready."

"Yes, my Lady." Caffin kept hold of Raffi, as though the servant might dart back into the office, and closed the door.

Lady Dewanne wore a long, elegant forest-green gown with silver trim, and a silver circlet above her ears, but Yilon's eyes were drawn to Dinah. She stood in the sunlight, in a similar gown with a pattern of silver beads on the shoulders which caught the sun in bright flashes as she turned. Her head, though, was bare. "Good morning," she said with a smile.

"You look beautiful," he said, pushing memories away. "What other guests?"

Lady Dewanne smiled. "Your parents arrived last night. You were already asleep, and considering the events of the past few days, we chose not to wake you."

"My...parents?" He looked back to Dinah's smile, then at the door. "Um...which parents?"

"Both of them." She didn't seem to realize that this didn't answer his question, at least not completely. "It was a surprise to me, as well. I had told them when the Confirmation was to take place, but I never received an answer."

He tried to picture his mother, or his father, here in Dewanne. It just didn't fit. This was the place where he'd known Dinah and Lady Dewanne, Corwin and Maxon and Min. They belonged here. But his father? Even stranger, his mother (if she'd arrived)? Though he'd not seen his mother in two years, and had said good-bye to his father only three weeks ago, they both felt equally distant from him, part of a different world. "They've been here since last night?"

"I spent some time telling them about the events of the last several days, but of course, I only know parts of the story. Dinah knows a little more, but I think they are anxious to spend time with you anyway."

Yilon's stomach growled. "I have the ceremony..."

"We'll dine with them, and then there will be a banquet tonight in your honor." Lady Dewanne smiled. "And after that, there will be time."

"Well, now that Yilon is here," Dinah said, "will you tell me—"

Caffin knocked at the door again. "Come," Lady Dewanne called.

And in came Yilon's father, striding quickly forward, with the tall white wolf behind him. They wore matching formal blue doublets with flower decorations down the sleeves, matching gold pendants around their necks, and matching wide smiles. To Yilon's surprise, his father stopped a few feet in front of him and didn't hold his arms out for an embrace. Yilon fidgeted, trying to reconcile the old resentment with the unexpected feeling of warmth. He saw then his father's upright ears, the proudly arched tail twitching, and the paws clasped behind his back, and realized that his father's restraint was solely for his benefit. Hesitantly, he lifted his arms and stepped forward, pushing resentment aside and letting the warmth take over in a smile.

Volle's smile widened. He stepped gladly into the embrace, bringing his arms around and his muzzle to brush Yilon's ear. "I'm so proud of you," he whispered, so softly Yilon was almost not sure he'd heard it. But then his father stepped back, with a quick brush of whiskers against his, and he saw the shine in his eyes and knew he'd heard right.

He folded his ears, trying to figure out how to respond, when he caught another scent. His eyes widened. "Mother?"

She stepped out from behind Streak, wiping her eyes, just as he'd remembered her. He didn't recognize the formal deep blue gown, but the bright eyes, the slender muzzle, the happy smile, all those were like coming home to him. Nothing felt out of place about her presence in the room, nor her scent against him as he rushed to her arms.

"My son, Lord Dewanne," she said.

"Not yet." He grinned. "How long did it take you to get here?"

"I left as soon as I got your father's note from Volyan. We met in Frontier. I'm glad we're in time. I was afraid we might have missed it." To Yilon's surprise, the look she exchanged with his father was affectionate.

"Did Volyan come with you?"

She rolled her eyes while Volle chuckled. "Your brother was supposed to ride with me. The morning we were to leave, I couldn't find him anywhere. I would be worried except that I heard from several people that he was at the Sheepshead until late in the night, with a lady on each arm."

"I'm sure he didn't mean to miss the carriage," Volle said.

"He's his father's son."

It was Volle's turn to roll his eyes. Yilon said, "That sounds like him."

"He cares about you," Volle said. "He just has trouble thinking beyond..." He glanced at his own groin.

"The present moment," Ilyana finished for him.

Yilon nodded. "I'm..." His tail was wagging back and forth, trying to drag his whole body with it. The bandage had been removed the previous night, and any small twinges of pain were lost in the moment.

"We heard what you've been through." His mother placed a paw on his left arm, and looked up. "Your ear..."

"We've heard some of it." His father, on his other side, glanced behind him. "You can tell us the rest as you're ready. And..."

Yilon turned. "This is Dinah. She might be Lady Dewanne. If she chooses."

She stepped forward and extended her paw. Volle took it with a courteous bow, and then presented his muzzle to exchange scents. Ilyana followed, and then Dinah looked up at the large white wolf, who was waiting with his ears folded partway back.

"And who is this?" Dinah said.

Volle spoke when Yilon didn't answer. "Streak, my companion."

Streak leaned forward. Dinah stood on tiptoe and touched her muzzle to his. "Pleased to meet you."

"Likewise." He took her paw carefully in two broad white ones.

As Dinah stepped back, she raised an eyebrow toward Yilon, which he interpreted as a question about the relationship between his father and Streak. The sourness he usually felt when thinking about that came to the fore again, but only as a habit, like a game he'd played as a cub for which he remembered the rules but had lost the drive. He gave Dinah a curt nod in answer, only then noticing Lady Dewanne, beyond her, regarding him with a thoughtful expression. He was about to say something when a small weasel walked into the room, dressed in the same deep blue finery.

"Yilon!" He bounced forward and took both Yilon's paws in his, pushing his muzzle forward.

"Corris?" Yilon extended his own muzzle, sniffing the familiar scent.

"Came along as your mother's bodyguard," the weasel said. "Dangerous for a lady to travel alone these days. Not to mention lonely. Hello, miss."

He bowed to Dinah, while Yilon looked at his mother, whose eyes were averted and ears half-back, though she was smiling. Dinah leaned forward to sniff muzzles. "Corris, was it?"

"Aye!" He beamed and nodded vigorously.

"Corris taught me all about using the short bow," Yilon said. "In Vinton, that is. I didn't know..." His mother still wouldn't meet his eye. His father and Streak were watching her, amused smiles on their muzzles. She did meet Volle's gaze, and her ears came up and she lifted her muzzle, smiling back archly. "It's great to see you."

"And a pleasure to see what a fine young lord you've grown into as well." Corris bowed again and then hopped back to take Yilon's mother's elbow. "Are we eating? I'm starved."

Dinah's eyebrows asked another question of Yilon, but he just smiled and held out his arm for her to take. "Yes, let's go to breakfast."

Although he knew how curious they were, he didn't want to talk about Kites, or Min, or Shreds, or even Maxon. The tale of his negotiation with Whisper was one even Dinah had not heard all of, so he spent most of the short meal telling that one. He tried to avoid mentioning Sinch, but whenever his name came up, he saw the glances his parents and Dinah exchanged. And then, just as the meal was drawing to a close and Caffin announced that they would be leaving for the church soon, Lady Dewanne, who had been quiet for most of the story, said, "So it was that simple. The bond between a fox and a mouse, down there and up here. A small gesture of love, to heal such an old wound."

Everybody fell silent. Yilon clenched his paws. He didn't want to ask, but the longer the silence dragged on, the less he was able to remain quiet. "How is he?" he asked her. "Is he...is he still..."

"We've had no word today," she said. "But Incic will do his best. Even if he could not save..." She looked down at the table.

"Corwin?" Yilon looked at Dinah and saw the answer in her muzzle. "I didn't know..."

"Last night," Lady Dewanne said softly, still not looking at him. "I asked Incic not to tell you then. There was nothing to be done."

"But Sinch was still alive when he arrived," Dinah said. "And they haven't sent any word yet. Colian was to move Valix there this morning as well. I'm sure he would have told me if..."

Yilon nodded. He opened his muzzle to ask if he could go see him before the ceremony, and then closed it again. It would be better not. As long as he postponed the visit, Sinch would still be alive, still be close to recovering, and he would not want to find out anything different until it was all over.

The plaza in front of the castle was filled to bursting with carriages, all draped with green and silver banners. Foxes in finery and livery bustled between them, stepping into them and guiding them up the hill to the church, one servant standing by each of them with a protective umbrella. A line of soldiers protected the area just in front of the castle, where four carriages waited with open doors and attentive servants.

Lady Dewanne guided Yilon and Dinah to the first one, while Yilon's parents walked to the second. An older couple stood talking by the third carriage, and then got in as they saw the others embarking. "My parents," Dinah said, seeing Yilon look at them.

He nodded, waiting until she and Lady Dewanne had stepped in before getting in himself. The footservant closed the door, but still it was several minutes before they were on their way. "We will wait until everyone else is seated before arriving," Lady Dewanne told them, and indeed, by the time the driver spurred their mounts to movement, the plaza was nearly empty.

Later, Yilon would remember little of the actual ceremony, which passed in a blur. But he would always remember standing outside the church with the two vixens on either side of him, their clothes and fur bright despite the rain, and Lady Dewanne's solicitous look as they prepared to enter. "Are you ready?" she asked him, and he knew she was referring not just to the ceremony, but to the memories they both would face inside. He saw the loss of Maxon in her eyes, saw the tiredness in her whiskers, and he was reminded in that moment, as he would be in many moments to come in his life, of the burden of a lord, or any leader.

He took her paw and stood as tall as he could. "I'm ready," he said. "It's going to be okay."

The inside of the church, glowing with candles, was as different from the day before as it could have been. Though it was just as bright, the light came from the hundreds of candles, not the cloud-covered sun. The windows had been hung with silver chains which scattered dots of light all over the interior. Green and grey banners with the crest of Dewanne decorated the wall below the upper tier of windows, the musty smell of their ancient cloth a thick background to the main scent in the church: the crowd of foxes packing the stone pews.

They were old and young, rich and poor, tall and short. Their scents mingled in a dizzying palette, but the air in the church was designed to circulate, to make sure that all scents were exposed and none was hidden. Their fine silks and velvet filled his eyes with color. The low murmur of their chatter died down as they turned to watch Yilon enter, hundreds of shining eyes turned to him.

He would remember those eyes, and the eyes of the Cantor, standing at the altar in bright white robes and silver armbands, as they met his in silent acknowledgment before any words were spoken. He would remember the words of the oath, the promise to rule the province of Dewanne in accordance with the laws of the Church and the kingdom of Tephos, and saying out loud, "I will serve the people of Dewanne and our Father Canis with all of my heart, my spirit, and my life."

He would remember Dinah's smile, when he turned to face the assembled crowd on his knees so that the Cantor could place the crown on his head, but more than that, the space she'd left between herself and his mother, holding her paw on the stone there. The weight settled on his head as he realized whom she meant to be sitting there, the thought of the mouse as painful as her gesture was touching.

The smell of the coronation robes, old and infused with the scent of Lords past. His mother breaking down in tears when the Cantor announced, "Rise, Lord Dewanne." His father's paw held in Streak's large white one, while his other grasped Ilyana's. The smiling vixen, whose name he didn't know, tears streaming down the sides of her cheek ruffs, both paws held out to him in supplication or gratitude. The deep bow of Caffin, manning the carriage, waiting for him, and the feeling when he said, "Tails down" and the servant relaxed on his command. The memory of Caffin and Min doing the same thing on his arrival.

And looking up just before he got into the carriage to return to the castle, at the rooftop of the building across from the church, seeing a small silhouette standing much more visibly than it needed to be, watching him. He raised a paw to it, but it did not respond. And that, he thought as he got into the carriage, was as it should be. He'd already received their loyalty, or at least the promise of truce; any more acknowledgments between them would have to be earned.

And then he was in the carriage again, and almost no time seemed to have passed. Dinah sat next to him, Lady Dewanne across from him. "How long do I have to keep the crown on?" He kept reaching up to adjust it.

"At least through the banquet," Lady Dewanne said. "Afterwards, you may leave it in the care of the Treasury."

"Lady Dewanne," Dinah began, but the older vixen held up a paw.

"That will be your title soon enough—should you choose," she added, with a smile. "I hope you do."

"You're still a lady of the land," Yilon said. "You always will be."

Her eyes sparkled. "Perhaps this one time I will not argue with you."

Dinah leaned forward. "Will you—"

She shook her head quickly. "After the banquet. Patience, dear. There will be time."

If the Confirmation had gone by in a flash, the banquet took forever. The castle gates stood wide open, with foxes walking in from the plaza where they were gathered in small groups talking. Because the banquet was open to the city, tables were set up in the great hall rather than in the dining hall. Yilon sat at the head table with Dinah, Lady Dewanne, and his parents, with Streak looming over the cheerful Corris at the end of the table. Through the window he could see the residents of Dewanne strolling in. They entered the hall in pairs, unannounced, and found their own seats at the multitude of tables. Long after the last space was filled, foxes continued to wander in, but nobody seemed upset at the lack of a chair; they simply stood around and talked in groups, in happy, excited voices. Many of them, Yilon saw, wore the uniforms of the guard, and whenever he met the eyes of one of those, without exception, he received a respectful smile.

The footservants brought loaf after loaf of fresh bread in from the kitchens, and their ears and tails had a perky air about them as well. Yilon had eaten two pieces of the bread when his father slid a jar down the table to him.

"We brought this for you. And something else, too, but we'll save that for later," Volle said.

Yilon picked up the jar. His mouth watered immediately at the scent of honey. "Oh," he said, and held it out to Dinah. "Try this."

She hesitated, holding a finger over it until he held out a piece of bread. She dipped hers in, then brought it to her mouth as he dipped his own into the jar. "Mmmm." She closed her eyes. "Sweet."

It hadn't been that long since he'd had honey, but the taste transported him. He smiled down to his father and Streak, who were both waiting for his reaction. "Thank you."

"Lord Dewanne used to take some back here from time to time," Volle said. "We thought you might like a taste of home."

Yilon let the sweetness fade from his muzzle. He picked up another slice of bread to dip in, and then stopped with the bread held over the jar. Dinah's parents had come up to the table and were standing behind Volle, across from Yilon. "Hello," he said.

"My lord," the vixen said, "Congratulations and welcome."

"Thank you," he said, rising to greet them.

"We won't stay," her husband said, and now Yilon noticed other foxes gathering behind them. "We just wanted to be the first."

"You have an extraordinary daughter," Yilon said. "She saved my life. Twice. Or more."

Dinah rose, her ears flicking back. "Well, someone had to take care of you."

Her parents looked at each other. "It's certainly nice to know she's put her skills to good use," her father said. "We had no idea."

Volle looked up at them with a grin. "Sometimes your children can surprise you."

"Indeed," Lady Dewanne said from the end of the table.

"And I understand we will have a wedding to arrange," Dinah's mother said.

"If she chooses." Yilon turned to her.

Dinah smiled. "We can talk about it later."

Her parents looked at each other with resignation. "Whatever her decision, we welcome you to our province," her father said.

"Thank you again," Yilon said, and impulsively lifted the jar of honey. "Please, have a taste of some Divalia honey."

And after that, he offered the honey to each fox who came up to introduce themselves. Most of them simply offered congratulations, or welcome. Many had brought small gifts, which footservants took to a side table. Some wanted to talk about their position in the town: the prim assistant head of the silver trade, the scruffy northern region mine surveyor, and the plump city planner. Two leaned in to tell him to take care of the mouse problem once and for all.

After the second, Dinah touched his shoulder and said softly, "Don't worry."

"I wasn't," he said.

"Well, your ears went down and your tail's all bristly," she said.

He made an effort to relax, noticing his father and Streak's ears similarly laid back. "It's the way they are here," he said.

"I know," Volle said. "It's just that seeing it in person..."

Lady Dewanne tipped her goblet to her muzzle. "With practice, you can view it as a separate place." The heavy silver goblet landed with a thud on the wood table.

"Careful of the wood," Dinah said, leaning over.

Lady Dewanne smiled at her. "It's not yours yet, dear."

Dinah folded her ears down and sat back. Yilon shot a sharp glance at Lady Dewanne, but the older vixen, if she noticed, did not react. And then there was another fox leaning forward to bow and say "welcome," and Yilon had to focus his attention.

The line died down, but foxes came up all through the roasted goat course, the mushroom and potatoes side, and the cheese and berries. Yilon sat back after greeting a vixen from the Heights and found a small wooden box in front of his plate. His mother, across from him, smiled when he looked up.

"I brought something as well," she said, and when Yilon opened the box, he found a small round Vinton goat cheese, surrounded by dried sunberries and spiced nuts. The familiar scents overwhelmed his senses so that he couldn't even bring himself to eat any of them at first.

"Thank you," he said. "I want to save these for later."

"I wanted to make sure you got to have them," she said, glancing at the nearly-empty jar of honey.

And after the banquet, there were barrels of wine brought out as the tables were cleared. The residents stayed until the sun went down, and Yilon walked around talking to many of them, soldiers flanking him discreetly. It was all a bit overwhelming, but Dinah accompanied him for much of the evening. She knew enough of the people that he trusted she would remember them later, even if he didn't. Still, he realized as the evening wound down, he felt comfortable in the castle, and he was looking forward to going back out into the city, to place all the foxes he'd met that evening in their proper settings.

His parents had retired, but told him they would be up for a while and that he should come say good night. When the last few foxes were lingering and nobody was pressing to talk to him anymore, he found Dinah and Lady Dewanne talking near the stairway to the second floor.

"No word from Incic?" he said.

"We haven't checked," Lady Dewanne said. Her words were slurred just enough that he noticed. "Would you like us to send a messenger over?"

Dinah laid a paw on his arm. "He would have come, if he were...I mean, if he had..."

Yilon nodded to her. "I'd like to—I have to go myself, I think."

"May I accompany you?" Dinah tilted her muzzle.

He started to say he would prefer to be alone, then changed his mind and nodded. Lady Dewanne held up a paw. "In that case, may I as well?"

Yilon raised his eyebrows. She smiled coolly down. "I have some things to say to you both. You will find that often the best place to discuss secrets is away from this castle." She brushed a finger up her long black ear and flicked it back, as if to indicate that someone was listening to them at that moment.

He'd expected Lady Dewanne to talk to them on the way over, but she kept silent all the way across the plaza, around the crowds of foxes still celebrating, some of whom cheered the small party as they walked by. She did not speak under the glow of the moon and the lamps that dotted the streets of the west side, and indeed walked behind them until they arrived at Incic's offices. There, she took the lead, rapping sharply just beneath the carved relief of the chirurgeon's emblem on the wooden door with the until a short vixen in a white robe came to open it.

"My Lady," she said, bowing.

"And your Lord," Lady Dewanne said, sweeping past her into the small foyer. "Is Master Incic awake? We wish to inquire after the condition of one of his patients."

"And visit, if we can," Yilon put in.

"He is with them now," the nurse said. "Please come into the waiting room. I will let him know you have arrived." She held aside the curtain, showing them into a small room with benches along either wall. She started to leave through the doorway opposite, turned and made a confused curtsy to Yilon and added, "My lord," and then turned again and left quickly.

The little room smelled strongly of lye and alcohol, though the smooth white marble benches were bare. Yilon was sure that the discolorations on the floor were spots of blood that had not been scrubbed completely clean. Dinah sat on one of the benches immediately, but Yilon couldn't bring himself to sit. Lady Dewanne, too, remained standing, but unlike Yilon, she did not pace between the benches. Rather, she stood over Dinah until the younger vixen looked up at her. "My Lady," she said, "Will you tell us—"

The far door opened, admitting a tall fox in a bloodstained white robe. His arms moved constantly as he talked, slender fingers hovering as though waiting for something to do. "You're here about the mouse, is that right? The male mouse? The female's doing well. Whoever treated her did all the right things. All except one or two, but minor, very minor. No way he could have known."

Yilon glanced at Lady Dewanne. The older vixen didn't react to the chirurgeon's failure to address them by their titles. "Incic," she said, "how is the mouse?"

He brought a paw up to his ear, rubbing the edge between thumb and finger. "Very tricky, very tricky. The humours are out of balance. Then again, for a mouse, who can say? Fascinating things. Wonderful opportunity. Took pages of notes." He looked around as if expecting praise. "But no dark humour. Very lucky that. The ancestors seem to have, for some reason, who knows? We cleaned him up, waited the night. Today, had to open the wound further to see. Some damage, some damage. But no dark humour. And having the other mouse seems to perk him up. One would expect that, of course. It's the same with foxes. Loved one nearby, that bond, that does things we cannot with all our tools and knowledge. One day, perhaps." His expression drifted.

Yilon shook his head, trying to make sense of the fox's babbling. "So... he's alive?"

"Of course he's alive." Incic brought his paw down from his ear and looked indignant. "I said, if he lived the night. Did I not?"

Yilon's head spun. He had to lean against the wall, while Lady Dewanne said, "You said there was a chance."

"Can we see him?" Yilon said. He was having trouble keeping his balance through the wash of relief.

"See him?" Incic fluttered his fingers. "He's asleep. The other is awake."

"I don't care." Yilon was starting to get control of his breathing. "I want to see him."

"Even the Lord of Dewanne—" the chirurgeon started.

"As of this morning," Dinah said, "he is the Lord of Dewanne."

"Even the Lord of Dewanne," the chirurgeon went on, "must not wake a patient of mine. The sleep of Canis, the sleep of Rodenta, whatever it is."

"I don't want to wake him," Yilon said. "I just want to see him."

Incic shook his head and perked an ear, as though Yilon were speaking a different language. "See him? Ridiculous. What good does that do? See him?"

Dinah stepped forward. "Can we talk to the other one?"

He stopped and stared at her, and then resumed his fidgeting. "Course you can talk to the other one. She's awake. Talkative too. She keeps asking if she's dreaming. Tchah."

Lady Dewanne leaned forward. "Take us to her, please, Incic."

He jerked his head. "This way." He vanished through the doorway.

They followed him up a set of stairs and down a hallway, to a small room with two beds. The smell of alcohol grew stronger as they walked into the room past a small stand which held several bottles and a small pile of bloody rags. Two of the multiple small drawers in the front of the stand were open, but Yilon didn't look to see what they contained, because his attention snapped immediately to the bed on the left and the small shape huddled under the blanket. He padded quickly across the stone toward it.

"'Bout time you showed up," a sharp voice came from the other bed.

He hadn't even noticed Valix there. She was sitting up, a robe wrapped around her shoulders, staring at him. He looked down at Sinch's sleeping muzzle and caught the faint citrus and rosemary scent of a sleeping draught coming from the empty cup next to the bed. "What do you mean?"

"He talks in his sleep," she said. "Keeps talking about you."

Incic stood off to one side, fingers tapping along one arm. As Yilon reached out to rest a paw on Sinch's shoulder, the chirurgeon coughed and shook his head when Yilon looked at him. "No touching," he said. "Definitely no touching."

"All right," Yilon said, returning his attention to Valix.

She rolled her eyes. "He kept saying something about the smell. I figured he must be talking about a fox, right?" Yilon's ears folded back. "Oh, all right, he might have said your name a couple times, too. That make you feel better?"

"Not really." Yilon stared down at Sinch. His muzzle looked so peaceful. He was breathing normally, and as much as Yilon wanted to see the wound, he would have to trust Incic's skill.

And then Sinch's eye opened. He yawned and turned his head.

Incic was at his side in a flash, his fingers now sure and quick now that they had something to do. He pushed Yilon aside. "Shouldn't be awake," he said. "How do you feel?"

Sinch's eyes tracked Yilon. "My side hurts," he said. "But I'm okay."

Incic snorted. "You are not okay. Perforated internal organs, mixing of humours, elevated temperature, no, no, not okay at all." He paused. "Even for a mouse."

"I will be," Sinch said.

Yilon nodded, and found Sinch's paw under the blanket, while Incic wasn't looking. He squeezed it as gently as he could, trying not to worry at the mouse's weak grip. He let go before the chirurgeon could see it. "Open your mouth," Incic was ordering Sinch, and Yilon stepped back to let him work.

Dinah touched his arm. "Yilon," she said.

He squeezed as gently as he could.

He tore his gaze from Sinch. She was smiling. "Is this a good time to tell you my decision? Because I think I just made it."

He knew what her decision was by her smile, but he nodded anyway and said, "Go on." Lady Dewanne and Valix were watching them too, now. Only Incic seemed oblivious, feeling Sinch's ears and then padding to the side table to mix another solution.

"I'll be Lady Dewanne," she said. "We'll figure out how to have heirs. I figure together we can work something out. But the condition is that you have to be happy about it."

"I am," he said, but even he could hear the flatness in his voice.

She nodded toward the bed. "It doesn't take Canis's Nose to sniff out what you've got with him, even if you won't admit it. It appears to be the one thing that makes you really happy."

"We don't have to get married right away," he said.

"Oh, stop it." She punched his shoulder. "I'm willing to do my duty to," she rolled her eyes, "my land, my people, and all that. But I'm not willing to be miserable doing it, and if you're moping all the time and I have to live with that, I'm going to be miserable."

"I can handle—"

"Will you stop trying to be so self-sacrificing?" She glared at him. "You've already as much as said you'd give him up to do your duty. You've proven you'll be a better lord than I or—or anyone else ever would. So allow yourself a little happiness. Didn't you say that the mice are your people too?"

"Yes, but—"

"Do males ever get easier to understand?" She leaned around him to ask Lady Dewanne that question.

"No more than we do, dear," the older vixen said.

She returned her attention to Yilon. "It's simple. Either you get me and him, or you get neither of us."

Yilon felt his insides thaw. For the first time, he looked at Dinah as a companion, and the thought made him smile. "That's the condition, eh?"

She put a finger to her muzzle. "And that you take me to Divalia."

Yilon smiled. He leaned forward to touch his nose to hers. "Will you be my bodyguard when he's not around?"

"We'll share that duty, I guess." She laughed. "I can't believe how hard it is to convince to you take something you want."

"I suppose I'm not used to having that." He felt too tired to argue about duty and responsibility.

She bumped his muzzle. "Is that a yes?"

He nodded and took her paws in his. “Yes. Thank you.”

Their muzzles hovered near each other’s, and then Dinah turned away, ears flicking. “Maybe we should save that for another time.”

Relieved, Yilon squeezed her paws lightly and let them go. They grinned at each other and then saw Lady Dewanne wiping her eyes with a finger, delicately. Both mice were watching them, too, Sinch over Incic’s arms, Valix with her arms folded. When she saw the foxes looking at her, she snorted. “How romantic.”

“*You’re* married,” Sinch said, but then his voice cracked. Yilon saw the tears streaking his muzzle and the smile he couldn’t hide.

“Well, what’s that got to do with anything?” Valix twisted a band on her wrist. “Anyway, I just told ya that to keep you from tryin’ anything. Never been married.”

“What about Balinni?” Sinch said, and then Incic turned to the rest of the room.

“What did I say?” he snapped. “Upsetting a patient. What are you all talking about? Death? Plague? Family?”

“Family,” Valix said, rather cheekily. “Balinni’s my father.”

“Out!” Incic shooed the foxes out. “And you,” he said to Valix, “quiet, quiet, quiet.” As they crowded out the door, Yilon raised a paw, and Sinch returned the gesture, both of them smiling hugely.

He was still smiling even as he bumped into Dinah in the waiting room. She’d stopped unexpectedly to confront Lady Dewanne. “It’s isolated here,” she said, drawing the heavy curtain along the doorway leading to the interior.

“Indeed,” Lady Dewanne said in her high voice. “And now that we have privacy and opportunity, I find...that what I had to say does not need to be heard.”

Dinah’s brow furrowed. “About your family?”

Lady Dewanne paced the length of one of the benches and then turned back. “I want to give you my blessing. Velkan is a good governor and you can trust him. But you will need to spend some time here in order to make the changes you wish. It will be a hard road.” She paused and waved a paw. “Too much time spent with Incic. My thoughts are scattered.”

“Just say it.” Dinah flicked her ears, impatient.

Lady Dewanne smiled. “The people of this land deserve better than I was able to give them. I feel confident that you will give them what they deserve. You, Yilon, your alliance with your father and brother will be important, both for yourself and for Dewanne.” She hesitated, and then smiled. “Having met you, I see that your father was right.”

"About what?" Dinah asked.

Lady Dewanne walked to the door and held aside the curtain. "I have one more matter to attend to tonight. Dinah, I will perhaps see you at breakfast tomorrow. Good night."

"It looked like fun."

Chapter 32: Sweetness

Dinah didn't move as the curtain fell behind the elder vixen. "What was your father right about?"

Yilon glanced back toward the inside of the house. He'd forgotten about his father's letter. "Something he said a couple months ago. A long story. Speaking of which...my mother wanted me to look in on her before it became too late. You don't think it is, do you?"

"I don't think it's ever too late." Dinah smiled. She walked over to the curtain and held it aside. "You can tell me the story on the way."

So on the way back, as they walked slowly through the streets, he told her about his mother's exile to Vinton, how his father had not known him until his fourteenth birthday, how he had not been designated the heir until two months ago. "Your father just sent your mother away so he could be with Streak?"

Yilon shrugged. "If we're to be married, we'll stay together. If I have Sinch, you'll have to find someone in Divalia."

She smiled. "Is that an order?"

"If I'm not allowed to be miserable," he said, and she bumped her shoulder against his. She laughed, and after a moment, he smiled too.

"It's only sex, after all." She looked sideways at him. "Is it really that important?"

He thought again about Sinch. "If you do it right," he said.

They walked on under the moon. As they reached the plaza, they heard the cheers and songs of revelers still celebrating. The square was just as busy as it had been when they'd left, the wine still flowing. Impromptu dances had broken out. "My Lord, my Lady!" Drunken foxes waved as they went by.

"My Lord, just one dance?" A vixen approached him. Her breath reeked of wine, and her ears were comically askew. She was smiling broadly.

"I have to get back," Yilon said, but Dinah laid a paw on his arm.

"One dance," she said. "I'll go ahead and tell them you're coming."

He would have hesitated longer, but the vixen grabbed his arm and whirled him into the plaza. The music never seemed to stop or pause, so he just joined in, hopping from one foot to the other, holding on to the vixen. She laughed and jumped back and forth with him, not so much a dance as a romp. "We're just all so happy," she bubbled, and hiccuped.

He danced with his vixen for a few moments, but then had to disengage, as the music kept on and on, the foxes with the fiddles and horns apparently tireless. She leaned forward to rub muzzles as he slowed down. "Thank you for the dance, my Lord," she said. "I'll not forget."

Her glistening eyes told him she truly wouldn't. "You're welcome," he said, and returned her smile. When he turned around, Dinah was still there.

"It looked like fun," she said. "Just a little longer." And she took his paws and swept him back out into the plaza.

What a thing, he thought, as the foxes around them cheered at their dance together. All this merriment, all this hope, all for him. He could easily have felt elevated or special, but more than anything, he felt the weight of responsibility, the powerful urge to protect the foxes in the plaza, to keep them safe and happy and joyful for as long as he could. But he wouldn't be alone. He smiled down at Dinah, guiding her back to the castle.

"It's a bigger celebration than Rekindling," she said, panting a bit.

"I'd hope this one doesn't happen as often." Yilon held the door for her to enter the great hall. The footservants were still cleaning up after the crowd, going about their jobs quietly and efficiently. But even they smiled as Yilon passed, perking their ears. He nodded and returned their smiles as he and Dinah mounted the stairs.

Dinah rubbed her whiskers. "I do wonder what she'd been going to say. About her family. I wonder if it was about her not having cubs. I could swear she had one that died, but in the church, she said..."

"She was afraid of Dewry. That doesn't make sense, either. They could have had the cub here while he was in Divalia."

Dinah nodded. "Or put out the rumor that he'd died. But she told you she was barren. Maybe she pretended to have a cub so Lord Dewanne wouldn't cast her aside?" She shook her head. "I don't know how she could do that, though."

Yilon sighed. "It's done. I suppose it isn't important anymore."

The west side of the second floor held four small guest rooms and the stair to the third floor, where Lady Dewanne had apparently already retired to her suite. Yilon's mother had been sent to the Garden Room, the first one on the right. He approached the door and heard the murmur of two voices inside.

He hesitated, then knocked, and heard his mother's voice say, "Come in."

"I'll leave you here," Dinah said. "Good night."

Yilon clasped her paws. "You're staying here?"

She shook her head. "I'm going back to the Heights."

"You should stay," he said. "I wouldn't want anything to happen."

She smiled. "I'll be safe."

"You don't have your sling," he pointed out.

She winked. "You don't know me very well yet, do you?"

He laughed. "If you really won't stay, at least take one of the soldiers at the gate to walk you home." She gathered her breath to protest, so he cut her off quickly. "Remember, all those residents in the plaza, and out there in the city, they're depending on you now. You have to stay safe."

"Oh, very well." She considered him, and then leaned forward to tap her nose to his. "Good night, Lord Dewanne."

He watched her walk toward the stairs, and then opened the door, with a little wag to his tail.

His mother and father sat together on the bed, smiles lighting up their muzzles as he walked in and closed the door behind him. They were sitting very close; they might have been holding paws before he walked in. To his surprise, Lady Dewanne sat in one of the chairs near the bed, sitting up straight. "We're so proud of you," his mother said.

"Not just for today," his father added. "For the way you've handled yourself the past few days."

"From what we've heard." They looked at Lady Dewanne.

She nodded. "You both have much to be proud of."

His mother and father looked at each other. "We raised him as best we could," Ilyana said softly.

Yilon took the other chair, his eyes on Lady Dewanne. She was watching him in turn, the corners of her mouth curved very slightly upright. "He is his mother's son, and his father's."

They both looked at him then, and he saw that she'd told them. He nodded. "She knew. And...Maxon did, too." He thought of Maxon's cry, "He *is* your brother," in the church, and winced inwardly. Despite his loyalty to the old lord, he'd lied to save someone else's son. For the benefit of Dewanne. Yilon said a quick, silent prayer to Canis for the steward.

"We came down to see you when you were two years old," Lady Dewanne said. "You wouldn't remember, of course. You," she turned to Volle and Ilyana, "were so proud, and you had fairly drenched him in rosewater. I remember thinking it odd. Sheffin, bless him, didn't. So I spent a short time among Yilon's private things in his bedroom here, and that was enough to confirm my suspicion. It also raised some interesting questions about mice, which have since been answered."

Yilon flicked his suddenly-warm ears. His parents turned to each other, and then Volle began to rise. "Delia—"

"Sit," she said. "Had I intended to take some sort of action, I would not have waited until after the Confirmation. No, I just find it extraordinary and beautiful, that this web of lies is untangled into truth with such a simple stroke. After all our pretense and preparation, it turns out that Yilon is exactly what he says he is. He is your son."

Volle sat back, slowly. Yilon brought his ears up. "Does anyone else know?"

She shook her head. "I have not told anyone. Maxon..." She paused, while her eyes drifted to stare at something not in the room. "It would not be in his nature to reveal that secret."

"Why are you telling us now?" Ilyana said, softly.

Lady Dewanne turned to her and smiled. "To reassure you that your secret is safe. And to congratulate you on your devotion. I did not know of any way to end a pregnancy save for wormwood, and that would prevent another until the following season. Incic tells me it is possible with certain herbs, but that it is a painful and unpleasant process. To have gone through that simply to ensure that your cub would have one father and not another shows far more strength than I possess." She bowed.

Ilyana looked at him, and then up at Lady Dewanne. "Thank you."

"And you," she said to Volle, "you stood by your wife, even though she allowed another into her bed."

He took Ilyana's paw, and nodded. "Would you not have done the same for Sheffin?"

"I would have done anything for him." Her muzzle assumed that faraway expression again. "He protected me his whole life, forgave me everything. Every room in this castle holds memories of him. I will be glad to be gone, tomorrow. But before I go..."

Yilon had not thought about that, that his mother had loved his father enough to double-cross Lord Dewanne so that her cub would be his. That his father had forgiven a serious transgression to remain with his mother. He rubbed his fingers together, staring down at his paws, thinking about Maxon's story, how Kayley had refused to end her pregnancy. Lord Dewanne's mistakes, now both erased for him by others, as cleanly as with...

...any way to end a pregnancy save for wormwood.

Lady Dewanne was standing over him, holding out a letter. He didn't take it.

Corwin recommended him. He's good with wormwood.

I've treated Lady Dewanne. Not with needle and thread, of course...

He stared up at her. "You could have had cubs," he whispered.

"I told you that I am not favored of Canis," she said, just as softly. "I am barren indeed."

His parents were trying not to look interested. "The wormwood," Yilon said, softly.

Pain flashed in a grimace across her muzzle. She bent over to his far ear and whispered, with no more than a breath, "Barren of courage."

Her sister died giving birth to a cub with a clubfoot...

"You let others..." he couldn't finish the sentence.

"I have made terrible choices," she said in the same whisper. "I have lost two dear friends this week because of them." She pushed the letter into his paw. "You are my atonement, to my land and my people. And this is my gift to you, meager though it may be. I pray you will not judge me too harshly."

He took the letter, never taking his eyes from hers. In them, he saw resolve, pain, tiredness. "It's not for me to judge." His voice felt detached.

She straightened. "Dewanne will prosper with your guidance, as you will prosper from your father's, I feel sure."

Yilon nodded. "Good night," he said, unable to keep a chill out of his voice.

She waved to his parents, and left. He sat staring at the wall, while his parents watched him. Finally, he unfolded the letter, noting the broken seal of Vinton on it. Opening the first fold, he recognized his father's handwriting.

My esteemed peer,

It is with great pleasure and pride that I write to you that Yilon has far surpassed any expectation we held for him. His history and diplomacy tutors say that they have not had a more gifted student in a generation. His bearing is noble and his judgment is beyond question, even at his early age.

Yilon felt a twinge of guilt at that line. In theory, it had been, until put to the test here. But he had learned.

He is in every way the model of an heir. Were we fortunate enough to have him as our first-born, we would not hesitate to hand over Vinton's rule to him and retire to Helfer's Vellenland estate. His mother and I agree that our only regret in writing this to you is that we shall lose the pleasure of his company for months out of the year, but our loss shall without question be the gain of the people of Dewanne. In the coming years, we look forward to a fruitful and long-lasting alliance between our provinces, as our families are joined in name and law.

Yours in the blessed Pack,

Volle, Lord of Vinton

Below the text of the letter, in the blank area, in a neat, regular script that smelled of fresh ink, was written, "Not every shadow is dark."

He folded the letter and looked up. "What is it?" his mother asked.

"The answer to a question," he said.

"What did you ask her?" his father asked.

Yilon shook his head. "I'm not sure."

When he didn't elaborate, Volle turned to Ilyana. "So she was barren after all?"

Ilyana frowned. "That doesn't sound right to me."

Yilon's eyes came to rest on his mother, her delicate muzzle, slender arms and legs. Her fragility felt unbearable to him. "She wasn't barren," he said. "She was afraid she'd die. So they risked *your* life." He got half out of his chair, not knowing why or what he intended to do, just that he wanted to run upstairs and pull Lady Dewanne out of her bed, make her answer to her actions.

His father half-rose with him, watching him; his mother waved them both to be seated. "We would have had another cub anyway," she said. "This was a blessing from Canis, to have another lord in the family."

Yilon was still working through the implications of Lady Dewanne's cowardice. "Min... Maxon... Corwin... Sinch wouldn't be in the chirurgeon's house right now..." He sank back down in his chair. He'd made mistakes, yes, and he would always bear part of the blame for Min and Sinch, if not the others, but he would not have been in Dewanne to make those mistakes if Lady Dewanne had done her duty.

"How is Sinch?" Volle asked gently.

"He'll live," Yilon growled."I wish I'd never been named the heir."

"So do I," his father said.

Yilon's head snapped up. "Have I made that much a mess of it?"

His father looked at him steadily, smiling. "You've done better than—no, you've done just as well as we hoped. As we knew you could."

Yilon struggled with the curious warmth those words ignited in him. His fingers rubbed the parchment of the letter. "But you wish I hadn't."

"Of course," his father said. "For your first fourteen years of life, I saw you four times, twice when you were too young to remember. I missed watching you grow into the fine young lord you are now. Don't you think I hated that?"

"I don't know," Yilon said. "Did you?"

He saw the reproach in his mother's eyes and laid his ears back, but his father put up a paw and spoke before she could. "A wise old friend of mine once said that I would have to cast my cubs out into the world without any help, and I swore never to do that. Your mother and...and Streak and I talked about it. We promised that one of us would always be with you and Volyan. Don't you think it hurt her as much to give up Volyan as it did for me to miss your childhood? But our positions required us to spend our time apart, and we made that sacrifice for our family."

"I'm sure you were crushed at having to live in the palace with *him*."

"I'd made enemies at the palace," his father said. "Long before I met Streak. They would have done terrible things to me."

"They did," Ilyana said softly.

"And to my family," Volle went on. "It was for their safety that they remained in Vinton."

"Didn't you like Vinton?" his mother said softly.

Yilon's ears went back. "I love it," he said immediately.

"I didn't, at first," she said. "I thought it was an exile, a remote place where I would have to raise cubs and then watch them grow up and leave me. But I grew to love it. I love working with Anton, being the lady of the town, but still having enough liberty to walk up the mountain in the morning to watch the sun rise." She looked down. "I always knew you would leave me, and that was the only thing that made me sad."

She squeezed his father's paw. He waited for Yilon to talk, but Yilon was thinking about Dinah, about Sinch, about Lady Dewanne. After a moment, his father said, "We did the best we could. Can you blame us for seeking happiness where we could find it?"

You could've told me more, explained it better, Yilon thought, but he found his thoughts turning in another direction. "Corwin said something like that, the last time I saw him."

Volle ducked his head. "I was sorry to hear of his passing. Dewanne and Delia spoke very highly of him."

"I would've liked to have had his advice," Yilon said. His eyes felt heavy, and for the first time, he felt the pressure of emotion behind them. "Maxon...he caused so much trouble, but he was devoted to his cause. Like Min."

"You should not have had to go through all this," Volle said, with a fierceness that surprised Yilon.

"It was...to be truthful...it was partly my own fault," Yilon said. "I didn't want to be here." He looked at his mother. "I suppose I've grown to like it a little more."

"It doesn't seem so different from Vinton," she said. "A little rougher."

"A lot rougher."

She nodded. "And I understand there are mice here, but I haven't seen any."

"There's some tension," Volle began, then let Yilon talk.

"They hate each other," he said. "That's one of the things I have to fix."

"You may not be able to," his father said. "Ancient enmities run deep. But sometimes all they need is for someone to show them the way, to help them take that first step. Show them new ways to think and act."

Yilon pressed the letter between his fingers. "I'm trying," he said.

There was a quick knock at the door, and it opened before anyone could answer. Streak stepped in, but stopped when he saw Yilon. He looked over at Volle. "Sorry. I was just going to bed." He looked around the room. "I'll go."

Yilon saw his father's expression. "It's okay," he said.

Streak tilted his head. "No, I'm tired." But he wasn't yawning, and his tail was twitching.

How would he feel if his son, his and Dinah's, hated Sinch? His heart twinged. But after all, Lady Dewanne had told him that lords spent most of their time making up for mistakes. And now he was a lord. "It's okay," he said. "You can stay. We're talking about family stuff."

The white wolf smiled, and closed the door behind him before padding over to sit on Volle's other side.

Volle smiled, one paw reaching down to clasp Streak's. "We'll be working together," he said to Yilon, "on many things, now that you're my peer. I won't force advice on you, but don't be afraid to ask for help. I don't know the politics here, but I have been a lord for twenty years." He smiled and tapped the side of his muzzle. "I know a few tricks."

Your peer. Perhaps it was just the fatigue of the long day, but Yilon saw for a moment Lord Dewanne on the bed next to his mother, the muzzle he'd seen on the bust in the office glancing aside at her, trying to figure out how to ensure the succession of his land with a bastard son he feared and a wife afraid to have cubs of her own, knowing the consequences if he died without an heir. He heard again his father's strict warnings to his brother about sleeping with vixens, and Corwin telling him about all the indiscretions of lords past, and Maxon sitting in the small room in the Strad house, the smell of blood still faintly in the air, telling them about the family whose lives had been ruined because of Lord Dewanne's carelessness.

Then it was his father again, his mother, and him, and, yes, Streak, a family that was perhaps not perfect but was still together, still whole, in the castle—his castle—in his province of Dewanne. His shoulders sagged, and that was definitely fatigue after the Confirmation, the banquet, the socializing afterwards, the visit to Sinch, and even this talk here. He realized that he hadn't said anything, that his parents were still looking at him. His mother covered a yawn.

"I'll be glad to have your help," he said.

Volle's smile widened. He glanced at Ilyana and said, "I think it's getting late."

She nodded and held his paw lightly before releasing it. She looked around at Streak. "Did you see Corris out there?"

Streak smiled. "He'd worn out three dance partners, last I saw. Would you like me to send him up?"

"If you would." Ilyana smiled. "If he's ready."

Yilon rose. "I'm going to go see Sinch. Spend the night there, if Incic will let me."

"Let you?" Volle rose along with him, Streak standing as well. "Did you remind him that you're his lord now?"

Yilon grinned. "He doesn't seem to care much for titles."

"We'll be here another day or two. If you'd like company on your way back to Divalia, I can wait until then."

Ilyana stifled another yawn. "I was going to suggest to Delia that she and I could travel together, but I think she does not want to wait as long as I want to stay. We have a week, perhaps two, before the passes risk being closed, and I would like to see this other city where my son is the Lord."

"Oh, I nearly forgot," Volle said. He lifted a small jar from beside the bed. "This is the other thing we brought. I know you like them raw, but, well, at least they're not cooked."

Yilon sniffed, catching the bitter tang of locusts, overlaid with sweetness. Not honey, but a kind of flavored sugar. He smiled. "They don't have those here yet. Are they coming west? Master Verian said they would."

"Slowly. Another year or so. It seemed long to wait." His father handed him the jar.

Yilon took the jar and fished one of the locusts out. "Again, thank you," he said.

"We'll have more time to talk tomorrow. But I'm glad we talked tonight."

Outside, Streak made for the stairs, to find Corris. "I'll see you in our room," Volle waved to him, and then rested a paw on Yilon's shoulder. "Good night. Give our best to Sinch. We'll all pray to Canis for his quick recovery."

"Thanks," Yilon said. "And thanks for these, and for...for coming. It's good to see you." He leaned forward.

Volle took the hint. "We are so proud of you," he said, wrapping his arms around Yilon. And Yilon thought, then, of all his father had gone through. Raising a son far away, so that the lord who thought himself the father would never suspect the truth. Writing a letter, which at first he'd thought was just his attempt to pawn off an undesirable son on a far-off province, but which in his father's presence glowed with the light of truth. Bearing his son's hatred toward the person he loved most in the world. Traveling across the country as the weather turned cold, an uncomfortable journey at his age, to be at his son's side.

He brushed his father's muzzle in parting, letting the embrace linger before stepping back. "Good night," he called as he walked back to his room to put away the jar of locusts. Volle disappeared into his room, leaving the castle quiet and nearly empty.

Yilon kept out one locust, which he turned over in his fingers as he walked down the stairs to the main castle hallway. It wasn't the same as catching them out of the air, but his mouth watered at the scent of the fruity sugar on it. He held it up in salute to the portraits of noble foxes as he passed them. When he walked out into the cool night, he popped the candied insect into his muzzle.

The bitter taste stirred his memories, even coated by the sweet crunch of hard sugar, but he only closed his eyes for a moment to savor it before opening them to take in the celebration still animating his city. As he raised a paw to the few foxes still dancing, swallowing the last pieces of the locust under the bright Dewanne moon, it was the bitterness that faded first, leaving only its memory and the taste of sweetness on his tongue.

About the Author

Kyell Gold began writing furry fiction a long, long time ago. In the early days of the 21st century, he got up the courage to write some gay furry romance, first publishing his story "The Prisoner's Release" in Sofawolf Press's adult magazine Heat. That led to a novel, ***Volle***, and a sequel, ***Pendant of Fortune***, set in the world of Argaea, both of which won the Ursa Major Award for Best Anthropomorphic Novel (2005 and 2006). His novel ***Waterways*** also won that award in 2008, and he has won the Ursa Major Award for Best Anthropomorphic Short Story three times (2006-2008). Other strange things he likes to write about include mystical decks of cards, superheroes, and sports; his novel ***Out of Position*** takes place in the world of professional football. ***Shadow of the Father*** is his third Argaea novel.

He was not born in California, but now considers it his home. He loves to travel and dine out with his partner of many years, Kit Silver, and can be seen at furry conventions in California, around the country, and abroad.

About the Artist

Sara Palmer is an elusive creature often found in the smaller states of northern New England, where she can be spotted nestled between a cadre of Egyptian Mau cats and a couple dogs. She is often trailed by smaller, louder version of herself that some scientists believe is the next generation of artist. Though shy by nature, she is a frequent denizen of Dealer rooms and Art shows, and her work has been known to inhabit many tomes published with the fandom and without. Careful watchers will spot her as the illustrator of previous Argaea novels. One can recognize Ms Palmer by her perserverence in the face of adversity, her strong work ethic, and a constant strive to improve at her craft.

About the Publisher

Sofawolf Press was founded in 1999 by Jeff Eddy and Tim Susman with the goal of bringing professional-quality publication to the best in furry fiction. Please browse our catalog at *http://www.sofawolf.com*.